CW00339120

# THE GIRL WITH THE EMERALD RING

Elise Noble

Published by Undercover Publishing Limited

Copyright © 2020 Elise Noble

v5

ISBN: 978-1-912888-24-5

Edited by Nikki Mentges, NAM Editorial

Cover design by Abigail Sins

www.undercover-publishing.com

www.elise-noble.com

For Janet, who so selflessly gave so much to others.
The sky has another star now.

# CHAPTER 1 - BETHANY

"BETHANY, WOULD YOU help that lady?"

I forced a smile for Henrietta, the gallery manager, a scrawny blonde with an addiction to mascara who'd hated me from the moment I started working at Pemberton Fine Arts.

"Of course."

Henrietta thought I wanted her job, and while I couldn't deny I'd have accepted if it was offered, I wasn't about to stoop to her level and make snide comments to Hugo Pemberton, the gallery's owner, behind her back. Not that I in any way expected an offer—despite being thirty-four years old, I was little more than a glorified intern. Henrietta had only asked me to help because she was busy with another client and the third member of our little team, Gemma, had disappeared. Again.

I glanced towards the door to see who "that lady" was and swallowed a groan. Mirabella Vallos was no lady. She might have had money, but she also had a drinking problem and a stinky attitude to go with it. Even at school, she'd been a cantankerous little witch.

"Mira, how lovely to see you."

"Bethie!" Oh, how I hated being called Bethie. "It's been months, hasn't it? Since before your divorce? Wait—you're not *working* here, are you?"

The word "working" obviously left a nasty taste in her mouth because she screwed up her face in disgust. Or at least, she screwed up the bottom half. The top half was frozen in place by Botox. Mine had long since worn off, and boy was I glad to have the ability to frown back.

Ladies like Mira didn't work—well, maybe the odd day of volunteering to give them something to post on Instagram—and I'd once been a part of that realm. It was only recently that I'd turned my back on it, and I was still trying to find my place in a new world.

"Yes, I work here now."

"I heard..." She lowered her voice to a stage whisper, and I saw Henrietta straining to listen. "I heard you got screwed over in your settlement."

Screwed over? That was the understatement of the century. Somehow, our family home had ended up in a trust fund controlled by my ex-husband's parents, the villa in Italy turned out to be "owned" by a business partner, the fancy cars were "leased," and in an unexpected turn of events, our savings had dwindled due to a series of bad investments. By the time our lawyers finished arguing, I was left with our pied-à-terre in Kensington, an extensive designer wardrobe I no longer needed, a horse that ate the little money I had remaining, and a reputation as a gold-digging bitch. And the best part? My ex also kept my family. My parents and sister still liked him better than they did me.

"The settlement could have been better," I admitted. "What brings you here today?"

"We've just redecorated the lounge that overlooks the indoor riding arena, and we need to spruce up the walls."

An indoor riding arena was a mere memory for me. Chaucer spent most of his time in a muddy field now, and boy did he love to wallow.

"What did you have in mind?"

"Something horsey. Old-looking. What's that guy's name, the one who paints the thoroughbreds? Stubbings?"

"Stubbs. George Stubbs."

"Do you have any of those?"

"I'm afraid not. We could find you a print, but I don't believe there are any originals on the market at the moment."

And even if there were, they'd cost hundreds of thousands of pounds. Hardly the thing to hang on the wall of an indoor school. The insurance would be astronomical.

"I don't want a print."

"We do have some lovely paintings with a similar feel about them. Perhaps you'd like to look at those? And can I tempt you with a cup of tea or coffee while you're here?"

"Have you got any wine?"

It was only ten a.m., but okay then. If I recalled correctly, Mirabella tended to get rather loose with her husband's credit card once she had a few drinks inside her. Give her a bottle, and she wouldn't even know what she was buying. She'd once purchased a stallion at auction that turned out to be a gelding, and the day it arrived, she'd invited a bunch of us over to see her prized possession, still totally unaware. I hadn't been popular when I'd pointed out the lack of balls.

"Red or white?"

"Rosé or champagne."

But of course.

We'd held a show last night, and thankfully, we still had half a dozen bottles of rosé left over in the fridge. I stifled a yawn as I trudged to the kitchen. The show had been a success in that we'd sold all but two paintings, but the artist was a pretentious bore and the event ran late. Midnight had been and gone by the time I shovelled the last guest out of the door and into a taxi.

Still, I couldn't complain too much. At least I had a job.

Between my complete lack of experience and Piers bad-mouthing me to anyone who'd listen after I left him, finding work hadn't been easy. Do you know how much use a degree in art history is in the real world? No other gallery would give me so much as an interview, but luckily for me, Hugo had read for his degree at Oxford University, my alma mater, and also once had a bust-up with Piers's father. The whole Fortescue-Hamilton family was mud in Hugo's eyes, which I suspected was the main reason he'd offered me the position.

A position that paid peanuts, but it was better than having to turn to my parents. They weren't short of money, and they'd even offered to bail me out, but their "gifts" came with so many strings attached that it was like wading through macramé. Never again would I be beholden to another person, not a blood relative and certainly not a man.

Which was why I poured Mirabella a generous glass of rosé and headed back to the gallery to find her studying one of the most awful examples of modern art I'd ever seen. Imagine if Picasso drew a pineapple, then put it through a shredder and gave the pieces to a toddler to reassemble. Even Hugo agreed it had no redeeming features. He'd bought it as part of a job lot from a house clearance to get a David Hockney sketch he really wanted, and it was a toss-up over whether to burn the piece or hang it in the gallery on the off-chance some schmuck with appalling taste came in.

"Isn't it something?" I said to Mirabella as I passed her a glass of wine. "It's by Vincent Crystalla."

"Who?"

"He won the Turner Prize for *Laughter Unchained*." Which was a vaguely horrifying sculpture of a clown in orange prison overalls, handcuffs and leg shackles lying on the floor behind him. "Are you familiar with his work?"

"I don't think I saw that one."

"It's a metaphorical representation of the constraints oppressive governments put on human enjoyment. Profound. What do you think of *Fruit: Reconstructed*?"

"It's, uh, interesting."

"Imagine having that on the wall at one of your parties—it'd be a real talking point."

"You think? It's not a bit...offbeat?"

"Well, you have to be a real art lover to appreciate it."

"I'm not sure it'd work in the riding arena."

"No, you'd want something more traditional for that spot. Andrea Edmunds is an up-and-coming artist who paints horses in a distinctive style—acrylic on bare canvas with minute attention to detail—and she also takes commissions. Would you like to see her portfolio?"

Two hours and four glasses of rosé later, I helped Mirabella into a taxi and went back inside to face Henrietta. Any other boss would no doubt have been thrilled by the sales I'd made—two countryside scenes, one custom painting from Andrea Edmunds, and the awful pineapple thing—but I knew Henrietta wouldn't see it that way. We got a bonus for each painting sold, and her client had left without buying a thing.

"Bethany, a word?"

"Let me just clear these wine glasses away."

Anything to put off the inevitable. What would she make me do this time? Rearrange the packaging supplies? Reply to comments on the gallery's Facebook page? Dust the back office? In the five months I'd worked there, Henrietta had proven herself to be a master at dreaming up trivial tasks to keep me busy, thereby minimising the possibility that I might beat her in the sales stakes. And I couldn't say a thing. Complaining would make me look like a troublemaker, and I needed to keep this job for a little longer. The only thing that would look worse on my CV than no experience at all was leaving a position after such a short period of time.

"No, no, leave that. Gemma can do it. Hugo's asked you to run an errand."

Translation: Hugo had asked Henrietta to run an errand, and she'd seen it as the perfect opportunity to get rid of me.

"What kind of errand?"

Oh, that sly smile... She tried to hide it, but just for a moment, it popped onto her face unbidden.

"He wants you to deliver a painting to a client."

"Which client?"

Henrietta passed me a piece of paper, and I recognised Hugo Pemberton's elegant cursive.

"Here—Hugo wrote down the address so you wouldn't forget."

So *she* wouldn't forget, more like. The week after I started, she'd delivered a painting to Christie's instead of Sotheby's and blamed it on Gemma's poor instructions. But I'd been standing next to Gemma when she jotted down the notes from Hugo to give to Henrietta, and she'd clearly written Sotheby's. When Hugo asked if I knew anything, I couldn't lie, and that was another reason Henrietta went out of her way to make my life difficult.

Except that today, I got the last laugh. Hugo's note gave the address of a hotel in Richmond, with an instruction to meet AJ Lonsdale in the bar at four o'clock. It may have been less than ten miles away, but in London traffic, it would take me over two hours to get there and back, by which time the gallery would be closing. Since there was obviously no point in me going back to work, I could carry on driving west to Ascot and visit Chaucer. Between the distance to the stables, the cost of petrol, and the overtime at work, I only got to see him three days a week now if I was lucky, so today's trip would be an extra treat. Still, I tried to look cheesed off in case Henrietta changed her mind.

"I'll be sure to memorise the address. Where's the painting?"

"In Hugo's studio. You need to leave soon or you'll be late."

Really? But it was only half past twelve, and I didn't need to arrive until four. Then the old-fashioned brass bell above the front door jangled, and I realised

Henrietta just wanted to get rid of the competition.

"Ooh, I'd better go and speak to this couple," she said.

See?

Hugo was seated at his easel, his face hidden behind a jeweller's visor as he retouched an old oil portrait. The rather stern-looking lady was the ancestor of a client's wife, and he'd decided to have the painting restored as a Christmas surprise. If the wife was anything like my mother—and I suspected she was since they played tennis together—she'd rather have some diamonds or a trip to the Caribbean, but since the husband was paying Hugo a lot of money, I wasn't about to mention that.

"Henrietta said you wanted me to deliver a painting?"

Hugo tutted quietly under his breath. "I asked *her* to go while you looked after the customers."

As I suspected. I saw my precious hour with Chaucer slipping away. "I could ask her to swap? But some people just came in, and she's talking with them." I leaned in closer to study the painting. The last time I'd seen it, there had been a two-inch tear in one corner, but now the damage was all but invisible. "Did you patch it?"

"I considered that, but there were flaky areas of paint on the subject's dress, and also the face, so in the end, I re-lined it instead."

Sometimes, when a painting had been neglected over the years and was almost beyond saving, the best option was to bond the whole thing—the damaged canvas and what was left of the paint—onto a new canvas behind using a heat-sensitive glue.

The number-one rule of art restoration was that any changes to the painting needed to be reversible. After re-lining, the whole thing would be coated in a synthetic, non-yellowing varnish that could be removed later with solvent if necessary. Only then would the delicate process of retouching begin. A restorer was a master in his own right—he had to be every bit as skilled as the original artist as well as schooled in chemistry, materials, and the history of art. Hugo Pemberton was one of the best.

Once, I'd hoped to follow in his footsteps. The way a seemingly lost cause could be transformed into its former glory by a process that at times seemed like magic had fascinated me for years, ever since my father had my family's own art collection restored when I was a child. But a lack of courage and marriage to the wrong man had put paid to those dreams, and now I was the errand girl.

"It looks great. About that delivery—I really don't mind making the trip. Best not to interrupt Henrietta when she's with potential customers."

"Yes, yes, you're right. As long as you're sure you don't mind." Hugo's lips pinched in concentration as he selected a tiny sable brush, a double-zero size, then changed his mind and swapped it for an even smaller triple-zero. "The painting's right over there in the corner."

He waved his other hand at a small wooden crate, roughly thirty inches by fifteen. From those dimensions, I knew the painting would be about two feet by one foot in size as we tended to allow three inches for packing materials, perhaps a little more if it needed to survive a plane trip. Inside, the painting would be wrapped in buffered, acid-free tissue paper and a layer of bubble wrap, with the remaining space filled by styrofoam peanuts.

"Is it the Stanley Spencer landscape?"

"No, I'm still working on that one. This is a Heath Robert, a birthday surprise for a friend in California. His assistant's in town today, and he's going to take it back with him."

Heath Robert—pronounced "Roe-bear," never "Roh-bert"—was a well-established artist fond of painting sailing boats. The last work of his we'd sold went for eleven thousand pounds, so it was a generous gift. But Hugo always had been generous. On my birthday, he'd given me a bottle of Veuve Clicquot, then taken me, Henrietta, and Gemma out for dinner at the fancy restaurant around the corner. Even Henrietta had been cheerful that night.

"Lovely—I'll take good care of it. Don't work too late, will you?"

"No, no, of course not."

Hugo would ignore me, just as he always did. It wasn't unusual for me to unlock the gallery in the morning and find him fast asleep on the old leather sofa in the corner of his studio, snoring quietly. Hugo got so engrossed in his work that he forgot about the time.

Outside, I carefully strapped the Heath Robert into the boot of my Ford Fiesta, a car I'd bought second-hand with proceeds from the sale of four Versace evening gowns and half a dozen hats I'd never worn. I still had clothes in the consignment store near my apartment, and every so often, money would trickle into Chaucer's carrot fund.

The four-year-old Fiesta was a bit of a come-down after driving a series of brand-new Mercedes for the last decade, but I didn't care. Better to own my car than to have Piers remind me who financed my lifestyle every five minutes. Or worse still, my parents.

I carefully closed the boot and squeezed through the narrow gap to the driver's door. According to my father, Hugo had inherited the gallery building from his parents, and it came with a tiny yard and half a dozen parking spaces at the rear—a real luxury in Chelsea. Since I didn't have parking at my apartment, he let me keep my car there, tucked in between his old Jaguar and Henrietta's BMW compact. Yet another reason to hang on to my job.

When I set the satnav on my phone, the route was one solid red line from beginning to end. No problem— thanks to Henrietta, I had plenty of time, and I could listen to an audiobook on the way. And stop off for a coffee. And pick up a bag of carrots for Chaucer. And perhaps grab a microwave meal for dinner. The big supermarket near Earl's Court had a café and free parking, so it seemed rude not to. Far better to get my caffeine fix at Tesco prices than pay through the nose in a hotel bar while I waited for AJ Lonsdale to arrive.

The painting would be okay in the car for a few minutes, wouldn't it? I'd heard of gadgets that could detect electronics—laptops and the like—but not canvas. Besides, there was CCTV. Surely even the most brazen of thieves would hesitate before breaking into a vehicle in broad daylight in a busy car park under the watchful eyes of a camera.

Should I head to the café first? Or the produce section? After I'd exited the car, I yawned as I carefully skirted around a homeless man and headed towards the store. Why weren't the doors opening? Oh. Because that was the exit. Duh. *Wake up, Bethany.* In four hours, I'd see the only male I still cared about, and then I could go home to get some sleep. Honestly, I was so over humans. Give me a horse any day.

# CHAPTER 2 - ALARIC

"FUCK, CINDERS—COULD you have found a more inappropriate surveillance vehicle?"

Alaric McLain watched in the rear-view mirror as Emmy Black closed up behind him in a sleek black Aston Martin. Even with his windows shut, he heard her approach.

"I'm sorry, okay?" Emmy's voice came through the speakers in his rented Honda SUV. "I've had two hours' sleep, and I'm barely functioning. I could've sworn there were more cars in the garage, but all that was left was this and a motorbike."

"Why didn't you bring the motorbike?"

"You want me to wear leathers in this temperature? I'd sweat like a pig." Granted, she had a point there. Early May, and the weather in London had gone haywire. The last two days had been like a cheerleader's pool party—wet and hot. "Plus there was nowhere to put my rifle."

Alaric didn't even try to hide his groan. "You brought a rifle? We're chasing an art thief, not a bunch of terrorists."

"You told me that terrorists steal art to finance their activities. 'It's not like in the movies,'" she mimicked. "'Forget *Ocean's Twelve* and *The Thomas Crown Affair*.'"

That was true. Many people shared a romanticised image of art thieves, fostered in no small part by Hollywood. In real life, men who took masterpieces didn't do it for the challenge or a bet—more often than not, they were hardened criminals after cold, hard cash, and paintings made easier targets than, say, a bank or an armoured truck. Narcotics dealers used them as trading cards. Thieves sold them through fences for a fraction of their true value. Or occasionally, they were stolen to order for people who ran roughshod over others to satisfy their selfish desires.

The police didn't tend to take art theft seriously either. As long as nobody got hurt and the insurance companies paid up, cultural crimes got put on the back burner. Despite the vast sums of money involved, museum heists got handled by the same squad as a common or garden burglary, and those cops didn't have the knowledge or the resources to recover stolen paintings.

How did Alaric know all this? Because he'd once been a member of the FBI's Art Crime Team, a small band of investigators and undercover agents who specialised in recovering treasures that would otherwise be lost forever. It had been a surprise transfer, a promotion, and it made a change from dealing with plain ol' RICO violations. Although the Art Crime Team worked out of Washington, DC, he'd spent much of his time overseas, skulking through the underbelly of society in search of missing cultural artifacts. Many of them made their way to the United States—it was the biggest market in the world for stolen treasures.

One day, Alaric might have masqueraded as a thief,

the next, as a middleman or a buyer. Undercover work was his speciality, the ability to hide in plain sight a skill he'd been perfecting since childhood. Colleagues called him a chameleon. His father was a diplomat, and moving from country to country had meant Alaric learned to fit in quickly. He'd lived everywhere from England to Italy to Tanzania to Poland, and as a result, he'd learned more about people than an entire anthropology department. It had been only natural for him to join the CIA after college and take his hobby of being places where he shouldn't be to a whole other level. Bureaucracy and a boss he couldn't stand led him to quit after four years, but the FBI had welcomed him with open arms. At least, they had until they'd fired him.

Hence today's little excursion.

With no Bureau backup anymore, Alaric had been forced to turn to Emmy—his ex-girlfriend and part-owner of Blackwood Security. His own private intelligence agency, Sirius, was still in its infancy, and all three of his business partners were men. They may have been experts in their field, but male-female surveillance teams tended to work better, other than the rare occasions when the female half turned up in a fucking supercar, obviously.

"I'd have preferred you in the leather outfit," he told Emmy.

"Of course you would, but the bike was a bright red Ducati. Look on the bright side—no sane person would run surveillance in this beast, so Blondie won't suspect a thing."

Blondie was a retail assistant named Bethany Stafford-Lyons. They'd met her last night during the

Pemberton gallery's latest exhibition, where they'd snooped around and planted half a dozen bugs in addition to gushing over the paintings and pretending to drink champagne. Her hair colour came from a bottle, the contents a shade or three too light for her complexion, and either she'd been on vacation recently or her tan was applied by hand as well. Stafford-Lyons took care of herself, but she wasn't a princess. When she'd handed Alaric a drink, she'd tried to hide the chips in her manicure, then blushed when she noticed him glance at a faint bruise on her calf still visible through her sheer pantyhose.

A preliminary background check showed Stafford-Lyons was a thirty-four-year-old divorcee who'd worked at Pemberton Fine Arts for the last five months, but apart from that, she hadn't held a job since she graduated from Oxford with a first-class honours degree in art history. Credit records were sketchy, mainly because she didn't appear to have paid for anything prior to her divorce. A kept woman. Her only sins had been an arrest at an animal rights protest when she was eighteen and a handful of parking tickets. One of Alaric's business partners, Judd, ran in those sorts of circles, and his assessment of her father suggested a manipulative man who'd stop at nothing to get his own way. The ex-husband? A "blithering idiot, a sycophant."

Was Bethany Stafford-Lyons hurting for money? Rumour said the divorce settlement hadn't been kind to her. Sure, her address was in Kensington, but 122c Carlton Terrace was a tiny apartment, a far cry from the Surrey mansion she'd lived in previously. The change in lifestyle must have hurt. Had she been tempted to get involved with Pemberton's side hustle to make some extra cash?

Alaric dropped back a few car lengths, letting Emmy take the lead through Chelsea. He hated to admit it, but the Aston fit in quite well there. They could swap positions after they left the area.

Where was Stafford-Lyons heading? He had no idea. The bug had picked up Pemberton talking on the phone earlier, and he confirmed he'd be sending his assistant to the meet with *Red After Dark* as previously arranged. Since the gallery manager was tied up with customers and the lazy brunette with the nicotine habit didn't have a vehicle, that left Stafford-Lyons. Certainly she'd carried a box of the right size towards the rear exit of the gallery.

"You really think this woman can lead us to *Emerald*?" Emmy asked. "She seems kind of... virtuous."

"You know who else seemed virtuous? Bernie Madoff."

"Fair point. Care to give me a proper briefing yet? I'm not completely in the dark, but it's definitely twilight."

"I would've done it last night over dinner if you hadn't lived up to your nickname and run out on me, Cinders."

The moniker had come about after Emmy lost one of her high-heeled pumps in a wine bar on their first date. Red-lacquered soles, size six. His first two wilderness years excepted, Alaric had bought Emmy a pair of designer heels for every birthday, remembering Bradley's instruction to go up a size in the Louboutins. Bradley was Emmy's assistant, a man who knew more about fashion than *Vogue* and who'd been responsible for the Brioni suit habit Alaric had never been able to break.

"Believe me, I'd rather have sat around drinking wine until the early hours, but when some fucker breaks into one of the properties we monitor..."

"Did you get him?"

Silence. If Emmy had been sitting in the passenger seat, Alaric knew she'd have been wearing her snarky "what do you think?" face.

"Of course you got him."

"I also got a lot of questions from the cops plus a whole ream of paperwork. They really don't love it when bad guys trip down the stairs."

"Hence the lack of sleep and the tetchiness?"

"I'm *not* tetchy."

"Whatever you say, Cinders."

"Briefing?"

Alaric swallowed a laugh. Nearly eight years, and Emmy hadn't changed a bit. Not like him. In many ways, he was grateful for that. How many other women would step off a jet at Heathrow, spend the night fighting crime, and then go straight out on a job with barely an explanation? Plus she still trusted him while many others didn't.

"Remember when *Emerald* went missing? That wasn't the only painting the thieves took—there were four others stolen in the same heist."

Collateral damage, no doubt snatched because of their proximity to the main prize. *The Girl with the Emerald Ring* had been the obvious target. Once held in the private collection of Ada and Gerhard Becker, it was moved to their namesake museum in Boston upon

Ada's death fifteen years ago. In her native Germany, Ada had grown up as the daughter of a wealthy industrialist, and with money no object, she'd spent years amassing art, a passion she'd inherited from her father and one that hadn't diminished when she emigrated to the United States at the age of thirty-seven. In her will, she'd insisted her collection go on show for the nation to enjoy when she passed.

It was from the Becker Museum that *Emerald* had been stolen thirteen years ago in a daring robbery involving smoke canisters and a rooftop escape. None of the guards from the surveillance room downstairs noticed a thing until it was too late, mainly because they were far too busy chasing a squirrel through the sculpture hall, which it later emerged had been released by the thief or thieves. The police found a box hidden behind a life-sized model of Aphrodite, complete with a remote-controlled locking mechanism and a handful of macadamia nuts. Presumably a "visitor" had left it there. Nobody noticed, and why would they? The security team had been concerned with people taking things out of the gallery, not bringing them in.

"Yeah, I remember. But the others weren't as valuable, were they?"

"No, but collectively they were still worth millions. And two weeks ago, a contact of mine believes they caught sight of *Red After Dark* in Hugo Pemberton's studio."

"That's the one with the red-headed woman running into the forest?"

"You remember?" Alaric was impressed, but then again, Emmy was fond of art herself, although her tastes tended towards more modern pieces. Her ability to appreciate a painting's beauty was yet another thing that had attracted him to her.

"We spent weeks looking for those paintings before you fucked off to who knows where. And Blackwood's still looking for them. We never stopped."

"Really?"

"Dude, I never give up."

True. Emmy always had been a tenacious bitch, which was both a good thing and a bad thing, depending on the situation.

"That makes two of us. If it's the last thing I do, I want to get *Emerald* back where she belongs and find out who took the pay-off as well."

*The pay-off.* Alaric's downfall. The day it disappeared had been both the best and worst of his life. After months of undercover work, he'd finally gotten a lead on *Emerald*, the jewel in the Becker Museum's crown. Negotiating the purchase had taken weeks, and together with his colleagues at the Bureau, he'd planned an elaborate sting operation involving a yacht, a helicopter, and a payment of ten million dollars—one million in cash and the rest in diamonds. Except things hadn't quite gone according to plan.

The first indication that the job was jinxed came when the helicopter the FBI had dredged up—the only one available that didn't scream "law enforcement"—developed an engine problem. The doohickey to fix it wouldn't be available for at least a week, apparently.

That presented a problem because when Alaric had spoken to the broker the evening before, he'd claimed to be in Florida, a thirteen-hour drive away but only two hours by air. If Dyson had men watching for

Alaric's arrival and he suddenly appeared in a car, rather than by helicopter as they'd previously discussed, that would arouse suspicions. Cue a call to Emmy, who'd offered up her Eurocopter plus a pilot for the short hop from her place near Richmond to Virginia Beach.

Issue number two had revealed itself the following morning as he ate breakfast with Emmy. The scheme called for two bikini-clad girls to accompany him— every rich asshole had them—but one of Alaric's would-be deck ornaments had fallen down the stairs at the Chesapeake field office and broken her ankle yesterday afternoon. By the time she got out of surgery and somebody thought to inform Alaric, it was too late to arrange a replacement.

"We're gonna have to call this off," he said, groaning into his oatmeal. "We can't go ahead without Gina."

"Why not?"

The FBI's team had been finely balanced—the staff that an unscrupulous businessman would be expected to travel with versus a team capable of taking down Dyson and his goons if the need arose. The few people who'd met the guy said he usually brought half a dozen men. As well as the bikini girls, Alaric's alter ego, Joseph Delray, had a captain and a deckhand for his yacht, plus a butler and a bodyguard. Any more and they risked scaring Dyson off.

The captain and deckhand knew boats, the butler was another agent from the Art Crime Team who spent most of his time behind a desk, and the bodyguard was a former marine picked out by Alaric's boss. Secretly, Alaric thought the marine was a bit of a dick. A call to his old college roommate, himself a captain in the USMC, confirmed Alaric's initial impressions— Corporal Hooper had been great at sucking up to the brass, apparently, but not so good in the field. Nobody had been sorry to see him go. That left the girls, one of whom had been selected for her shooting skills and the other for her rack.

"Gina was our best marksman, and the job's risky enough as it is. I had to fight like hell to get it approved, and now the program manager's getting cold feet. Quite frankly, so am I."

"So you need a girl who can shoot?"

"Yes, and they're in remarkably short supply."

"What time do we leave?"

Alaric did a double take. "You?"

"I think I'm qualified to wear a bikini, and I certainly know how to fire a gun."

"You said you had a meeting at ten."

"A meeting I've been looking for an excuse to ditch, and this one's perfect. Would I rather sunbathe on a boat or freeze my tits off in an air-conditioned conference room in Langley while a bunch of spooks argue with each other? Hmm, let me think for a nanosecond..."

"I'm not sure the boss'll go for that."

"No, but his boss's boss will. I won't even charge the FBI for my time." Emmy grinned, and Alaric had never been able to resist her smile. "This is gonna be fun."

# CHAPTER 3 - ALARIC

EIGHT PHONE CALLS and two hours later, Emmy and Alaric had boarded her helicopter together. That was the only reason he was still alive today.

Off the Virginia coast, he feigned relaxation while the captain motored the Seaduction—a nice fifty-footer confiscated from a drug dealer and his fifth wife—out to sea to meet their prey. The trip took on a jovial air as the girls lay out on the sun deck and the guys sipped drinks from the cooler, and Alaric dared to hope that the exchange might even go smoothly. By all accounts, Dyson was an honourable guy—for a thief, anyway— and he didn't have a habit of double-crossing his buyers. Tough but fair, Alaric's sources told him. If Dyson said he had *Emerald*, then the painting was in his possession.

Four miles off the coast, the captain shut off the engine and waved Alaric over.

"This is it, boss. These are the coordinates, but there's nothin' here." No, there wasn't. Just a blue sky and gentle swell as far as the eye could see. "What now?"

"Now, we wait."

A half hour ticked by before a small scallop vessel appeared on the horizon. Alaric thought at first that it would pass them, but it turned to circle them once before it approached.

"This is it," Emmy said from her position on a sunlounger. "A shitty fishing boat. Nice move."

As the scalloper came closer, Alaric saw that the occupants were anything but fishermen. He counted six men, all wearing jackets despite the heat. The muscle. The main man, the man Alaric had dug through the dark reaches of society to find, was nowhere to be seen. Rumour said he was older, a nondescript shadow.

"You have a tender?" the tallest of the crew barked.

They did—a small Zodiac RIB with a powerful outboard motor. Drug dealers had the best toys, everything from planes to sports cars to mini-submarines. It was almost enough to make Alaric rethink his career. The FBI paid peanuts. He had a little family money to fall back on so he wasn't exactly on the breadline, but he hated feeling undervalued.

"Yes, we have a tender."

"You'll come alone."

Go alone? No problem. He'd been ready for that. He'd been ready for almost anything except what actually happened.

From the deck of the Seaduction, the waves hadn't looked like much, but as he bumped towards the scalloper in a dinghy, they seemed a whole lot bigger. Unlike Emmy, he hadn't spent much time on the water, and his stomach threatened to heave its contents overboard as he approached the bigger boat. *It's just seasickness*, he told himself. Nothing to do with the fact that the assholes on board most likely had guns and he didn't. He'd considered bringing one along in an ankle holster, but Dyson had specified that he go unarmed, and the information Alaric had managed to glean suggested the man wasn't dangerous unless provoked. The risks of carrying a concealed weapon outweighed the benefits.

Emmy, on the other hand... Not only was she a weapon in her own right, but when they'd arrived at the marina, she'd hefted a duffel bag up the gangplank onto the Seaduction and dumped it beside the bed in the master stateroom. She hadn't volunteered what was in it, and Alaric had known better than to ask.

Now he secured the tender's painter to the bottom rung of the metal ladder attached to the side of the scalloper, then faced the challenge of climbing the damn thing carrying a briefcase in one hand. If Emmy had been in the Zodiac, she'd have laughed her fucking head off. Probably she'd also have brought some kind of strap to secure the briefcase to her back if she'd been the one doing the handover. There was a reason Alaric had chosen to specialise in information gathering rather than hands-on operations. Let him talk his way into a fancy party over bobbing around in a dinghy any day.

Fortunately, the crew of the scalloper saw his predicament and lowered a rope.

"Tie the briefcase on," the tall guy ordered.

Alaric hesitated. With the money on board, there was a risk they'd cut him loose, or worse, shoot him. His heart hammered in his chest as he evaluated the risks, but ultimately, he came to the conclusion that Dyson had a reputation to protect, even if it was a slightly shady one.

The briefcase disappeared over the metal railing above, and Alaric quickly stuck a tracker to the scalloper's hull just above the waterline, then clambered up the ladder, puffing as he neared the top. The last month had been manic, and all those missed gym sessions were starting to show. Emmy had given him a workout last night, but that combined with only a couple of hours' sleep hadn't exactly helped his energy levels, and he was grateful when two of the crew members helped him onto the deck before giving him a thorough pat-down. They missed his subvocal earpiece and the microphone built into his watch, but he sure was glad he'd left the gun behind.

"Mr. Dyson is downstairs," the tall guy said, handing the briefcase back to Alaric.

Below decks, their target was working at his laptop in the crew quarters, a four-berth stateroom now converted into a makeshift office with a desk crammed between the bunks. Dyson was undoubtedly not his real name, but it was the only name Alaric had for him. Considering the man's reputation as one of the art world's premier fixers, Alaric had been expecting something more than a diminutive guy in his fifties sporting thinning brown hair, flip-flops, Bermuda shorts, and a T-shirt advertising a brand of beer Alaric had never heard of. But when the picture in his head didn't match up with reality, he mentally chided himself. After years working undercover, he of all people should know that appearances were deceptive.

Dyson looked up. "Mr. Delray. We meet at last."

That line came from a bad action movie, which unbeknown to Alaric at that moment, was exactly what the situation was about to turn into. He smiled and nodded. The smile was tense, and deliberately so— Alaric's alter ego hadn't been keen to meet in the middle of the fucking ocean.

"Difficult trip?" he asked. "The sea's a little rough today."

"On the contrary—it's always a pleasure to get out on the water, even in a boat like this. Do you have the money?"

"Do you have the painting?"

Dyson chuckled. "All in good time. Can I interest you in a drink?"

He waved a hand at a glass-fronted mini-fridge on the floor in one corner, and Alaric spotted a bottle of Dom Perignon as well as soft drinks and a six-pack of beer. Dyson was an enigma, a ghost with many faces, much like Alaric himself was to become after that day.

"Let's save that for after we've completed the deal, shall we?"

"As you wish." Dyson closed the laptop and tucked it into a drawer, then tapped his hand on the desk. "Let me see."

Alaric hefted the briefcase onto the table. One million bucks in hundred-dollar bills weighed twenty-two pounds, not much for what amounted to a lifetime's work for many people. The remainder of the pay-off, the diamonds, consisted of sixty-five stones of three to four carats each, all rated in the top two categories for clarity—IF or VVS1. Alaric had learned a lot about gems over the last few months, and not just because of this case. No, last month, he'd bitten the bullet and bought a ring for Emmy. Would he ever give it to her? He didn't know. He wanted to. But there was one big obstacle standing in the way, and his name was Black.

Emmy's husband.

The two of them had never been married in the

traditional sense. There was no big white wedding with a kiss and a honeymoon at the end. From what Alaric could gather, it had started off as a green-card deal, a way to tie Emmy to Blackwood Security and her job for good, but the arrangement had lasted for seven years and counting. The pair lived together, and even though Emmy assured Alaric that there was no romance involved, he'd seen the way Black looked at her. The asshole wouldn't let Emmy go easily.

Did Alaric feel guilty about dating another man's wife? Not really. It wasn't as if Black stayed celibate. Emmy said he had a fuck pad in Richmond, an apartment where he took women, but when Alaric did some digging, he found it was so much more than that. Black didn't just have the occasional hook-up, he had a whole damn harem. The women lived in an apartment complex in Rybridge, usually half a dozen at any one time, and they even had a concierge to look after them. When Black needed to get his rocks off, he just picked out a piece of ass and had her sent over. Did Emmy know all that? Alaric was fairly sure she didn't. The beck-and-call girls signed NDAs.

And tempting though it had been to let the information slip, he didn't want to win Emmy's affections by driving a wedge between her and Black. She obviously cared for the man despite his many faults. No, Alaric needed to tread carefully and bide his time.

The night before the handover, before they'd flown to Virginia Beach and picked up the yacht, Emmy had fallen asleep in his arms for a few minutes, something she never normally did. He'd whispered that he loved her. Did she hear? He wasn't sure, but when her eyes flickered open, she'd kissed him sweetly, almost tenderly, and he'd sensed her hesitation before she headed back to her own bedroom. She'd wanted to stay.

Why hadn't she? Because she was dangerous. A combination of nightmares, instinct, and lightning-fast reflexes meant she was capable of killing a man in her sleep, and she'd come damn close once. Ever since that night, she'd slept alone.

But maybe if she got away from Blackwood, away from the source of the strife...

Alaric pushed the thought out of his mind as he unlocked the briefcase. That was a problem for another day.

The first inkling that something was wrong came with Dyson's sharp intake of breath. What was the issue? Alaric had watched the accountant at the Bureau pack the cash himself, and the amount was spot on— one million dollars exactly, taken from a slush fund that didn't officially exist. Alaric's boss hadn't been thrilled about him borrowing it, or the conflict diamonds confiscated from a crooked lobbyist, but since they'd be coming right back, he'd grudgingly agreed.

An FBI team would be monitoring the scalloper's movements by now, thanks to the tracker Alaric had installed. The agents were stationed on a coastguard patrol boat just outside the marina. They'd decided it was too risky to have more vessels in the area in case they spooked the target, and that was a good call judging by the marine radar unit mounted above the scalloper's bridge. As long as Alaric got *Emerald*, Dyson and his friends would be arrested as soon as they set foot on the shore. And if the sale turned out to be a scam and Dyson attempted to steal the money? Same outcome—handcuffs and a nice vacation in prison. Sure, there was a chance they'd try to dump Alaric's body overboard, but what was life without a little danger? He wasn't worried. He'd been in worse situations, and he had Emmy as backup. Oh, and the other FBI agents, but Emmy was worth ten of them.

"This money is fake," Dyson snapped. "Do you think I'm stupid?"

What? *This* was the scam? They'd lured Alaric into the middle of nowhere, only to accuse him of a double-cross? As if he'd do that. Not when Dyson was their best—and only—lead to a ring that had stolen hundreds of millions of dollars' worth of art. Rumour said the School of Shadows had been involved in the *Emerald* heist as well as the disappearance of a Van Gogh last year and numerous other high-profile thefts over the past four decades, but nobody knew who they were or where they came from. Alaric couldn't afford to screw this up.

"It's not fake."

"I wasn't born yesterday. These bills all have the same serial number."

A chill started in Alaric's toes and worked its way up his body. Duplicate serial numbers were amateur hour, and they hadn't even been sequential let alone identical when he left FBI headquarters in Washington, DC. He grabbed one stack and thumbed through them, and the chill turned to a full-on glacier seeping through his veins. The notes *were* forgeries, and not even good ones. Instead of puffy clouds drifting over Independence Hall, there was a fucking tempest brewing.

"What the hell?" he muttered under his breath.

Meanwhile, Dyson had tipped a couple of the rocks out of their velvet pouch and begun examining them with a diamond tester, a small electronic device that measured the electrical and thermal conductivity of the stone. Diamonds wouldn't conduct electricity, whereas some imitations would.

Such as the ones in Dyson's hand, for example.

"This is cubic zirconia," he said. "I negotiate in good faith, and you, my friend, are a fraud."

*No, no, no.* Those damn stones were diamonds. According to Alaric's boss, every single one had been authenticated by a jeweller when they were confiscated, and they'd been sitting in a safe at the Bureau ever since. Alaric knew it was possible to tamper with a diamond tester, to rewire the inside to skew the readings, and if that had been the only problem, he'd have suspected Dyson was trying to pull a fast one. But the hundred-dollar bills... Sometime between the originals being loaded into the briefcase at headquarters and that moment on the boat, they'd been swapped. What if the real diamonds had been taken too?

He was trapped in a fucking horror story.

"I don't know where those stones came from."

At best, the operation was blown. At worst, his entire career had been flushed down the toilet. He'd been entrusted with ten million bucks' worth of loot, and now it was gone. How the hell would he explain things to his boss? His brain froze, which gave Dyson enough time to get to the door. At that point, Alaric realised that losing his job wasn't actually the worst-case scenario; losing his life was.

Dyson shook his head, dismissive. "Enrique! Get rid of this man."

Fuck.

Enrique, the tall guy, appeared with another five henchmen behind him, all with guns in their hands and pissed expressions on their faces. Their bearing said former military, their willingness to accept orders said they'd turned mercenary, and Enrique's malicious grin said he was enjoying this.

"With pleasure."

From another world, Emmy's voice registered in Alaric's ear.

"Got your back, Prince."

Her tone said what her words didn't—he also had her trust, and that meant everything.

When Enrique jabbed the muzzle of his pistol into the small of Alaric's back, he moved towards the narrow staircase, careful to keep his hands in sight. No sudden moves. No twitches that could encourage Enrique to pull the trigger too soon. Whatever Emmy was planning, he needed to trust her in return and let her do her job.

Except muffled voices told him things weren't going to plan on the Seaduction either.

"Stand down, Marine," Emmy said, presumably to Hooper. "We don't need any heroes."

"Ma'am, you're not in charge here."

"Neither are you."

"This is an FBI operation, and you're a civilian. In McLain's absence, I'm assuming command."

"No, you're making a difficult situation worse."

*Fuck, fuck, fuck.*

Alaric blinked in the daylight as they emerged onto

the deck, and the first thing he saw was sunlight glinting off the gun in Hooper's hand. Enrique saw it too—only a damn mole could've missed it. His pistol shifted to the side of Alaric's head in order to use Alaric's body as a shield, and the other men dived behind whatever cover they could find when Hooper began firing. Emmy charged him and pushed the jackass into the water, but not before the damage was done. The mercenaries shot back, and a blossom of red formed on the captain's shirt as he crumpled to the deck. The last thing Alaric saw before Enrique dragged him behind the pilot house was Emmy taking a running leap across the gap between the two boats. In a gold fucking bikini.

By the time she'd finished playing cat and mouse, six men were dead, Hooper was spewing curses, the helicopter was on its way to pick up the injured captain, and Dyson was nowhere to be found. *Emerald*, the laptop, the Zodiac, and the briefcase? They were gone too.

# CHAPTER 4 - ALARIC

"EARTH TO ALARIC," Emmy said, her voice loud and clear through the Honda's speakers. "Don't zone out, dude. You owe me a briefing."

Right. A briefing on the job. The whole reason they'd come to London in the first place.

"Sorry."

"The gallery? *Red After Dark*? I didn't see it last night."

"No, it was never for sale or even on display. Alessandra got 'lost' on her way to the bathroom and wandered into Pemberton's upstairs studio out of curiosity. When he found her in there, she said she was interested in buying it, but he told her it was with him for restoration on behalf of a client."

"Alessandra? Your contact's a woman?"

Was it Alaric's imagination, or was there a hint of jealousy there? Emmy had no right to feel that way— *she* was the one who was married.

"Why the surprise? I've heard I can be very charming when the need arises."

"No reason. So, the painting? Why did we plant bugs instead of searching for it?"

"One, Pemberton's got hidden cameras all over the gallery, the private areas and restoration room included." Alessandra had spotted them—it was her job, since she was an undercover officer with Italy's Carabinieri. "And two, he told Alessa that the owner was picking it up today."

"Except the owner asked for delivery service?" Emmy guessed.

"Exactly. I overheard Pemberton talking on the phone this morning, before the gallery opened, and he offered the services of his assistant."

"Where's the handover?"

"I don't know—the owner said he'd email the final details within the hour, and the bug in the hallway by the bathroom picked up Pemberton giving instructions to that bitchy manager chick. Seems he wrote the address down."

"Your team hasn't hacked his email?"

"Not yet. He doesn't appear to use it all that much."

Up ahead, Stafford-Lyons passed the site of the former Earls Court Exhibition Centre and slowed for the traffic lights, positioned in the middle lane. Alaric let a Porsche cut in between them, the driver too busy on the phone to notice when the lights turned green. Ten seconds passed before Emmy got impatient from two cars behind and leaned on the horn.

"Where are you going, lady?" she muttered. "Holland Park? Hammersmith?"

No, Tesco.

Stafford-Lyons signalled and pulled into the parking lot, then slotted her Ford Fiesta neatly into a space near the back. What the hell was she doing? Stopping to buy groceries? Surprise turned to incredulity when she exited the vehicle with only a small purse. Where was the painting? Had she left it in the trunk? *Red After Dark* was worth a million dollars.

"What the fuck?" Emmy asked.

"I have no idea."

"Did we get this wrong? Nobody in their right mind's gonna leave a painting by Edwin Bateson in a parked car while they go into a bloody supermarket."

Alaric was beginning to wonder the same thing himself. "I guess it's possible we made a mistake."

"Maybe the other assistant was meant to deliver the painting and this one's just out to buy lunch? Did you actually see her load the thing into her car?"

"No, I didn't," he admitted. "She carried a package in that direction, and the other girl's with customers, so I just assumed..."

"Never assume—"

"It makes an ass out of 'u' and 'me,'" he finished. How many times had she told him that? "This job's cursed."

"Want to go back?"

"We'd better."

"Okay, but let me grab some food first. I skipped breakfast, and my stomach's protesting."

Emmy was the only girl Alaric had ever dated who ate more than he did. Probably because she spent half her life in the gym and ran a marathon every week. He worked out, but he'd always struggled to keep up with her. Did he mind? No way. That stamina meant she'd blown his fucking mind in the bedroom, as well as other parts of his anatomy.

"Hurry up, Cinders. And bring me back a sandwich, would you?"

Emmy bleeped the locks on the Aston and strolled into the store, following in the footsteps of Stafford-Lyons. Damn, that ass. It had only gotten better over the years. Mind you, Alaric had always been a leg man, and Stafford-Lyons gave Emmy a run for her money in that department, especially in those pumps. *Don't be so fucking shallow, McLain.* He forced his gaze away from his ex and focused on the surveillance app on his phone. Last night, they'd taken advantage of the crowd cover to install small, wireless bugs, Russian-made, easy to hide but poor when it came to battery life. He'd set them to voice-activated mode to conserve power, and a quick check revealed everything was operating as it should. Any conversations within range would come through the car's Bluetooth speakers.

If he got the chance, he'd go back to the gallery at some point and retrieve the spent devices. They weren't cheap, and Alaric was funding this fool's errand on his own dime. Time and time again, his business partners had told him to let it go, to focus on the future, and he knew they were right, but...he just couldn't. Even after all these years, he still felt a compulsion to clear his name, to prove he wasn't a thief to everyone who'd doubted his word. His colleagues, his parents, his former friends... The only person from his old life who truly believed in him was Emmy. Sure, the others at Blackwood had tried to help in the aftermath of the Seaduction disaster, but they'd never trusted him again, no matter how hard Emmy had fought his corner.

The sting of that would never fade.

At the gallery, Henrietta encouraged a couple to buy a painting. A landscape, one that would look just darling above their fireplace, or so she claimed. If it was the one Alaric was thinking of, the horses looked like donkeys and the clouds bore more than a passing

resemblance to the Stay Puft Marshmallow Man.
Silence from Hugo Pemberton. He seemed to be a man
of few words.

Alaric was about to call Emmy and ask her to pick
up a packet of chips for him too when he spotted a girl
heading for Stafford-Lyons's car. A blonde teenager
wearing torn black jeans and a faded hoodie over a T-
shirt that showed her midriff. Even from forty metres
away, Alaric could see the holes in her sneakers. A
fashion statement? Alaric had never understood the
attraction of adding ventilation to perfectly good
clothes.

The girl didn't look behind her, didn't hesitate as
she unlocked the Fiesta and slid into the driver's seat.
Who was she? Alaric didn't have time to consider the
question before he frantically dialled Emmy.

"Get your sweet ass back here. This *must* be a
handover because the car's on the move."

# CHAPTER 5 - SKY

IT STARTED LIKE any other Wednesday morning, with borderline exhaustion and an errand to run for Digger, a guy who made his money doing questionable things for questionable people. Two or three times a week, sometimes every other day, he gave me an envelope to run across London and twenty quid for the "favour." I didn't know what was in the envelopes. I didn't want to know.

Then my phone rang, and a tedious day turned worse.

"Sky, can you pick me up? Pleeeeeeease. If I could get back to Lambeth, you know I would, right? But I've got no money and..."

"And what, Lenny?"

I'd heard it all before. Every damn excuse under the sun, but each time he called pleading, I still gave in. Out of the many, many foster siblings I'd had, Lenny was the only one who'd treated me like a human being rather than an opponent. My childhood had been one big competition, with kids vying to stay with the good families and escape the bad. I first met Lenny when I was eight and he was fourteen. We'd clicked straight away despite the age gap, and for the first time in my life, I'd had a friend. Someone to eat snacks and watch movies with. Someone to walk me to school and help me with my homework. Someone who'd comfort me when nightmares woke me up. Then Lenny had whacked our foster father over the head with a chair when he saw the fucker with his hand down my knickers. Again. His hand down my knickers *again*. I'd lost count of the number of times that bastard molested me, but after the chair episode, Lenny and I got split up and sent to opposite sides of London to ensure it didn't happen again. The chair thing, not the sexual assault. Nobody seemed to care much about that.

My new family were arseholes too, but more in the "we don't give a shit as long as you keep out of our hair and we get our money" way. Lenny drew the short straw and got slung into a group home. So I owed him. I owed him big, and no matter how many stupid things he did and how much I complained, we both knew I'd always bail him out.

This time, he paused before elaborating on his situation. "I've lost my clothes. Like, I've got underpants, but I dunno where my trousers went."

For fuck's sake. "What have you taken?"

He giggled, a feminine sound from the boy who'd never quite grown into a man. "Uh, I just had a few drinks."

Yeah, right. "Sure, Lenny."

"Will you come?"

"This is the last time. You can't keep getting wasted like this."

"I'll be good from now on, I promise."

There was that damn giggle again, and I knew that the next time a mate offered him a can of beer or a fat joint, he'd tag along to the party. And they were always in the middle of bloody nowhere. Of course, I knew why

—if there were no neighbours to moan about the noise, there was less chance of the cops getting called—but I wished that just for once, they'd pick a house near a train station.

I scrabbled through my pockets for something to write with and came up with a half-empty cigarette packet and a stubby eyeliner pencil.

"Gimme the address."

I heard mumbles in the background as he tried to work that out. Once, I'd spent two hours looking for him at "the big white house with the pool near Tonbridge." The pool turned out to be a duck pond, and Tonbridge was actually Tunbridge Wells. I needed one of those tracker thingies they used in the James Bond movies to clip to his belt, although that wouldn't have helped me today seeing as he'd lost everything but his bloody underwear.

"It's, like, an old house near Windsor. White Horse Farm. Some little village... Birmingham?"

"Dude, that's a city."

More muttering. "Try Burnham."

I scribbled it down. "I'll be there as soon as I can."

"Can you bring crisps? Man, I'm hungry."

If he had the munchies, that meant he'd been smoking pot. Brilliant.

"Yeah, I'll bring crisps. Just don't wander off, yeah?"

"I won't, I swear."

That bloody man-child. I glanced at my new watch. The old one had died last week when I jumped out of a window and smacked it off the brickwork on my way to the ground, and I'd acquired my new "Cucci" timepiece in exchange for a couple of fags and a Coke. As in Coca-

Cola. I'd tried powdering my nose once or twice, but it didn't agree with me, so now I steered well clear. It was almost two in the afternoon. The number three had fallen off, and now it rattled around by the hour hand as I dropped my arm by my side. I wasn't due at work until eight, which gave me plenty of time to find Lenny, study for the GCSEs I wanted to take if I ever had time to go back to school, and still fit in a run with my crew before it got dark. Exploring abandoned buildings with them had become a bad habit, and an addictive one.

But keeping to that schedule meant finding a set of wheels quickly. Luckily, I was passing through Kensington and there were cars parked all over the place. I just had to pick one. Something newish because I needed a satnav. The maps app on my phone had been a bit dodgy lately. The whole phone had been a bit dodgy. Hmm... A tall brunette stepped out of a BMW on the other side of the road, and I watched as she tucked her keys into her handbag. Thick leather with a flap-over top. Too tricky.

A wave of tiredness washed over me, and I didn't bother to cover my yawn, even when a hoity-toity woman in a too-tight skirt suit minced past me. Who cared about her dirty look? She probably slept on a bed of feathers and had a butler to dress her every morning.

Coffee. Before I went anywhere, I needed coffee. That glorious hit of caffeine. Thanks to a housemate's snoring, I'd been up since six, and I hadn't gone to bed until four last night. Same as every night. Usually, I caught up on a few hours' kip after Stumpy buggered off to do his lunchtime shift, but thanks to Lenny, I wouldn't have that luxury today.

Tesco came up on my left, and I nipped inside.

Lenny could bloody well wait for five minutes. Queueing up in the café, I could have been any other college student longing for her morning fix. Over the years, I'd learned to blend in—black trousers with a blouse or polo-neck jumper if I was hanging out in the Square Mile, leggings and a fitted T-shirt for parkour, jeans for the casual look, and a pussy pelmet and glorified bra when I worked at the club. I leaned my head down to pick an imaginary piece of lint off my trousers as I walked under the CCTV to the right of the counter. No sense in starring on *Crimewatch* if I didn't have to.

As I got closer to the barista, I quickly checked my wallet—a genuine Louis Vuitton I'd plucked out of a handbag in this very establishment almost a year earlier—but it only contained a fiver and a handful of change. Mental note: make sure I borrowed a car with a full tank of petrol because I couldn't afford to buy any more.

"An Americano, please," I told the barista when he raised an eyebrow. I always picked the cheap option.

"Syrup?"

I shrugged and gave him the shy smile that had worked last week.

He returned it. "On the house?"

I dialled the smile up a notch. "Caramel, and thanks."

His eyes followed my ass all the way to the table, but I didn't care. I hadn't been blessed with many assets, so I had to make full use of those I did have.

My stomach grumbled as I sipped my coffee, and the sight of the guy next to me eating a chocolate muffin didn't help. Three hours had passed since I'd eaten bread and jam for breakfast. It should have been toast, but the toaster was broken, and I refused to fork out for another one. Someone would only trash it again.

I'd chosen the table by the window for a reason, and as I sipped, I kept an eye on the comings and goings in the car park outside. A Toyota hatchback pulled up—a possibility because I preferred smaller cars—but the woman bleeped the doors locked before disappearing along the street. No go.

"I haven't seen you in here before," the guy at the next table said.

*Please, not now.* I didn't have time to get hit on this morning. Things to do, a car to purloin.

I put on a puzzled expression. *"Nie rozumiem."*

There were advantages to having a Polish housemate. Paulius may have struggled with the washing-up, but he offered free language lessons and his plumbing skills were on point. "I don't understand" was one of the first phrases he'd taught me, and it came in mighty handy on occasion. The guy beside me shrugged and went back to his muffin while I carried on with one of my favourite activities: people watching.

Not to brag or anything, but I'd got good at reading people over the years. My survival depended on it. I knew which guys would buy drinks off me in the club and which would try to cop a feel. I could pick out the arrogant assholes who'd be so busy staring at my tits that they wouldn't notice as I nicked their wallet. And I could spot the subtle tremor of a junkie out for his next fix from a hundred yards away. Sure, I made the odd misjudgement—and once, a monumental fuck-up—but my instincts were generally right.

Today, I watched a girl drag a poodle past on a

fancy leash, pink and sparkly. Not her own dog. Nobody who'd spent thousands on a designer pooch and accessories would yank the thing along like that. A businessman walked by clutching the handle of his briefcase so tightly his knuckles turned white. He had something important in there. Cash? Jewellery? We were in a posh part of London, after all. Or just that one big contract he couldn't afford to lose?

A slender blonde climbed out of a Fiesta and tucked the key into the side pocket of her tailored jacket. Pale pink, and it looked like silk. She obviously had money to spend on dry cleaning, yet she drove a cheap car? A contradiction in terms, but when she tried to go in through the exit and had to backtrack, I figured she was the type of woman to own a satnav.

I hastily drained my coffee, grabbed a basket, and caught up with her in the produce section, where she was comparing a bag of regular carrots to the more expensive organic ones.

Oh, to have that luxury. Most of the time, I survived on instant noodles and whatever leftovers Stumpy brought back from his job in the pub. To me, vegetables were a treat. She went with the organic version—no surprises there—and as she turned, I hip-checked her hard enough to send her handbag flying.

"Gosh, I'm sorry! I'm so sorry."

So far, so good. That shit went everywhere. The woman carried an entire fucking department store in her damn purse, including—I shit you not—a can of mosquito repellent. Where did she think we were? The bloody rainforest? I bent to help her scoop up all the junk and bumped her again.

"Oops, I'm such a klutz."

"It's fine." Her words were polite, but her tone was...not angry, more jaded. "Accidents happen."

In the confusion, it was easy for me to slip the car key out of her pocket and into mine, and I smiled inwardly as I fished a pair of tights out of a display of cucumbers, handed them to her, and backed away. Phase one: complete.

Where would the blonde go now? If she planned to head straight back to her car, I'd have to abort, and I kept an eye on her while I grabbed a packet of crisps for Lenny and paid. Yes, I considered nicking them, but I figured two crimes in one day would be pushing my luck.

The blonde picked out a bag of apples to go with her carrots, then headed deeper into the store, towards the convenience food and all the other goodies I couldn't afford. Excellent. Things were going smoothly so far.

Still, I couldn't shake the niggly feeling that something was wrong as I approached the car, checking carefully for watching eyes. A mum pushing a stroller, more businessmen, a group of teenagers who should have been in school. They hung out in packs. A woman exiting a flashy black sports car caught my eye, not only because of the vehicle but because of the way she walked. Confident. Self-assured. *Don't fuck with me.* I waited until she passed before I carried on.

The lights flashed as I unlocked the Fiesta, and I slid behind the wheel. Every time I did this, I got an irrational fear that the car would blow up when I started it. Damn Digger and his endless supply of knock-off action movies. But the engine turned over smoothly, and I took a second to familiarise myself with the dashboard—satnav, headlights, indicators, fuel gauge. A full tank of petrol. My lucky day, other than the fact that the interior reeked of Shimmer body spray. One of the bar girls at work tended to apply it rather liberally and it always made me sneeze, but this was a hundred times worse. It seemed the posh bird bought the damn stuff in bulk.

The first spots of rain fell as I pulled out of the parking space, and I flicked on the wipers. How far was Burnham? I'd figure that out on the way. A guy in a Honda SUV glanced in my direction as I went past, a phone to his ear. A salesman married to his job?

I let a black cab pull out in front of me, feeling charitable since part of my afternoon had gone to plan. My *new* plan, anyway. When I woke up, I hadn't envisaged having to rescue Lenny from a farmhouse, although it didn't come as a complete surprise seeing as I'd had to haul him out of a mausoleum last winter. He'd been doing lines off a coffin, for fuck's sake.

Time and time again, I'd asked myself why I bothered, but the answer was always the same. Lenny was family, or at least, the closest thing to family that I had.

I closed my eyes briefly at a red traffic light. Some days—okay, every day—I wished I had a normal life. But there I was, in a stolen car because I couldn't afford to pay the train fare, and I didn't even have a driver's licence.

At least the blonde had picked all the options when she specced the car. Decent speakers, AC, pale grey leather seats so comfortable I longed to stop for a snooze. But I couldn't stop. Not yet. Maybe not for years. See, I had this big idea. Lenny called it crazy, but I preferred to think of myself as ambitious.

I wanted a home.

That was it. Just a home. Nothing huge or flashy, but a place I could call mine. I'd lived in nineteen different places during my childhood, and since the start of the year, I'd already moved twice.

I was tired.

Tired of the constant upheaval, tired of having to babysit Lenny, tired of always working or studying or dealing with arseholes. Tired of the hustle. Tired of life.

I just wanted a tiny flat of my own so I didn't have to carry my entire life around in my pockets in case someone decided to evict me. Which meant I socked away every spare penny I made as a shot girl in Harlequin's nightclub, I never paid bus fares, and my current home was an empty pub shared with twenty others, most of whom spent their days stoned out of their tiny little minds.

The light changed, and I eased forward, heading west out of London. Who knew? One day, I might even take my driving test too.

## CHAPTER 6 - BETHANY

WHERE THE HECK was my car? Okay, I was forgetful sometimes, but I'd parked it right next to the canary-yellow SUV with the surfboard sticker in the back window. I *knew* I had. Unless the driver of the SUV had moved their car. Or there were two colour-blind surfers in Kensington. Or...or... No way. Who would want to steal a Ford Fiesta? It was hardly a Ferrari, and the boot didn't even hold that much shopping.

And *how* would they have stolen it? I mean, I had the... I patted my jacket pocket. The key was missing. Dread washed over me, and the coffee cup slipped out of my hand. Warm cappuccino splattered all over my shoes and the homeless person sitting next to me.

"Hey, lady. Watch it!"

"I'm sorry. I'm so sorry."

Hold on. Where had I heard those words before? The girl who slammed into me in the produce section had apologised profusely, and at the time, I'd thought nothing of it. People got clumsy. Had my key fallen out of my pocket in the store? Was it still lurking among the vegetables? Or worse, had somebody else picked it up?

The homeless man clambered to his feet, or rather, to his foot. Too late, I noticed the crutches next to him and realised he only had one leg, but he was still much taller than me and kind of intimidating. A grubby tartan blanket slipped off his shoulders and landed in a heap on the ground, and I took a step back. Usually, the store staff moved beggars on, but clearly they'd missed one. Slackers.

"These clothes were clean on today."

I sincerely doubted that, judging by the state of him, but I forced myself to be polite. *Politeness doesn't cost anything*, my mother always said, even if she didn't often practise what she preached.

"I'll pay for them to be dry-cleaned. Uh, I don't suppose you recall somebody driving away in a small red car? A Ford Fiesta?"

"Aye, about ten minutes ago. A young blonde lass. Your daughter?"

Not likely. After years of trying, I'd come to the conclusion that a baby wasn't on the cards for me. The doctor had referred us for tests, but Piers didn't relish the idea of "jerking off into a cup," as he put it, and he'd cancelled three appointments before telling me he'd changed his mind about having a child anyway. His mother blamed me for my failure to conceive—she didn't say as much, but I knew she did—and every time we'd gone for dinner, his father muttered something about needing an heir. By that point, Piers had started spending more time away, and the rest... I didn't want to think about it.

"No, not my daughter. Was she wearing ripped jeans and a hooded sweatshirt?"

"That's her, aye."

Chaucer's treats slid out of my hands and landed in the puddle of coffee as my knees threatened to buckle. That rotten delinquent had stolen my car. And Hugo's painting. *A ten-thousand-dollar freaking painting.* I clutched at a nearby signpost to stay upright, and only then did the small print on the sign itself register. *Tesco Stores accepts no responsibility for valuables left in cars.*

Shit, shit, shit.

The disclaimer wasn't a surprise, but it hammered home the fact that I only had third-party insurance. A comprehensive policy had been too expensive after I had a tiny prang in my last Mercedes. Okay, it was a little more than a prang—I drove it into Piers's Porsche after I caught him screwing Andromeda Bartrop *in our marital bed*—but the insurance company hadn't looked too kindly on my claim of mitigating circumstances. And I was normally such a careful driver, or so I thought... Oh, what was the point? I couldn't turn the clock back, which meant I'd lose my job for sure, and I wouldn't be able to keep Chaucer without grovelling to my parents, and now I was bloody crying.

The homeless man handed me a surprisingly clean tissue.

"Are you okay, love?"

"Does it look like I'm okay?"

"Shouldn't that girl have taken your car? She had a key."

"She stole the key! And then she stole the car."

"Reckon you should report that to the police. Give 'em summat to do besides botherin' innocent citizens."

The police. Of course, the police! I rummaged through my handbag in search of my phone, but I couldn't find it. Had the blonde girl taken that too? I screwed my eyes shut, trying to remember if I'd picked it up. Or if I'd even had it in the store at all. The last time I'd seen it, it had been sitting in that little dip in the Fiesta's centre console, readily to hand if I needed to check my messages at a traffic light.

And it was most likely still in the exact same spot.

"My phone's in the car," I said hollowly. "I'll probably never see it again."

On the bright side, that meant I could put off speaking to Hugo for a while longer. Confessing that I'd lost his friend's birthday gift promised to be one of the most excruciating conversations of my life, second only to asking my father to bail me out of jail when I was eighteen. With hindsight, I should have stayed there. Daddy had agreed to fix the problem on one condition —that I split up with my then-boyfriend, and doing so had broken my heart. Rowan had been the sweetest man, an artist, but my parents said he had no class and no prospects. Faced with the threat of a prison sentence for breaking into an animal testing facility, I'd panicked and sent him a Dear John letter. He'd served three months for releasing a dozen rabbits and never spoken to me again.

I figured Piers was karma's way of kicking me in the butt.

"Here." The homeless man reached into the pocket of his tattered jacket and drew out an old-fashioned flip phone. "Borrow this. Sorry it's not one of them fancy things."

"Th-th-thank you."

Gah, I'd turned into a blubbering fool, which only lent credence to Piers's claim that I was "too emotional." Even my own mother had told me I was overreacting about his affair. Every man had his little indiscretions, she told me. It was just part of married life.

I'd tried looking the other way. For two months, I'd climbed into a cold bed in the spare room and waited for Piers to come home, listening for the *click* of the front door, wondering where he'd been and who he'd been with. Eventually, I couldn't stand it any longer.

Cue the ostracism.

People judged me from afar, condemned me for my poor life choices without even knowing me. I heard the whispers behind my back, saw the way former friends avoided me at gatherings. At my little sister's engagement party, I'd hidden in a bathroom while she and two of her friends discussed how ridiculous I was being right outside the door. Fancy giving up my lifestyle to be poor—absolutely unthinkable.

But then it struck me as I dialled the police with shaking fingers—hadn't I judged the man in front of me? Yes, his clothes weren't very clean, but he was kind, and I was fast coming to learn that kindness was more important than laundry soap or a phone with all the apps.

Oh my gosh. Apps!

Didn't iPhones come with an app to locate them? I'd never used it, but I was fairly sure I'd set it up one lonely evening soon after I left Piers. My previous phone had come to a nasty end when I threw it at him.

"Should I call someone for you, love?"

"I need somebody with a smartphone. There's a tracking app on mine."

I racked my brain for someone, anyone, who might be able to help, but with only a handful of friends left, I had precious few options. Hugo was out, obviously, as was Gemma. Gemma had been weirdly cagey about her phone lately. She never used to be that way, but a month ago, I'd seen a message pop up from her new boyfriend, asking her to cancel plans to spend the evening with him instead. Still raw from Piers's betrayal, I'd opened my big mouth to tell her that no man was worth giving up her independence for, and since then, she'd acted off with me, changing the subject whenever I asked if she had any plans for the weekend. And last week, when I'd noticed a bruise on her arm and asked if she was okay, she'd told me to mind my own business and then locked herself in the bathroom for fifteen minutes. When she came out, her eyes were red, and she'd avoided me for the rest of the day. In truth, I was worried about her, but right now, I was more concerned about my car. Who else had a phone I could borrow? Henrietta would only take joy in the fact I'd screwed up. Pinkey from the stables was too far away, and Sarah, my neighbour's housekeeper, had gone to Portugal for the week.

Another tear rolled down my cheek, and I cursed both myself and the mess my life had become.

"You should call the police," the homeless man advised. "They can track your phone."

"They *can*, but will they? My friend Madeleine—my ex-friend now—her Maserati got stolen from right outside her house and she had one of those fancy tracker systems, and by the time the police followed up on the report, the car was in Bulgaria."

Madeleine, who had more money than sense because her husband was chief of something or other at an investment bank, had been bloody-minded enough to hire a Bulgarian PI, but when he got there, all that was left of her SUV was the badge and the steering wheel. I had visions of my Fiesta being hacked into little pieces, and what would happen to the painting?

Mind you, the blonde girl hadn't looked like a hardened criminal, more an opportunist thief, a skinny waif who shied away from an honest day's work. If I confronted her and informed her of the error of her ways...

My new friend nodded. "Know what you mean about the old bill. They spend most of their time moving me on instead of catching crooks." He plucked his phone out of my hand, pressed a few buttons, and held it to his ear. "Rafiq, you busy? No? Do me a favour and meet me at the big Tesco store?"

"Who's Rafiq?" I asked, curiosity getting the better of me.

"A mate of mine. He drives a taxi, and he's got a smartphone."

"He'll drive me to my car?"

"Aye, he will if you pay him."

"Uh, does he take credit cards?"

"That he does." The gentleman shook his head. "Pretend money, I call it. Back in my day, the only money worth having folded."

I tried to swallow the lump in my throat, but it wouldn't shift. And the pesky tears kept coming too.

"Thank you. I don't even know your name."

"Mungo. My name's Mungo."

"And I'm Bethany."

I never carried much cash, but I rummaged around in my wallet and gave the forty pounds in there to Mungo. He deserved it and more.

"Will that cover your laundry?"

Mungo grinned, and his teeth were better than I

expected. *Dammit, Beth, you have to stop judging people.*

"Plenty enough. Do you have a spare car key?"

"At home. Why?"

"Because if you have another key, you can wait until the girl looks away, then steal the car back again."

What a great idea! Teenager or not, avoiding confrontation seemed like a good plan. I'd always shied away from arguments. Until the night I walked in on Piers and Andromeda, I'd barely raised my voice, and we'd been married for ten years at that point. With hindsight, that was about nine years too long.

"I guess it wouldn't take long to stop off and pick it up."

Mungo nodded, then tipped an imaginary hat. "Good to meet you, Bethany. Best of luck with your car."

# CHAPTER 7 - SKY

TRAFFIC ON THE M4 came to a standstill before Heathrow, and I crawled the last few miles while praying that Lenny hadn't a) wandered off or b) found something else to smoke, both of which had happened when he'd pulled similar stunts in the past.

Over the last couple of years, he'd spent more time high than lucid, and although he tried working every so often, those jobs never lasted long and he drank most of his wages. He'd given up. I saw it in his eyes. Lenny only got that spark back with a little pharmaceutical help, and I couldn't blame him. Once, after we'd shared a cheap bottle of cider and a couple of cigarettes, he'd confessed what had happened to him in that group home, and I wished with all my heart that I could have turned back the clock and kept my experiences with the pervert secret. I'd have coped, but something inside Lenny broke after we got moved, and I wasn't sure I could ever fix it. I only knew that I had to try.

Satnav told me to exit at junction seven, then sent me through several villages and a small forest on my quest to find my wayward foster brother. At times, I thought it would be nice to live in the country. Get a hut in the woods and hide away so nobody could bother me. Live off the land and all that. I choked out a laugh —I couldn't help it, seeing as the only experience I had with plants was minding a cannabis farm for a few quid when I was fourteen. Humid as fuck, and the place had stunk. And speaking of stink, I must've sneezed a hundred times on the journey, even though I'd opened every window. I'd be smelling Shimmer in my sleep. But at least the rain had come to nothing.

White Horse Farm showed up on my left, and I groaned at the sight of the "For Sale" board at the end of the driveway. *Lenny, what have you done?*

I kept my fingers crossed that they'd just broken a window and then hung out with a few drinks, but as soon as I saw the front door hanging off its hinges, I knew I was out of luck. Idiots. They'd have left fingerprints everywhere, and when the owners found out... Lenny had already been arrested twice, mainly for being in the wrong place at the wrong time, so it wouldn't take much effort to work out who'd been involved. The only saving grace was that he didn't have a fixed address, so the police wouldn't be able to find him straight away.

I rooted through my pockets for the thin leather gloves I kept in there, well worn from years of use. No way would I be making the same mistake.

The distinctive smell of pot wafted out at me as I pushed open what was left of the front door, and I groaned when I saw the mess in the hallway. The house was stuck in a time warp, with flowery wallpaper and scratched linoleum on the floor, but someone had taken the time to draw an oversized cock on the mottled mirror hanging on the opposite wall. Lipstick, by the look of things, which meant they'd brought girls out here too.

A cough from my right made me turn towards the

kitchen, also outdated but dominated by a scarred table that some designer in Chelsea would label as "rustic" and slap a four-figure price tag on. A person was slumped over it, one cheek resting in a pool of vomit, but the shock of blond hair told me it wasn't Lenny. I backed out and tried the next door. One, two, three, four bodies lay jumbled around, two on the floor, two on an old sofa. High as a giraffe's nuts. A ginger guy glanced up as I walked in, mumbled something unintelligible, then closed his eyes again. I spotted Lenny's pasty body in front of the window, attired in only a pair of Bart Simpson boxer shorts. He hadn't been kidding about that part.

"Lenny, we have to get out of here."

He grinned through his drunken stupor. "Sky! You came...best...cigarette?"

"Forget cigarettes. Where's your sweatshirt?"

He shrugged one shoulder and tried to look around, but his eyes wouldn't focus.

"Stay there. I'll go and look."

Stay there? He couldn't have moved if he tried.

I paused by each body to check they were all breathing as I hunted for something, anything, to cover Lenny up. If a cop saw a half-naked man riding around in my passenger seat, it would result in raised eyebrows, a stop, and a night in the cells once they realised I'd pinched the car. No, I needed to find Lenny a T-shirt at least, and preferably something to put on his feet.

The rest of the house was trashed, and the upstairs bathroom made me gag when I peered around the door. No toilet paper meant some animal had used the curtains as a substitute. Living in a squat, I was well used to substandard hygiene, but this took it to a far deeper level.

A prickle of uneasiness ran through me as I checked each bedroom, but all I found was a skinny brunette passed out on a dusty bed, minus most of her clothes. Tell me Lenny hadn't tapped that? I spotted a familiar sweater in a crumpled heap by the bed, and I didn't know whether to be disgusted or impressed that he'd managed to get it up in the state he was in. At least the used condom on the floor suggested he hadn't been entirely stupid.

And now we could leave. I stooped to pick up the garment, breathing a sigh of relief when I found his trousers and trainers underneath. No vomit, thank goodness. Still, I held the lot at arm's length as I headed for the door.

I needed to get Lenny dressed, haul him to the car, drag him home, then handcuff him to something solid so he couldn't cause me any more damn problems.

Five minutes. Five minutes and we'd be—

Oof!

I didn't see the person approach, only felt the arm snake around my chest, pulling me backwards and squeezing the breath out of me. Panic set in, but only for a second. I'd practised for this with Reuben from my parkour group. Practised over and over and over and over. I'd met Reuben on the worst night of my life, and I never ever wanted another experience like that one. Neither did he, and when I'd refused to go to the police about what happened, he'd, well, taken me under his wing, I guess. Dragged me out every Monday evening and Saturday morning when all I'd wanted to do was curl up in my sleeping bag and cry. We'd run, we'd jumped, we'd climbed, and after my arms and legs had turned into silly string, he'd drilled me through self-defence 101 until I could barely walk.

And his persistence paid off.

Instinct took over, and I threw my weight backwards, jerking my head so my attacker got the full force of my skull in his face.

A harsh, "Fuck!" came from behind me.

Wait a second—*his* face? That curse had sounded decidedly feminine. The arm around my chest loosened slightly, and I clawed at it, registering the slim wrist and bright red fingernails. A woman. It was definitely a woman.

But why?

And who?

Not one of the drugged-out losers Lenny hung around with, of that I was certain. Had the owner of the farmhouse come home? The TAG Heuer the woman was wearing on her wrist looked as out of place here as Lenny did, so I guessed not. But I had no time to dwell on the puzzle because when her grip eased, I ran.

# CHAPTER 8 - SKY

I RAN, BUT I ran the wrong damn way.

Instead of bolting down the stairs, I ended up at a dead end, a hallway with three closed doors leading off it. A hard tug opened the first one, and I swore under my breath at my bad luck. An airing cupboard. A fucking airing cupboard.

Door number two led to a bedroom filled with more dusty furniture like downstairs. A bed, a chest of drawers, a chair with one leg missing. No key for the door lock, and the bitch was already coming after me. I heard her muffled footsteps running as I wedged the chair under the handle and contemplated my next move.

The window. It had to be the window. There was no other way out, but fortunately, I'd had plenty of experience at jumping out of buildings.

In keeping with the rest of the house, my escape route had been built about a hundred years ago and not updated since. No fancy double glazing here. Five generations had painted over the old sash frame in thick yellowed gloss, and the damn thing was stuck shut.

On any other occasion, I'd have thrown the chair through the window, but the door handle rattled behind me as my pursuer caught up. No, the chair was otherwise engaged.

Her voice floated through the door, taunting, playful almost. "Nowhere to hide, you little bitch."

Nerves got the better of me. "Leave me alone! I haven't done anything."

Humourless laughter came, muffled by the wood, and then the door shook in its frame as she threw herself against it. At least in the nineteen-whatevers, they'd built houses to last. I hoped she broke her damn shoulder.

But the door jolted again, and fear raced through me. I hated that feeling, one I'd felt too many times on the streets over the last few years. At least in London, there was a chance somebody would hear me scream. Out here in the sticks, I only had Lenny and a few semi-conscious partygoers for company, and in Lenny's present state, he wouldn't be playing the hero.

There was nothing else for it—I'd have to go out the window. While the woman pounded on the door, I drew one foot back and aimed a sharp kick. Then another, and another. First the glass shattered, then the wooden frame gave way and tumbled fifteen feet to the ground outside. I didn't hesitate. I couldn't, because as I leapt from the window, tucking and rolling on impact, the bedroom door gave way and the woman came after me.

A quick glance behind showed blood streaming down her face, but that didn't slow her down. She was the bloody Terminator in tight jeans and a black leather jacket. And me? Normally when I practised parkour, I felt like a character in a computer game—which is to say kind of invincible but always on the verge of using up a life—but now? I moved with all the grace of a

Teletubby.

By the time I realised she was jumping after me, I'd lost precious seconds, and she'd halved the distance between us. Worse, by turning to look back, I missed the gnarled old tree root sticking out of the leaves in front of me, hooked my foot under it, and went flying. I felt as well as heard the knee tear out of my jeans—my *only* pair of jeans—taking a good chunk of skin with it. But panic overrode the pain, and I kept running.

So did she. Her footsteps sounded louder than the rush of blood in my ears as I headed for a tumbledown barn fifty yards from the house. When did it last get used for animals? Not recently, that was for sure. The giant doors hung askew on the hinges, gaping and dark like a shortcut to the underworld. Or a trap. Instead of running inside, I headed to the right, only to be faced with an impenetrable barrier of brambles. Left with no choice, I switched direction to the back of the barn, where a rickety wooden staircase led up to a hayloft. Was she following? Yes. Good. If I could just get ahead of her, I could run through the barn, jump down to the ground floor, and leg it out of the front doors while she hopefully impaled herself on a piece of rusty farm machinery. Maybe she deserved it, maybe she didn't—all I knew was that I'd never been chased through a farmyard by a freak-slash-supermodel before, and if I didn't lose her soon, I'd have more than a cut knee to worry about.

I feared the half-rotten steps might give way beneath me as I bolted up them, but I made it through the small door at the top with the bitch hot on my heels. The cavernous space was filled with a delightful stench of dead rat—a smell I was all too familiar with from some of the places I'd lived back in London.

*Why me?*

It wasn't as if I went out looking for trouble, despite what my former foster parents might have said. Trouble just had an uncanny knack of finding yours truly. Like the time I crawled into a warehouse to sleep and accidentally found myself in the middle of a drugs bust, or that night when starry-eyed me joined an up-and-coming pop star for drinks and came to getting raped in the back of his limo. With that in mind, on a scale of zero to the pinnacle of my fucked-up life, today's episode rated as a mere blip.

A blip getting closer with every step.

I kicked over a pile of wood, booby-trapping the way to a narrow ladder before I shinned down it. *Fuck, ouch, that hurt my damn toe.* The open doors gaped ahead of me, giving me hope, and I sucked in a ragged breath as I stumbled forward. *Let me out.* With a bunch of spiders and a lunatic as my witnesses, I was never gonna nick a car again. I stretched for the line where darkness became daylight, and just as I made it outside, the clatter of metal reached my ears, followed by the sweet sound of cursing. Maybe somebody up there was smiling down on me today after all?

That was the last thought I had before a pair of arms closed around me—a man's this time—forcing me down, down, down to the ground. The newcomer was careful not to make the same mistake as the blonde bitch with regard to requiring facial reconstruction because he knelt on my back, pinning me against the damp earth so I couldn't move.

I turned my head to the side, wincing at the pain in my neck, and even though I couldn't look up more than a few inches, I felt *her* glaring down at me. She shifted, and a shadow fell across my face. I waited for her to say something, but it was the man who spoke.

"I should be mad, but it's not every day I get to watch Action Woman versus GI Jodie." His American accent was a surprise, but the tightness in his voice wasn't.

"Who are you?" I asked, but it came out as a mumble because my face was still smushed into what might have once been a lawn but was now mostly mud.

"She broke my fucking nose," the woman snapped.

"Shit. We should—"

His grip loosened slightly, and I tried to wriggle free, but I soon regretted it when the woman bent to twist my arm behind my back. I bit my tongue to stop a yelp from escaping. No way was I giving that bitch the satisfaction of knowing she'd hurt me. Who the hell was she? And more importantly, how was I going to get away?

"Keep her still. I'll be back in a sec."

Drops of blood splattered onto the ground beside my face as she straightened, and a wretched fear began to claw its way through my guts. The last time I'd been trapped like this, a man had torn me to pieces, both physically and mentally. The panic welled up, threatening to overflow, and I made one last-ditch effort to throw my captor off, but this time he was ready. He held me in place until the woman came back with a pair of handcuffs and snapped them around my wrists.

Wait, handcuffs? Were they cops? For a moment, the crushing weight lifted, and the prospect of being arrested had never felt so good. How much trouble would I be in for stealing a car? It wasn't as if I'd damaged it, so maybe I'd get off with community service if I apologised? Judges liked offenders to show remorse, or so I'd heard.

Then I realised no one had read me my rights, and when the woman began duct-taping my legs together, the overwhelming sense of dread came rushing back. Even if I could scream, nobody would hear me. Nobody conscious, anyway. Where was Lenny? What about his friends?

Part of me wanted him to rush in to save me like a white knight, but deep down, I knew he was incapable. He could barely walk straight on a good day, and this pair didn't mess around. Better for him to stay hidden, then raise the alarm. If he even realised I was in trouble, that was.

"Wh-what do you want?" I managed to choke out. My mouth was full of gritty mud, and my stomach threatened to heave.

"We'll ask the questions," the woman said. "Let's start with your employer. Who do you work for?"

Should I tell them? My job at Harlequin's wasn't exactly a secret—my arse was on their website home page—but why did they want to know? My boss had the odd dodgy dealing, but he'd given me a job when nobody else would, and I didn't want to cause him any problems.

"Fuck you," I mumbled.

I half expected a kick in the ribs, but what came was silence. Silence broken only by the quiet purr of an engine followed by the crunch of gravel. Another visitor?

"Who the hell is that?" the man muttered. "Are we

expecting anyone?"

"Nope. I'll wait here with our friend while you find out who it is."

"Me?"

"Dude, I look like I've been playing in a slaughterhouse. Take my knife and your charming personality and get rid of them."

"I brought my own knife."

"Then what are you waiting for?"

The woman hauled me upright, careful to keep to the side of me this time. She'd taped my knees rather than my ankles, and she propelled me forward as I took little shuffle-hop-steps towards the barn. Now I got a better look at her. I'd done a good job on her nose if I said so myself, between the wonky, swollen bridge and the blood splattered across her face and clothes. She would have been pretty otherwise. Beautiful, even. And also...she was vaguely familiar. Ah, fuck. She was the woman I'd seen getting out of the sports car at Tesco. Up close, the air of toughness was all too evident, hardness combined with sharp edges, and being honest, I couldn't see myself getting the jump on her again. I was surprised I'd managed it once.

She produced more handcuffs from somewhere—how many pairs did she have?—and secured me to a solid-looking metal bracket inside the old building. A second later, she slapped a strip of duct tape over my mouth.

"Shh."

Like I had a choice.

Something glinted in her hand, and as she stepped towards the barn door again, I realised it was the aforementioned knife. Bloody hell. Who *was* this psycho? And what did she have planned for whoever was outside?

# Chapter 9 - Bethany

"MAM, I AM not sure this is a good idea. What if the thief is dangerous?"

Rafiq was a worrywart. He'd spent the whole trip making dire predictions about my fate, which I found kind of ironic considering the way he drove.

"It'll be fine." I tried to sound more confident than I felt. "I'm not going to confront her or anything. Hey! That's a red light!"

Instead of slowing down, he hit the accelerator. "Is okay. It has no camera. Mam, you have the asthma?"

No, just possible cardiac arrest. I forced myself to stop hyperventilating and focus on Rafiq's phone screen as my heart threatened to hammer its way through my ribcage. Was it better to be unemployed or dead? That seemed like a decision I might need to make in the near future. At least my will was in order—I'd carefully written Piers out of it and left all my worldly goods in trust for Chaucer, with anything left over going to an equine charity at the end of his life.

"I'm perfectly healthy. Have you considered sticking to the speed limits?"

"Time is money. Benjamin Franklin say this. You know Benjamin Franklin?" Not personally, no. "He was the president of the United States of America. My cousin lives there."

"Lovely." Americans came into the gallery on occasion, and they were always so loud, so pushy. Give me a quiet, reserved Brit any day. Apart from Piers, of course. As far as I was concerned, he could take a running jump off the white cliffs of Dover and good riddance. "I think in this instance, it might be preferable to get to our destination just a teeny bit slower."

And also alive.

"Which way we go now?"

"Right at the roundabout."

Five minutes later, Rafiq slammed on the brakes as we approached an overgrown driveway, and I crossed myself as I lurched forward. I wasn't even Catholic, but it seemed like a good idea to hedge my bets.

"We are here?" he asked.

"According to the phone, we are."

"You should call the police now."

And risk losing Hugo's painting again? Not a chance. "I've got a better idea. You go down the driveway, and if the car's empty, I'll jump behind the wheel and we can quickly drive away."

Rafiq was the master at that.

"What if it is not empty?"

"Uh, perhaps you could say you're lost, and then we'll have a rethink?"

"You mean lie? I do not lie. It is rude."

"Ordinarily, I'd agree with you, but do you think you could make an exception today? Say you took a wrong turn? Just a small fib?"

"A fib is not as bad as a lie?"

"No, no, definitely not. I fib all the time."

For years, I'd complimented Piers on his

appearance when in reality, he'd turned into a beluga whale who'd stumbled across Saville Row. Day after day, I'd assured my sister she wasn't overreacting when she wasn't just a drama queen, she was a supreme overlord. And as for my mother, every single room in her house looked like a death match between Trump Tower and the Palace of Versailles. Twenty-four-carat over-the-top opulence. I told her it looked fabulous.

"Okay, then I will fib. Should we go down the driveway right now?"

Good question. A brave person would probably have got out of the car and snuck through the trees commando-style for a recon first, but I wasn't brave and I was also wearing stilettos. Running would be a problem. Why hadn't I changed my stupid shoes when I stopped to pick up the spare key? And my pencil skirt. That wasn't conducive to a swift escape either.

Dammit, I really wasn't cut out for this.

"Yes, drive slowly. If you see a red Ford Fiesta, stop as close to it as you can."

I'd sat in the back of the cab like a regular passenger, and the seat blocked my view as we trundled forward. Should I hide? What if the girl recognised me? She'd only seen me for a brief moment, and hopefully she'd been more focused on stealing my key than memorising my face. I arranged my hair so that it masked my features and scooched down in the seat a bit.

Trees met overhead, giving the tunnel-like driveway a foreboding appearance. Between terror and the humidity, I was sweating like a pig in a sauna, and I almost told Rafiq to turn around. This wasn't my life. I was born to make small talk at cocktail parties, not hunt down teenage hoodlums.

An old brick-built house came into view, battered by time and the elements, shutters hanging crooked by the windows. The front door sagged open. Was the girl inside? Surely nobody actually *lived* there?

A flash of red at the side of the building caught my eye, and I sagged with relief. My car! And the boot was still closed, so hopefully that little brat hadn't found Hugo's painting. Not that she'd know what to do with it if she did. A girl of her ilk probably couldn't tell the difference between paint-by-numbers and a Picasso.

"I see the car," Rafiq said, a hint of excitement in his voice. "This is excellent news."

"Yes, it is." Honestly, the best part was that I wouldn't have to ride back in the taxi with him. "Just pull up alongside it."

I fumbled in my pocket for the key, eager to get away from this horrid, horrid place, but Rafiq's sharp intake of breath stopped me. What now?

"There is a man."

A *man*?

"Where?"

Rafiq pointed past the house, where the corner of an old barn was just visible. Sure enough, a tall, well-dressed man was walking towards us, and if it were at all possible, he looked even more out of place than I felt. Who was he? Why was he here? Was he involved in the theft of my car?

As he came closer, I realised there was something familiar about him. I'd seen him before, but where? I considered telling Rafiq to reverse, but then what would happen to my car? The man didn't look dangerous, not in a serial-killer way, in any case.

Dangerous to a girl's heart, perhaps. Mine skipped as he got closer.

Then I remembered where I'd seen him. At the gallery. *The freaking gallery.* Last night, he'd been at the show with a stunning blonde, and I'd been trying to sell him a sculpture until Henrietta had practically elbowed me out of the way. An American. Slightly brash but not at all suspicious, and yet here he was, incongruous among the undergrowth in a blue button-down shirt, grey flannel slacks, and polished brown brogues. What the hell was going on?

A thousand possibilities flew through my mind. What if I'd got this wrong and my car hadn't been stolen by an opportunist thief? Perhaps they'd lured me here as part of a kidnap plot? My family had money, although I wasn't convinced my father would shell out for a ransom payment.

"Uh, I think we should leave."

"But your car is here."

"Yes, but—"

Too late. The blonde from last night parked a black car behind Rafiq's taxi, blocking us in. Shit! I fumbled for the lock with trembling fingers, but the man pulled the door open before I could find it.

"Ms. Stafford-Lyons, this is an unexpected pleasure." He was still smiling, and it was quite disarming. "Good drive?"

"No, it was bloody terrifying." The words popped out before I could stop them. Did I mention my tendency to babble when I got nervous?

He motioned for me to exit the vehicle, and then Rafiq piped up.

"We are lost."

Good grief. The man rolled his eyes, and a hysterical giggle bubbled up my throat. My accomplice and I were so bad at subterfuge it was laughable.

Just for a second, I wondered if this could all be a bad dream. If the American and the blonde and the teenage car thief were figments of my overactive imagination. I dug a pink-lacquered fingernail into my arm, and it hurt. Dammit.

I climbed out of the car slowly, hesitantly, because I didn't have much choice in the matter. The blonde exited her car too, and was that *blood* on her?

What the hell had I got involved in?

# Chapter 10 - Alaric

LOST? ALARIC HAD met a lot of bad liars in his time, but this guy won the trophy. Who was he, anyway? Another fool Pemberton had suckered into his sly little game?

On the plus side, it wasn't the owner of the shitty farmhouse who'd arrived home, but making up a story to get rid of Stafford-Lyons and her sidekick wasn't an option. She knew too much, perhaps even more than him.

The curse of *Emerald* had struck again.

"Lost? I'd say that's unlikely. You didn't trust your middleman?"

Alaric motioned at Emmy to hang back. Whatever happened, he needed to resolve the situation quickly so she could get to a hospital. Broken noses could be nothing or a whole heap of trouble.

"My what?"

"Your middleman. The girl who picked up the painting."

"Picked up? What?"

"The painting." Alaric said the words slowly. "At the grocery store."

Stafford-Lyons looked genuinely confused. A world-class actress, or denser than the bronze statue she'd tried to sell him last night? Back then, he hadn't realised just how involved she was in Pemberton's scheme, and he didn't want to admit how close he'd come to buying the damn thing. Judd always said he was a sucker for a pretty smile.

Guilty as charged.

But Alaric wouldn't let that impact on work. Not when *Emerald* and his ruined reputation were at stake.

"Nobody picked up a painting. My car got stolen out of the car park, and I realised it must've been the girl who walked into me in the store, and I was going to call the police, but I left my phone in the car, and then I remembered I could track the phone with an app, so I called a taxi. Well, I didn't call the taxi, a homeless man did, and—"

Alaric turned to the guy behind the wheel. "You're a cab driver?"

"Yes, we are lost."

"Cut the bullshit, okay?"

This was so messed up. Could Stafford-Lyons genuinely have been that unlucky?

"You've got a painting with you?" Alaric asked her.

"In the boot of my car? Yes, a Heath Robert gouache on paper."

"You're certain of that?"

"I put it in there myself."

"I meant, are you certain it's a Heath Robert?"

"Well, yes. It's a gift for a friend of Hugo's. Hugo Pemberton," she added. "He owns the gallery where I work."

"I know who Hugo Pemberton is." Could Alaric have made yet another *Emerald*-related fuck-up? It was entirely possible. So many times, the universe had tried to tell him that the masterpiece was lost for good, but he just couldn't take the damn hint. "You saw the painting?"

"The colours are stunning. Robert captured the sunrise over the Serengeti perfectly, and the trees... Uh, you don't care about that, do you?"

"*When* did you see the painting?"

"Last week, when Hugo had it on display in his workroom. At the time, I didn't realise it was intended as a gift, but Hugo's always been generous with his friends."

"You didn't see it today?"

"Hugo packed it ready to travel. You can't just throw a piece like that into a frame and hope for the best." She checked her watch. "And I need to deliver it to Richmond. I'm already late."

Alaric revised his earlier assessment. He'd put money on the fact that Stafford-Lyons wasn't lying, and she didn't come across as stupid either. More naïve. No matter, letting her drive off into the sunset with a questionable package clearly wasn't an option.

"How long have you worked for Pemberton?"

"Five months." Correct. "But why all these questions? Who are you?"

"I'm a private investigator. A client hired me to search for a missing painting."

After decades of practice, lies rolled off Alaric's tongue with ease. Especially ones that weren't too far from the truth.

"Well, I don't have your painting. Whoever told you I did was wrong."

How confident was he that *Red After Dark* was in the back of Stafford-Lyons's car? Alessandra had her own agenda, but Alaric was ninety-five percent certain she wouldn't have called him with a bogus tip. How would it benefit her if he went after Pemberton? The answer: it wouldn't. She'd only been at the gallery because the drug-peddling asshole whose inner circle she'd worked her way into had wanted to buy a gift for his mother, and for the past five years, she'd worked narcotics, not property theft. Of course, she could have made a mistake. She wasn't an art expert.

And even if Alessandra had identified the painting correctly, Pemberton could have been lying when he told her it would be picked up today. That ninety-five percent chance dropped below fifty-fifty once all the variables were taken into account. Bad odds. Worse was the fact that Alaric had been outed. There would be no more skulking around the Pemberton gallery, no more covert visits while posing as a customer. He'd have to send Judd or Ravi or possibly Naz, and they had enough of their own shit to deal with without embarking on a wild goose chase after a painting more elusive than any ghost.

Or he could take a chance. All or nothing.

Maybe it would work out and maybe it wouldn't, but what did he have to lose?

One thing was for sure—they couldn't hang around. As well as Emmy needing medical attention, they had a teenager trussed up like a bondage victim, and...what the fuck? A guy stumbled through the front door of the farmhouse wearing only a pair of boxers. Emmy leapt from the car and went after him before Alaric could blink, but Stafford-Lyons's eyes bugged out of her head.

"Who on earth is that?"

"I was about to ask you the same question."

"Have I wandered into an alternate universe?

Today's been the most disastrous day of my life, and if you'd met my family or my ex-husband, you'd know that was a big deal."

And Alaric was about to make it worse. She was right—there was a man waiting for the painting in her trunk, and he wouldn't wait forever. They only had a tiny window of time in which to act.

"I know all about bad days, believe me. And the painting you have in your car isn't the one you think it is."

*If you're confident, they'll believe you*, Alaric's old mentor at the CIA had told him. And most of the time, the advice worked, today included.

"No, you're wrong," Stafford-Lyons said, but she hesitated first. She wasn't sure. "Hugo told me it was the Heath Robert."

"Then Hugo was lying."

If it turned out not to be the case, Alaric would apologise profusely, but he had to know.

"Why? Why would he do that? My family's known him for years, and he's got an impeccable reputation."

"The best criminals often do."

She gasped. "Hugo's not a criminal!"

"If he's got you driving a million bucks' worth of stolen art around under false pretences, he's hardly a pillar of the community."

"The Robert isn't stolen, nor is it worth a million dollars. Heath himself brought half a dozen paintings into the gallery a fortnight ago, and they go for around ten thousand each. I made him coffee. Quarter of a teaspoon of sugar, no more, no less," she mimicked. "And just a splash of cream."

"If the painting in your trunk's a Heath Robert, I'll

buy you dinner." What the hell was Alaric saying? Dinner? That hesitant smile Blondie wore when she got nervous was fucking with his mind. "Any restaurant you want."

"Are you crazy? Why would I want to eat dinner with you when you've practically kidnapped me?"

Alaric spread his arms wide. "I'm not keeping you here."

"Your girlfriend has blocked my car in. And Rafiq's."

The taxi driver was still sitting in his vehicle. Probably had the meter running.

"She's not my girlfriend. She's a colleague." Sort of.

A glance towards the house revealed no sign of Emmy. Still, he hadn't heard any screams, and he couldn't see her letting her guard down twice in one day.

"You're missing the point I was trying to make."

"And you're missing mine. I've told you there's a stolen painting in your car. The moment you leave this property, you'll be aiding and abetting a crime."

"You're delusional."

"Prove it."

"Fine. *Fine.* I'll prove it."

She produced a key from her pocket, then nearly broke an ankle when she tripped over a clump of grass. On a scale of zero to how-the-hell-can-she-walk, those pumps rated off the chart, but Alaric wasn't complaining. He did the gentlemanly thing and caught her, chuckling to himself when she pushed him away. Yeah, her instincts were on the money. *Damaged goods, baby.*

He waved a hand. "After you."

Stafford-Lyons managed to get the trunk open, and a sickly aroma wafted out. Cotton candy mixed with synthetic flowers and...pineapple? He wrinkled his nose before he caught himself, and of course, she noticed.

"It was an accident. I didn't realise how hot the car was, and a can of body spray exploded in the boot. I'm kind of used to the smell now."

"That's global warming for you. Hottest May on record, so I hear."

Alaric didn't miss the way her hands shook. This broad was way, way out of her comfort zone. Probably she didn't leave the Royal Borough of Kensington and Chelsea very often. Pemberton had packaged the painting well, which was only to be expected, and Stafford-Lyons cursed when one of her false nails broke as she tried to pick the tape apart.

"Allow me."

Alaric never went anywhere without a knife, but she gasped again when she saw the blade. This girl definitely led a sheltered life.

"Don't worry, I carry this for craft projects only." It was Emmy she needed to watch out for. "I promise I'll be careful with the painting."

If she'd looked closely, she might have noticed his hands trembling too. Eight damn years. Would he be a step closer to *Emerald* after today? Or a step farther away?

He pulled on a pair of white cotton gloves, then carefully removed the outer layer of brown paper to reveal a wooden box underneath. Once he'd pried it open, he found a bubble-wrapped frame nestled among styrofoam peanuts. Under the bubble wrap was a thick poly bag, and beneath that, layers of glassine tissue. It reminded him of birthday parties as a kid. Pass the fucking parcel.

But today? Today, the victory was Alaric's. Even before he peeled away the glassine, he saw the distinctive moody hues of *Red After Dark* peeping through. *Serengeti sunrise my ass*. Still, he didn't quite believe his eyes until he'd revealed the full painting, a masterpiece he'd never seen in the flesh before. Angry, textured brushstrokes, pain on paper as the artist captured the beauty of the woman who'd broken his heart. The love of his life. He'd died by suicide soon afterwards, a tortured soul gone too soon.

The work was as pristine as the day it'd been painted, and Alaric had to give Pemberton credit for doing an excellent job with the restoration. Too bad the fucker was crooked.

"Guess we won't be going to dinner now," Alaric said.

Which was strangely disappointing.

"This...this isn't *Dawn Over the Plain*," Stafford-Lyons whispered.

"No, it's *Red After Dark*, stolen eight years ago..."

"From the Becker Museum. I know." Her voice registered horror. "Unless...unless it's a copy?" She reached out, then caught herself. "Do you have more gloves?"

"In my pants pocket."

He leaned to give her access, and she hesitated for a moment before she fished around for them. Alaric carefully turned the painting over, unable to look away. There it was. The hidden secret few had ever seen. Before Edwin Bateson ended his life, he'd written an ode to his lost love, his muse, on the back of the canvas, poured his heart out in slanted script.

*My darling,*

*Absent your smile, my heart grows cold,*
*Your fair virtues I mourn.*
*Without your touch, I wish not to grow old.*
*To see another dawn.*

*No more tomorrows, grace lost to a thief,*
*And sorrow's distant eye,*
*Watches a love, now turned to grief.*
*Each night alone I lie.*

Between the poem and the exquisite workmanship, there was little doubt the painting was the real deal, but Alaric allowed Stafford-Lyons to take a look too. She had an art degree, right? Which meant she most likely knew as much about provenance as he did, perhaps even more. His knowledge came from lessons at the Bureau, a course at a museum or two, and a desire to learn once he realised he genuinely liked the subject.

While Stafford-Lyons studied the Bateson painting, Alaric called up *Red After Dark*'s entry on the National Stolen Art File and zoomed in on key areas. Every detail matched.

And the expert's verdict?

"If it's not the original, it's an excellent copy."

"Does Pemberton paint from scratch?"

"Surely you can't think...? No, he doesn't paint from scratch. I've only ever seen him work on restorations, and he spends ridiculous hours in the studio. All night sometimes."

"Which means he could easily work on the illegal side of his business after dark."

"I just can't believe Hugo's a thief."

"You're holding a stolen masterpiece in your hands."

"Maybe he didn't realise?"

For fuck's sake. "It's his *job* to realise. And if he's so innocent, why did he tell you it was a Heath Robert?"

"I... I..."

Movement to the right caught Alaric's eye, and Emmy strode out of the old house. Oddly enough, she didn't look happy. She paused on the way to toss her leather jacket through the open window of the Aston Martin, leaving her white T-shirt complete with its scarlet Rorschach in full view. Stafford-Lyons's eyes widened as Emmy stopped a few feet away.

"Houston, we have a problem."

"What problem?"

"The house is full of stoned teenagers, and they're starting to wake up. It's like the zombie fucking apocalypse in there, except they're hunting for weed rather than fresh meat. Seems the one who made a bid for freedom belongs to the bitch in the barn."

"Her boyfriend?"

"Brother."

"Uh, are you okay?" Stafford-Lyons asked. "You have a little..." She motioned to her nose.

"No, I'm not fucking okay. I should be sitting in a conference room drinking bad coffee, but instead, I'm chasing your accomplice all over the countryside."

"She's not an accomplice," Alaric explained. "The kid stole the car."

"Seriously? Nobody's that unlucky."

"Told you that painting's cursed."

"Dude, I'm beginning to believe you." Emmy nodded past them to where *Red After Dark* sat in the trunk of the Ford. "Is that what we're looking for?"

"Sure seems like it."

"An elaborate suicide note," she murmured, leaning forward for a closer inspection.

Alaric quickly pulled her back before her blood made *Red After Dark* even redder.

"Hey, what are you doing?"

He handed her a handkerchief. "Use this for your nose first."

"Oh, ta." The white cotton quickly turned crimson. "So, now what? This whole operation's been a clusterfuck of epic proportions, but it's not over yet."

No, it wasn't. They may have recovered a stolen painting, but it wasn't the one Alaric wanted. For eight years, he'd been focused on *Emerald*. Only *Emerald*. Any other successes along the way were incidental, although he couldn't deny the reward money for the two Rembrandts and the Vermeer he'd recovered had been a nice bonus. Emmy was injured, plus they had a flaky gallery assistant and an all-too-crafty car thief to deal with. Not to mention a bunch of stoners. "Clusterfuck" didn't even begin to cover it.

But they couldn't quit. The next link in the chain was waiting in Richmond for Stafford-Lyons to deliver the painting, and the question was, should they let her? Should they turn *Red After Dark* over to the authorities, or instead use it as bait for *Emerald*?

There was only one decision Alaric could make.

# CHAPTER 11 - BETHANY

A MONTH AGO, I'd gone for a long ride on Chaucer, a jaunt along little bridleways bursting with spring wildflowers—blackberry blossom, cow parsley, foxgloves, late snowdrops, and bluebells—the two of us trotting along in the dappled sunlight with just a few rabbits for company. I'd taken a picnic and eaten it by a stream while Chaucer nibbled on the long grass beside me, and that day, I'd dared to hope that the worst was behind me. The divorce papers were signed, I had my new job, and nothing could possibly beat the horror of finding my husband in bed with another woman.

I'd been wrong.

The one man I'd still trusted had lied to me, and not only that, Hugo was involved in some nefarious scheme I didn't understand. *Red After Dark* stared up at me, taunting me with its malevolent beauty. Every brushstroke screamed emotion. No fake could make a person *feel* in the way that painting did.

The dizzying revelation that my time at the Pemberton gallery was over hit me like a runaway Clydesdale. The American was right—I'd be complicit in illegal activity if I set foot over the threshold again. Although the mere thought of returning was laughable —once we'd handed *Red After Dark* over to the police, I'd be fired on the spot anyway. Would Hugo be arrested? Possibly, but he'd most likely wriggle out of any charges by pleading ignorance—mud rarely stuck to men with old money and influence. I'd seen it a hundred times over... A friend of my father's having assault charges dropped right after a party the judge attended. Piers's brother's drink-driving case getting thrown out on a technicality. Everyone siding with my ex-husband during our divorce despite the fact that he'd cheated.

*And it wasn't over yet.*

"I'll make a statement to the police," I said, desperately trying not to sniffle. I had enough cash in the bank to cover another month's worth of expenses, but no more.

"That won't—" the American started, but he didn't finish because the blood-covered blonde took off running.

What the...? A girl bound with black tape was hop-shuffling towards the woods at the rear of the property, a loose handcuff dangling from one wrist. Was that...? Bloody hell. That was the girl who took my car!

The American put his head in his hands. "Fucking cursed. Shoulda cuffed her to a damn railroad track."

"Uh, I'm really not sure what's happening here. Am I actually awake?"

"We all are. Wish we weren't."

"Why is that girl covered in tape?"

"Because she was in your car."

"You made a citizen's arrest?" That made a degree of sense, although where did the handcuffs come from?

"Something like that."

Wait a minute... "But you didn't know she'd stolen my car until I got here."

"We attempted to discuss the matter with her, and there was an altercation. It seemed safest to incapacitate her while we spoke to you."

The blonde managed to get the handcuffs back onto the car thief, and she half dragged, half carried her in our direction. Rats. What was I supposed to say? I wasn't sure whether to feel sorry for the teenager or give her a piece of my mind.

"Get the hell off me," she groused as she got closer.

"Shut up and walk."

"I'm sorry I took the car, okay?"

"No, you're sorry you got caught. There's a difference."

"I was gonna put it back. I just needed to pick up my brother."

"Ever heard of a cab?"

"Ever heard of being poor?"

"Yes, actually, I have."

I glanced across at Rafiq, who was watching the little scene with undisguised curiosity, nose pressed against the glass. Probably it wasn't every day he drove to the middle of nowhere with a freaked-out female only to be thrust into the middle of a bad B-movie. The blonde woman followed my gaze and sighed.

"Let's lose the audience, shall we?"

I stiffened. Surely she didn't mean...?

"He's not involved in this, I swear. He's just a taxi driver I met this morning. Please don't hurt him."

Her laughter surprised me. She didn't look like the sort of woman who'd have a sense of humour.

"Relax. I'm just gonna pay the fare and send him back to London."

"You are?"

"I'll even give him a tip."

She motioned for Rafiq to roll down the window and peeled four fifty-pound notes off a roll from her trouser pocket. Apart from drug dealers and billionaires, who carried that kind of cash around with them?

Wait. What if she *was* a drug dealer? I only had the American's word that he was a private investigator, and I'd learned during my degree that stolen art was often used as collateral in drug deals. Had I walked into the middle of something far worse than I'd ever imagined?

"Maybe I should go back with him. Here..." I held out the keys. "Do what you want with the car."

"No, we need you as well."

Rafiq picked up on my anxiety, bless him. "I will take the lady back."

Another laugh. "Chill, pal. I'm a plainclothes police officer." The blonde flashed an official-looking badge in a leather wallet—phew—and Rafiq bobbed his head in understanding. "You've interrupted an operation, unfortunately, but it's all under control now. We're finishing up, and then we'll be off too. Ms. Stafford-Lyons here is assisting with our enquiries."

"Yes, mam. I should go back to London?"

"Just return to your job and forget this ever happened."

"Okay, yes."

No! If the police impounded my car as evidence, how would I get home? "Wait—"

The blonde peered at Rafiq's windscreen. "Hey, did you realise your private-hire licence has expired?"

"I am leaving right away. I forget everything, no problem."

She moved the sports car back far enough to let him past, and I choked on the cloud of dust he left behind. Gravel from his spinning wheels pebble-dashed the front of my Fiesta. The teenager glared at me as if this were all my fault.

"Why didn't you stop him?" she asked.

"How?"

"Grab the keys? Jump in the car?"

"That lady is a policewoman," I hissed. "I'd have been arrested."

"Bitch, please. If you believe she's a cop, I've got a bridge to sell you."

Uh-oh. "A-a-aren't you a police officer?"

"Fuck no. I got the badge off the internet for a fancy-dress party. Can't believe he fell for it."

The brat rolled her eyes. "See?"

"The bickering's cute, but we don't have time for it. Chances are, that dude's gonna call the cops anyway, and none of us want to be here when he does. Thanks to Miss Fisticuffs here, I need to see a doctor, and you, Ms. Stafford-Lyons, need to deliver a painting." She raised an eyebrow at the American. "Right?"

He paused before speaking, as if he couldn't make up his mind how to answer. Finally, he nodded. "Right."

"Hold on... You want me to deliver a *stolen* painting?"

"Yes, because how else will we know who picks it up?"

"But...but...surely it should be turned over to the police?"

"*Red After Dark* isn't our target. It never was. We're more interested in one of the other paintings that was taken that day, and this is the first lead we've had in a while. We need to make the most of it."

"Which painting? *The Girl with the Emerald Ring*? *Fool's Gold*?" I couldn't quite remember the other three. Did one have a shepherd in it?

"*The Girl with the Emerald Ring*."

"I know *Emerald* was the most valuable, but I've always loved the Klimt. It was on a par with *The Kiss*. Exquisite."

"I don't disagree, but let's just say we have our reasons for going after *Emerald*."

"You really are private investigators?"

"Yes, we really are."

The woman reached through the window of the sports car and came back with another wallet, this one slim black leather with well-worn corners. I realised it was a reflection of her. She wasn't quite as polished as she'd made out at the show last night. Her accent had switched from RP to East London, and up close, there was a tiredness in her face she couldn't hide. Plus her nose was swelling rapidly. She needed ice.

"Here." She passed me a business card printed on thick cream stock. "That's me."

*Emerson Black*

*Director*

*Blackwood Security*

"And I'm Alaric," the American said.

"Do you work at Blackwood Security too?" The card had a London address and phone number, and his accent definitely wasn't local.

Emerson answered for him. "We have branches all over the world."

"And the Becker Museum hired you?"

"I can neither confirm nor deny." She shrugged. "Client confidentiality."

Of course. But it made sense—from what I'd heard, the police didn't treat art theft as a priority. And why would they? They were too busy dealing with knife crime and terrorism, and budgets had been cut to the bone if the newspapers were to be believed.

"I'm not certain it's a good idea to just hand the painting over to a stranger. Well, Hugo told me the man's name, but if he lied about the painting, he probably lied about who I'm meant to be meeting too."

"The alternative is to hand it to the police, and they'll want to know where it came from... It's up to you. How do you like jail?"

"Are you threatening me?"

"Think of it as gentle encouragement."

I really didn't like that woman, and I didn't trust her either, but her words did spark a glimmer of hope. If I delivered the painting, Hugo wouldn't fire me. I could avoid that particular black mark on my CV. Continuing to work at the gallery wasn't an option, obviously, not if he was handling stolen goods. Even if he did it unknowingly, Alaric was right—Hugo should have taken more care to check *Red After Dark*'s provenance. What if it happened again and the police turned up? As an employee, my reputation would be trashed even more than it was already. Far better to leave on my own terms and get a reference. Then at a later date, perhaps I could report what I knew to the police anonymously?

And what if these PIs *did* manage to get *The Girl with the Emerald Ring* back as well as *Red After Dark*? The art world would owe them a debt of gratitude, and another generation would be free to enjoy some of the world's most spectacular treasures.

"You want me to deliver the painting, and that's all?"

"Deliver the painting and then go back to work. As I said to your driver, forget today ever happened. But if you spot any more stolen artifacts in the Pemberton gallery, I'd appreciate a heads-up."

That didn't quite fit with my plans, but I wasn't going to argue. Not when I just wanted to get out of there. Fortunately, the brat took Emerson's attention, which gave me room to breathe.

"What about me? She's got her car back, so no harm done, right? If you let me go, I promise I'll keep my mouth shut about the painting and all the other shit."

"Let you go? Oh no, sweetheart. I've got plans for you."

"Plans? What plans?"

For the first time, a hint of worry came into the teenager's voice. Even though I was still mad at her for taking my car, I also felt pity because I wouldn't have wanted to be on the receiving end of Emerson's "plans" either.

"I need to see a doctor and have a very awkward conversation with my husband." Her husband? Poor guy. "Since you've sidelined me, you get to make amends by taking my place on the surveillance team."

Alaric opened his mouth to argue, but Emerson silenced him with a sharp look. That didn't stop the brat from protesting though.

"Are you kidding? I don't know the first thing about surveillance."

"Maybe not, but you're street-smart, and that's something you can't learn by taking a course. Just do what Alaric tells you and don't steal any more cars. How old are you?"

"Eighteen."

"How old are you really? Don't lie to me. I'll find out the truth, one way or another."

"Seventeen." Her tone turned sulky. "But I'll be eighteen in two months."

Emerson nodded to herself, and I couldn't read her smile. Cunning? Satisfied? Whatever, it made me nervous.

"Your name?"

"Sky."

"Your *real* name?"

"That *is* my real name."

"Full name?"

"Sky Malone. I don't have a middle name. My birth mother was too busy smoking crack to think of one."

Emerson's smile only grew wider.

"Alaric, meet Sky. You can bond in the car. A father-daughter surveillance team—how does that sound?" Then to Sky, "Don't forget to call him Daddy, sweetheart. He likes that."

Alaric's face clouded over. "Shut the fuck up, Emmy."

"What happened to your sense of humour?"

"I lost it eight years ago."

"Ooh," Sky said. "Have we wandered into a domestic?"

This time, they both turned to her and spoke in unison. "Be quiet."

She ignored that. "Look, I'd love to help, but I

can't."

"I wasn't giving you a choice. A couple of hours, and it'll be over."

"No, you don't understand. I *can't*. I only came here to pick up my brother, and he doesn't do well on his own."

"Yeah, I know. We met. Find him some clothes, and I'll drop him off in London on my way to the doctor."

"No offence, but I don't trust you."

"I get it. Believe me, I understand how hard it is to trust people in your position, but sometimes you have to take a chance. The other option is for me to call social services and the cops. Technically, you're still a minor, and I'm sure between them they can put you through hell for the next two months."

"You're a bitch."

"I'm not disagreeing with you, but I'm a bitch with enough contacts in London to make your life a misery if you cross me. I'll take your brother home, but you *will* do this job. Get your knee cleaned up. There's a first aid kit in the boot of my car." Sky's expression turned mutinous, but Emerson didn't care, and now the woman turned her attention on me. "Do you need to call your contact to explain you're running late?"

I couldn't decide whether to be envious of her self-confidence or disgusted by the way she ordered people around. But I realised I had to do as she said. I was the wrong side of thirty so threats of social services wouldn't work on me, but she'd surely think of a way to make my life even more of a misery than it already was. And as she said, it would all be over in a couple of hours.

"Yes, I should probably call."

"Gimme five minutes to round up the right junkie and organise a team to come and clean up this shithole, then we'll get going."

## Chapter 12 - Sky

"FOR THE RECORD, Emmy was bullshitting about the Daddy thing," Alaric said as we followed Bethany Stafford-Lyons's car along the M4 towards Richmond-upon-Thames with the AC blasting. *Stafford-Lyons*. I'd been dead right about the posh part. Who needed two surnames?

"Yeah, I figured that. She looks like she talks a lot of bullshit. All I can say is that she'd better take Lenny home the way she said."

Otherwise, it wouldn't be her hunting me down. London was my home turf, and I'd find that bitch, starting with a trip to Blackwood Security's building in King's Cross. I'd seen the card she gave to Bethany and memorised the address out of habit.

"She will."

"How can you be so sure?"

"Because I've known her for a long time, and she's a woman of her word."

"I figured you two had some weird kind of history. Do you, like, know her, know her?"

"None of your business, kid."

"So that's a yes, then."

I took some satisfaction when Alaric scowled, his pinched brows and flattened lips reflected in the windscreen. So far, he seemed slightly less unpleasant than Emerson, but she'd set a pretty low bar so that wasn't saying much. And I still didn't fully understand what was going on. Something about a stolen painting and a pickup, and Alaric needed a sidekick because a lone male watching people would stick out like a sore thumb if he hung around for more than a few minutes. Fine, I could stand next to him for a bit. I got that Emmy was pissed at me—her nose had looked like Rudolf's by the time she drove away in that fancy car of hers, swollen across the bridge and turning a nice shade of red. Considering the way she'd trussed me up afterwards, I was oddly proud of myself for managing to inflict so much damage.

Lenny, of course, had no recollection of the incident whatsoever. We'd found him in the living room, seated in a dusty velvet armchair wearing only those damn boxers and a vacant expression. When I saw him, that was the closest I'd come to crying in months. Years, even. I just wanted him to get better, but apart from picking him up every time he fell, I didn't know what to do. Drugs had taken ahold of him, and I was fighting a losing battle to break him free. Life had turned into a vicious circle—the more trouble he got into, the more it cost me to get him out of it, everything from paying off his dealers to making sure he ate. Lenny hadn't been able to hold down even the most menial of jobs for months. And the more hours I worked, the less time I was able to spend babysitting him, which meant he got into even more trouble.

The selfish part of me was grateful that Emerson had taken charge of him because it meant that for an hour—just one damn hour—I could leave the worrying to somebody else. Helping some American to follow a painting was child's play in comparison to watching my wayward foster brother. Especially since that painting was the one from the boot of the Fiesta. I mean, the thing was in a hefty wooden box. Nobody could slip it into a pocket or swallow it if the heat got too much.

And while I might not have had any formal training in surveillance, I'd gone through a phase of following Lenny's dealers and shopping them to Crimestoppers. Half a dozen of them had been arrested, and those assholes had been sneaky fuckers. I'd only stopped because Lenny had a knack for finding suppliers and each new one was worse than the last.

"So, what's the plan, boss?" I asked.

"Stafford-Lyons is going to hand over the painting to a man in the bar of the Ash Court Inn at four o'clock. The hotel's website says there's a parking lot around the back, so I'll drop you off and let you get in position in the bar while I find a spot for the car. Stafford-Lyons will circle the block a couple of times before she goes inside to give us time."

"What should I do in the bar?"

"Relax. Buy a drink."

"With what? In case you haven't noticed, I have literally no money."

Turned out the American carried twenties the way Emerson carried fifties. He peeled one off the wedge in his wallet and handed it over. Did he want the change? Because if he didn't ask for it, I planned to keep it.

"Nothing alcoholic," Alaric instructed. "Bar snacks are okay, but don't order anything that requires cooking. Chances are, we'll need to make a quick exit. Just follow my lead."

I'd get food? Perhaps I should volunteer for this

surveillance lark more often. My stomach grumbled in agreement, and I wondered if it would be rude to buy a dozen packets of peanuts to go. If only I had more pockets...

"Hungry?" Alaric asked.

"Starving. I skipped lunch."

"There're snacks in the glove compartment. Help yourself."

He wasn't kidding. I practically dove to open it, and a dozen bags of sweets fell into my lap. Had I died and gone to heaven? Unlikely. After the shit I'd got up to, I had a spot reserved in hell, but who cared when it came with jelly beans and gummy bears?

"That's some sweet tooth you've got."

"It's all Emmy's. She stashes candy everywhere her nutritionist won't find it."

I did the same, except with ramen noodles and a bunch of hungry housemates. Who had a freaking nutritionist, anyway? Emmy's junk food habit meant dietary advice was obviously a waste of time, so she clearly had more money than sense. Still, I wasn't about to look a gift horse in the mouth. I tore open a packet of Skittles.

"Want one?" I offered the bag to Alaric.

He shuddered. "No, thanks."

Ah well, more for me. I'd got through the entire packet plus half a dozen melted peanut butter cups by the time I saw the sign for Richmond. Two miles to go, and I ran a thumb over the cracked screen of my phone. Lenny had promised to text me when Emmy dropped him off, but so far, there was nothing. How long would it take her to drive to Lambeth? And would Lenny even remember a word he'd said? Dammit, I just wanted to know he was safe.

But I couldn't get distracted, not now. I spotted the Ash Court Inn on the right, a cream facade with a sign in curling black script over the portico. Four stars, rooms, bar, conference facilities, and the holy grail— free Wi-Fi. Someone must have been watering the flowers in the pots outside because they were the only plants around that weren't brown and crispy, and a porter walked past pushing one of those fancy luggage trolleys stacked high with suitcases that matched my wallet. Except they probably weren't stolen. In short, the Ash Court Inn was the sort of place I'd never have walked into on a regular day on the basis that I'd get kicked straight back out again. Bet Emmy hadn't thought of that when she came up with her fucking plan.

Still, I waited until the doorman turned his back, then slipped through into the bar where the opulence continued. Everything was leather or crystal or polished wood, and the place stank of money and expensive perfume. Bet they didn't have happy hour. Not a single person smiled, not even the barman when I sidled up and took a seat in front of him.

"Coca-Cola, please. Ice, no lemon." I imitated Bethany Stafford-Lyons's upper crust accent, something I'd become accustomed to doing before I got the job at Harlequin's, back when I'd had to hustle for a living. I didn't enjoy scamming tourists or picking pockets, but when it came to a choice between stealing or starving, or worse, going back into foster care, it wasn't difficult to tuck my guilt away and do the necessary. When the barman looked down his nose at me, I produced Alaric's twenty-pound note and stared right back. "And a packet of salt-and-vinegar crisps."

*Any time today would be good.*

"Of course, Miss."

I didn't see him make a call, but he was still fixing my drink when a guy in a suit appeared at my elbow. Polyester, by the look of it, and it didn't fit too well. Staff, then, not a guest, and from the pretentious manner, I pegged him for a manager. Brilliant. So much for me surreptitiously studying the patrons. Everyone was staring at me now, everyone except the preppy guy sitting by the window who kept his attention firmly fixed on the door. He was waiting for somebody. Bethany?

"Can I help, ma'am?" the manager asked.

*Yeah, you can ask that prick to pour faster.* "No, I'm fine, thank you."

"Can I ask why you're here today? I don't recall you checking in."

See? Welcome to being poor. "I'm waiting for someone."

"I'm afraid Ash Court Inn isn't that sort of establishment."

For a moment, I was confused, but then I wanted to punch him in the face. He thought I was a hooker? No, asshole, that was my mother.

# CHAPTER 13 - SKY

IT TOOK ALL my self-control to muster up a bland smile for the manager. "I'm sorry? I don't understand."

Spell it out, you pretentious git. Explain your nasty comment.

"Uh, well..."

"Is there a problem?"

I didn't recognise the voice, which was a male version of Bethany's, super posh, and I was fully prepared to have another argument until I turned around to find Alaric standing behind me. *Nice accent, dude.* Since I couldn't imagine him ripping off idiots in the West End, I was curious where he'd got it from. He'd also dredged up a sports jacket from somewhere and slicked his light brown hair back. At least one of us fitted in perfectly at the Ash Court Inn.

"Do you know this young lady?"

"She's my daughter. Did you get what you wanted, sweetheart?"

"Service is kind of slow. And I'm waiting for this guy to explain something."

"Explain what?"

Now the manager turned the colour of Emmy's nose and backed away. "Terribly sorry for any misunderstanding. It's just that you don't look like our usual clientele."

Alaric sighed. "She's going through a phase."

"It's not a phase, *Daddy*."

He ignored me and signalled to the barman. "Sparkling water, light on the ice and heavy on the lime. Sweetheart, did you pay?"

"Not yet."

"I'll get it." Bonus. "Would you mind bringing our drinks over to the table?"

"Of course, sir."

Alaric steered me towards the far corner of the room, where a potted palm meant we could see without being seen. I rubbed one of the leaves. Real, not fake. About the only thing in this place that was.

"Anything?" he asked.

"Ten quid says it's the WASP by the window."

Ten quid of his money. Should I up it to twenty? I knew I was right.

"Since I agree with your assessment, I'd be stupid to take that bet."

"Did you even look? Or are you just scared of losing?"

"I looked."

"Prove it. What colour shirt is he wearing?"

"Pale blue with thin white stripes. Turned-up jeans and loafers, no socks. No wedding ring either. At first glance, his watch looks like a Rolex, but I'd bet it's a cheap imitation since it doesn't quite fit his image. He fidgets. Picks at his shirt cuffs." Alaric took a seat and motioned for me to do the same before he continued speaking softly. "How many people are in here?"

"Why does that matter?"

"It doesn't. I'm testing your powers of observation."

Oh. I tried to picture the bar without looking

around. "Seven."

"Including us and the bartender?"

"No, excluding."

"Close. Eight. We can rule out the two women sitting by the door because Stafford-Lyons is here to meet a man. Likewise the lady beneath the reproduction of Stubbs's *The Countess of Coningsby*. The man by the door with the laptop is either hotel staff or here for a meeting—"

"How do you know that?"

"Because the document on his screen has the hotel's logo at the top. The men next to the grandfather clock are here on a date, which leaves two. Our man by the window and the guy in the suit. But suit guy has a briefcase at his feet that's too small to fit the painting, and he wouldn't have brought it knowing he had to carry something sizeable." Alaric smiled. "You shouldn't interrupt. It makes you memorable for all the wrong reasons."

No problem. I'd run out of things to say.

"Tell me," he continued. "Why did you pick out the man by the window?"

"Because when the manager accused me of being a prostitute, he was more interested in gawking at the door than at me."

Alaric's expression hardened. "Rest assured I won't leave a tip."

"Forget it. Today's not the first time some toffee-nosed twat has tried to kick me out of their fine establishment. Most of the time I deserve it, although I'm definitely not a hooker, Daddy."

"It wouldn't take much for you to blend in. You've already mastered the accent. Where'd you learn it?"

"A combination of *Downton Abbey* and *Made in Chelsea*."

"You didn't get tempted by *House of Cards* and *Jersey Shore*?"

"Like I can afford to pay for Netflix right now. But I can do Polish. *To miejsce jest tak pretensjonalne*." This place *is so* pretentious.

Alaric smiled, genuinely it seemed. "You're right. *Czy chcesz później dostać burgery*?"

Did he seriously just ask me if I wanted to get a burger afterwards? Or had I misunderstood? He didn't miss my hesitation.

"Don't freak out—this isn't a *Daddy* situation." He motioned at the empty crisp packet in front of me. "You just seem hungry, that's all."

Sometimes, it was the good things that crept up and caught me unawares. Not often, but occasionally. I quickly wiped my nose with my sleeve. Stupid sniffles.

"Allergies," I said. "Probably the furniture polish."

"Right. So, dinner?"

"Why are you being nice? I mean, Emmy's properly mad at me, and she's your 'colleague.'"

"Emmy's not mad at you. She's mad at herself for letting you get close enough to do that sort of damage."

"What about the car I took?"

"Emmy would be a hypocrite if she condemned you for that."

"You mean *she's* stolen a car?"

"You're not the only one with a misspent youth."

This day got stranger and stranger. "I didn't mean to break her nose, honest. She grabbed me, and I just wanted to get away."

"I know. You almost managed it too."

"Yet here I am."

"Here you are. And you didn't answer my question."

"About dinner?" My mouth watered at the thought because I bet when he said "burger" he didn't mean the McDonald's Saver Menu, but I had to turn him down. "Can't. I have to work."

"Work where? What do you do?"

"I'm a shot girl. You know, one of those bimbos who parades around in hot pants with tequila bottles on her belt? I serve overpriced alcohol to horny assholes from eight until the place closes."

Technically, I was self-employed—Howie, the owner of Harlequin's, liked to avoid paying taxes whenever possible—but I was there almost every night. The way it worked was that I bought a bottle of alcohol at full price from the bar, then sold it by the shot glass at a markup. If I smiled and flirted, the idiots I was serving didn't even notice that the glasses weren't full.

"You can't take a night off?"

"No, Mr. Moneybags, I can't take a night off. If I don't work, I don't eat, and Lenny... He's not so good at looking after himself."

"So I gathered."

A subtle change came over Alaric, nothing I could pinpoint, more a shift in energy. I almost swung around to see what was happening behind me, but I realised at the last second that it would be a schoolgirl error. And I didn't want to make another mistake in front of him.

"Our lady's just walked in," he murmured.

I grabbed my glass because I didn't want my drink to go to waste, but Alaric stopped me from knocking it back with a tiny shake of his head.

"Don't rush. There's no hurry."

I hated not being able to see, but then I realised that if I looked at the painting on the wall opposite, I could make out Bethany's reflection in the glass. She stood just inside the doorway, eyes searching, and I groaned when she focused on me and Alaric. *Look away, you daft mare.* Thankfully, her gaze didn't linger too long, and she headed to the bar. The asshole barman smiled at *her.*

"We were right," Alaric murmured.

The preppy guy left his table by the window and joined Bethany. Her smile was tight, and they didn't exchange more than a few words before he ordered her a drink, picked up the box she'd brought and tucked it under one arm, then strolled towards the lobby.

"Now you can finish your drink," Alaric told me, draining his own glass.

It was weirdly exciting. I'd never had a partner in crime quite like this before, especially one so competent. Most of my tricks of the trade had been learned from kids I'd met on the street and an endless succession of housemates, and half of them were in jail now. The biggest miracle was that me and Lenny weren't.

Alaric rose and studiously ignored Bethany as we left the bar. The preppy guy was on his way out the front door when we reached the lobby, but Alaric still found time to smile at the receptionist and ask the doorman if it was meant to rain. The painting was fifty metres ahead by the time we hit the pavement, and I was tempted to jog after it.

"Relax. It's not a race."

"What if he gets away?"

"This is a good distance. Trust me."

Alaric kept his pace steady, but he had deceptively long strides, and I felt as if I was speed-walking in the bloody Olympics as I hurried along beside him. At least I'd worn trainers today. In my work uniform of high-heeled boots, I'd have broken a damn ankle.

"What do you think of that tie?" Alaric asked, pausing to glance in a shop window. "Would it suit me?"

Who gave a shit about a tie? "Sure, if you want to look like a double-glazing salesman."

He just laughed.

When we moved off, his fingers grazed the small of my back, and I suppressed a shudder. Not because of the Daddy thing—that wasn't how he meant it—but because of my past. Even on the rare occasions a man treated me civilly and with respect, the smallest touch could make me stiffen unintentionally. I'd learned to live with it in Harlequin's because the bouncers would come running at a snap of my fingers, and I didn't mind the odd back-slap or bro-hug from the guys in my parkour group, but caught unawares in the wild...

I forced myself to relax. To breathe.

Anyhow, it looked as though my time with Alaric might come to an end sooner rather than later when the preppy dude cut left into another hotel, this one a more modern cousin of Ash Court. Five glittering stars this time, with the addition of valet parking and a spa. How the other half lived.

"Do you think he's staying here?" I whispered to Alaric.

He quickly scanned the lobby through the glass facade. Our target had taken the elevator, and I watched the lights above the doors as it rose. One, two, three floors, and then it stopped.

"Wait here. I'm going to speak to the receptionist."

"On your own?"

He gave me a sheepish smile. "She's female."

And damn lucky. If I'd been a decade older, I'd have liked a dose of Alaric's brand of charm.

"Fine, I'll stay outside. Try to keep your dick in your pants."

On the plus side, that gave me time for a sneaky cigarette, which served two purposes. One, I'd get a nicotine hit, and two, I'd have a perfect excuse for loitering. Nobody questioned a smoker. We just got dirty looks. And before you ask, I never *bought* the cigarettes. There were always dropped packets kicking around at Harlequin's, and I made the most of it.

My phone buzzed as I lit up, and I quickly checked my messages. Lenny. Thank fuck.

*Lenny: Man, this car's the bollocks. And the bitch bought me three Happy Meals.*

*Me: Are you home?*

*Lenny: Yeah. Someone trashed the microwave again.*

Bloody hell. The microwave was less than a month old, and guess who'd paid for it? That's right—muggins here. But at least Lenny was safe. A weight lifted, and I closed my eyes and took a long inhale.

"Do you have a light? I apologise—I didn't mean to startle you."

The speaker was a man in his mid-thirties, maybe a touch older if he took care of himself. Short brown hair. Clean-shaven. An American accent with a hint of something else—French?—a suit that was definitely *not* polyester, a pink shirt, and a family-sized suitcase by his side. I thought men travelled light? The overall effect was slightly effeminate.

"Sure." I offered him my lighter. "Checking in?"

"Out, actually. All good things must come to an end."

"You were here on holiday?"

He took a long drag before he answered. "A little business, a little pleasure."

"You picked the right week for it—the weather's never normally this warm."

"So I've heard. Do you live in London?"

As if on cue, a breath of wind blew smoke in my face, and a band of black cloud appeared over the building opposite, plunging us into shadow. This morning's rain shower might have fizzled out, but the oppressive humidity signalled a thunderstorm was coming. I didn't fancy being caught out in it.

"I'm from Nottingham. My dad's here on a business trip, so I tagged along for some father-daughter bonding. He says I'm going through a phase."

My companion chuckled. "We all have phases. When I was a teenager, I grew my hair long and learned to play the violin."

Another gust, and this time, I didn't get smoke. I got something almost as unpleasant and oddly familiar. Flowers, candy floss, and overly ripe pineapple. I'd only just managed to get the stink out of my nostrils, and now it was back. My imagination? Or...or... I glanced at Pink-Shirt Guy's suitcase. It was certainly big enough to fit Bethany's painting, but was I overthinking this? I took another surreptitious sniff. There was definitely a hint of Shimmer body spray in the air. Was it on my clothes? I hadn't smelled it in the bar.

Pink-Shirt Guy stubbed out his cigarette and extended the handle of the case. "Enjoy the rest of your trip."

"You too."

Shit, what should I do? I fumbled for my phone to call Alaric, but the damn thing slipped out of my hand and landed on the brickwork at my feet. The screen went dark, and I cursed under my breath. *Another one bites the dust.* Me and phones didn't have a great relationship. We broke up on a regular basis, emphasis on the "broke."

The guy was at his car now, a black Mercedes parked to the left of the hotel entrance. I memorised the registration number, but would it be enough? *Long strides, don't hurry...* I got to the front of the hotel, but there was no sign of Alaric in the lobby, or the receptionist either. Tell me he wasn't trading party favours for information?

What should I do? There were no taxis in sight, and even if there had been, cabs cost a fortune and I only had twenty quid and change on me. Then I saw it. A white delivery van parked outside the entrance, the window down and the keys in the ignition. Ah, fuck it. I already knew I was going to hell—at that point, I figured it was go big or go home.

The Mercedes paused, an indicator on, and turned left into traffic as I slid behind the wheel of the van. There was a hi-vis vest on the passenger seat, and I shrugged into it, then jammed the baseball cap beside it onto my head. If Pink-Shirt Guy looked in his mirror, hopefully he wouldn't recognise me.

The van started with a quiet purr, and I eased out

after the Mercedes. Fuck my damn life. I should've kept the handcuffs from earlier because when I got ahold of Lenny, he was never going out by himself again.

# CHAPTER 14 - EMMY

"DID YOU EVEN go to Vinnie's birthday party?" my husband asked. On screen, his dark eyes had turned into two hard chips of granite, and the rest of him didn't look happy either. I propped my elbows on the desk in the study we shared at Albany House, our London home, and rested my chin in my cupped hands. Funnily enough, I hadn't been thrilled by today's events either.

"Yes, I went." For all of twenty minutes after I left the gallery yesterday. Enough time to hand over a gift and take a couple of photos before I met Alaric for dinner. But then the office called and I had to go chase assholes. "I didn't lie."

"So Alaric just happened to be in town?"

Black was pissed, as I knew he would be. When it came to Alaric, he suffered from an irrational jealousy that clouded all reason. Other men got him wound up too, but with Alaric, the green-eyed monster was more like Godzilla. Day to day, I lived with it. Sometimes it could even be fun—jealous, possessive sex was wild like nothing else—but mostly, I wished he'd get over himself and accept that I was able to spend time in the same room as Alaric without wanting to stick my tongue down his throat.

Which was why I may have led him to believe I was

coming to London to attend an old friend's fortieth birthday celebration rather than hunting for a missing painting with an ex-lover.

"I knew Alaric was here," I admitted. No matter how many lies I told other people, I never lied to Black, not outright. "He asked me to help out for a few hours, and I could hardly turn him down. I don't care what everyone says—he didn't take that money, and if he can get *Emerald* back, it might go some way to restoring his reputation."

Alaric jointly ran a private intelligence agency now, but there were still a lot of people who didn't trust him, and trust was everything in our business. It was the difference between landing contracts with government agencies and skulking around in the shadows. At the moment, Alaric's involvement in Sirius was mostly a secret, even though he owned a quarter of the company. One of his business partners fronted the operation while he did what he did best—collected secrets and ferreted out information. He was good, but *Emerald* had been his nemesis for eight years now, and I was beginning to believe his claim that the damn painting was jinxed.

I touched my nose gingerly. Another victim of the curse? I'd felt the fucking thing crunch when Sky slammed her head into it. Blackwood had an arrangement with a London doctor who'd treat our people without asking questions, and she'd checked out the damage after I got back. The verdict? A fracture in the bridge. Hopefully, it should heal without needing further treatment, but in the meantime, I had a face like a clown, an economy-sized packet of ibuprofen, and an upset husband.

"You don't know for sure that Alaric didn't take the contents of that briefcase," Black said.

"Oh, please. Firstly, he had no motive. He wasn't exactly hurting for money thanks to his parents. And if he *had* nicked it, he'd have got straight on a plane to the nearest non-extradition country, not hopped on a yacht and sailed out into the middle of nowhere to get shot at."

Alaric knew how to disappear. I'd found that out first-hand. The aftermath of the shooting had been brutal, weeks of questioning and a fruitless search for cash, diamonds, and a painting that had vanished from the face of the earth. In the chaos of the battle, I'd gotten a fleeting glimpse of Dyson off the stern of the scalloper in the Zodiac boat, but Alaric's colleagues had been too busy panicking to track him. After the way Hooper behaved, I'd been tempted to shoot him myself, motor back to shore, and use my own helicopter to give chase, but Alaric overruled me and insisted on taking the former marine to the hospital. The prick had made a good recovery, and the last I heard, he was working as a mall cop, which as far as I was concerned was too much responsibility for a man with the impulse control of a toddler. Actually, that was unfair to toddlers.

Black had helped with the investigation, but grudgingly. I got the impression he was more annoyed at Alaric for dragging me into the case than at the various thieves. And his suggestion that the cash and diamonds might have been swapped before the pay-off left FBI headquarters hadn't gone down well with the brass, although they didn't have any better ideas. At one point, they'd fingered me as a suspect, and I thought Black was gonna take the director's head off in *that* meeting. To say the atmosphere had been strained was an understatement.

Anyhow, after a month of daily interrogations and with his termination from the FBI imminent, Alaric had simply vanished. Gone. Poof! Believe me, I'd looked for him. At first, I'd been terrified he'd done something stupid, worried that the next call from an unidentified number would be news of a body. Eleven months had passed before the first pair of shoes arrived. Just cheap things, more like embroidered slippers really, but there was a clock drawn onto the box with the hands pointing to midnight, and I knew who they were from. Over the years, slippers and doodles turned into birthday cards with Louboutins, and I figured Alaric was doing okay.

But I'd almost given up hope of seeing him again until he'd materialised in the quarantine unit where I was busy cheating death, and I couldn't even kill him for abandoning me because there was a glass wall between us.

And now? Now here we were, dancing around each other, whatever relationship we had still kind of awkward and off limits for discussion. Turning back the clock wasn't an option because Black and I were a thing now, but I didn't want to lose Alaric as a friend. Not again.

Which meant I had to deal with Black's jealousy.

"Alaric nearly got you killed," he griped. "And today, he got you hurt."

"Bullshit. What happened on the boat was unfortunate, but I'm trained for that. *You* trained me. Are you doubting your abilities?"

Silence.

"And today was my fault. I let my guard down and underestimated the opposition. Does that remind you of anyone else we know?"

More silence.

I'd met Black seventeen and a half years ago on a dark night in London, a night when I'd stolen his wallet and broken his nose. He'd miscalculated my abilities back then, although there *had* been a certain amount of luck involved too.

"Well, enjoy Belize. I'll see you back in Virginia."

I hung up, and when he tried to call again, I shut the lid of my laptop and left the room to lick my wounds. Let him think about things for a while. I sure needed to.

Upstairs, I had my "thinking window," a glass oval above a window seat at the far end of a second-floor hallway. Bulletproof glass, of course. Black had insisted, although he swore he wasn't paranoid, just careful.

The spot overlooked the garden, and I watched a flock of sparrows attacking the bird feeder as I considered my next move. A lot would depend on how Alaric and Sky got on in Richmond. How long had it been? Four hours? So far, there'd been no news, but I knew better than to interrupt Alaric in the middle of a job. He'd call when he was ready. Either that or he'd fuck off to Outer Mongolia or somewhere again, which would sting like hell but would actually make my life easier.

"Hey."

I whipped around to find Alaric standing at the other end of the hallway, hands in his pockets.

"How did you get in?"

"Ruth."

Ruth was our London housekeeper.

"I sent her home."

"Yeah, she said you did, but she also said you looked miserable so she's making you dinner."

Alaric appeared thoroughly cheesed off too.

"What happened in Richmond?"

"Got any wine?"

"That bad?"

"On second thought, I might start with whisky. How's your nose?"

"Less painful than the chat I had with Black."

"Empathy isn't exactly his middle name."

"It was partly my fault. I might have forgotten to mention I was meeting you here."

Alaric snorted. "Ever ask yourself why you didn't tell him?"

"We're not having this conversation, okay? Richmond? I half thought you might've brought Sky back with you."

She seemed to like Alaric. More than she liked me, at any rate.

"Maybe I would have if she hadn't done a disappearing act."

"She ran out on you?"

That revelation annoyed me more than I let on. Sky interested me. And I hadn't sent her out with Alaric because I was incapable of going myself—I'd battled through more than a broken nose in the past—I'd sent her because I wanted to see how she coped. To hear she'd bugged out was...disappointing. Sure, I could find her again by staking out the squat she called home, but I wasn't sure I wanted to.

"I left her outside the second hotel, and when I finished in there, she'd gone. She may also have taken another vehicle. The receptionist said a delivery van went missing around the same time Sky did."

Sadly, that didn't surprise me. "Second hotel?"

Alaric started at the beginning with the tale of how they'd followed the guy who met Bethany at the Ash Court Inn to another establishment nearby. Alaric had charmed the man's room number out of the receptionist, only to find things weren't quite as they seemed.

"An out-of-work actor?" I asked. "Are you serious?"

"Some guy hired him via email. Said it was for a low-budget spy movie."

"Didn't he wonder where the cameras were?"

"Apparently, it was 'raw and real,' so they were using hidden cameras. They just told the guy to act natural and he didn't question it."

"Not the brightest crayon in the box, eh?"

"Not even if you set him on fire. I've got copies of the emails, but they came from a free-to-use webmail account."

"I can get Mack to check into it."

"We both know it'll be futile. He was told to collect a key from the desk and check in to room 312, zip the box with the painting into the open suitcase on the bed, and then have a drink in the bar before he left. That's where I found him. Candace checked with her colleagues, and one of them saw him walk in there."

"Candace?"

"The receptionist."

"Tell me you didn't get her phone number."

"Why would it matter if I did?"

Why indeed? I had no right to get snippy about shit like that anymore. But even so, it felt as if there was unfinished business between Alaric and me. We hadn't so much broken up as been forced apart by circumstances. There'd be no going back to the way things were, but the transition to the friend zone wasn't as simple as flipping a switch.

Still, I wasn't about to start that discussion.

"Because we're meant to be working."

"Sometimes, mixing business with pleasure gets the best results, wouldn't you agree, Mrs. Black?"

Ouch.

*When you don't have a good comeback, change the subject.* "Who booked the room?"

Alaric's smirk said he knew exactly what I'd done. He didn't see into my soul the way Black did, but once upon a time, he'd certainly been tuned in to my thoughts. Seemed not much had changed.

"Our favourite gallery owner."

"Pemberton?"

"Unless there's another one you haven't told me about."

"Shit. Did anyone see who went into the room after the actor?"

"Not that I could find. There weren't any security cameras on that floor, and it looks as though he left via the rear fire escape."

"It wasn't alarmed?"

Alaric grimaced. "Apparently, the housekeeping staff propped it open because of the heat. The AC's been faulty lately, as have the cameras at the front of the building. Budget cuts. The place got a shitty review from a lifestyle blogger with ten million followers, and business has been bad for months."

"What about the buildings across the street? Surely one of them must have CCTV?"

"Everything's closed now. I'll go back tomorrow and start asking questions."

"Do you need manpower? Blackwood might have a spare person or two."

"Thanks."

"And if nothing turns up, then we've got one option left."

Pemberton. The possibility of him being merely negligent with regard to the restoration of *Red After Dark* had all but vanished. Firstly, he'd lied to Bethany about which painting she was delivering, and secondly, he'd booked the hotel room. But who for?

"Yes, I know." Alaric sighed. "But Pemberton reminds me of my grandpa. I feel like I should be making him cocoa, not interrogating him."

"Fine, then I'll do it. I don't have any grandpas."

"The other issue is that if we talk to him, it'll tip off a bunch of art thieves that somebody's after them. Fifty bucks says *Red After Dark* isn't the first stolen painting he's restored, and we might be better served snooping around again instead."

"Bethany knows who we are now."

"Bethany won't tell Pemberton."

"How do you know?"

Alaric just shrugged and gave a wan smile. Ah, the old McLain charm.

"Okay, she might not tell him deliberately, but she'd probably gawp and drop her tray of champagne if we turned up at another exhibition."

The smile faded because he knew I was right.

Albany House was full of cameras and wired for sound. I'd deactivated everything but the perimeter security when I arrived, but if Black thought Alaric might be there, chances were he'd override the system to check up on me. Even so, I took a step closer and squeezed Alaric's hand.

"I know why you want to find *Emerald*, but don't let this shadow hang over the rest of your life."

"Sometimes...it feels like I can't find the light switch, you know?"

"I'll go to the gallery with you, and I'll catch the damn champagne."

"What about Black?"

"I'll deal with Black." Easier said than done, but I'd manage somehow. After the initial *Emerald* incident, I'd offered to replace the ransom out of my own money, and Black had been furious. Alaric refused to accept, and even if he had, a lot of the damage had been done by that point anyway. Everyone thought he was a thief. "Come on, let's go out. If we stay here, we'll both end up miserable and drunk."

"Out where?"

"Dinner?"

"Ruth's making you macaroni and cheese."

My comfort food, and her recipe was the best. She put onions in it, and usually bacon too. "Okay, we'll eat and then go out. How about a show? Or a club? Not my club, obviously."

Black's, my London nightclub, had too many eyes and ears as well, and guess who monitored the cameras? Yup, Blackwood. I didn't particularly want to fuel the office gossip for the next month.

"A jazz club?"

Not my favourite—I preferred my music to come with a tune—but Alaric had always told me that jazz wasn't about the words, it was about the feelings. If it made him happy, I'd go.

"Okay, jazz."

But no sooner had I uttered the words than my phone rang with the theme song from *The Office*. Fuck. If this was Black's doing... I wouldn't put it past him to invent an emergency to give me something to do that didn't involve Alaric.

"Yeah?"

"Emmy? It's Tom."

He didn't need to tell me that. Tom's voice never wavered, never changed in tone. A tranquil lake in a raging sea. No matter how much shit hit the fan, he remained unflappable, which made him the perfect choice to be one of our control room managers. With the day shift over, he'd be in charge of the building at the moment.

"What's up?"

"There's a young lady asking for you at the front desk. Says her name's Sky Malone?"

Ever had one of those moments where despair turns to hope? My heart gave a weird skip, and I felt my lips curve of their own accord. Perhaps I hadn't misjudged Sky after all?

"I'm at Albany House. Can you get somebody to drive her over?"

"Now?"

"Right now."

"Zander's just about to leave. I'll see if he'd mind a detour."

I could get Alaric to meet them downstairs rather

than showing off my messed-up face to Zander. One of my eyes was going black too. I could hide it with make-up—I'd had plenty of practice over the years—but I was still pissed off about it. But you know what they say—out of darkness cometh light. Which sounded all very biblical but was actually the motto for the city of Wolverhampton.

"What are you smiling about?" Alaric asked.

"Sky's just turned up at the office."

His eyes brightened too. "Really? Why?"

"Tom didn't say, but he's sending her over here."

Except when Tom called back a minute later, it turned out he was no match for a strong-willed teenager.

"Sorry, boss, but Miss Malone doesn't want to go with Zander."

"Why? He's hardly an axe murderer."

"Apparently, she's already late for work."

Well, I had to give her points for being conscientious in at least one area of her life.

"Can you put her on?"

"One moment."

I held the phone out to Alaric. "You need to convince her to come here instead of going to work."

"Why me?"

"In case you hadn't noticed, she isn't my biggest fan."

"She just doesn't know you the way I do, Cinders." He flashed me a grin as he took the phone. "Hey, Sky. We're about to eat dinner. You like macaroni and cheese? Call in sick, and I can order a pizza too if you want."

A pause.

"How much will skipping work cost you? ... Then I'll give you that much in cash. Yes, as many toppings as you want. ... See you in half an hour." He passed the phone back. "She's on her way, and we owe her fifty pounds and a pizza with everything. The way to her heart is through her stomach."

"Actually, it's better to go through the armpit. Less resistance."

"Please, Emmy."

"Or through an eye socket to the brain."

"Just be quiet and order the damn pizza."

# CHAPTER 15 - SKY

THE HEAVENS OPENED as we pulled out of the underground parking garage at Blackwood Security's fancy office building. If that wasn't a metaphor for my life, I didn't know what was.

The guy driving me—Zander, he said his name was —didn't seem bothered by the storm, just switched on the blowers to de-mist the windscreen and turned the wipers onto fast. He had a black sports car too. Was it mandatory for getting a job at that company? Probably.

I didn't appreciate being summoned across London, but I was so damn hungry, and there wasn't any food at home. I'd spent Alaric's money on three different bus fares, and the prospect of going straight to the club and working for eight hours straight in boots that pinched my feet was more than I could bear, especially when he'd offered to give me more cash. The way I felt right now, I'd probably do something stupid like faint in Harlequin's.

No, I'd go to Emmy's place, eat the pizza and the macaroni and cheese, tell Alaric what he needed to know, collect the cash, then get the hell out of there.

And at least I didn't have to ride on another bus to get there.

"Do you know Emmy?" I asked Zander.

"Yup."

"Is she always so demanding?"

"Yup."

"Do you ever say anything but 'yup'?"

"Yup." He glanced at me quickly, eyes crinkling. "Sorry, couldn't resist. How do you know Emmy? Are you one of the foundation kids?"

"What foundation?"

"Guess not, then."

"I only met her this morning. We...uh, we had a fight."

"Like a slanging match?"

"No, more of a punch-up."

"And you lived to tell the tale?"

If I wasn't mistaken, there was a hint of awe in his voice.

"Yeah. Why?"

We stopped at a red traffic light, and he turned to take a closer look at me. Why did I feel like I was under a microscope? Finally, he spoke again.

"Most people who take on Emmy end up with more damage. All you got was a few holes in your jeans?"

"Those were there already."

Zander started laughing. "You're ballsy, kid."

"I'm not a kid. I'm eighteen." Practically. "Can I borrow your phone?"

"Why?"

"Mine broke, and I need to call my brother."

Zander reached into his jacket pocket, pulled out a slim smartphone, and tapped in the code to unlock it.

"Here you go. Brothers worry—I know that from experience."

If only. When Lenny got high, he forgot I even existed. I punched in his number from memory then cursed under my breath when it rang and rang. Finally, voicemail clicked in, the generic greeting he'd never bothered to change.

"Lenny, it's me. I'm gonna be out for a few more hours, and my phone broke so you can't call me. Please, just go home if you're out. *Please.*"

I passed the phone back to Zander, ignoring his look of concern. Sympathy didn't help me. Not one bit.

"Younger brother?" he guessed.

"Older."

"Yet you feel responsible for him?"

"I don't want to talk about it, okay?"

Zander waited a beat, then shrugged. "Fair enough. What sort of music do you like?"

"Whatever."

A moment later, the sound of classic rock filled the car, and I leaned back in the leather seat, trying to block out the world for five minutes at least. How much longer could I carry on with things as they were? The last decade had worn me down to the point where I felt like giving up, like closing my eyes and sleeping for eternity, but where would that leave Lenny? Once, I'd thought that if I could just get a decent job, I'd be able to fix the problem, fix *him*, but now? He needed professional help. I'd got him into two treatment programs, but he'd relapsed after both of them, the second time within days, and now we were right back at the bottom of the waiting list again.

Meanwhile, I was self-studying to retake the GCSEs I'd screwed up the first time because I was too busy hustling for money and dodging Lenny's dealers, and I couldn't remember what it felt like not to be exhausted.

*How much more?*

"We're here." Zander shook my shoulder, and I jolted awake. Shit. I'd fallen asleep in a stranger's *freaking car*. Last time that happened, I'd woken up with a man groping me, and things had only got worse from there. *Bloody hell, Sky*. What happened to my sense of self-preservation?

My heart sped up as I blinked a few times, trying to work out where I was. Another underground parking garage, by the look of it. I recognised Emmy's black sports car next to Alaric's SUV, and there was a bright red motorbike in the far corner. The other six spaces were empty. Guess everyone else was out.

Zander walked around to open my door, something I couldn't recall a man ever doing before, then motioned to the left.

"Elevator or stairs?"

"Stairs."

I'd been stuck in an elevator once. What a miserable three hours that had been. The intercom didn't work, the lights went out, and I couldn't even sit down because some filthy scrote had peed on the floor.

When Zander opened the door at the top, I expected to see a hallway full of doors, because that was how every other apartment building I'd been in worked, but instead, I found myself in an art museum. An air-conditioned palace. Everything was white—the walls, the floor, the side table, the couch along one wall —except for a huge multicoloured chandelier made from blown glass and a painting of a woman who'd been put together all wrong. I looked around in case there was a pickled shark too, but thankfully no.

"What is this place?" I whispered.

"Emmy's home. Hmm, is that..." Zander stepped

closer to the painting.

"A Picasso?" Alaric's voice came from behind us. "Yes. Bradley rearranged the art collection."

"I heard a rumour they had one, but... It's impressive. Surprised they've put it on display like this."

"Art's made to be enjoyed, not hidden away in vaults."

"Alaric. It's been a long time."

"Zander." The men shook hands. "Life treating you well?"

"Not bad. I got married."

"Congratulations. Your sister okay?"

"Define 'okay.' She's dating a rock star, and I'm not sure whether to go all big brother or welcome him to the family."

"Travis Thorne? I thought the girl in the gossip columns looked familiar. Wasn't his band involved in some sort of murder investigation?"

"All resolved now, thankfully. I guess as rock stars go, he's not such a bad guy."

His sister was dating *Travis Thorne*? Most of the time, I listened to the electronic shit Howie played in the club, but I'd still heard of Travis freaking Thorne. The guy wasn't just a rock star, he was a rock god.

A buzzer sounded, and a screen lit up beside what I assumed was the front door. The picture was surprisingly clear, and my mouth watered when I saw the outline of a pizza delivery bag in the caller's hands.

"The rest of dinner's here," Alaric said. "Good to see you again, buddy."

Zander vanished back down the stairs, and Alaric left me alone in the hallway while he went to fetch the pizza. Alone with a freaking Picasso. I was surprised he trusted me not to steal it after the vehicle incident. *Incidents*. Did he know I'd borrowed the van this afternoon? I figured I'd find out soon enough. If he decided to kick me out, hopefully I'd manage to snarf down most of dinner first.

When Alaric returned with not one but three pizzas plus a trio of sides, he herded me towards the back of the house. I was basically lost by the time we reached a kitchen bigger than the former pub I lived in. Emmy stood on the far side with a steaming dish in her hands. She cooked as well?

I tried to look at her nose without being obvious. It didn't seem to be any more swollen than earlier, but I spotted an ice pack on the marble island in the middle of the room.

"Eat in here?" she asked. "I can't be arsed to carry stuff to the dining room and all the way back again."

The kitchen table seated twelve. There was a dining room as well? Oh, who was I kidding? Of course there was a dining room.

"Fine by me," Alaric said.

Was I supposed to chime in too? "I'm just here for the pizza."

"You're clearly not, since you showed up at the office before we ordered it." Emmy set the dish down on a leather mat, and the delicious aroma of cheese drifted in my direction. "And I'm curious—why were you so keen to leave this afternoon that you stole a van, yet you came back?"

"Because I thought I'd better follow the dude with the painting, and I wasn't sure I'd have enough cash for a taxi."

"Why didn't you call Alaric?"

"Because my stupid phone broke." I slapped it onto the table just in case she didn't believe me, and another crack appeared in what was left of the screen. "And I couldn't see him inside. Look, it was either borrow the van or lose the guy. Spare me the lecture on morality, okay?"

Emmy held up her hands. "No lecture from me."

"What dude with the painting?" Alaric asked.

"Some American guy. At least, I *think* he had the painting." I paused to grab a slice of pizza. There was no Hawaiian, but in the gourmet chow stakes, peppers, sweetcorn, tomatoes, olives, and extra cheese came a close second. "He stopped for a cigarette, then drove to the airport. I did what you said—stayed well back and didn't crowd him—and I'm pretty sure he didn't spot me."

"Why do you think he had the painting? You saw the box?"

"No, I smelled it. His suitcase whiffed of the body spray that exploded in Bethany's car. I guess he could just have liked eau de candy floss, but it would've been quite a coincidence, don't you think?"

"What do I think? I think I want to kiss your feet. Did you see which terminal the man went to?"

"No, because some arsehole blocked the van in and I couldn't follow. But the dude got picked up from outside the car hire place by a big black BMW with 'VIP Service' on the door. Guess he's rich."

"You're not wrong there," Emmy said. "The VIP lounges are hidden away in Terminal Five, and they're bloody expensive." But I bet she'd been in them. "If you don't know they're there, you won't find them. The entrance is just a plain white door in a nondescript corridor. Getting the client list won't be easy, but we can try."

"Might be easier to go for the rental agency," Alaric said. "Did he return a car?"

"Yup." I channelled Zander, then took another bite of pizza.

"Which company did he use? Maybe we can find a name."

"London Luxe, and his name's Stéphane Hegler."

Oh, how satisfying. Alaric's mouth dropped open, and even Emmy looked gobsmacked.

Finally he asked, "How do you know that?"

I put my slice of pizza down long enough to root through my handbag and slid the crumpled rental agreement in their direction.

"Because of this. But I guess he might've used a fake passport. Money can buy you anything, right?"

Sometimes even taste. I wanted to hate Emmy's home, but if I'd had about a zillion pounds to spare, I'd have picked out furniture just like hers.

"How did you get this?"

"Waited until Hegler left, then went up to the counter and pretended I'd left my jacket in a rental car the week before." The idiot behind the desk didn't even question why I'd bothered to visit the office rather than phoning like a normal person. Probably because he was too busy staring at my tits. Pervert. "When the guy on duty buggered off to check the lost-property box, I swiped the paperwork and left. And yes, I kept my head down so my face isn't on camera."

The driver's baseball cap sure had come in handy. Perhaps I should start wearing one more often?

"Nice move," Emmy said. "That'll save us a ton of work."

Why was she being nice to me all of a sudden? I didn't understand her.

"Where did you leave the van?" Alaric asked.

"In the car park at the airport. I wiped the steering wheel first. Someone'll find it, probably a traffic warden."

Three slices of pizza down, and I decided to try the macaroni and cheese. How long since I'd eaten the proper stuff and not the dried version that came in a packet? One of my good foster mothers had made it for me, but I'd only been with that family for two months before I got moved on again, everything I owned stuffed into a black plastic bag. Unwanted, like last week's rubbish.

Oh boy, this stuff was good. There was *bacon* in it, which basically made it heaven on a plate.

"You should've become a chef," I told Emmy, and for some reason, both she and Alaric found that hilarious. He nearly choked laughing. "What? What's so funny?"

"The...the idea of Emmy cooking something edible."

"Huh?"

"My housekeeper made this," she explained. "Cooking isn't my strong suit. If it's not microwaved or flambéed, you're shit out of luck, but I do have an excellent collection of takeout menus. Want me to order anything else?"

It was tempting. So tempting. But I couldn't. "Nah, I have to get back to Lenny. I tried calling him from your mate's phone, but he didn't answer, and he gets into trouble if I'm not around."

"You need a new phone? I'll get you one."

Without another word, she rose from her seat and vanished into the bowels of the house, leaving me to wonder if I'd dropped into an alternate universe. What had happened to grouchy Emmy, and who had spare phones lying around in their house?

"Is she for real?" I asked Alaric.

"She always used to break phones with alarming regularity, and I don't suppose much has changed. She'll have a stack of spares somewhere."

"What do you mean, used to?"

"We haven't seen much of each other for a few years."

"Why not? Did she piss you off too?"

Alaric shook his head. "It's a long story, and not one I'm about to tell."

Fair enough. Everybody liked to keep their secrets, especially me. The less I told people about myself, the less shit they had to throw back in my face later on. Anyhow, it only took a couple of minutes before Emmy reappeared with a brand-new smartphone in a box. She slid it across the table in my direction.

"Here you go. It's already charged."

Bloody hell—it was one of the newest models, and far more expensive than I'd ever be able to buy. I didn't tend to steal pricey phones either because I hated the feeling of guilt that came with them. I was doubly glad I hadn't gone to Harlequin's now. A ton of food and a new toy sure beat traipsing around for hours on aching feet.

It only took a moment to insert the SIM card from my old phone, and the moment I did, the screen lit up with a dozen text messages and missed calls. Strange.

I'd never been that popular.

Before I could go through them, the phone rang again. Paulius, my housemate, and he only ever called if he wanted something. Shit. Tell me we hadn't run out of lightbulbs again, because I hated arriving home in the pitch black.

"It's Sky. What?"

"You need to come home. Lenny, he is not well."

Ice prickled up my spine. "What do you mean, not well?"

"He won't open his door, but we heard him moaning. And now he is quiet."

Oh, fuck, fuck, fuck. *Lenny, what have you done?* He'd been vaguely coherent when Emmy loaded him into the car earlier, and he'd managed an intelligible text message, which meant whatever it was had happened recently. My guess? He'd taken something, and I dreaded to think what.

"Okay, I'm coming." I shoved my chair back and gave the pizza one last longing look. "Gotta go, sorry. Uh, you said you'd give me money for missing work—can I get it?"

I didn't have time to mess around with buses and Tubes. If Lenny had OD'd again, I needed to get there fast, which meant taking a taxi.

Emmy and Alaric looked at each other.

"Sky, we still have questions," Alaric said.

"Then I'll come back tomorrow or something. My brother's sick."

Emmy raised an eyebrow. "Really? He seemed okay earlier, relatively speaking. Is he hungover?"

"Nah, it's not that." The last thing I wanted to do was spill Lenny's problems to two relative strangers, but I figured I owed them an explanation. "Sometimes...sometimes, he takes drugs, and he's not always as careful as he should be."

Another glance between them, and Emmy nodded once. "I'll drive."

"Huh?"

"At this time of the evening, the fastest way to your place from here is by car. I'll drive."

She paused for long enough to grab a green duffel bag out of a cupboard, and then the three of us were running through the house and back down the stairs to the underground garage. Alaric bleeped his SUV open, and we all piled in.

When Emmy said driving was the quickest way, she wasn't kidding. By the time we arrived, I was hanging on to the seat belt with one hand and the grab handle with the other, muttering prayers to any god I could think of and Satan as well since the woman drove like a demon. The smell of burned rubber permeated the air as I stumbled out of the back seat on shaky legs.

Paulius was standing by Lenny's door on the top floor when we got there.

"We tried to open it, but it's stuck."

Emmy and Alaric didn't hesitate, just ran at the door together and shouldered it open. It bounced off the wall, and a chunk of plaster fell from the ceiling and landed on Lenny's motionless body. I froze for a moment, taking in the scene. He was lying on the floor in boxer shorts and a T-shirt, pale, so pale, and the little collection of items beside him revealed my worst nightmares had come true. A metal spoon. A lighter. A shoelace. A hypodermic syringe. He'd fucked up again, and big time.

An ambulance. We needed an ambulance. Thank goodness I had a new phone.

"My brother's overdosed," I told the 999 woman when she answered. "He needs a doctor."

"Is it an emergency?"

"Yes, it's a bloody emergency!"

How did Emmy and Alaric stay so calm? They knelt next to Lenny, one on each side, checking his vital signs. *Please, let him be alive.*

"No pulse," Emmy said. "Is he breathing?"

Alaric's answer was to start chest compressions as he shook his head.

Fuck. How long did ambulances take?

"Average response time in London is seven minutes," Emmy told me. I hadn't even realised I'd spoken out loud. "But St. Thomas's is only a mile away, so we might get lucky. Let's try this in the meantime."

She opened the duffel bag, and I realised it was a first aid kit. A giant first aid kit. A quick rummage, and she drew out a syringe of her own.

"Wait! What's that? What are you giving him?"

"Naloxone. It reverses an opiate overdose by binding to the body's opioid receptors instead of the heroin."

I could do nothing but watch. It was clear both Emmy and Alaric knew what they were doing, and I definitely didn't. I'd never felt so helpless in my life. Next, Emmy produced a green box and tore Lenny's shirt off, the ripping sound the loudest thing in the room. He was dying, yet it was so quiet.

"What's that?" I whispered.

"A defibrillator. If there's still electrical activity in his brain, there's a good chance we can shock his heart into restarting." She stuck two sticky pads on Lenny's chest. "Clear."

Alaric rocked back on his heels for a moment, Lenny jolted, and Emmy studied the screen on the machine.

"Okay, as you were. Sky, can you go outside and show the medical team up when they arrive?"

I didn't want to leave Lenny, but I also knew what Emmy said made sense. Every second counted, and I had to play my part. My knees almost buckled as I staggered down the stairs, past Paulius and the others who'd gathered in front of the old bar.

"You should've called an ambulance earlier," I snapped, unable to help myself.

None of them said a word.

## CHAPTER 16 - ALARIC

"I TAKE YOU to all the best places, Cinders."

"Technically, I think you'll find I took you."

"And your driving hasn't improved in the slightest."

Alaric paused the chest compressions to switch to rescue breaths. If he'd timed it right, he'd get through five cycles of thirty compressions and two breaths in two minutes, by which point the naloxone should have begun to work and the AED would be ready to shock again if necessary.

"How are we doing?" he asked Emmy, who'd spent most of the time singing "Stayin' Alive" by the Bee Gees —badly—to keep him in time.

"Five seconds... Okay, pause." She studied the screen for a moment. "No shockable rhythm." Smoothly, she pressed two fingers to the kid's carotid artery. "Moment of truth."

No shockable rhythm meant one of two things— either there was a pulse, or there was no electrical activity left to shock and they'd both be attending a funeral soon. No matter that they'd only known Sky for a day—she'd made a big impression, and Alaric knew that Emmy wouldn't let her deal with the aftermath of this evening alone any more than he would.

What was it to be?

Emmy closed her eyes for a moment.

"Thank fuck," she said on an exhale. "Get him into the recovery position."

Emmy tipped the kid onto his side while Alaric wiped his mouth with a sleeve. He'd started without a resuscitation mask, and Lenny tasted of old beer and tomato ketchup, neither of which was pleasant. Still, he was alive. Good thing too, because Alaric's black suit was in a storage locker in Florida along with most of his other belongings. At heart, he was a nomad, and his feet got itchy if he stayed in one place for longer than a few months. Emmy was the only person he'd considered putting down roots for, and when that didn't work out, he'd gone back to his transient ways. Here one week, gone the next. At some point, he'd rent another house for a while, but where? Florida was too hot in the summer.

Before he could consider his options any further, Emmy's phone rang with Bryan Adams's "Black Pearl." Alaric had taken her to one of Adams's concerts a lifetime ago, and she'd danced along to the track next to him, far more relaxed than she was nowadays. It didn't take a genius to work out who was calling.

But she surprised him by cursing.

"Bad timing?"

"Nope. Well, yes, but that's not why I'm pissed. Eight thirty in the evening? Black's checking I'm not having a cosy dinner with you. Trust me—I know him."

Checking up? That sounded like the asshole's MO. But Emmy would never cheat, and Alaric would never put her in a position where she might be tempted to do so. He liked her too much to ruin her relationship. Maybe even loved her still. No, he'd never hurt her, but he'd be damned if he lost her as a friend just because

Black decided to throw his considerable weight around.

"You gonna answer?"

"He can wait. Okay, this asshole's breathing on his own now, and his pulse is stronger."

A siren sounded in the distance, quickly drowning the music out as it drew closer. It wasn't long before footsteps thundered up the stairs. Sky burst in first.

"How is he? Is he...? Is he...?"

"He's alive." Emmy straightened, allowing the EMTs room to work. "He had four hundred micrograms of naloxone at eight thirty-two, followed by one shock. Pulse and respiration appear to have stabilised now. We found him unconscious, and we don't know exactly what he's taken or how much, but..." She waved a hand at the drug paraphernalia littering the room. "Opiates of some kind seemed like a fair bet."

This morning, even after the altercation with Emmy, Sky had been full of confidence, verging on cocky, but now she looked lost. Bewildered. This was a reminder that she was still a child, albeit fast approaching adulthood.

"Are you planning to take her back to Albany House tonight?" Alaric quietly asked Emmy. "Because if not, I'll find her somewhere to stay."

"Too damn right I am. This place is a shithole. I've lived in worse, but not by much, and it's fucking terrifying going to sleep because you never know what you'll wake up to. Can you help her to pack while I clear this kit up? Watch out for needles."

"What shall I tell her to bring?"

"Anything she wants to keep. She's not coming back here. Not ever again."

# CHAPTER 17 - SKY

AWAKE OR ASLEEP? It was hard to decide, and for five minutes, maybe ten, I just lay on the most comfortable bed I'd ever set my ass on and stared at the ceiling high above me. Last night had been the worst of my life, more awful even than being raped and left for dead myself. A sob welled up in my throat just from thinking about the past. Usually, I managed to block out the pain, but that jump out the window yesterday had shaken loose all sorts of emotions I didn't want to feel.

And then Lenny... It was the closest I'd come to losing him, and the scariest part was that I had no idea how to stop him from doing it again. If Alaric and Emmy hadn't been around... I didn't have an outfit suitable to wear at a funeral. And I certainly didn't have a defibrillator or a bag full of magic drugs.

At the hospital, Lenny had needed another dose of naloxone—the doctors had explained the effects were only temporary, and once it wore off, Lenny could keep overdosing until the drugs worked their way out of his system. I'd stayed with him until the early hours when he'd woken up and mumbled a string of half-assed apologies and the doctors said he was out of the woods. "Sorry, Sky" really didn't cut it, not this time, but I couldn't bring myself to yell at him. Not to mention I'd probably have got myself kicked out of the hospital if I'd given him a piece of my mind the way I wanted to.

And now? Now I was back at Emmy's house, and much as I wanted to hate being there, I also didn't want to leave. The fridge was full of food, and I didn't have to worry about waking up and finding a stranger standing over me. If I hadn't been so stressed over Lenny, I could've rolled over and gone back to sleep for the rest of the day, but I needed to know how he was, and also work out what was next for us. When Alaric started shoving my belongings into bin bags yesterday, I'd been too stressed to pay much attention, but did that mean he'd try to stop me from going back to the pub? Because where the hell else did he think I was going to live? I couldn't afford rent in London, and I also had to find a new job, one where I could keep a better eye on Lenny. Some companies allowed pets, or so I'd heard. I needed one that would let me bring my damn brother to work.

I rolled over, found the number for St. Thomas's and dialled, then did my best to sound polite when a woman answered.

"Hello? Can you tell me how Lennon Powell is?"

Alive, upset, and going into withdrawal was the verdict. Shit. Why had he gone back to the junk? The drink and the pot I could handle, but not heroin.

*Dammit, Lenny.* Every time I thought I was coping, things went tits-up again.

What was the time? Ten o'clock, and with Lenny staying overnight at the hospital again, I could at least get out and earn some money. Move my stuff back to the pub, run an errand or two for Digger, then head to Harlequin's. Schoolwork would have to wait.

My room came with its own bathroom, like a hotel, and I stood under the hot water until my fingers went pruney. Then I pulled on my grubby clothes, which spoiled the feeling of being clean, and ventured off to find Alaric. And Emmy. I needed to thank them, both of them, even if the words might stick in my throat when it came to the latter.

Last night, I'd memorised my way from the hallway to my bedroom, and now I reversed the route. Turn right, go around the corner, head down two flights of stairs, follow the corridor to the left, walk through the door by the painting of a horse, and there I was, back in the art gallery. I stared up at the Picasso again. I'd only ever seen stuff like that on the telly, and although the picture was all wonky, it was also kind of impressive to be standing in front of something a hundred years old that still looked so fresh.

The house was quiet, insulated from the sounds of traffic on the road outside. I couldn't ever remember experiencing that kind of silence in London. Even in the middle of the night, there was usually some idiot yelling or slamming a door. Was I alone? It felt like I was alone. But then I caught the merest whiff of bacon and figured someone was cooking. Not Emmy, apparently.

But she was the only person in the kitchen when I finally found it again, sitting at the table with a plate of crumbs and a laptop in front of her.

"Morning. Hungry?"

Always. "Is there any food?"

"Help yourself to whatever's in the fridge, or Ruth's left bacon in the oven."

"Where's Alaric?"

"Out. He's gone to talk to people about Hegler."

"Do you know where he put my stuff?" He also owed me money, but I wasn't sure how to ask for it after everything they'd done last night.

"Yes."

"Can I have it back?"

"Later. I want to talk to you first."

"Then can you hurry up? I've got things to do."

"Get some food."

*I'm not hungry anymore.* The words hovered on the tip of my tongue, my annoyance at being ordered around warring with my need to eat. In the end, hunger won. How long since I'd had a proper bacon sandwich? Months. The pub didn't have a working kitchen, just a now-defunct microwave. It only had electricity at all because Tyson had found a way to wire us into next door's supply. He was good at stuff like that. If he'd had actual qualifications, he could've made good money, but since he was an ex-con, nobody would employ him, so he made cash rewiring cannabis farms instead.

I found four types of bread in the fridge, along with ketchup, HP Sauce, and two kinds of orange juice. Emmy stayed seated, but even without looking, I felt her gaze burning into me as I moved around the kitchen. Talk about uncomfortable. The intensity could melt steel.

Finally, I took a seat opposite her, and sauce squished out the other end of my sandwich as I bit into it, splattering onto the white china plate.

"Where's my stuff?"

"GCSE maths?"

"You went through my things? Don't you understand the concept of privacy?"

"The bottom of the bag split and your textbook fell out." Oh. "Having said that, I did take the liberty of running a quick background check. You've stayed out of trouble with the police. Fuck knows how."

That bitch.

"I never did anything illegal until yesterday."

"Bullshit."

"What do you want? Look, thanks for saving Lenny and all that, but I just need to get out of here."

"What do I want?" She pushed the laptop to the side and watched me, elbows propped on the table. Yep, intense. *Don't squirm, Sky.* "What I want is to make you an offer."

"Huh?"

"I want to make you an offer."

"What kind of offer?"

"You remind me very much of myself eighteen years ago."

"Yeah, right."

"I sat opposite a man with a broken nose, and he made me a similar offer. I'll adjust for inflation, of course."

What was she talking about?

"You've got a lot of potential, Sky, and I don't think you realise quite how much. Come and work for me for six months. Let me train you. At the end of that period, either one of us can terminate the contract if it isn't working out, and I'll pay you three hundred grand either way."

"I'm sorry?"

"Three hundred thousand pounds for six months of your life." Was she for real? "And I'll also pay for Lenny to go to rehab. My assistant tells me the Abbey Clinic's the best place in London. Lenny's an addict, Sky, and with the best will in the world, you can't fix him by yourself."

Didn't I know it? I'd tried and failed. And I knew all about the Abbey Clinic too. It cost over two grand a week, and you couldn't even get an appointment without connections.

"Why me? I don't have a single qualification, and my work experience is basically shady shit and serving shots to drunk people."

"It's the shady shit that interests me. And you also have other qualities." She ticked off points on her fingers. "You're loyal. You take care of Lenny no matter how many problems he causes. Plus you have a conscience. In Richmond, you could've walked off into the sunset, yet you came back. And you're driven. Why else would you be pushing yourself to do schoolwork and keeping so fit in your spare time? You've got gifts, and I want to exploit them."

At least she was honest about the exploitation part. But even so... "Three hundred grand? Are you crazy?"

"If it works out the way I hope it will, it'll be the best money I've ever spent."

This was insane. I stared down at my rapidly cooling sandwich and found I suddenly *had* lost my appetite.

"What would I have to do?"

"Learn. You'd be taught everything from diving to flying to shooting to fight skills to languages to trigonometry. I'm assuming we could skip the parkour and the pickpocketing lessons?"

I managed a nod.

"Lock-picking too?"

"I can do the basics."

"Good. You'd be expected to maintain an excellent level of fitness, and discipline is key. Some days, it'll feel like you're being asked to do the impossible, but you'll dig deep and do it anyway. You'll be tested in every way you can possibly think of. It'll hurt, mentally and physically. And then there are the soft skills. You'd have to learn to deal with people, which might be the hardest part for you."

"Gee, thanks. You're not exactly selling the job. Apart from money, why exactly would I agree to this?"

"Because if you make the grade, in a year or two, you'll be able to do any fucking thing you want."

"How do you know?"

She just smiled at me. And then I understood.

"You want me to be your sidekick?"

"No, I want you to be my replacement. I've got a few years left in me yet, but nobody can do this job forever."

"And what exactly is your job?"

"I fix problems that other people can't. There are small groups of people fighting behind the scenes to keep the world on an even keel, and I lead one of them."

"Fix problems? How?"

"By whatever means necessary."

I thought back to the shooting she'd mentioned. Surely not? "But you don't kill people, right?" I asked, just to check.

Again, she smiled.

Holy shit.

"I'm not sure..."

"Believe it or not, I have a conscience. So do you,

and I won't ever stop you from following it. Take some time to consider things, okay? This isn't the kind of decision you make lightly."

"Would I have to work at that office in King's Cross?"

"No, you'd have to move to Richmond. As in Richmond, Virginia, not Richmond, London. That's where I'm based now. There'd be some travel involved."

Travel? I'd never even left London before. The closest I'd got to a holiday came six years ago when Lenny had still been clean and mostly sober. In the middle of a mini-heatwave, he'd snuck me out of my foster home and we'd caught the Tube to Hyde Park, then sunbathed and stuffed ourselves with ice cream by the Serpentine for the whole day. I'd got a bollocking when I arrived back home, but it'd been worth it. It was another of the memories that stopped me from abandoning Lenny. Those brief moments of respite he'd brought me on gloomy days.

"What if I say no? I'll be on my own?"

"No. I'm a bitch, but not that much of a bitch. I'll help you to get Lenny enrolled in a community detox program and provide you with a flat for three months so you can get back on your feet. I also run a charitable foundation, and its mentoring scheme has good success at helping participants to find stable jobs. *Legal* jobs."

Another stupid sob threatened to escape. Three months of accommodation and detox for Lenny? That was a good offer, and if somebody had dangled it in front of me this morning, I'd have bitten their arm off. But the first option? The thought of working for Emmy both scared and intrigued me. I had no doubt she'd be a hard master, but the idea of being moulded into her image? Last night, she'd taken charge and saved Lenny, then used her calm authority to get him a private room at the hospital. Every time someone asked me a difficult question, she'd jumped in and deflected, and nobody had dared to argue. I didn't much like her, but I'd envied her. And now she was offering me the chance to become her?

Honestly, I doubted I had it in me, but I only had to stick it out for six months. Six months, and I'd have enough money for a down payment on a flat. Perhaps even enough to buy outright in the suburbs. Then me and Lenny wouldn't have to keep moving from squat to squat, constantly looking over our shoulders. And if he went to the Abbey Clinic, maybe I wouldn't have to spend the rest of my life watching out for the telltale signs of addiction either.

"Why are you helping me? I broke your nose."

"That was a wake-up call. I underestimated you. Trust me, it won't happen again." She got up, closed her laptop, and tucked it under her arm. "Think about it," she said over her shoulder as she headed for the door. "You're welcome to stay here while you decide."

Hmm... How long could I stretch this out? Emmy said I could stay at her house while I considered my options, and since I didn't have to go back to the pub now no matter what, I wondered if a month was a reasonable amount of time to make a decision.

Six months. Twenty-six weeks, one hundred and eighty-two days. That was a long time in hell. Realistically, yesterday's chase had only taken a minute or two, but it had felt like an hour. Could I hack it?

And would community detox work for Lenny? He'd already tried it twice before and fucked up by drinking, and I couldn't supervise him every second of every day. I'd still have to work. He'd narrowly survived last night's overdose, but would he live to see twenty-five?

Quiet footsteps sounded behind me, and I spun in my seat to see a grey-haired woman in the doorway. She looked like somebody's grandma, all smiley and kind and a tiny bit plump. Probably not my grandma, though, although since I hadn't met either of them and I barely even remembered my mother, I couldn't be sure.

"You must be Sky?"

"Yeah."

"I'm Ruth, the housekeeper here. You didn't like your breakfast?"

"No. I mean, yes, it was really good. I just lost my appetite."

"Anything I can help with?"

"Not really. I don't think so."

"Well, I'm always here if you need an ear. Did Emmy leave?"

"Just a minute ago."

"Ah."

From the way she said it, I knew she'd put two and two together about my lost appetite and Emmy's recent departure. I wasn't one for sharing my problems, but if Ruth had worked in the house for a while, maybe she could give me some information?

"Have you known Emmy for long?"

"Over seventeen years now."

Really? Seventeen years? That meant she'd met

Emmy right about when Emmy started doing her "problem fixing."

"She says I remind her of the way she used to be."

"Well, dearie, I've only just met you, so I'm not the best judge of that, but I can tell you that Emmy's changed considerably in that time. She was one step up from a street urchin when she first arrived, and she gave Black a good challenge. Although secretly, I think he enjoyed it."

"Black?"

"Her husband."

"Her husband? Was he the person who..." Who what? "Who...recruited her?"

"Oh, yes, dearie. They didn't get married right away. No, they spent two years at each other's throats first. Do you want something else to eat? I'm just about to start on lunch."

I shook my head. "Do you like working for her?"

"For the both of them, you mean. I wouldn't have stayed for so long if I didn't. They're good people."

Good people. Good people who occasionally did bad things. Wasn't that me as well?

Emmy was right—I did have a lot of thinking to do.

## Chapter 18 - Bethany

DELIVER THE PAINTING and then go back to work, Emerson had said. Forget today ever happened.

How? How was I supposed to do that?

The fact that I'd handled stolen goods preyed on my mind for the rest of Wednesday and most of Thursday, and I found myself scrutinising every painting in the gallery, wondering about their provenances. When I took Hugo his morning tea, I'd barely been able to look him in the eye. He was busy touching up a landscape with a tiny paintbrush. Who owned it? Where did it come from?

I'd breathed a sigh of relief when he'd locked and alarmed his workroom at lunchtime on Thursday and headed out for an appointment. At least I could avoid facing him for another day. And at three o'clock, Henrietta tapped me on the shoulder.

"Hugo just called. He's been delayed at the hospital, so he won't be back until late."

"The hospital?"

"I think it's some routine scan. I saw a letter on his desk the other day. Anyhow, he wants one of us to lock up, but he also asked me to run an errand, so that means you."

An errand? I'd bet Chaucer's last bag of carrots that Henrietta's "errand" involved a hot yoga class followed by happy hour with her equally obnoxious friends, but I honestly didn't care because it meant I wouldn't have to put up with her for the remainder of the afternoon.

"Sure, I can lock up."

"Get Gemma to help you. Although I'm not sure where she's gone."

Neither was I. I recalled her "popping out to pick up a salad" at lunchtime, but I hadn't seen her come back. I typed out a quick text message.

*Me: Hey, are you okay? Henrietta's gone out, and I was wondering if you could help me lock up?*

Five minutes later, I got a reply.

*Gemma: Sorry, I had a headache, and Hugo said I could go home.*

*Me: Is there anything I can do? Want me to pick up some paracetamol and bring it over when I finish?*

*Gemma: Ry's looking after me, but thanks for the offer.*

Ry. The boyfriend. A bulky man who towered over me and bore a passing resemblance to The Rock, but with more hair. I'd only met him once—Ry, not The Rock—when he came to pick Gemma up after work one day, and he'd rubbed me up the wrong way. The man was too slick, too charming, and while Gemma spoke about him in glowing terms, I worried that things were happening too fast between them. She'd changed since he came onto the scene. When I first met her, she'd been sweet, bubbly, a bit ditzy, but always friendly. Now she was quieter. Meeker. She'd lost weight too, half a stone or so, and she'd been slim in the first place.

But what could I do? She claimed to be happy, and if Ry was spending his evening taking care of her, perhaps I was anxious over nothing.

*Me: Hope you feel better soon! See you tomorrow
x*

The gallery was quiet, and with Henrietta out of the way, I sat myself at the front desk where I could see the door and began hunting through recruitment websites. I'd come in early this morning and updated my CV, but it was still woefully inadequate. Everywhere wanted experience, experience, experience even for an entry-level position, and I didn't know how to use a franking machine or set up databases or navigate the latest CRM systems. Plus explaining the total absence of gainful employment throughout my twenties and the fact that I'd lasted less than six months at my last job promised to be awkward, and that was if I even made it to the interview stage. I sent off half a dozen applications for roles I didn't particularly want, then turned to YouTube.

*Dammit, Beth, stop wasting your time on horse videos.*

I should be doing something constructive instead. Something work-related since Hugo was paying me. Like...checking the art theft database for stolen paintings. Would that count for the "IT skills" section of my CV? My hands hovered over the keyboard. No, I really didn't want to look at that list, but once I'd had the idea, I couldn't shake it.

With no customers around, I tried searching, only to find there were in fact a bunch of databases and most of them required registration. Well, no wonder so much stolen art slipped through the cracks. The FBI's database was open to the public, so I clicked through the paintings, both sad and horrified that so many masterpieces had been lost. Then guilty when I saw

*Red After Dark's* entry.

What had happened at the hotel after I left? I wished I'd thought to get Alaric's number so I could ask. Yes, I had Emerson's card, but quite frankly, she scared me, so I figured I'd just keep checking the papers for news instead.

And there was *The Girl with the Emerald Ring*, still stunning even on a computer screen. I hoped whoever had her was treating her well. It would be sacrilegious to roll up a painting like that and stuff it into a closet, but I'd heard of that happening.

Then I saw it. A small still life, a plate of fruit and a deer skull, nothing particularly special on the surface except it was an early Pieter Claesz and it had been stolen three years ago, estimated value $150,000. And soon after I began working at the Pemberton gallery, I'd seen a remarkably similar painting in Hugo's studio.

I clicked frantically through the list, breathing a sigh of relief each time I reached the bottom of the page without seeing another piece I recognised from upstairs. And then my heart stuttered. There, front and centre, was an oil-on-canvas of a Venetian bridge, and Hugo had been working on one just like it last month.

"What are you looking at?"

At the sound of the voice, I jumped out of my skin and knocked over my coffee cup. The contents sloshed across my keyboard, and the laptop began making a horrible whirring noise before the screen went dark.

Shit!

"H-h-Hugo, I'm so sorry. I thought you were at the hospital."

"They made me wait for two hours, then cancelled the appointment. Damn bureaucrats." He dropped his handkerchief onto the rapidly spreading puddle while I rummaged in my handbag for the packet of tissues I knew was in there. They didn't help much either, and I ran to the bathroom for paper towels. When I got back, Hugo was still staring at my blank screen.

"What were you looking at?" he asked again.

"Oh, nothing important."

"The Stolen Art File?"

"I-i-it's important to remain diligent."

"Yes it is, and I see from your flustered demeanour that you think you recognised a painting?"

"Uh, that Francesco Guardi did look similar to one you were working on last month."

"Not the same painting at all. The one upstairs was in for assessment, but it proved to be a reproduction. A worthless copy. The workmanship was sloppy, and the pigments..." He shook his head and tutted. "Far too modern. I prepared a report for the auction house saying so."

I should have been relieved, but Hugo's explanation seemed too smooth, almost as if he'd prepared the spiel in advance just in case. Was he telling the truth? I wanted to believe him, but I wasn't sure I did.

"That's a relief."

What else could I say?

"Rest assured, if I had any inkling a painting brought here was stolen, I'd have reported it myself. And there's no need for you to keep checking the database. I do so regularly."

"Okay, I won't."

"Congratulations for being on the ball though, Bethany." He tilted the laptop to one side and lukewarm coffee ran out of the USB port. "I'm not sure this is recoverable."

"I'm so sorry."

"Let's leave it to dry overnight, shall we? Can you lock up on your way out? It's gone six o'clock."

So it had. I kicked myself for not keeping an eye on the time—I should have left half an hour ago, and then there would have been no coffee spillage and no awkward moments with Hugo. Mental note—set an alarm on my phone to remind me to go home.

"Absolutely. And again, I apologise about the laptop."

I poured myself a large gin and tonic the moment I got home, which I most certainly needed because my phone rang right after I took the first mouthful. I'd been staring at it as I turned Emerson's business card over and over in my hands, wondering whether I should call her about the other two paintings I'd seen.

Reporting my suspicions would be the responsible thing to do, wouldn't it? Plus I'd absolve myself of any further responsibility. But what if I'd been mistaken about the Pieter Claesz? And what if Hugo had told the truth about the Guardi?

I was still agonising over the conundrum when my mother called.

Oh, hurrah. Just when I thought a bad day couldn't get any worse.

As usual, there was no preamble. She got straight to the point. Small talk was for acquaintances at parties, not her own daughter.

"Bethie, you haven't forgotten your father's

birthday get-together on Saturday, have you?"

Of course I hadn't forgotten. I'd been dreading it for weeks. Why? Because Piers's parents were friends of the family, which meant they'd be invited, and that invitation would extend to Piers himself. And Piers was insensitive enough to attend if there was free booze involved. I'd been hoping for some last-minute illness or accident that might give me an excuse to skip the party—perhaps I could accidentally fall off Chaucer or have him stomp on my foot? A broken toe would be far less painful than having to face my ex-husband.

"No, no, I'm looking forward to it."

"Good. Don't be late again—we need you to help serve the canapés."

That was my parents—stingy to the last and always looking for an opportunity to exert control. Why hire an extra waitress when I could be pressed into duty? They'd probably make me help with the washing-up afterwards too. It wouldn't be the first time.

"It's in my diary. Er, is Piers coming?"

"And his new fiancée too, I believe."

*What?*

"His fiancée? He's *engaged*?"

"Just last week. Andromeda's such a darling girl. An actress. You remember her?"

"Yes, I remember," I said through gritted teeth. The image of Piers pumping away on top of her would be burned into my retinas forever.

"Bethie, you should stop being so bitter. After all, it was you who left him, not the other way around."

"Mum, he *cheated* on me."

"Oh, not this again. Men are like that, I'm afraid, darling. You just have to learn to live with it. Seven o'clock sharp."

She hung up, and I stared at the screen, wondering not for the first time how I could possibly be related to that woman. Yes, we looked quite similar—even now, thanks to my mother's endless nips and tucks—but inside? Claudette Stafford-Lyons was so heartless I was amazed blood still circulated in her body.

# CHAPTER 19 - SKY

STAY OR GO? Stay or go? Stay or go?

I'd slept on it, and although I knew logically what I *should* do—put up with six months of hell while Lenny got better, then take the three hundred grand and run—the thought of quitting London for the unknown left me nauseous.

And killing people? Although Emmy hadn't said the words, she'd intimated them, and I wasn't sure I could do that. Yeah, I knew that sort of shit must go on—the Russians had been caught doing it often enough—but assassins had always been nameless, faceless ghouls, not pretty blondes who lived in mansions and wore designer outfits. And certainly not girls like me.

I'd called Reuben this morning to talk about it. Not the killing part, obviously, but the possibility of moving to America to be...well, I'd told him I'd be a glorified private investigator. At first, he'd been supportive, happy I'd found a job that would utilise my skills.

"Always said you had the moves, love," he told me. "'Bout time someone else saw your potential. America's a long way, though, and what about Lenny?"

"Lenny's rehab comes as part of the package."

"Ain't never heard of a job offerin' that before."

"Me neither. But he needs more help than I can give, and this might be the only way. He overdosed last night." I swallowed to keep the sob inside. "He bloody died, Reu, and the woman who would be my boss, she saved him."

"Where is he now?"

"In the hospital. I need to find somewhere for him to go when he comes out. Somewhere without dealers on every damn corner."

"Like a rehab place," Reuben finished for me. "They payin' you too? Or is it one of those internships where you gotta make your own way?"

"They'd be paying me. Really well, actually." I took a deep breath. "Three hundred thousand for six months."

Even over the phone, Reuben's disappointment was palpable.

"Sky, what I tell you about scams? You a smart girl, and you still fallin' for this shit?"

"I know, I know, it's crazy. And if I wasn't standing in this woman's freaking mansion, I'd be laughing about it with you over Maccy D's on Saturday morning. But she's loaded, Reu. She's got a fucking Picasso hanging in her hallway. Hell, she probably spends three hundred grand on shoes every year."

"You know I only ever want what's best for you, love, but I'm not sure this is it."

"But what if it is? What if this is my only chance to make something of myself, and I turn it down? I don't want to spend the rest of my life living in shitty squats and praying Lenny doesn't self-destruct while I go out to work."

There was a long silence.

"Reu?"

"I know I can't talk you out of this. You too

stubborn. So just promise me you'll be damn careful. If you take the job and it turns to shit, you come back here. Shavonne's still on the couch, but we'll find space."

Shavonne was Reuben's sister. She'd made the stupid mistake of falling in love, or so she said—personally, I thought it was more a combination of lust and alcohol—only for the prick to hightail it out of Dodge when she got knocked up. For the last three months, she'd been sleeping in her big brother's studio apartment while the council tried to find her a flat. At least her baby daddy had promised to cough up for child support—I'd acted as lookout when Reuben paid a visit to remind the one-shot wonder of his obligations.

"I'll be okay, but thanks." My voice dropped because getting all mushy made me feel super awkward. "Thanks for everything you've done for me. I don't think I'd have survived...you know...otherwise."

"Leave it in the past, love. Don't let it poison you."

"I will, but—"

"Focus on the future. And if this job's on the up and up, you gonna be a rich woman."

"If it works out, the Happy Meals are on me."

Reuben's deep guffaw made me smile. "Just don't gimme none of them apple sticks."

"Fries all the way."

Although at that moment, I wasn't certain I could stomach either. My appetite had deserted me, which was perhaps the worst part of this whole adventure. Food, food everywhere, and I didn't want any of it. Maybe I'd just have a coffee...

In the kitchen, footsteps sounded behind me as I hung up, and I sagged with relief when Alaric came into view and not Emmy. I didn't need the pressure of her presence right now.

"Not hungry?" he asked.

I'd opted for pastries in the end, years of hunger leaving me unable to walk past free food without swiping whatever I could. There were three dainty Danishes on my plate, each with a bite taken out of it. Nothing tasted good at the moment, not even a cinnamon whirl.

"I'm thinking."

"About Lenny?"

"Sort of."

He didn't pry, just walked to the coffee machine, and it soon started beeping and hissing. When Ruth was out, I stuck to instant because that thing had more buttons than an aeroplane cockpit.

"Want a drink?" Alaric offered.

"Can you make it do mocha?"

"I'll have a try. Your brother's gonna be okay— Emmy spoke to the hospital earlier."

"I know." I'd been with her when she called, and I'd even spoken to him. He'd sounded miserable, depressed and uncomfortable as he went through withdrawal, but he'd be released soon. The question was, where would he end up? Where would *I* end up? "Did Emmy tell you she offered me a job?"

"Yes, she mentioned it. You don't know whether to accept?"

I shook my head. "What would you do?"

"In your position?" He picked up two cups from the machine and set one down in front of me, then took a seat opposite. "What are your ambitions? What do you want to get out of life?"

"Until yesterday? I just wanted a permanent roof over my and Lenny's heads and a job that didn't involve doing dodgy stuff."

"With Emmy, you'd get the former, but there'd be a certain amount of risk involved with the job. But it strikes me that you're the kind of girl who thrives on taking chances. How did you feel after you followed Hegler to the airport and got hold of his rental car paperwork?"

Pretty freaking elated. Who wouldn't if they managed to get one over on a thief without being caught?

"Happy," I admitted. "Satisfied that I'd got the job done."

"Multiply that by a thousand. How would you feel then?"

"Higher than I'd ever get on drugs."

"There's your answer."

"But..."

"But what?"

"Emmy said...well, not said, exactly, but suggested...that she might kill people."

Alaric fell silent, staring into his coffee.

"You didn't know?" I asked. "I'm not sure murder sits well with me."

"No, I knew. I'm just trying to work out how much to tell you."

Oh. "Like, because it's classified or something?"

"Emmy's work goes beyond classified."

"You could tell me, but then you'd have to kill me?"

"I prefer not to get my hands dirty anymore."

"Wait a minute... *You* kill people too?"

"Killed. Past tense. Sometimes, in our world, death

is a necessary evil." Alaric sighed and put his cup down on the table. "If these words go any farther than this room, we'll both have to face Emmy's wrath. Got it?"

"Got it."

Emmy's wrath was *not* something I'd risk voluntarily. My lips would stay firmly sealed no matter what Alaric told me.

"Three years ago, Emmy planned and executed a raid on a drug compound in Colombia. She neutralised the leader of a major cartel and disrupted the supply of tainted cocaine to a large part of the eastern seaboard. Two years ago, a group of terrorists got damn close to carrying out a biological attack at Dulles airport. Emmy tackled the terrorist and stopped thousands of people from getting infected with a virus you don't want to hear about. Three months after that, she led a team to Siberia and terminated a rogue general who had, among other things, a nuclear weapon in his possession. *That's* what Emmy does, and yes, occasionally people die. But because people die, the rest of us get to sleep a little more soundly at night."

"I didn't realise..."

"Not many people do, and that's the way it has to stay."

"Wait. She thinks I can do that stuff?"

"Apparently she does."

"But...but... I don't know the first thing about drugs —apart from maybe trying them a time or two—or viruses, or freaking Siberia. I never even sat my GCSEs because I was too busy trying to take care of Lenny."

That had been after his first overdose. I'd literally handcuffed myself to him while he went through withdrawal because it was the only way I could stop him from scoring more drugs. He'd even threatened to kill me once if I didn't let him go, but I still refused to do so—I *couldn't*—although I'd been terrified the whole time.

"If you want to learn, Emmy'll make sure you get the best teachers, that much I can tell you. She never settles for second best."

"What if I'm not good enough?"

Yes, I planned to quit after six months, but on my terms. If I *failed*? I hated losing.

"If you're not good enough for her Special Projects team, then I'm sure she'll find you a more appropriate role. Maybe something in the London office. If you do your best and don't mess her around, she won't kick you into oblivion if you don't quite make the cut."

"The London office?"

That would bring me back to Lenny, and if I had three hundred grand plus a steady income, I'd be set. Even if I got to work as a cleaner, it would still be better than serving tequila dressed as a slutty cowgirl.

But six months of hell...

I needed to change the subject. I needed space to *think*. Alaric had helped to clarify the situation, but could I overcome my own doubts and fears enough to go to the US? Damned if I didn't, damned if I did...

"Did you find Hegler?" I asked.

"Not yet, but we're working on it. People are checking into anyone with that name, and we're also trying to get hold of the flight plans for all private jets that left Heathrow on Wednesday afternoon. Something'll shake loose."

"Do you regret delivering the painting?"

Alaric considered the question for a moment. "No, I

don't. If we hadn't let it go, I'd always have regretted not trying."

I knew at that moment that I'd take the job with Emmy. Why? Because if I didn't, *I'd* always regret not trying.

## CHAPTER 20 - BETHANY

"BETHANY, CAN YOU bring us drinks, please?" Henrietta smiled as she asked, but it was fake, and I knew the "please" at the end pained her. "And do you know where Gemma is?"

"Sorry, I don't. What would you like?" I asked her clients. "Tea? Coffee? Wine? A soft drink?"

"Do you have Scotch?" the husband asked.

At eleven in the morning? "I'm afraid not."

"A glass of red, then. And Belinda will have mineral water with a twist of lemon, won't you, darling?"

Belinda nodded. I hadn't heard her say a word since they arrived, just like I hadn't seen Gemma do any work. When I first started at the gallery, she'd flitted about constantly, always busy, but now? Henrietta had asked her to dust the tops of all the frames, but the only evidence of her presence was a step-stool and a cleaning caddy abandoned by a limited edition Hockney print. At least I knew the Hockney wasn't stolen. It had been traded in by a big shot at a London law firm who wanted "something with more gravitas" after he got promoted to senior partner.

Last night, I'd barely slept, agonising over whether I should phone Emerson and mention the two suspicious paintings. That way, the problem would be out of my hands, but if Hugo found out I'd reported him... Bye-bye reference.

Perhaps I could wait until I found a new job and then make the call? It wasn't as if the paintings were still at the gallery in any case. They were both long gone. My tired hands shook as I slopped wine into a glass. A little alcohol loosened the purse strings—that's what Henrietta always told me—so I stopped just short of the brim. Water, fresh lemon, cappuccino with caramel syrup for Henrietta... I could come back and make a drink for Hugo afterwards.

To call or not to call, that was the question.

The question I was still agonising over as I stubbed my toe and stumbled in the main gallery. The tray went flying, and wine, water, and coffee splattered over the wall, the floor, and—oh, *fuck*—a Heath Robert original. Shocked gasps came from all around, from Henrietta, her clients, and Gemma, who'd materialised out of nowhere together with the cleaning caddy, which she'd dumped right in my way to trip over. And Hugo. Of course, Hugo had to be walking past too.

Gentleman that he was, he offered me a hand, and I staggered to my feet, wincing as I put weight on my twisted ankle. But his face had blackened with the fury of a winter storm, even if he tried to hide it in front of our customers.

"Gemma, would you get this cleared up, please? Take the Robert to my studio. Bethany, I'll see you in my office."

"Of course, Hugo," Gemma said. "The cleaning supplies are— Oh, they're right here."

That little... How dare she act surprised to cover up her own carelessness?

I didn't miss Henrietta's smirk as I slunk from the

room. If she hadn't been with the red-faced boozehound, I might even have suspected her of moving that caddy herself.

Could the Robert be saved? It was protected by glass, but if any liquid had seeped under the edges of the frame... I wanted to go back and help, to make sure Gemma had blotted everything she could, but I didn't dare. First last night's laptop incident and now this. Luckily, the laptop had come back to life again this morning, although the "C" key was still being a bit temperamental.

I willed my foot to stop tapping while I waited for Hugo to arrive, fidgeting in his visitor's chair as I prepared my apology in my head. I was never normally careless like that. Never. This week had taken its toll. The theft of my car, *Red After Dark*, what I'd found on the FBI's website. Sky. Emerson. Alaric. Yes, perhaps I'd thought of Alaric a little more than I should have. But in an afternoon filled with chaos, he'd acted with decency.

It wasn't long before I heard the *click* of Hugo's leather wingtips on the polished wooden floor. How bad would this be? Henrietta had dropped a painting last month and cracked the frame, and she'd got away with a rather peeved lecture according to Gemma, who'd listened at the door.

"Bethany."

"Hugo, I'm so sorry. I tripped, and it honestly was a complete accident. If there's any damage, I'll pay for the repairs." Somehow. I had no idea quite how since I barely had any money, but maybe Hugo could deduct it from my pay?

"This is two accidents in two days."

"The laptop's working almost perfectly now. I promise I won't place drinks on the desk again."

"No, no, I appreciate that." He took a seat opposite me and adjusted his bow tie. "Let's not beat around the bush, eh? You're still on your probationary period, and I'm not sure this is the right position for you long-term. If the painting you just soaked had been an unframed watercolour..."

What? His words slowly sank in, and I vaguely recalled something about an initial six-month trial in my contract. Hugo was letting me go?

How would I pay my bills? What would happen to Chaucer? And worse, how would I explain this to my parents? There'd be no avoiding it—Hugo ran in the same circles as my father, and if past gossip was anything to go by, every guest at tomorrow's party would know I'd been sacked by the time I walked through the front door.

My parents would start applying the pressure again. Toe the family line or face poverty. The only asset I had left was my apartment, but even if I put it on the market tomorrow, it wouldn't sell in time for me to pay Chaucer's next livery bill. And once that money was gone, then what?

"But I love working here," I tried, even though I knew my pleas would be in vain.

"I just feel that it might be better if you moved on. It's nothing personal."

"There's nothing I can do?"

"I'm sorry, Bethany. I'll pay you until the end of the month."

*I will not cry.* Eyes prickling, I managed to make it to the break room and stuff the few belongings I kept there into my handbag. Lipstick, spare tights, a framed photo of Chaucer. Then I got in my car and started driving. I didn't have a clue where I was going, and even if I'd wanted to go home, I had nowhere to park.

My brain was barely functioning, and on autopilot, I ended up on the M4 heading out of town. Just sitting with Chaucer would make me feel better. It always did.

Crawling along behind a lorry on the elevated section, I felt hurt. I felt panicky. And perhaps I felt a tiny bit angry too. Until today, Hugo hadn't shown the slightest indication that he wasn't happy with my work. Yes, I realised I'd made two mistakes, but Henrietta messed up on occasion as well, and Gemma had barely done a thing for weeks.

That anger was why I ended up with my phone in my hand when traffic came to a standstill. I'd saved Emerson's number just in case, and I jabbed at the screen until I heard ringing through the car's speakers.

"Emmy Black's line, Sloane speaking."

I'd been psyching myself up to speak to Emerson, not an assistant who, from her accent, sounded as if she was in the United States, and now I stuttered.

"I-I-is Emerson, uh, Emmy there?"

"I'm afraid she's in a meeting right now. Can I help or take a message?"

"How about Alaric? Is he there?"

"Alaric...McLain?"

Why did she sound so surprised by the question?

"I don't know his last name. He was with Emmy two days ago. They said to call if I had any information, so here I am, calling."

"Oh, uh, yes." Surprise turned to fluster. "Yes, I guess it must have been him."

"Is he there?"

"At Blackwood? Well, no. He doesn't work here."

"But he said he was a private investigator. Doesn't Blackwood do investigations?"

"We certainly do, Ms.... I'm sorry, I didn't get your name?"

"Bethany Stafford-Lyons. I really need to speak to either Emmy or Alaric."

And I needed to speak to them before I either chickened out or passed out from the limited supply of gin I had left in my kitchen cupboard. I'd have to leave my car at the stables and catch a train back to London, except that would be awkward because I had a pile of dry cleaning in the boot, and—

"If you give me your number, I can ask one of them to call you as soon as they're available. Will that work?"

"I suppose it'll have to." *Dammit, Beth, don't sound so snooty.* I wasn't at home anymore, so there was no need to put on airs and graces to please my mother. "Yes, thank you."

# CHAPTER 21 - BETHANY

I THOUGHT I'D have a long wait. After all, when I'd left urgent messages with the receptionist at Piers's dental practice, I'd been lucky if he got back to me the same day. But I'd barely stepped into Chaucer's stable when my phone rang with an unknown number.

"Hello?"

"Ms. Stafford-Lyons." He said it as a statement, not a question.

"Alaric?"

"Sloane said you wanted to speak with me?"

"Yes. I...I... About Hugo. More paintings."

"You sound upset." Another statement.

"Well, yes. Yes, I am."

"Start at the beginning. What happened?"

I blurted out the story, and as I got to the part about the coffee, it began to rain. Big, fat plops that splattered onto the concrete yard outside and quickly formed puddles. Guess who hadn't changed out of her stilettos before she went into Chaucer's stable? That's right: this girl. Now I had two choices—walk barefoot back to my car or ruin a pair of shoes I couldn't afford to replace. A tear slipped out, and of course Alaric sensed it.

"Hey, it's just a laptop. I knocked a glass of water over mine once, and when it dried out, it worked okay."

"No, you don't get it. Hugo caught me looking at the pictures. The FBI's stolen-art database. And when I asked him about one of the paintings, the Francesco Guardi, he said it was just a copy, but today he fired me and...and... I wasn't a bad employee, I swear. Except I tripped over a cleaning caddy this morning and spilled some more drinks, but it was an accident. Then Gemma insinuated she hadn't put the cleaning caddy in the way, but Henrietta was with clients and it certainly wasn't me, so who else could have done it?"

"Maybe Hugo was looking for an excuse to let you go?"

"But why? I know my sales weren't as good as Henrietta's, but she kept making me run errands to keep me away from the clients." Alaric's suggestion sounded more like a conspiracy theory plucked from a dark corner of the internet. Would Hugo really stoop so low? Why hadn't he given me some warning? I could've worked overtime, called around our customer list. "And now I have to find another job, and somewhere to park my car, and I have literally no other work experience and my only qualification is an art history degree and I'm stuck in a stable and it's raining."

Add "and I sound like a whiny idiot" to the list. Another sob slipped out, and Chaucer nuzzled closer. Brilliant. Now I had horse slobber on my jacket.

"Whoa, whoa, whoa. One thing at a time. You're stuck in a stable?"

"Not stuck, exactly. Like, I can get out, but I'm wearing leather-soled Manolos and there are puddles." Could I come across as any more spoiled? "Honestly, it's fine. I'll just take them off."

Alaric muttered something that sounded like, "We'll

see," then spoke more clearly again. "Why do you need to find somewhere to park your car?"

"Because I live in Kensington and my apartment doesn't come with parking. Hugo let me leave my car at the gallery."

"You can ditch it at Emmy's house for now. Her place is in Belgravia, but it's only a few stops on the Tube."

"Shouldn't you check with her first?"

"No need. I already know what she'll say. Now, your job. Do you want to work in another art gallery?"

"I want to work anywhere that pays me enough to keep my horse. They're so expensive, and Chaucer more or less eats money."

"You say you haven't worked much since university, but I bet you didn't sit around doing nothing all day, did you?"

"Well, no. I ran the house. Did the shopping, coordinated the staff, arranged dinner parties, that sort of thing. It took most of my time. Piers liked everything to be just so."

"So you're organised, good at talking to people, and used to working to exacting standards. What else?"

That tight knot of tension that had been bouncing around in my stomach for the last three days gradually began to loosen as Alaric translated my life for the last decade into something appropriate for a résumé, as he called it. I realised I'd done more than I thought. All those charity luncheons I'd coordinated. The annual ladies' golf tournament I'd co-hosted. My volunteer sessions at Riding for the Disabled before circumstances meant I had to quit.

I *hadn't* been a layabout, as Piers had accused me of

in several of our arguments. I'd done more than shop and go to the bloody hairdresser. Unloading on a virtual stranger, one with no agenda when it came to my personal life, I began to realise that. Isolated from everything I knew after my divorce, I'd struggled to see past the snide comments that still echoed in my ears. The only thing that had been worse was the pity.

I also realised another thing. I liked Alaric. He listened and didn't judge, and although our first meeting had been a little unorthodox, he was kind.

"Bethany? Are you still there?"

I noticed we'd progressed from Ms. Stafford-Lyons to my actual name, and I couldn't help smiling like a lunatic. Chaucer gave me a curious look before snatching another mouthful of hay and dropping most of it onto my hair.

"Yes, I'm here."

A pause, and I heard a car door slam. "Where, exactly?"

A giggle bubbled out of me, which fifteen minutes ago would have been impossible. "In a stable, as I said. I have a horse, Chaucer, and being with him is my happy place. I realise that probably sounds—"

"No, I meant which stable? I can see a clock on a wall, and a bunch of wheelbarrows lined up."

I froze, then whirled around to look at the clock high up on the end of the hay barn, an oversized decorative thing that hadn't worked for as long as I'd been there. Truth be told, the whole yard was a bit shabby now, but Chaucer got well cared for, and it had been affordable until this morning.

My gaze dropped slowly, and I saw a familiar figure standing below the clock, looking somewhat lost and most definitely out of place in a pair of dove-grey tailored trousers and a navy-blue sports jacket. What the actual hell?

"What are you doing here?" I managed to utter.

Alaric turned and saw me staring over Chaucer's door. "I figured somebody should come and save your shoes, and since I was more or less passing..."

Wow, that was... I was about to say gentlemanly, but as I processed his words, I quickly amended it to invasive. Creepy. Slightly alarming. Fear spider-walked up my spine as I realised I was alone at the yard. Pinkey, who ran the place, had passed me in her Land Rover as I trundled down the drive, probably on her way to the feed store, and it was too early for the after-work crowd, too late for the ladies who lunched.

And now Alaric was within touching distance.

"H-h-how did you know I was here?"

He pointed to the phone, still clamped to my ear. "Bad habit, I'm afraid."

"You...what? You traced my phone?"

"It's easy when you know the right people."

"That's so rude!"

"I was worried about you."

"I'm fine."

"You're not fine." He glanced down at my feet, smiling. "Nice shoes. If I'd offered to come and help, would you have taken me up on it?"

"Of course not. You've got far better things to do with your time, I'm sure."

"How about you let me be the judge of that? What else do you have to do here?"

"Nothing. Not really." A pencil skirt and stilettos definitely weren't suitable for riding, and I hadn't brought any horsey clothes with me. "I'm not even sure why I came."

"When times are tough, we turn to the things that comfort us." He turned away as he spoke, and the sadness in his voice made me wonder whether he spoke from experience.

"What comforts you, Alaric?"

The pause stretched out to the point of discomfort, and I regretted asking the question. The answer was none of my business. I barely knew this man, and hadn't I just accused *him* of being invasive?

But he answered, his voice soft. "Freedom. Freedom to think what I like and do what I want. But you can have too much of a good thing. There's only so much solitude a man can take." His gaze flickered for a moment as he came back from wherever his head had been, his return no doubt assisted by the *crack* of thunder overhead. The rain came down again. "Ah, shit."

I quickly unbolted the stable door and held it open. "Want to join me?"

"Is your horse safe?"

"Chaucer? He's a sweetheart. Just watch out for his feet because he doesn't always look where he's putting them."

Alaric slipped inside, sticking close to the wall as he eyed up Chaucer. Chaucer, of course, walked straight over and nudged him into a corner. A corner filled with cobwebs.

"Uh..."

"He's only looking for treats. Chaucer! Get back." I gave him a prod, and he obliged, grudgingly. "You're not a horse person?"

"The only other horse I've been near is Emmy's, and he tore the ass out of my pants."

I started laughing because that was the stuff of cartoons, not real life, but then I made the mistake of picturing the scene. If Alaric's ass in trousers was any indication, his ass out of them would be very pleasant indeed. My cheeks burned. Dammit, the man was practically a stalker, and I should *not* have been picturing him naked. I desperately tried to straighten my face.

"Sorry," I choked out. "So, Emmy has a horse?"

"His name's Satan, which gives some indication of his charming personality. Mostly it gets shortened to Stan, though."

"He sounds like the perfect horse for Emmy." I clapped a hand over my mouth. "Again, I'm sorry." Alaric and Emmy worked together. They were probably friends. "I really ought to think before I speak."

"No, you're right. Emmy would get bored with a regular horse." He gingerly reached out and patted Chaucer's neck. "This one seems friendlier. How long have you had him?"

"Eleven years. I got him as a three-year-old and broke him in myself."

"Eleven years? Long time. Do you jump over stuff with him?"

I shook my head, a lump forming in my throat. "Dressage mainly, but I sneak in a few fences on occasion."

"You don't enjoy jumping?"

"I used to love it, but everyone says it's too dangerous."

"Everyone?"

"Piers. My parents. Before I got Chaucer, I had a bad fall eventing and broke my ankle. My old horse... It wasn't his fault, he just spooked at a fox, but my parents sold him while I was in the hospital." I squashed my hands against my eyes to stop myself from crying, then regretted it when my fingers came away covered in mascara splodges. Goodness only knows what my face looked like. "Polo would be seventeen now. They refused to tell me where he'd gone, and I never managed to find out what happened to him."

I'd never forgiven my parents either. It was the last bloody straw. The final nail in the coffin. With hindsight, my marriage to Piers had been a rebound relationship, me grieving for the loss of my beloved horse as well as a way to escape from my parents. Out of the frying pan and into the damned fire. Piers had bought me Chaucer as a gift soon after we started dating, although he'd sided with my parents over the risks of jumping. Back then, Piers had been so attentive, so complimentary, I hadn't seen what an arsehole he truly was.

"Want me to take a look?" Alaric asked.

"A look? For Polo?"

"Yeah."

I choked up again. How did this man I barely knew make all the emotions I'd spent years keeping locked up for appearance's sake overflow into a mess of smudged make-up and—oh, hell—snot? I tried to sniffle without sounding like a complete peasant.

"Thank you for the offer, but it's impossible. It's been so long, and I'm sure Daddy changed the name on his documents." Because he'd paid for Polo and put himself down as the registered keeper, he'd been able to make amendments without my permission, and worse, data protection rules meant the people who ran the registry refused to tell me any of the details. "I still look at pictures from all the events I can find just in case I spot him somewhere. Although he's probably retired now, I keep hoping..."

"Just give me whatever information you have."

"Why would you help me?"

"Call me a sucker for a pretty face."

I knew I was pretty—my mother always said it was one of the few things I had going for me. *Shame the inside doesn't match the outside, Bethie.* If I had a pound for every time I'd heard her say that, Chaucer's stable would have central heating and a television. But it still made me smile inside to hear the words come out of Alaric's mouth.

"I have an image of his passport," I whispered.

"Horses have passports?"

Oh, this wasn't going to go well, was it? Still, I appreciated the sentiment. "Yes, all horses in the UK and Europe do."

"Then send me the details."

He extracted a business card from his inside pocket and passed it to me, navy-blue cardstock with cream print. *Alaric McLain. Sirius Consulting.* Sloane been right—he didn't work for Blackwood—and yet he'd referred to Emmy as a colleague. Did he freelance?

A chink of light shone through the clouds, distracting me. The rain was still coming down, albeit not quite so hard, and vivid colours lit up the sky.

"Look—a rainbow," I said before I caught myself. Piers had always poo-poohed me when I'd tried to show him nature's gifts. Called it childish. But Alaric turned and leaned on the stable door beside me, his expression a mix of contentedness and awe.

"The world never ceases to amaze me. That out of darkness, we get such beauty."

It was a moment. One Chaucer interrupted by pushing his head in between us to see what all the fuss was about.

"Hey, you big oaf!" I ducked under his neck to get back to Alaric, only to find he'd got tangled up in yet more cobwebs. "Uh, you have a little... Actually, a lot... Here, let me..."

As I brushed Alaric down and picked dusty bits of cobweb off his back, head, and trousers, I realised that being on my own at the yard wasn't so bad after all. If anyone had seen us, I'd have had to answer a million questions, and knowing my luck, word would somehow get back to my mother as well. And I also realised that up close, Alaric's backside was every bit as nice as I'd suspected.

Be still my dirty mind.

"Okay, all done. The rain's eased off, so we should probably leave now."

He didn't answer, just caught me by surprise when he swept me into his arms, bridal style. Chaucer leapt back at the sound of my shriek.

"What the hell are you doing?"

"The shoes, Bethany. Have you forgotten why I came here in the first place?"

Oh, yes, the shoes. They really were very nice ones. I might have got rid of most of my dresses, but the shoes were a different story. Selling them would be a last resort, and they wouldn't raise much anyway. Not many people wanted to buy used footwear. Much as I disliked being manhandled, I hated the thought of ruining a pair of Manolos more.

"You can make it the whole way to my car?"

Alaric just looked at me. Oops. Maybe I shouldn't have insulted his masculinity? Men took that sort of thing very seriously, which Mother assured me was the reason Piers felt the need to go out and shoot at things every other weekend. Clay pigeons mainly, but occasionally grouse. Luckily, he missed most of the time.

I reached for Chaucer, and Alaric stepped closer so I could pat my horse on the nose. Then I fumbled with the bolt on the door while Alaric waited patiently. About halfway to the car, I became conscious of two things. Firstly, that Alaric must spend plenty of time in the gym because his hard chest matched his arse perfectly in terms of muscles, and secondly, I didn't mind being carried after all. Which was perhaps why my left arm found its way around Alaric's neck and clung on as he picked his way around the puddles in the car park. It struck me as odd that he obviously took care of himself and yet he wasn't wearing any aftershave. All I could smell was his own musky scent, which wasn't a bad thing in the slightest.

"Got your car key?" he asked.

"Yes." I'd zippered it into an inside jacket pocket this time, and my shirt rode up as I tried to tug it free. Yes, it was a very good thing Pinkey wasn't back yet. "Right here."

Between the two of us, we got the car door open, and Alaric lowered me gently into the driver's seat. But he didn't release me right away. No, he stayed there with one arm around my back and the other under my legs, his lips just inches from mine. Was he... Was he going to kiss me? I held my breath as my heart thudded against my ribs. What would I do if that mouth touched mine? Pull him to me or push him away? Logic said to shove him back and slam the door, but my fingers itched to curl around his lapels. Or tangle in that thick brown hair. Or explore the muscles rippling in his back.

How would he kiss? On a scale of Piers's sloppy mauling to Audrey Hepburn and George Peppard's rain-drenched smooch at the end of *Breakfast at Tiffany's*, I bet Alaric would rate at least as high as a Mr. Darcy.

But I never got to find out. He withdrew his arms and stood, bracing his hands on the car roof as he studied me.

"I'd better give you Emmy's address," he said finally.

"What?" It came out as a whisper, and I sucked in air when I realised my lungs had none left.

"To park your car?"

"My car? Yes. Right. Car."

"Are you okay?"

The lie came automatically. "Of course. Thank you for saving my shoes."

"Can you drive in those things?"

"I've had plenty of practice. Hey, where are you going?"

Rather than answering, Alaric pushed away abruptly and stepped back. Why? What had I done? Was it something I said?

# CHAPTER 22 - ALARIC

ALARIC STALKED AROUND Bethany's car, cursing under his breath. What was he playing at? He'd come to her in an attempt to fix some of the problems he'd caused, not to complicate his life even further.

Those fucking shoes.

Delicate feet, slim calves, strong thighs...

Shit, he'd almost kissed her. That hadn't been part of the plan.

He took a breath to steady himself, one hand on the passenger door handle. When Bethany told him she'd been fired, he knew at once that *Emerald*'s curse had struck again. Until he crossed paths with that damn painting, he'd never believed in bad luck or negative energy, but on his travels, he'd met everyone from a Chinese philosopher to a Malaysian shaman, and he'd come to the conclusion that there were forces at work in the world that he didn't fully understand. That no one understood. Dark and light, day and night, good and evil, yin and yang.

Bethany stared at him as he slid into the passenger seat, her eyes the colour of the lightening sky flecked with the deeper blue of Mogok Valley sapphires. Alaric had visited there on his sabbatical, seen the city and met the locals, all the time wondering whether he'd ever return to his old life or anything like it. Now, he was closer than he'd ever been before, but those stubborn fugitives—love and reputation—still remained out of reach.

Although...

Bethany's head tilted in confusion, but he wasn't planning to answer her unasked question about his own stupidity. He busied himself with her satnav instead.

"I'll be in front of you all the way, but I've set the postcode in case we get separated."

"The postcode. Okay."

She knew, didn't she? She knew that his self-control had almost deserted him. What would be next to go? Willpower and any sense of rational thought? Dammit, he needed to keep his faculties.

"The traffic always seems to snarl up close to London. Just call if you get lost, and I'll find you somehow."

He didn't mention that "somehow" would involve calling Naz and asking him nicely if he'd mind tracking Bethany's cell phone again. Or one of Emmy's team if Naz had decided to take a nap. The guy went through fads like Alaric went through underwear. Last month, he'd been eating blueberries with every meal because a woman he met on the train told him he needed to detox. The month before that, he'd taken up roller skiing, then left all the kit in Judd's basement when he went to visit his grandma in Georgia. Georgia the country, not Georgia the state. And this month? This month saw Naz extolling the benefits of polyphasic sleep, which basically meant he was kipping whenever anyone wanted him to do anything.

Perhaps Alaric should get Naz to speak with

Bethany? Exhaustion ringed her eyes, circling a resigned sadness that no make-up could hide. First she'd had a divorce to deal with, then Pemberton's retaliation. And it *was* retaliation. Last night, he'd discovered one of his assistants had both sharp eyes and morals, so of course he'd wanted to get rid of her. What if she questioned things further, kept checking the stolen-art databases? There was no way the gallery would stand up to that kind of scrutiny. No, she'd had to go. She said she tripped over a cleaning caddy? Alaric would put money on the old bastard having moved it into Bethany's path himself.

"Thank you for doing this. I won't need the parking space for long, I promise. Just until I can make other arrangements. I'll update my CV again this evening, and—" Now what was wrong? She'd gone quite pale. "I can't."

"Can't what?"

"Can't update my CV. My laptop died two months ago, and I've just been using the one at the gallery. But I had to leave it behind." Unexpectedly, she thumped the dashboard, then leaned her head against the steering wheel. Her breath steamed onto the windscreen, fuzzy little circles of despair that matched Alaric's mind. "Sorry. I'm sorry."

"I've got a laptop. Let's drop the car off, then we can work on your résumé." We? *For fuck's sake, McLain.* "I'll even buy you dinner."

It was official: his mouth was no longer connected to his brain, and the latter had ceased to function. In fact, the only parts of him that were still working were his tongue and his dick, which had clubbed together to toss difficulties into his path like confetti at a wedding.

"Dinner?" Bethany asked.

"We've got to eat, right?" *Just. Stop. Talking.* "What kind of food do you like?"

"Anything I don't have to cook myself."

Slowly, deliberately, Alaric forced one foot out of the car. What the hell was he doing? The last time he'd let his little head overrule his big one, he'd ended up with Emmy, and look how that had turned out. He'd ended up hurting both of them, not to mention making an enemy out of her husband. Marriage of convenience his ass. Deep down, he'd always known Black would claim Emmy in the end, but still he couldn't stop himself from falling head over heels. Quite literally, he mused, remembering the number of times he'd fucked her in stilettos.

Alaric's gaze strayed towards the driver's side footwell, sliding over a pair of smooth legs he had no business looking at. If he didn't get a grip, he'd be forced to check himself into a damn monastery until he came to his senses. Honestly, he didn't usually behave like a horny teenager. That was Judd's job.

Alaric made a mental note not to let him anywhere near Bethany.

"Are we going now?" She turned listlessly in her seat.

"Unless you want me to get pizza delivered to the parking lot." He glanced out the door, taking in the tangle of brambles surrounding the potholed blacktop. Stray pieces of straw scudded past, tumbling in the stiff breeze that blew from the north, and a squirrel balanced on a wooden post, a rotting totem of a fence that had once separated the space from a bare paddock. Now white electric tape marked the boundary instead, and a small brown horse shook a frothy tangle of hair away from its eyes and stared hangdog at them from its makeshift prison. "The ambience isn't much, and there's a nosy diner at the next table, but the view's nice."

"Really? I always thought it was a bit overgrown." Ah, such innocence. She didn't get the double entendre? "Pinkey's always saying she's going to cut it back, but then a horse goes lame or a water drinker malfunctions and floods the place or the roof of the tack room falls down, so she runs out of time. And Twiggy's meant to be on a diet. He used to be in the paddock by the footpath, but people kept bringing him carrots."

"Somebody called that horse Twiggy?"

He was a whisky barrel with a leg at each corner, about as far from a twig as it was possible to get. Walk him up a hill and he'd block out the sun.

"Technically, he's a pony rather than a horse, but... yes, I suppose there *is* a certain irony. His name's actually Lord Ferdinand, but he escaped and got tangled in a blackberry patch. It took us an hour to cut him free and two more to pick the bits out of his hair. Pinkey called him Twiggy for a joke because it was either laugh or cry while we all got our hands cut to shreds, and it stuck."

Before his brain caught up, Alaric had reached out for one of Bethany's hands, turning it over in his to examine the skin on both sides. At least he knew why her nails were chipped now—caring for her horse trumped manicures.

"What are you doing?"

"Checking for damage."

"Damage? From the blackberries?"

"Plants can be vicious."

He'd found that out the day Emmy convinced him it would be fun to make a parachute jump. He'd only agreed because she promised he'd be strapped tightly to her the whole way down. The first thirty seconds of free fall had been terrifying, but once she pulled the chute, he'd actually begun to enjoy himself, aided in no small part by her legs wrapped around him and the filth she'd been shouting in his ear over the wind noise. Then thirty feet from the ground, a last-second gust had tossed them sideways into a briar patch. And it only added insult to injury when Black glided in like a steroid-addled ballerina, landing neatly in the field to their left.

Emmy had been pissed, really pissed, mostly at herself but partly at the undergrowth. She'd cursed in at least six different languages as she hacked through the bushes with a machete. A fucking machete. To this day, Alaric didn't know where she'd got it from. He'd covered the important bits with his hands when they landed, which meant he'd retained the ability to have children at least, but rather than going out for dinner, they'd spent the evening tweezing thorns out of each other's asses.

"Who says romance is dead?" Emmy had joked. Laugh or cry, right?

Their romance might not yet have been dead at that point, but when Alaric looked back now, he understood there had been a tumour growing.

Bethany pulled her hand away, gently rather than snatching. "It happened six months ago. The scratches don't show anymore."

Why couldn't he get involved with a woman who had a safe hobby for once? Not that he was *involved* with Bethany, exactly. He owed her, that was all. And he wasn't about to make the mistake of suggesting she take up flower arranging.

No, he was going to get away from the damn car and take her back to London where she belonged.

"Are you still in London?" Ravi asked through the Honda's speakers.

"Just outside and going nowhere fast." The M4 was backed up. Again. Bethany was right behind Alaric, and every so often, she leaned across to fiddle with the radio. Trying to find out what the delay was? Or just listening to music? Yesterday, he'd have pegged her as a classical fan, but she'd already surprised him once with her choice of hobby. Perhaps she liked hard rock?

"Heading into town or out?"

"Into town."

"Good—can you do me a favour?"

"What kind of a favour?"

"I ran out of time to buy Rune a birthday gift, and my flight doesn't get in until late tonight."

Rune? Birthday? Alaric checked his watch just in case Ravi was wrong, or joking, or... Sure enough, it was May twelfth. Oh, sweet mother of fuck. How could he have forgotten?

He managed a weak, "That's tomorrow?"

"You forgot your *daughter's* birthday?"

Alaric wasn't Rune's biological father, but that didn't matter. It was his name on her fake birth certificate, which meant he had certain responsibilities, albeit shared with the other men of Sirius. If it weren't for Rune, there would *be* no Sirius.

"I'll get a gift. Of course I'll get a gift." What was the time? Almost four o'clock. "Or maybe I could ask Barbara to pick something up."

"Uh... No."

"Why not? Running errands is literally part of her job."

At first, they'd done all the admin themselves—organised meetings, answered the phone, booked travel, typed up reports—but as they got busier, they'd missed calls, missed flights, and missed spelling errors. A shared PA had seemed like a worthwhile investment, although they'd been through four in the last year thanks to Judd.

"Judd didn't tell you?"

"Tell me what?" Alaric asked through gritted teeth.

"Barbara quit."

"What? When? I spoke to her yesterday afternoon, and she was fine."

"This morning."

"Say he didn't..."

Judd had managed to drive away every single one of Barbara's predecessors, mostly by sleeping with them and then breaking their hearts, but occasionally by not sleeping with them and breaking their hearts. This time, Alaric, Ravi, and Naz had banned him from participating in the recruitment process entirely and hired a sixty-year-old spinster who hadn't been genetically blessed in the looks department. Surely there wasn't enough alcohol in the world for Judd to make a move on Barbara?

Ravi snorted out a laugh. "No, he went one better this time. After he got back from Brazil, he forgot to reset his watch, so when he woke up jet-lagged at eleven a.m., he thought it was seven o'clock and went downstairs to make himself a coffee."

Alaric couldn't hold back his groan. "He got dressed first, right? Threw on a robe or something? Underwear?"

"What do you think?"

"I'll speak to Barbara. Promise it'll never happen again. Did she run screaming?"

"No, she fainted and hit her head on the kitchen table. After Judd drove her to the emergency room, she made one of the nurses bring her a sheet of paper and a pen so she could write out her resignation letter. Judd said he'd pay her three months' severance. Apparently, she needed eight stitches, and she's moving to Sheffield to recuperate with her daughter."

"We need to get a proper office." Using Judd's spare living room wouldn't work anymore, and they were making decent money now. "There must be enough in the budget. Judd can hire someone else to water his plants and feed his cat while he's away, and maybe, just maybe, we'll be able to keep an assistant for longer than three months."

"There's enough in the budget, but don't you think an assistant would get lonely on her own? None of us would ever use an office. At least at Judd's place, there are people to talk to."

That was a fair point. Judd had a constant stream of people going in and out of his Kensington townhouse. The cleaner was a regular fixture, and then there was his personal trainer, the decorators that always seemed to be working there, and an endless series of women. When Barbara wasn't being treated to the sight of Judd's bobbing cock, she'd spent half of her mornings organising cabs and occasionally providing a shoulder to cry on. Something else she hadn't been happy about, and who could blame her? She'd signed up for typing and filing, not counselling.

"So what do you suggest? We just carry on as we are?"

"What about some sort of chastity device?"

"Sirius is an intelligence agency, not a BDSM club."

The echo of a tannoy drowned out whatever retort Ravi made, and Alaric caught the words "gate" and "boarding."

"Is that your flight?"

"Yeah, and it's already late." A woman said something to Ravi in the background. "What, I can't take the water with me? But I just bought it at the kiosk right here." More muttering. "Okay, okay, I'll drink it. Alaric? You there?"

"Still here."

"So, can you get a gift for Rune? I looked in duty-free, but I figured she'd get expelled if I brought her a bottle of Jack Daniels and a carton of cigarettes."

"I'll find something."

"And we need a new assistant too. Could you call the agency?"

"Why me?"

"Because you're the most diplomatic. Or do you want Judd to turn a job interview into a date again?"

Alaric sighed. "No, I don't."

"Then you'll call?"

"Yeah, I'll call. See you tomorrow."

As Alaric hung up, he glanced in the mirror again. Maybe there was a better solution? Bethany was organised and she needed a job, but Alaric would be damned if he'd let Judd get his dick into her. The woman had been through enough already this month. Which meant he'd have to train her himself, then find her an office. Did he have the time? He'd kept his schedule light after the *Emerald* lead came in, so technically he did. The bigger problem? Alaric would have to keep his own hands off Bethany. Firstly, he didn't shit where he ate, and Judd would never let him forget it if *he* scared off an assistant. Secondly, he didn't need any emotional entanglements, not when he was focused on building up Sirius and finding *Emerald*. Trouble was, his hands seemed to have a mind of their own right now. Should he make the offer or not?

# CHAPTER 23 - BETHANY

"I HATE TO ask this, but can we take a rain check on dinner?" Alaric said as I hurried towards him in Emmy's parking garage. "I'll still give you a ride home."

I'd spent the trip back from Chaucer psyching myself up to spend an evening with a man for the first time since my divorce, so to hear he'd changed his mind felt oddly disappointing. Not really surprising, but disappointing.

At least he'd come through with the parking space, and that was the more important thing. A safe, brightly lit underground spot beside a rather nice Aston Martin, which left me more worried about accidentally scratching a supercar than about venturing into a deserted parking garage. And I hated skulking around London alone. Once, I'd tripped over a slumbering homeless man in the yard behind the gallery, and I'm not sure who was more startled—him or me. Certainly I'd dropped the leftover cupcake I'd been carrying.

"Of course, it's not a problem. I'm sure I've got something in the fridge at home."

"Tomorrow night instead?"

Huh? Usually, asking for a rain check meant "I want to cancel, but more politely." Alaric really did want to go out? That *was* unexpected.

"I wish I could, but I can't. Not tomorrow. I have a

family thing."

"You don't look too thrilled about that."

Oops, did I grimace? "My father's birthday celebration. I'm sure I'll survive."

"Aren't parties meant to be fun?"

"Not in my world, and especially not when my mother's invited my ex-husband and his new fiancée."

"She's done *what*?"

"He's a family friend."

"I was under the impression your divorce was acrimonious?"

"It was. He...he cheated on me."

"Then how the hell is he still a family friend?"

"Because..." Where did I start with explaining the Stafford-Lyons family dynamics? And more to the point, why was I waffling on about it with a virtual stranger? "It doesn't matter."

"Yes, it does, because you're upset."

"Honestly, I'll be fine. If I park my car along the road from my parents' house, nobody'll block me in and I can make an early exit once the brandy starts flowing."

"Sounds as if you've done that before."

An embarrassed giggle burst out of me. "I tried, except I made the mistake of parking on the drive. Then I couldn't get out, and I had to hide in the tack room until everyone else went home."

"Why not decline the invite?"

"You haven't met my mother. I'd never hear the end of it. It's bad enough that I went rogue and got a job, without skipping social functions too. I..." *Stop chewing your lip, Beth.* "I have to stay in my parents' good books in case things get so bad financially that I can't afford Chaucer's livery. They have stables, but if I use them, I'll be expected to play by their rules. Which means smiling politely when Mother tries to set me up with another moneyed worm more dickish than Piers and most likely stepping back into my role on the country club social committee. I can't lose Chaucer. I *won't*. Plus..."

"Plus what?"

"I guess there's just a tiny part of me that wants to show everyone that I haven't fallen apart the way they expected. They're all going to be talking about me anyway, and if I don't show my face, the gossip mill will go into overdrive. Bethany's at home crying into her wine. Bethany's checked herself into rehab. Ooh, what if she's topped herself? When I missed Mother's last party, someone started a rumour I'd had a nervous breakdown." I took a deep breath. "I'll be fine." Who was I trying to convince? Alaric or myself? "Sorry for burdening you with my problems like that. I really should think before I speak."

I expected him to back away the way Piers had every time I got overly emotional, but he just smiled. And not a "there, there, go take a Valium" smile—no, this was almost...cunning?

"How do you feel about a late dinner tonight?"

"I'm sorry?"

"I have an errand to run first."

"Uh, okay." Dinner was back on?

"Great. Can you do me a favour and make a reservation? Anywhere you like—I'm paying."

"I... I... Of course. What time?"

Now it was his turn to look unsure. "Can you tell me where there might be stores open this evening? I've been to London plenty of times, but I tend to avoid shopping."

"What do you need to buy?"

"A birthday gift. For a teenage girl."

"What age? There's a big difference between thirteen and nineteen."

"She'll be fifteen."

"And how well do you know her? Is she a relative?" What age was Alaric? Late thirties at a guess, too old to have a fourteen-year-old sister unless his parents had started very young. Or maybe his father had remarried? A good number of my father's friends were on their second or even third wives, and they were invariably younger than me. "A half-sister?"

He guided me towards his SUV with a hand on the small of my back, and the gentle touch sent a nervous shiver up my spine. A late dinner? I'd stay up until midnight if necessary. Hell, make it breakfast.

"Do you want me to go and buy the gift? It's the least I can do after you saved my shoes. Most of Oxford Street stays open till eight, and Selfridges doesn't close until nine. I honestly don't mind. In truth, I quite like shopping, but I don't have the money to go much anymore." I gave a shrug as he opened the passenger door for me. "Buying groceries just isn't the same."

He watched me for a moment, hands braced on the roof as he stared into the car. Finally, he nodded, although it seemed more of an affirmation to himself than an answer to me.

"I'd appreciate your help. Wait here while I run upstairs and find you a key card for the gates?"

It wasn't as if I could escape. The shutter door had rolled down again, leaving the cavernous room as secure as a tomb.

"I'm not going anywhere."

He flashed me a tight smile. "Back in five. And the gift?" He spoke softly. "It's for my daughter."

His *daughter*? As Alaric strode towards a set of elevator doors in the far corner, my mouth opened wide enough to catch flies. A daughter? Did he have a wife or girlfriend to go with her? He wasn't wearing a ring, but that didn't seem to mean much nowadays. The crushing band around my chest made me realise just how much I'd been starting to like him, and I thought he'd been flirting with me too. Had I misread things that badly?

"Did you ask your daughter what she might like?" I queried, silently thanking Piers and my parents for all the awkward situations they'd put me in over the years. If nothing else, they'd allowed me to perfect the mask I'd hurriedly slammed into place when Alaric emerged from the elevator holding up a small black key fob, and I'd listened attentively as he explained how to use it to open the gates. The garage door itself used facial recognition, and apparently, they'd coded me in already from the cameras lurking in each corner. Good for safety, I had to admit, but also mildly creepy.

Alaric started the engine and headed for the door. "I wanted to surprise her. Didn't really think it through, did I? And I actually need two gifts—one from me and another from one of my business partners. They're... honorary uncles, I guess. The two of us are going to see her tomorrow morning."

"Going to see her?" My heart leapt, and boy did I feel shitty about that. "She doesn't live with you?"

"No, she's at boarding school."

Oh. I desperately wanted to ask about her mother, but how could I bring that up without sounding either nosy or insensitive? Answer: I couldn't.

"I see. Boarding schools can be a little restrictive on what pupils are allowed to take. Is your daughter a girly girl? A tomboy?"

"She likes science stuff. Math, that sort of thing. Ravi tried to give her a chemistry set last year, but she wasn't allowed to keep it. Too dangerous, so they said."

"When I was at boarding school, a group of girls stole lithium from the lab and set fire to the dormitory." I still remembered the alarms, the smoke-filled corridors and the screams as we'd stumbled outside. "It was bloody terrifying."

"Rune hasn't set fire to anything yet. Maybe I could get her a laptop?" Alaric quickly shook his head. "No, Naz already got her one at Christmas."

Was Naz another business partner?

"How about a book? Does she like reading? Or play any musical instruments? What about chocolate? You can't go wrong with chocolate at boarding school."

"Actually, you can. Rune's diabetic."

Shit. "Sorry."

"Hey, you weren't to know. And she's not musical, but yeah, she likes reading. Is there a bookstore on Oxford Street?"

"Not on Oxford Street itself. Foyles is nearby, but... No, it doesn't matter."

"But what?"

Was it my place to say? Oh, what the hell. "As I

mentioned, I went to boarding school, and my father often used to send me gifts." Or rather, his secretary did. "But what I really valued more than anything was his time. I barely remember all the clothes and candy and toiletries, but I'll never forget the day he picked me up and took me to Hickstead to watch the showjumping one afternoon."

I later came to realise he'd done it out of guilt after Mother found out about his latest affair, but still... I'd enjoyed myself.

"So you think I should take her out somewhere?"

"If you have the time. And your business partner too, if she's fond of him."

"Ravi. I'll talk to him tonight. So, the sixty-four-thousand-dollar question—where should we take her? We normally just go for lunch."

"What about an activity you can do together and then lunch afterwards? Is she at school in London? You could go to the Science Museum?"

"About an hour north of London. Ridgeview was the best place we could find."

And quite possibly the most expensive too. "Ridgeview Prep? I went to Marlborough Ladies' College—we used to play Ridgeview at hockey."

Mostly, they'd beaten us. Okay, they'd thrashed us in every match except one. We'd been so overjoyed at winning that Rebecca Mornington had opened the sloe gin she'd snuck in for a special occasion, and we all got a hangover and a detention.

"I heard the team's pretty good, but Rune isn't into sports."

"There's bound to be something in the local area. How about I look while you drive? Although I wouldn't recommend driving to Oxford Street."

"I need to drop my car back at Judd's place. Another business partner," he explained. "I'm staying there. Then we can take the Tube."

It was still rush hour, which meant we'd be packed in like sardines, but with Alaric beside me, I couldn't get too upset about that. I pulled my phone out to research gifts, but before I could consult Google, it buzzed in my hand.

*Gemma: OMG, I heard what happened! Henrietta said it was my fault, but I swear I don't remember leaving that cleaning caddy by the Heath Robert. I told Hugo he should fire me instead, but he just said that management decisions were final and slammed his office door. The painting wasn't even damaged. I reckon he's got PMT >:(*

I was fairly certain men couldn't get PMT, not unless it stood for Pocketing Money from Thieves. But I didn't want to leave Gemma upset over something that wasn't her fault, no matter what Henrietta might have said.

*Me: You're probably right—he's been a bit weird lately. And at least I don't need to bow down to Henrietta anymore.*

*Gemma: I'll miss you. If it's just me and Henrietta all day, I'll probably get arrested for murder.*

*Me: I'll miss you too. Meet up for dinner soon?*

*Gemma: Or a coffee? One lunchtime? Ry always likes us to eat dinner together.*

Control freak. On the plus side, Gemma sounded chattier than she had in ages, and since I had no job, coffee was actually a much better idea.

*Me: Perfect. I'll call you next week :)*

"Everything okay?" Alaric asked.

"It's just Gemma. You remember her from the gallery? Apparently, she offered to get fired as tribute, but Hugo turned her down."

"Well, we both know why." He reached across and gave my hand a kindly squeeze. "Sometimes, the dark days are fate's way of making the light seem brighter."

"I hope you're right. Because right now, I'm all out of matches."

# CHAPTER 24 - ALARIC

ALARIC GRASPED THE overhead rail and wrapped his other arm around Bethany's waist, using the gifts they'd bought for Rune as a shield between her and the rest of the rabble. Yes, he'd vowed to keep his hands to himself, but they were on the Tube, and punks kept bumping into her. What else was he meant to do? Okay, so he could have hailed a cab, but he was an asshole.

"So, activities for tomorrow..." he said as they headed for Shoreditch. "Any ideas?"

"I came up with three options near Ridgeview. Ten-pin bowling, adventure golf, or an escape room. But the adventure golf's outside, and there's a sixty percent chance of showers."

Attention to detail. Alaric liked that, and it made justifying a job offer that much easier. They needed an assistant who didn't cut corners.

"Then scrap the golf. We can do that some other time."

"Megabowl's a fifteen-minute drive, and they serve food, so you could combine it with lunch depending on the menu. Breakout's twenty minutes away, and I've found two restaurants nearby that look fun for a teenager—Noodle Nation and Pizzaland. All the places have parking available, and Pizzaland has a low GI option with a crust made from almond flour. That's suitable for diabetics, isn't it?"

Yes, it was. There was that attention to detail again. Seemed that pizza was the best choice for food, but what about the activity? Alaric had taken Rune bowling in the US, and she'd landed the ball in the gutter enough times that she'd gotten frustrated. Rune being Rune, she'd tackled the situation like a science problem rather than having fun, although her mood had improved after she'd drawn a dozen complex mathematical equations on napkins to work out the best angle and velocity for the ball. Fuck only knew who the asshole was who'd impregnated Rune's mother, but he must have been a geek of some kind.

"Tell me more about the escape room."

"You get shut in for sixty minutes, and you have to find clues and solve puzzles to unlock the door."

Which all sounded great apart from the "shut in" part. He didn't want to remind Rune of her past.

"Could you get out early if necessary?"

"It says there's a panic button, and the room itself looks quite big. There's a picture on the website. The only thing is that they recommend teams of four to six people. Does Rune have a friend she could bring?"

A good question. Rune was a loner—it came up at every parent-teacher conference. She said she was happy, but Alaric still worried that she spent more time in the library than hanging out with her peers. There didn't seem to be any bullying, and she got on fine with her lab partners, or so she said. And she'd willingly spend time with the guys from Sirius. She just didn't socialise with kids her own age.

"I don't think there's anyone."

"So perhaps the bowling..."

"What are you doing tomorrow?"

Bethany went doe-eyed. "Me?"

"Or I could always put an advert on Craigslist. Do you have Craigslist over here? Wanted: willing victim for pizza, puzzles, and present-opening."

He couldn't exactly ask Emmy, could he? Not when he hadn't quite gotten around to mentioning Rune's existence to her yet. During his time away, his biggest regret had been the loss of what they'd had together, and if he wanted to salvage a friendship out of the smoking remains of their relationship, then he had to take baby steps. When Alaric first showed up in her life again, she'd been prickly, and until recently, they'd kept their interactions on a strictly business footing. Emmy had been supportive of Sirius but steered clear of personal territory. In the last few days, Alaric had detected a change, but he didn't want to push her. And she didn't like surprises.

"We have Gumtree," Bethany said. "Maybe I should try an ad myself? 'Brave soul needed to attend sixtieth birthday party. Must be willing to act as pretend date; hirer will provide cover story, cocktails, and as many canapés as a man can eat.' Actually, I'd need to give him a riot shield too."

"How about a deal? You come to my party, and I'll come to yours?"

"Are you serious?"

"What kind of man would I be if I let you get eaten alive by a bunch of rabid socialites?"

"It's a very kind offer, but you don't understand how painful it could be."

"Yeah, I do. I spent half my life bullshitting at those

kinds of affairs." Alaric shrugged, figuring he might as well reveal a snippet of his past. "My father's a diplomat, and my mother comes from a long line of British aristocrats. I grew up offering canapés to pompous pricks."

A group of kids pushed past, and Bethany squashed tighter against him. Her fingers curled under the lapels of his sport coat.

"And yet you turned out okay," she murmured.

*If only she knew.*

The train shuddered to a halt, and a tinny voice announced they'd reached Liverpool Street. Their stop, although Alaric was tempted to carry on to who knew where. But Bethany came to life and tugged him towards the doors.

"We need to get off."

Never more so in his life. Alaric's cock was straining at his pants, and he hoped Bethany hadn't noticed. That could be awkward, especially if she accepted the offer he planned to make over dinner.

"Are you going to tell me where we're going yet?" he asked.

"It's a surprise."

It sure was. Alaric had expected something fancy, upmarket French or traditional British, perhaps Italian at a push. Not...ping-pong and pizza?

"This? This is the place?" he asked, just to be sure. A touch of incredulity leaked into his voice. Pop music blared out of Bounce as a couple fell through the doors, laughing, and the aroma of pepperoni and garlic made Alaric's stomach grumble.

Bethany's face fell. "Do you hate it? We could go somewhere else."

He quickly regained his composure. "And miss you playing ping-pong in stilettos? Not a chance. Won't you cripple yourself?"

She mimicked his earlier words. "I grew up wearing heels and smiling at pompous pricks."

"You're smiling now. Does that make me a pompous prick?"

"Of course not! I'm sorry... I didn't mean..."

Damn, she was cute when she got flustered. Her cheeks pinked up, and she did these breathy little gasps, and yeah, provoking her probably did make Alaric a prick. Just not a pompous one.

"Relax, I was kidding."

What was it about Bethany that made his dick twitch? He hadn't had this sort of visceral reaction to a woman since he met Emmy, and the two of them were about as different as it was possible for two people to be. Where Emmy was sharp and abrasive, Bethany was soft and sweet. Kindness versus cunning. Etiquette versus street smarts. Perhaps that was why he liked Bethany so much? Because she *was* so different. An old proverb sprang to mind—once bitten, twice shy.

That was quickly followed by a Nietzsche aphorism: *Was mich nicht umbringt macht mich stärker.* What doesn't kill me makes me stronger. Venom still coursed through Alaric's veins from the *Emerald* battle, and if he ever got his hands on the motherfucker who'd switched that pay-off...

"Are you okay?"

He forced himself to take a deep breath when he saw Bethany looking at him strangely.

"I'm fine. Just recalling parts of my past that I'd rather forget. Come on—let's go inside."

Bounce certainly lived up to its name. Bethany was slender except for her chest, and Alaric might have suspected she'd had work done if she hadn't been pressed so tightly against him on the Tube to Oxford Street. All hail the gods of rush hour.

"I'm terrible at this." She giggled, diving sideways as another ball headed for the floor. It was a miracle she hadn't split her skirt. "Have you ever played before?"

"No, and I'm not much better. Want to get some food?"

"I think we've earned it. And a glass of wine too."

"Hold off on the wine for a few minutes. I need to talk to you about something first."

Her smile faded, and Alaric hated that. "Nothing bad. I just have a proposal for you."

"A...proposal?"

"A business proposal," he clarified. "And have you made up your mind about tomorrow yet?"

"Sort of. I'll gladly come to the escape room if you need an extra person, but I couldn't in all good conscience inflict my family and their friends on you."

"You wouldn't be inflicting anything on me. I offered."

"If you met them, you'd probably never speak to me again." Bethany glanced sideways at him from under long lashes. "And I like speaking to you."

Fuck, someone up there wasn't making this easy. But business was business, and growing Sirius took priority over his personal life right now.

"That's good. How would you like to do it more often?"

Alaric guided her to an open table in a quiet corner,

or at least, as quiet as it got at Bounce. The music from the ping-pong room was still loud enough that he could hear every lyric.

"I think I'd enjoy that?"

"Good. You're polite, you're organised, and you're looking for a job, right?"

"Well, yes."

"My company's looking for a new executive assistant. How do you feel about working with us?"

The happiness in her eyes turned to confusion. "You... Huh? I thought... A job?" She smacked her forehead. "Dammit, I'm so stupid."

Now it was Alaric's turn to be confused. "No, you're definitely not stupid. I thought you wanted a job?"

"A job, yes, not a pity offer."

"A... Hold on, you think I'm offering you a job out of pity? That couldn't be further from the truth. Our last assistant quit this morning, and...honestly? We're kind of desperate. Shit, that came out wrong."

Bethany narrowed her eyes. "Oh, really? Why did she quit?"

"Because of Judd. He has a problem with women."

"He doesn't like them?"

"Quite the opposite, in fact. Historically, our assistants have worked out of an office on the ground floor of his townhouse, and he has trouble keeping his clothes on around them."

"So, what? You want me to be the latest fodder for your man-whore of a colleague?"

"Absolutely not. This time, I'd take responsibility for all the training, and then either you could work from home or we'd find you an office far, far away from Judd. We can't keep losing assistants. It causes chaos with the admin."

"I see. So I'd have to spend time with you to start with, and that was what you meant by talking more?"

"Yes, and we might have to travel. I'm not always based in the UK, and I'm still hunting for this damn painting. Would you be able to leave your horse for a while?"

"A short while. Pinkey takes excellent care of him." Bethany chewed on her bottom lip, thinking. "What about you, Alaric? Do *you* keep your clothes on around your colleagues?"

Was that a hint of disappointment in her voice?

"Business and pleasure are rarely a good mix."

Alaric walked a fine line with Ravi. They had an agreement. Rules. One wobble with Bethany, and he'd lose his balance entirely.

"Oh. Tonight isn't pleasure?"

"Tonight's fun. Pleasure's entirely different."

*Dammit, stop looking at her breasts.*

"So it's an either/or situation," she murmured, so softly that Alaric barely heard her over the chatter from the table next to them. A bachelorette party, judging by the outfits and the number of empty wine glasses.

"I've been giving off the wrong signals, and for that, I apologise. I'm not in the market for a relationship or even a hook-up. And you..." He reached out and cupped her cheek. "Deserve a man who treats you like a queen. So the only thing on offer is a job, one I think you'd be good at. And the occasional bit of fun."

Bethany turned away, trying to hide the way she wiped one eye as she did so. Alaric was in two minds whether to offer a handkerchief. The manners drilled into him dictated he should, but at the same time, he didn't want to draw attention to her tears. Perhaps *this* was why he'd been attracted to Emmy? She didn't cry. Although when she got pissed, she tended to head out the back of her house and unload her favourite Walther at one of the targets she had set up. Last time Alaric had been to Riverley, she'd pasted a photo of his former boss over the bullseye at the fifty-yard mark. There hadn't been much left of the man by the end of the day.

Before Alaric made up his mind, Bethany pulled herself together with a smoothness that suggested she'd done it many times before. The perky smile, the way she folded her hands in her lap... Fake but polished.

"Can I take your order?" a waitress asked. Was there a special class waitstaff took to ensure they interrupted at precisely the wrong moment?

"Give us five minutes?"

"The kitchen's about to close."

Bethany's expression didn't change. "I'll just have a margherita, thank you."

"Pepperoni for me, plus a bottle of white."

"Would you like any—"

"No." Alaric forced himself to be polite. "No, thanks. Nothing else."

The girl threw him a dirty look—so much for service with a smile—and flounced off.

Now, where were they?

"Could you tell me more about what the role would entail?" Bethany asked.

Great. She'd switched to job-interview mode. The perfect fucking candidate, emphasis on the perfect and the fucking. Or so Alaric imagined. Still, with no way he'd let himself find out for sure, he matched her smile with an equally phoney one of his own.

"The four of us are often difficult for clients to contact, partly because we travel a lot but mostly because when we're working, we can't stop to take phone calls. So you'd relay messages as and when our schedules allow. You'd also arrange transport and accommodation, plus carry out basic admin tasks—proofreading and formatting reports, printing and mailing hard-copy documents, and screening initial enquiries. And there would be an element of personal assistance—buying Rune's birthday gifts, for example. Plus possibly feeding Judd's cat and watering his plants while he's away."

"And the salary?"

"What were you on at the gallery?"

She named a figure so low it made Alaric wince.

"Hell, we were paying Barbara twice that, and you'd be worth the same."

"You don't even know if I can do the job yet."

"Yes, I do. I've just spent most of the day with you, Bethany. You've got the right attributes, and anything else is just training."

"And by attributes, you mean...?"

She glanced at her chest. Busted.

"I mean you have the right personality."

"How much travel would be involved?"

"I'll need to show you the ropes, which'll take a few weeks, and depending on where the hunt for *Emerald* takes me, I could end up anywhere. Potentially, the others could help, but I don't trust Judd not to eat you alive."

A spark of jealousy flared in Alaric's gut, and for the first time, he understood how Emmy's husband had felt all those years ago. When he hadn't taken Emmy for himself, but he hadn't wanted anyone else to have her either. If only the current circumstances were different. If Sirius were five years older, if Alaric didn't have an unstoppable compulsion to find *Emerald*, if he'd picked a place to settle and bought a house. But circumstances were what they were. Alaric had visited twenty-three countries in the last year, and the longest he'd spent in one place was three months. That had been Florida. He'd rented a villa so Rune could stay with him for Christmas, then got tangled up in Emmy's latest mess— a sex trafficking ring masterminded by the Mafia's favourite money launderer, both now thankfully defunct.

"So potentially a month or so of travel, and then I could work from London?" When Alaric nodded, Bethany continued, "And what does the company do? Sirius Consulting? That's kind of vague."

"Deliberately so. It's a private intelligence agency. Basically, our clients pay us to find them information that might otherwise be difficult to obtain."

"So you really are a private detective? Piers hired one to dig up dirt on me during our divorce, but there wasn't any dirt to find. He seemed quite disappointed."

"Yes and no. We cater to a different market— businesses, mainly. We advise on strategy if they want to enter new markets, analyse risks, and provide regulatory guidance. Plus we can assist with investigations—due diligence, fraud, asset tracing, and whistle-blower allegations."

Translation: they evaluated whether corrupt officials or dodgy competitors were likely to sink a project before it got started, and if necessary, worked out which palms to grease. Plus they dug into all the sordid details of people's lives and companies' histories that they didn't want to share, and sometimes, for variety, Sirius got to hunt down thieves.

In short, Judd and Alaric talked to people. A lot of people, many of whom would only deal face to face. Naz dug around electronically, and if they needed to get into somewhere tricky in the physical sense, that fell under Ravi's remit.

Judd was the frontman. Former MI6, charismatic, and far too charming for his own good. Alaric, Naz, and Ravi worked in the shadows, and they made damn sure that when their activities crossed that blurry line between grey and black, they didn't get caught.

"So you're a corporate spy?" Bethany asked.

"'Spy' is such a dirty word, don't you think? I'm a businessman."

"Piers used to send me to the country club to gather information on his investments from the other wives. At first, it used to be quite fun, but when I realised what an arsehole he was, I might have fibbed a bit."

"Insider trading?"

"Such a dirty phrase, don't you think?" A sly little smile cracked her plastic expression. "I just liked to gossip."

Be still his beating heart.

"About the job...?"

"I can start on Monday."

## CHAPTER 25 - BETHANY

EEK, THIS WAS worse than the first day of school. Back then, the worries about which clique I'd join and whether or not I'd make the hockey team had seemed like the be-all and end-all. Funny how such things seemed so unimportant these days, wasn't it?

I checked my watch again. Alaric should have arrived by now, but he'd called to say he was running a few minutes late. Climate change protesters had blocked the road with a giant plastic duck, apparently. I thought he was winding me up at first, but when I turned on the news, there it was. Eight feet tall, green, with half a dozen shaggy-haired youths superglued to each wing. Caring for the environment was important, but couldn't they have picked a spot that didn't inconvenience hundreds of ordinary Londoners just trying to go about their business?

Finally, the SUV pulled up on the double-yellow lines outside, and I grabbed my handbag and Rune's presents. I'd gift-wrapped them myself after Alaric escorted me home. Even once he'd friend-zoned me, he was still chivalrous.

Ravi had clearly been to the same school of etiquette because he hopped out and opened the back door for me, and wow... He was the most beautiful man I'd ever seen. Beautiful. Handsome didn't do him justice. A couple of inches shorter than Alaric and a slighter build, but still muscular. His biceps strained his short sleeves as he reached to shake my hand, and his pecs were outlined clearly under his T-shirt. But his face... Delicate, fine features, with a perfectly straight nose and high cheekbones. The deep tan of his airbrushed skin suggested mixed heritage, and his black hair gleamed in the sunlight. But all that paled into insignificance beside his eyes. A vivid blue, they reminded me of the Maldivian sea. Several years ago, I'd spent two weeks sitting beside it alone while Piers golfed.

"You must be Bethany?"

"Bethany? Uh, yes. That's right." I gave myself a mental slap. "Bethany Stafford-Lyons. Pleased to meet you."

"Ravi Wells. It's a pleasure."

I felt my cheeks flush on the last word, spoken in a smooth American accent, and my gaze cut to Alaric before I could stop it. Yes, he'd had the same thought. And dammit, I needed to learn some self-control. Thankfully, a taxi tooted behind us, and I leapt into the back seat as the driver made a rude gesture.

"Take it easy, buddy," Alaric muttered as we pulled away. "You don't own the street."

"If you want to avoid the climate protesters, take the next left," I said. "Inconsiderate fools."

I caught Alaric's smile in the rear-view mirror. "That's exactly what they want you to think."

"What do you mean?"

"That particular group's funded by the automobile industry. By pissing everyone off, they turn climate change into a pesky annoyance rather than an important topic that should be on everyone's agenda."

"How do you know that?"

"It's our job."

Wow. And I guessed now it was mine too.

If you'd asked me to picture Rune McLain before we arrived, I'd have imagined a tall, all-American cheerleader type with glossy hair and white teeth, confident and outgoing like her father. So the reality was somewhat of a surprise. Rune was tiny, a church mouse of a girl in leggings and a baggy sweater who hurried along beside Alaric, head down, then hugged Ravi fiercely when she got to the car. And she wasn't all-American either. Her features tended towards Asian, but I couldn't place her accent.

Alaric introduced us. "Rune, this is Bethany, Barbara's replacement."

To me, she said, "Hello," then to Alaric, "Barbara quit?"

"Yesterday."

"Oh." Her eyes widened, and she made a soft choking noise. "Judd?"

"Not in the way you're thinking."

The exchange surprised me a little, that they were so open with Rune, especially given how hands-off Alaric appeared to be with regard to his daughter. Boarding school, a last-minute birthday gift... It reminded me of my own upbringing, except my parents left me to find out about the birds and the bees through trial and error. Mostly error, if I was honest.

"How's school?" Ravi asked.

"Mostly good. Mock exams start next week. And I have to write an essay for the final of a biology contest."

"Mostly good? What isn't good?"

"Netball. I'm too short, and I can't run fast enough." She made a face. "I only get Cs for sport."

But I bet she got As for every other subject. When the four of us stood outside the escape room an hour later, I didn't miss her calculating expression. It matched Alaric's, so it seemed they had one thing in common at least.

An employee approached, bouncing jauntily in neon trainers, the chains in his hands jangling. Wait... chains?

"I'm Keiran, and I'll be your guide today. If you'll just hold out your hands, I'll join you together, and then we can get started."

"Join us together? It didn't say anything about that on the website."

"All part of the fun," he said, entirely too cheerfully. He'd already confiscated our phones and our watches, replacing them with a single electronic widget with a digital display on one side and a button on the other. Rune wore it on a lanyard around her neck.

Alaric grasped my hand in his and held it out, smirking. "You heard the man—it's all part of the fun."

I swallowed my groan, and it lay in my stomach like a rock. I'd hoped that in my new role as executive assistant I could manage to retain some iota of decorum, but it seemed that wasn't going to be possible. This time last week, I'd been happily pouring drinks and showing pictures at the gallery, sworn off men for good, and now I was chained to not one but two hot guys, because Ravi was on the other side of me with Rune at the end. How did everything go so wrong?

"Everyone comfortable?" Keiran asked. *Not even a little bit.* "Then let's get started. The year is 2025, and following World War Three, you've been kidnapped by mad scientist Igor Krankov to use in his experiments. An attack by rebels distracted him into leaving your cell door unlocked, and you've got one hour to escape from his lair before he returns. Are you ready?"

Refer to my previous answer.

"Aaaaaand go!"

Keiran stepped back, the door slammed behind him, and the wall in front of us slid to the side, revealing a set of thick iron bars. Our prison. Alaric squeezed my hand and took a step forward.

"Well, he said it was unlocked," Rune reminded us.

The door was, but our chains weren't. The good news was that the keys to the padlocks were most likely in the tiny chamber outside. And the bad news? There had to be at least two hundred keys hanging neatly on hooks on the wall. Were we expected to try all of them? Because that would take an hour on its own.

Alaric picked the nearest key off the board. "They don't have any codes on them."

"Are either of you girls wearing bobby pins?" Ravi asked. "Shame they're not regular handcuffs, or we'd be out of them by now."

Really? How?

Rune elbowed him. "No cheating. Is that other door locked?"

Alaric tried it. "Yup. There has to be some kind of clue…"

"But there isn't," I said. Why had I ever suggested this? "Just a hundred keys and a freaking light switch."

Suddenly, Alaric smiled. "Turn the lights off."

"Huh?"

"Just do it."

Rune hit the switch, and what do you know? Five of the keys glowed, four green and one pink. Alaric snatched them off their hooks, and then Rune turned the lights back on and held up the lock securing her to Ravi. A quiet *click*, and she was free.

"Good thinking," I said to Alaric.

"I remembered Emmy's tattoo. She has a skull on her arm that only shows up under black light."

A secret tattoo? How clever. That's what I should have done. Instead, when my family had sold Polo out from underneath me, I'd got his name tattooed across my heart in black ink. Piers had gone bananas. He'd even got a therapist to come to the house while I still had my bad leg propped up on the sofa, but thankfully, the woman had reassured me that my expression of grief was perfectly normal.

Alaric freed my hands, then rubbed a thumb over my wrist. "Okay?"

"We should open the door."

Turned out the mad scientist wasn't a bad housekeeper. His living room was quite tidy, albeit filled with a strange selection of objects. Including a mechanical parrot that greeted us with a squawk.

"Pieces of eight," it screeched. "Pieces of eight."

"Is there anything gold in here?" Alaric asked. "That could be a clue. Let's take one side of the room each— say what you see."

What I didn't see was a door. How were we meant to get out?

"I've got a fireplace with a mirror over it and a

painting either side. One's a weird abstract thing, and the other's a poor copy of the *Mona Lisa*."

Alaric studied the bookshelf on an adjacent wall. "The guy has bizarre taste in reading material. Dostoevsky, Tolstoy, and a Russian dictionary just in case he forgets any of the words. Science books, algebra, a zoology manual, and *Fifty Shades of Grey*. Someone must've put that here as a joke, surely?"

"Or an instruction manual," Ravi muttered. "I've got six pairs of shoes next to the desk, parrot food in one of the drawers, a pair of glasses, a notepad, and a bunch of pens."

"Anything on the notepad?"

"Not unless it's written in invisible ink. The shoes have numbers on the bottoms—twenty-three, fourteen, fifty-seven, and so on, all two digits—but I have no idea what they mean."

Rune held up a box. "There's a jigsaw. Is that what the parrot meant? Pieces?"

"That's a good possibility. How many pieces?"

She already had the lid off the box. "Not many. Twenty?"

"Good. You do the jigsaw with Bethany, and we'll carry on looking."

"The parrot has an empty dish," Ravi pointed out. "What if we're meant to feed it?"

I joined Rune at the desk, pushing any discomfort over the weirdness of the whole affair to the back of my mind. I hadn't spent much time around kids, especially teenagers, and I didn't want to get off on the wrong foot with her. That could make working for her father somewhat awkward.

"It's a picture of this room," she told me. "Here's

the parrot and the *Mona Lisa*. Can you see any more corners?"

If she was feeling any of the same uneasiness, it didn't show. Then again, she was probably used to her father's assistants coming and going. Emphasis on the going. I didn't want to leave like the others, but since I had no desire to jump into bed with a smooth-talking playboy, I considered myself one step ahead of my predecessors.

Gradually, the jigsaw took shape, and we both realised at the same time that there was one big difference between the picture and the actual room. A moment later, the two of us leapt for the rug.

"There's a trapdoor under here!" Rune said, breathless.

A trapdoor with five dials, each engraved with the numbers one through nine. A combination lock, except we didn't know the combination.

"Good going," Alaric said as he poured birdseed into the parrot's dish.

"Two-six," it shrieked. "Two-six."

Ravi knelt and turned the second dial to the number six. "Guess this is how we get out. Somewhere in here, there are four more combinations. One's on the shoes, but we need to narrow it down."

"Wait, wait," Rune said. "There's a piece of the jigsaw left over. A brown boot, left foot."

That gave us four-nine. Three numbers left to go, and now that I knew what we were looking for, I had a good idea where to find one of the codes.

"Where are those glasses?"

Alaric passed them over, and I slipped them on. Sure enough, the abstract picture changed under the tinted lenses, revealing two definite digits. I'd had a book of puzzles like that when I was a child, even had a go at creating them myself.

"Three-one."

Two to go. But we'd tried everything obvious. What about the books? I pulled a copy of *War and Peace* off the shelf, checking for any hidden compartments or perhaps a scribbled note. Nothing.

Then Alaric breathed on the mirror, and two ghostly digits appeared. One-seven. My jaw dropped.

"How did you know to do that?"

He gave me a wink. "Just a trick that us businessmen use occasionally."

Businessmen my ass.

"There's only one number left," Rune said, a little breathless.

But Ravi shook his head. "No need to look for it. We have four definite numbers, which means there are only nine possible options for the remaining dial. All we have to do is cycle through them slowly, and...voila." The lock clicked, and he heaved the trapdoor open, revealing a black hole. Spooky, but we'd come this far, and I wasn't about to chicken out. "Who wants to go first?"

Alaric stood at the edge, peering into the gloom. "There's a ladder. I'll go down first, then help the girls."

Teenage me, the tomboy my mother hated so much, would have insisted on going it alone, but as I'd got older, I'd been schooled into accepting assistance gracefully. Rune already had her manners, and she stood to the side with Ravi, who nodded for me to go next.

Good thing I'd worn trousers.

Alaric disappeared into the darkness, but it didn't stay dark for long.

"Ah, fu—" He obviously realised Rune was in earshot. "Fiddlesticks. There must've been a pressure sensor."

Rune snorted a laugh, and it was the first time I'd heard her sound anything other than reserved.

"Fiddlesticks? Have you been reading parenting books again?"

"Just trying to do things right."

"You already do everything right."

"Guys," Ravi said. "Can we have this discussion later when the clock isn't ticking? How much time do we have left? And what's down there?"

Rune checked the timer. "Fifteen minutes gone."

"Down here?" Alaric's voice sounded a bit echoey. "Remember that part in *Ocean's Twelve* with the laser grid?"

Ravi grinned. "Best scene in the movie."

"Well, it's like that except the lasers are green rather than blue, and there's no music."

I'd seen that movie too. What on earth had we gotten ourselves into?

## CHAPTER 26 - BETHANY

I LOWERED A foot, feeling for the ladder with my toes, and once I'd got down a few rungs, Alaric's hands rested lightly on my hips, steadying me. I didn't particularly need steadying, but I liked the feel of them so I didn't say anything. Yes, I understood nothing could happen between us, but still... Those little touches sent flashes of heat through me.

Swiftly followed by a chill when I turned to see the lasers. How the hell were we supposed to get across that? A big button glowed white on the other side—presumably we had to press it? Alaric reached out a hand and cut one of the beams. A buzzer sounded, and the button turned red and began a countdown from thirty seconds. Did that mean we couldn't complete the task until the clock hit zero? When he cut the beam a second time, the timer increased by a minute.

"Perhaps leave it?" I suggested.

"Just seeing what would happen."

Rune climbed down and quickly took in the scene. "Ravi can do this one?"

"I'd put my back out if I tried it," Alaric said. "Unless Bethany wants to have a go?"

I might have worn sensible shoes today—black suede boots with gold zippers on the sides—but that didn't qualify me to be a contortionist.

"Ravi's welcome to—" I jumped as I realised he was standing right beside me. How had he come down the ladder so quietly? "Uh, be my guest."

He studied the array of lasers for maybe ten seconds, then leapt, skipped, and limboed around the beams, finishing with a freaking backflip. The buzzer stayed silent, and the countdown reached zero a second before he punched the button. Perfect timing.

"Show off," Alaric muttered.

"What the...? Did he do gymnastics as a child?"

"Something like that."

"Wow."

The lasers vanished, and a door in the far wall swung open, revealing Krankov's lab. A ceiling fan whirred overhead, casting eerie shadows over the room. Bubbling flasks of coloured liquids lined one wall, and another held a bunch of animal skulls in glass cases, each with a plaque underneath. Were they real? A scarred wooden bench spanned the room, complete with three sets of electronic scales holding empty glass beakers. Brilliant. Science had always been my worst subject at school, and dead animals gave me the creeps. Dubious specimens floated in jars, atomic models sat on shelves, and I hoped to goodness the DANGER: RADIATION sign was a fake.

"What's that on the chalkboard?" Ravi asked. "Is that algebra? Or Russian?"

"Both," Rune told him.

I had an "aha" moment. "That's what the books are for upstairs. Russian and algebra. They're to help us down here. I'll go and get them."

"Time is of the essence," Alaric said.

"I know. I'll be quick."

"No, that's what the Russian says. It's a red herring."

"You speak Russian?"

"Enough to get by."

"Oh." Colour me impressed. "That's...that's... But we still need the algebra book. All those x's and y's are like Greek to me."

"Thirty-seven," Rune said.

"Huh?"

"The answer is thirty-seven. I can't speak Greek, but I can speak English, Thai, French, German, Spanish, and algebra."

Flipping heck. I turned to Ravi, questioning, and he backed away with his hands in the air.

"Hey, don't look at me. I can only speak English, Spanish, Hindi, and enough French to get laid."

Alaric glared at him, then cut his eyes to Rune, and Ravi took another step back.

"Shit, sorry."

Rune just giggled, high-pitched and musical. "Time's ticking. What do we do with the thirty-seven? Do you think it's something to do with these atomic models? Thirty-seven on the periodic table is rubidium."

"No, not that. There isn't a copy of the periodic table in here, and they can't rely on us knowing that information. We're not all smart-asses."

"Are you supposed to say 'ass'?"

"Dammit, probably not." Alaric smacked his forehead. "Sh— Shoot."

"We do swear at school, you know. And I'm fifteen now."

She looked younger, although I wasn't about to

point that out. "Only a couple of years until your dad'll be fighting off the boys with a stick."

If I hadn't been looking right at Rune, I might have missed it. The flash of fear in her eyes. I was sure I hadn't imagined it, but she quickly shook it away.

"No, no, that's no problem. I'm not interested in boys. No, never."

"Shall we get on with the game?" Alaric asked, and there was nothing subtle about his change of subject. Should I apologise? I wanted to because I'd obviously upset Rune, but at the same time, I didn't want to prolong the pain by pushing a topic nobody wanted to discuss. Maybe I'd ask Alaric later, see what he thought was appropriate.

Ravi followed Alaric's lead. "It has to be the beakers. We need to put something in them—thirty-seven of something."

"Thirty-seven millilitres?" I suggested. "Thirty-seven grams?"

Rune moved to the back wall, to the flasks of coloured liquid. "If this is water, then one millilitre equals one gram, so it doesn't matter which. And I can't see thirty-seven of anything else unless we start popping hydrogen atoms off all these hydrocarbon molecules, and I don't suppose they'd thank us if we did that."

Alaric grinned at her, the proud papa. "No, I don't suppose they would. Do you want to measure?"

Now Rune looked like the kid she was as she gleefully poured exactly thirty-seven grams of blue liquid into the nearest beaker. Nothing happened. No flashing lights, no hint as to whether we were correct. Did we just trust that we were on the right track? I didn't see we had a lot of choice.

"We need two more numbers," Alaric said. "Look for anything out of place, and say what you see the way we did upstairs."

We fanned out, and as luck would have it, I got the animal skulls. I peered closer and breathed a sigh of relief when I spotted a telltale moulding line—they were plastic, not real bone.

"Methane, ethane, propane, butane, hexane, octane..." Rune said, picking up models that could have come from any high school science lab. "No pentane and no heptane. Do you think that means anything?"

"It's possible, but again, not everyone would know that."

"Can I try fifty-seven?"

"Why not?"

Rune got pouring again while Ravi picked up a black box. "There's some kind of electronic thing, but I don't know what it is or what it does. Do you think these scribbles on the wall mean anything?"

Alaric went to check while I studied the skulls. They ranged from the size of a grape to bigger than a watermelon, and out of all of them, I only recognised one—a horse. Except the plaque underneath said *Tamias striatus*. Now, I had no idea what a *Tamias striatus* was, but it certainly wasn't the scientific name for a horse. That was *Equus caballus*, which was attached to something the size of a fist.

"I think these skulls are mislabelled." When I picked at the top plaque, the Velcro behind it loosened, and it came away in my hand. "I think we're meant to rearrange them. Should I get the zoology book from upstairs, or...?"

Alaric leaned over my shoulder. Usually, I hated when people invaded my space, but he was welcome to as much of it as he wanted.

"*Simia paniscus*—that has to be some sort of monkey. The top one? Rune?"

Rune managed to match five more. *Nandinia binotata* and *Nyctereutes procyonoides* were a mystery to all of us. But it didn't matter anymore because I suddenly realised the connection.

"Look at the first letters. We've got two N's left, and it really doesn't matter which is which."

*Simia paniscus*
    *Equus caballus*
    *Vulpes vulpes*
    *Eudyptes chrysocome*
    *Nandinia binotata*
    *Tamias striatus*
    *Erethizon dorsaum*
    *Enhydra lutris*
    *Nyctereutes procyonoides*

Rune's face lit up. "Seventeen! I'll pour it out."

We had three filled beakers on three scales, but nothing happened. No bells, no whistles, and certainly no way out of the room magically revealed itself.

Rune muttered under her breath. It sounded like "ai-shia," and from the delivery, I suspected it would be frowned upon by the Thai language version of Alaric's parenting book. Luckily, she'd spoken too quietly for him to hear.

"The fifty-seven's probably wrong," she said more loudly. "We're missing something. What else doesn't fit?"

Ravi picked up the black box again, and this time, a light started flashing, bold and bright, like something out of a disco. He started jigging around, and Rune groaned.

"Did you read the 'dad dancing' chapter from Alaric's book?"

She used his forename rather than calling him Dad? Odd. Mind you, a girl in my ballet class had done the same, although her parents followed some sort of new-age religion that meant they didn't wear shoes or wash their hair. Rainbow Starshine, she'd been named, although her parents were Bob and Susan.

"Would you rather do the foxtrot?"

Rune giggled as Ravi twirled her around, and I was surprised to note that he actually was dancing the foxtrot. Where had he learned to do that? This trio kept surprising me, yet I knew I'd only scraped the surface of their personalities. Working for Sirius promised to be far more interesting than my time at the gallery, and infinitely more fun than a decade of playing the perfect hostess. I started laughing too, not just because of Ravi's dancing but out of relief. When Hugo fired me, despair had threatened to overwhelm me again, the way it had after I walked in on Piers and his floozy, but somehow, I'd managed to land on my feet, even if the job interview had been a little unorthodox.

Alaric caught my eye, then rolled his. "Do you guys want to get out of here or not? Next time, I'll book dance lessons."

Ravi gave Rune one last spin, and Alaric caught her before she stumbled into the wall of flasks. I was so glad to see her enjoying her birthday. My own fifteenth had been a disaster. I'd wanted to go for pizza with my friends, but Mother had insisted on a marquee, a string quartet, and a finger buffet. As if trying to stomach caviar wasn't bad enough, I'd fallen asleep in the sun the day before and turned the colour of a lobster. My dress chafed against my burned skin with every step I took, so I'd snuck out in tears at seven thirty and hidden in the hay barn until everyone went home.

"We have twenty-six minutes left," Rune said. "What are strobe lights used for?"

"In the FBI, we used them to stun criminals."

Alaric had been an FBI agent? I suppose I should have guessed he'd been law enforcement of some kind before he moved into the private sector. What about Ravi? He didn't exactly scream "cop," but perhaps he'd done undercover work or something.

"When I worked in nightclubs, the strobe lights slowed down movement. Either that or they made people vomit."

Okay, definitely not a cop.

"What movement are we gonna slow down?" Alaric's forehead creased into a frown, then relaxed as he glanced upwards. "The fan. It's the fan. See the AC ducts? There's no reason to have a fan too, so it must be part of the game. Can we adjust the speed on the strobe?"

"There's a dial." Ravi held out the unit to Rune. "Care to do the honours?"

It was like magic. The fan flickered and flashed, and then suddenly, it stopped. Not really, but it looked as though it did. Eighty-four. The numbers were clear on the blades.

"Yeeeah!" Rune shoved the strobe back at Ravi and

grabbed the flask again, measuring carefully. This time when she stood back, the entire blackboard lifted up, revealing a set of stairs leading upwards. Ravi hopped through the hole first, and Alaric lifted Rune through to him, her feet clearing the remaining three feet of wall.

"Need a hand?" he asked me.

"It'll be an ungainly scramble otherwise."

I'd expected just a hand, as he said, but he shocked me by swinging me off my feet, bridal style again. I ended up nestled against his dark grey cashmere sweater. I'd say it reminded me of my wedding night, but when Piers had attempted the same move at Château de la Messardière in Saint Tropez, he'd put his back out, then spent the whole of our honeymoon zonked out on painkillers prescribed by a local physician. With hindsight, that was probably when his habit started. On again, off again, worse whenever things weren't going his way at work. Of course, he always denied there was a problem, but nobody had that many tennis injuries. What he did have was a number of doctor friends who'd write him prescriptions with no questions asked.

Over the years, I'd given up trying to help him. It only led to arguments, and quite frankly, he was easier to live with when he was under the influence.

What was Alaric like to live with?

*What was I even thinking?*

Rune belted up the stairs, and the rest of us followed as she pushed through the door at the top. I half feared we'd find ourselves in another freaky room, but no. Keiran was slouched on a plastic chair with his phone in his hand, and judging by the hasty way he shoved it into his pocket, he hadn't been expecting to see us quite so soon.

"Uh, that was quick. Maybe even the quickest." He checked his twin of Rune's electronic widget. "Yes, that *was* the quickest. Congratulations! You win a prize."

Over the course of thirty-seven minutes, Rune had gone from shy to animated. "Yay! What prize?"

"A free go in one of our other escape rooms. Wanna try the dungeon? The asylum? The haunted house?"

"Today?"

"Well, we'll give you a voucher, and you've got a year to use it."

"Then I think we'll come back. Okay?" She checked with Alaric, and he nodded. "I'm starving."

In the car, Rune opened up a tiny crossbody bag she'd been wearing under her sweater, pricked her finger, and pressed a drop of blood onto a strip of paper sticking out of a digital doohickey.

"It's a glucose meter," she explained. "I'm diabetic."

"Your father told me."

Ravi twisted from the front seat to look at me. "But perhaps not forever. Rune wants to become a scientist so she can find a cure, right, Einstein?"

"Einstein was a theoretical physicist, not a biochemist. Think Rosalind Franklin, Marie Curie, Alice Ball..."

Now that I'd met Rune, Alaric's choice of birthday gift—a biography of Peggy Whitson, a biochemist and astronaut—made perfect sense. Ravi? He was giving her sea monkeys, also picked out by Alaric. Which she was just as thrilled with when she unwrapped the box in the restaurant an hour later. For a small teenager, she sure could eat. She'd binged on crudités, put away more pizza than me, eaten two scoops of frozen yogurt, and now she was matching Alaric in the coffee stakes. We'd sat in a booth, Rune and Ravi on one side and Alaric and me on the other. Although we weren't close enough to touch, I could still feel every move he made. He gave off a weird energy that made me want to slide across the cheap red vinyl until I moulded against him, and no, I hadn't drunk a single drop of wine. It was all down to magnetism or pheromones or possibly overwhelming stupidity. Certainly I wasn't the only girl in history to have been attracted to her boss, but I hadn't even officially started work yet. Not to mention the fact that he'd been a bit of a prick when we first met. Honestly, this was ridiculous.

"Science was never my strong point," I admitted. "I always preferred the arts and humanities."

"I dropped most of those last year," Rune said. "Now I just do geography. Uh, while we're talking about geography, where am I staying this summer? Are you gonna rent a house again?"

Alaric turned to me. "It looks like we've found your first project. I'll need a short-term rental, three months from June first, maybe four."

House-hunting? Well, that was something different, but definitely more fun than serving refreshments to Henrietta's clients. Before I started at the gallery, I used to watch too many of those daytime property shows, and if push came to shove, I could probably make a half-decent attempt at renovating a rundown Italian farmhouse. Several times, I'd tried to convince Piers that it could be a fun project, especially as we could rent the property out for extra income afterwards, but he only ever wanted to stay in five-star hotels or my parents' villa in the Algarve.

"Whereabouts? London?"

"Rune? Where do you want to go?"

"Wherever you need to be for work. And near some restaurants? If Naz goes on one of his weird diets again, I'll have to order takeout."

"So maybe New York? Or a town near DC? Northern Virginia, Maryland, West Virginia..."

"Are your parents still in Germany?" Ravi asked.

"*Ja*, thank fu— goodness. No bratwurst for me any time soon."

So, Alaric had family problems too. I should have felt bad for him, but what I actually felt was a weird sense of camaraderie because I wasn't the only one with screwed-up relatives. And perhaps that was why, after we'd taken Rune back to Ridgeview and dropped Ravi off at a very nice townhouse not too far from my apartment—Judd's home, apparently—I didn't argue too much when he said he'd pick me up again that evening.

"Are you sure? My mother's worse than the CIA when it comes to interrogating people. Or so I'd imagine, anyway. It's not as if I've actually seen a real interrogation, or even met anyone who works for the CIA, but don't they waterboard people? There was a TV special— I'm rambling again, aren't I?"

Alaric just smiled. "I'll be back at six. If you want to thank me, wear fancy shoes."

Fancy shoes... Of course I could do that, but...why?

# CHAPTER 27 - ALARIC

"ARE THESE SHOES fancy enough for you?" Bethany asked.

Fuck yes. Silver strass Louboutins. Red soles, uppers sparkling with crystals, four-inch spike heels. Fifteen hundred bucks a pop. Alaric's first gift to Emmy had been a similar pair, back when he'd still had access to his trust fund. His gaze rose slowly, taking in slim ankles, toned calves, and the soft drape of Bethany's knee-length black cocktail dress. Silk? It looked like silk. She hadn't gone overboard with the jewellery either. Just a pair of diamond stud earrings, a carat or so each. Blonde hair flowed in waves down her back, and she'd fastened one side of it away from her face with a simple silver clip.

He was in trouble.

"On second thought, you should change into ballet flats. Or tennis shoes. Or slippers."

Her face fell. "What's wrong with the stilettos?"

"The men at this party won't be able to keep their eyes to themselves."

And Alaric didn't want to get thrown out or arrested.

"Right now, the only man looking at me is you."

"Yes."

His gaze settled on her feet again, and he imagined

those heels digging into his ass. Felt his dick twitch and forced himself to focus on her face. He'd almost forgotten what this feeling was like—the tumble over the cliff edge, clutching at rocks and branches until he gave in and slid all the way to the bottom. With Emmy, he'd dived head first, only to land in white-water rapids. It'd been one hell of a ride until he got tossed into a fucking whirlpool.

With Bethany, he needed to land on his feet. Couldn't afford not to. He'd lost everything once, and he wasn't sure he'd get through it a second time.

"The shoes?" She tilted her head to one side. "You really want me to change them?"

*Get your damn dick under control.*

"No, keep them on."

"I've hardly ever worn them. My parents gave them to me for my twenty-fifth, and I should've sold them, I know I should, but I'd only have got a fraction of what they cost, and...and I like them. So much of the time, I'm in riding boots, and... Listen to me. I'm sure you don't care."

Judd always reminded him of the need to vet employees, so Alaric could justify his desire to know every single thing about Bethany as work-related, right? Okay, it was a stretch, but as she hooked her arm through his and headed for the elevator in her apartment building, he just didn't care. Tomorrow. He'd get back to business tomorrow. Tonight, his role was to play the adoring boyfriend, and like with any job, he'd give the task his all.

He reached out and touched one of the earrings.

"And these?"

"I inherited them from Grandma. My mother would

never forgive me if they disappeared in the post-divorce cull. I guess if I got really desperate, I'd have to replace them with paste and pray she never found out. They make good fakes nowadays, don't they? It's hard to tell the difference sometimes."

Unless of course your name was Dyson and you were on a scallop boat off the coast of Virginia. Or at least, he'd claimed the diamonds were fake. Alaric had relived that day more times than he could count, and he still wasn't sure how that pay-off had gone so wrong. The cash had certainly been swapped, but the stones... What if the real ones had still been in the case? The diamond tester could've been rewired to give a false negative, and in the melee, Dyson had taken the case with him when he escaped. Could the counterfeit cash have been a distraction?

Would Alaric ever find out?

He'd been so close to *Emerald* and then *Red After Dark*, only to have both of them slip through his fingers. "Frustrated" didn't even begin to cover it.

"You won't ever be that desperate."

"How do you know? I'm basically one vet bill away from disaster."

"Because you're part of Sirius now, and we take care of our own."

Alaric wasn't rich, not by Emmy's standards, anyway, but he was comfortable again. Sometimes, he regretted kissing his inheritance goodbye, but his father's ultimatum—admit he'd stolen the *Emerald* pay-off and take his punishment like a man or be cut off—wasn't something he could contemplate going along with. Instead, he'd slung a few belongings into a bag, booked a ticket to Cambodia, and headed to the airport with Bancroft McLain's words echoing in his ears. *Stop embarrassing this family.* Alaric had been more worried about embarrassing Emmy. The theft had put her in an awkward position, especially after the FBI ruled out the possibility of the switch having taken place in their building and began to whisper about Alaric's overnight stay at Riverley. Better for him to vanish into the ether with the cloud of suspicion still hanging over him than let the woman he loved become a suspect.

Until he met Judd, Ravi, and Naz, he figured he'd be a beach bum for the rest of his days. He'd had the beard and the long hair and everything. But it had been all too easy to slip back into his old life—into *their* old lives—and once he felt that surge of adrenaline again...

Bethany's gasp drew him out of his thoughts.

"The Aston Martin is yours?"

"No, I borrowed it from Emmy." He gave the parking enforcement officer hurrying towards them a jaunty salute as he opened the passenger door for Bethany. Not that a ticket would be much of an issue. Emmy collected so many parking fines they were a line item in her accounts. One more wouldn't make much difference. "I don't stay in one place long enough to justify buying a car at the moment."

She ran a finger over his lapel as she slid into the seat. "And yet you own a made-to-measure tuxedo."

"There are three things every man should own, and a well-cut tuxedo is one of them."

"What are the other two?"

"A good watch." Alaric's Breitling had been a gift from Emmy, one of the few possessions he'd kept throughout his travels. "And you don't want to know the other."

The switchblade nestled securely at his waist, ready for those little emergencies. Four years had passed since he last killed a man. Unlike Emmy, he didn't make a habit of it, not anymore. And he was damn picky about the lives he took. Those scruples might have ended his career at the CIA, but at least he could sleep at night. When thoughts of pretty blondes in Louboutins didn't haunt his dreams, that was. It had been too damn long since he spent quality time with a woman. Or a man, for that matter. He'd been known to dabble.

When Bethany didn't push for an answer, Alaric relaxed. Emmy would've frisked him and found the knife by now, and he'd have returned the favour. The only difference? She'd have been carrying at least two blades. One tucked into her bra, usually, and another at her waist or inner thigh, depending on the cut of her dress. Or perhaps in the heel of her shoe.

Bethany's only weapon was her smile.

"Tell me more about this party," Alaric said. "What can I expect?"

"My parents throw half a dozen of these shindigs a year. Father's birthday is just an excuse, really. The men drink Scotch and boast about the size of their stock portfolios and yachts and mansions, while the women strut around like they're on a catwalk and gossip about anyone who isn't within earshot."

"So basically a dick-measuring contest?"

It reminded him of home. And Bancroft McLain had always been the biggest dick.

Bethany's cheeks turned delightfully pink. "Something like that."

"And you mentioned before that you wanted your family to see you hadn't fallen apart?"

"Exactly. I guess I just want to prove that I haven't turned into a lonely spinster intent on collecting cats." She shifted in her seat, turning to face him. "Thanks for coming."

"Any time. Although for the record, I do like cats."

That got a chuckle out of her, but no crude joke about him liking pussy too. Another difference between Bethany and Emmy. Bethany's shoulders dropped an inch as a little of the tension left her, but she was still too stiff. Too full of pent-up stress. Alaric wanted to turn her into warm putty by the end of the evening, purely for her own well-being, of course.

"We've got cats at the stables. Piers isn't keen on animals at all, but he put up with Chaucer because he didn't live at home."

"Sounds like a real charmer."

"Please, don't remind me. Somehow, he didn't seem bad at first, and my parents still think he's wonderful."

"You mentioned a fiancée?"

"Yes, Andromeda. She's two years younger than me. I went to primary school with her older brother."

"Say that again."

"I went to school with her older brother."

"No, not that. The name. *Andromeda*?"

"Her father's an astronomer."

"Her father's a sadist. What's the brother called?"

"Jupiter, but he changed it to Peter. Andromeda's an actress, so I guess it's good to be memorable."

"She doesn't call herself Andie?"

"No, she gets quite annoyed if you shorten it."

Alaric would have to remember that. "And Piers is a

dentist, right?"

"How do you know that?"

"We never hire anyone without a background check."

"Oh." Her quiet surprise followed by silence said what she didn't: that she wasn't happy he'd been poking into her history. But there was no anger, probably because she had nothing to hide apart from a poor choice of husband and a tendency to let her family walk all over her. "Guess you found out I'm quite boring."

"You just haven't had your time to shine yet."

"Are you always this sweet?"

"Depends who I'm talking to."

Bethany settled back in the seat, watching the London streets go by as they headed south towards Surrey. The Aston wasn't a city car. Crawling along in first gear was a jerky affair, the V12 a thoroughbred forced to do the job of a carthorse.

Finally, Bethany spoke, her voice softer than before. "Yes, Piers is a cosmetic dentist. Plus he helps to manage his family's property portfolio, which sounds rather grand compared to the reality. Think student housing rather than mansions."

"But it's still profitable."

"Yes. A little *too* profitable. I heard him on the phone from time to time, and he wasn't always nice. Looking back, I realise I should have said something, but..."

"It was difficult when you were depending on him financially."

"I know. Which is why I want to earn my own money from now on. I don't want to be beholden to anyone."

Alaric knew that feeling. For years, his father had dangled his inheritance as a carrot while beating him with the proverbial stick. And it was yet another reason he had to lock down any affection he might be developing for Bethany and keep their relationship on a professional footing—she shouldn't feel beholden to *him* either.

"You won't be." He cleared his throat. "Who do you want me to be tonight?"

"What do you mean?"

"What sort of man do you want on your arm?" Alaric switched to a French accent. "A Parisian banker?" Another swap. "Russian oligarch?" This was one area in which moving country every other year as a child had paid dividends. "Hungarian porn star? Apparently, I'm quite good at that one."

Bethany sounded younger when she laughed. Or perhaps it was just that her ex had piled a decade's worth of shit onto her?

"Where did you learn all those accents?" she asked.

"I've lived in a lot of places."

"And do you speak the languages too?"

"My Hungarian's slightly rusty. It's been a while since I went there. How about an Italian doctor? I'll jump-start your heart any time, *tesoro*."

"Can't you just be yourself?"

Be himself? That was a rare occurrence nowadays. During his time away, Alaric had grown to embrace his inner chameleon, to hide behind whatever character he'd morphed into that morning. All the masks and borrowed personas acted as a shield between him and his old world, or so Judd said. And he should know—he did exactly the same thing, and his therapist had analysed his proclivities to death.

"I'm not sure that's a great idea."

"Please? If I hadn't sworn off the dating game, I'd go for Alaric McLain over a Hungarian porn star every time. And I'm not interested in rich men anymore either."

If Bethany knew the real Alaric, would she still feel the same way? So far, she'd barely scratched his surface, and sometimes, even he didn't like the man who lurked beneath. But he found he couldn't deny her.

"Sure thing, my sweet. I'll just be myself."

# CHAPTER 28 - ALARIC

"WHO'S THIS, BETHIE?"

Bethie? She wasn't a Bethie. A Beth, maybe, but not a Bethie. Her father of all people should have known that, but the asshole probably spent more time on the golf course than with his daughter. Still, at least he hadn't called her Saturn or Galaxy or Starburst or something equally ridiculous. *Andromeda*?

"This is Alaric."

"Alaric McLain. Good to meet you."

"And you're dating my daughter?"

*My daughter.* He said it as though she belonged to him. Bertram Stafford-Lyons was a man who liked to be in control, and it must irk him to no end that Bethany had stepped out of line.

"We haven't put a label on it yet."

But the hand a mere inch above her ass said more than "just friends." She hadn't seemed bothered when Alaric put it there. In fact, she'd wrapped an arm around his waist, winked, and muttered, "Just getting into the spirit of things."

*Kill him now.* She fit perfectly against his side. An inch shorter than him in *those* shoes, soft in all the right places.

"We've been seeing each other for a few weeks," Bethany said. "I thought it was time I moved on."

Her glance at Piers and his blonde didn't go unnoticed. Nobody could have missed Andromeda. Her dress was a skintight sheath of satin in fire-engine red, and she'd worn enough jewellery that anyone short-sighted might mistake her for a chandelier. Then there was the laugh. In Tanzania, Alaric had been fortunate enough to stumble over a clan of wild hyenas, and for a moment, he thought he was back in the Serengeti.

"Moving on...with an American?"

"What's wrong with Americans?"

"You live in England. You shouldn't waste your time on a man who won't stick around."

For fuck's sake, Alaric was standing right there. "I actually have dual nationality. My mother's British."

"So you live here?"

"Right now I do." For another few days, at least. "I like to move around. See the world."

"And your parents?"

"What about them?"

"Where do they live?

Why did that matter? "In Berlin."

"Berlin? Interesting choice."

And a poor one, judging by the man's tone. Alaric allowed himself a tight-lipped smile.

"My father's the US ambassador to Germany."

Alaric may have disliked his father, but he did appreciate the way Bancroft McLain's position left Bertram Stafford-Lyons fumbling for words.

"Oh, right. And what do you do, Alaric?"

"I'm a consultant."

Which covered a multitude of sins. And yes, he did mean *sins*.

"Profitable?"

"Daddy, this isn't an interrogation."

Stafford-Lyons draped an arm over Bethany's shoulders and pulled her away from Alaric, a move she was clearly uncomfortable with, but short of starting a tug-of-war in the middle of the living room, Alaric couldn't get her back.

"I just want what's best for you, Bethie. A suitor needs to be able to take care of you. To provide."

"I can take care of myself."

It was as if Stafford-Lyons hadn't even heard her. "He's, what, thirty-eight? Thirty-nine?" Close. Alaric had turned forty last December. "And he 'moves around.' A man should be putting down roots in his twenties. Buying property. Planning for the future, not gallivanting across the world."

No wonder Bethany hadn't wanted to come tonight. Her father wasn't just a prick, he was a walking, talking, gonorrhoea-infected cock. He'd probably get on famously with Bancroft McLain.

Still, Alaric refused to let himself be cowed. "I have an estate in Italy. Does that count?"

Bethany's mouth dropped open, but she quickly shut it again as she shrugged off her father's arm.

"Daddy, I promised to show Alaric the gardens before it got dark. You'll have to excuse us."

With that, she grabbed his hand and practically strong-armed him through the house, her mouth set in a hard line as she ignored a woman calling her name. Only when they reached the lawn and her heels sank did she stop.

"Shit." She choked back a sob as she tried to free herself from the earth's clutches. "I knew we shouldn't have come. He's like this every damn time. Rude, condescending, just all-around obnoxious. I'm so sorry."

"Shh, it's okay." Alaric plucked her free and swung her into his arms the way he had at the stables. "If you met my old man, I'd be the one apologising."

"Is your father really an ambassador?"

"He is."

"Is that why you speak so many languages? Because you grew up overseas?"

Alaric nodded. "We used to move every couple of years, and I had to learn to fit in fast. I preferred hanging out with the locals to being just another privileged kid who shuttled back and forth between a residential compound and the international school. My parents never understood it. They both love the lifestyle—parties, prestige, a smattering of politics."

They reached the terrace, and Alaric set Bethany on her feet again. He didn't particularly want to. No, he wanted to carry her along the driveway, slide her into the Aston, and get the hell out of there. But then her father would have won.

"Thanks," she whispered. "I tried hanging out with the locals once. When I was sixteen. I snuck into the pub with some friends from the Pony Club."

"You got drunk?"

"No, one of my father's friends saw me there and I got grounded. But I might get drunk tonight. That seems like a good option."

Tonight, Alaric was driving, so it didn't matter. "Then let's get the mud cleaned off your heels and find you a drink."

"Oh no!" She stared at her feet and gasped. "My poor shoes."

"Where's the sink?"

She took his hand and led him towards the house. "This way."

In the utility room off the kitchen, Alaric lifted Bethany onto the counter beside the sink and removed her shoes. The water wouldn't do the leather much good, but it was better than being caked in dirt. He picked up a sponge and dabbed gently.

"Bethie?" he asked.

"He's called me that since I was little, and even then, I couldn't stand it."

"How about Beth?"

"Beth's okay. Do you really own an estate in Italy?"

Did he? It was a good question. "That, dear Beth, is a long story."

"Well, now that I'm here, I need to stay until the birthday cake comes out."

Alaric swallowed a sigh. How much of his past did he want Beth to know? Now that she was working for Sirius, she'd find out parts of it at least. He'd never tell her about the really dirty stuff, but too many people knew of his time with Emmy for that to stay a secret.

"Technically, I own part of an estate."

"Technically?"

"As far as I know, my name's still on the papers, but I haven't been there for years."

Eight years, to be precise. He'd bought it six weeks before the *Emerald* incident. *They'd* bought it. Emmy and him. He'd had business in Rome, and she had a job in Milan, only they'd both finished early. The sun was shining, and it was as if fate had dictated they have a dirty weekend. Or as Emmy had put it, "I need a good dicking. Meet you in Tuscany."

She'd picked him up from the railway station in a Ferrari. He never did find out where she'd got it from, but there was a picnic basket in the trunk and a blanket on the front seat.

"Where are we going?" he asked.

"Fuck knows. I've had the week from hell—again—and I just want to get lost. Okay?"

He ran a hand up her bare leg. "Okay. Ever fucked in a Ferrari?"

"No, but I like a challenge."

The adventure took them through tiny villages, down quiet country lanes in their quest to find a secluded spot where they wouldn't get arrested because, face it, the car didn't exactly fade into the background. Then they happened across the cracked walls and sagging gates of Casa Malizia, a faded *Vendesi* board screwed to one gatepost.

"Here?" Alaric asked, hard already because Emmy had driven with one hand for most of the way.

"Why not?"

It turned out that getting busy in a Ferrari was technically feasible but not exactly pleasurable, and after Emmy had hit her head on the roof for the third time, she huffed and climbed out.

"Where are you going?" His balls were tightening. So damn close. "I'm nearly there."

"And I'm nearly concussed. Bring the blanket."

She vaulted over the wall before he had a chance to argue, and they finished in the grass beside an old olive grove, the twisted trees providing respite from the midday sun. And after lunch, they snuck farther onto the estate, discovering a tumbledown farmhouse, crumbling outbuildings, a small lake, and rows of overgrown grapevines.

"This place was beautiful once," she said, a hint of sadness in her voice.

"It still is beautiful. A different kind of beauty, like an old black-and-white movie theatre or a retired racehorse."

Emmy lay back on an old stone bench, staring up at the sky. A single puff of cloud drifted on the breeze, and the only sounds were the rustle of the olive trees and the occasional bird call. Rustic peace, almost eerily so. The calm before the storm, he now knew. But that day, they'd both been happy. Emmy smiled more when she was away from Black. When she wasn't weighed down by the pressure he put on her.

Alaric sat on the ground, leaning one elbow on the bench as he watched her. "Sounds corny, but I wish we could stay here forever."

He'd meant stay in that moment, that mindset, but she took him a little too literally.

"Then let's buy it."

The moment skittered away. "What?"

"This place. It's for sale. Let's buy it. Then we can come back whenever."

Whenever they weren't working, which meant roughly once a decade. It was a crazy idea. Insane. They both lived a world away, and Alaric didn't know a thing about grapevines or olive trees. The house was a wreck. He opened his mouth to say "absolutely not," but what came out was, "How the hell do we buy an estate?"

In rural Italy, it turned out that you went to the local café and asked who the owner was. By the end of Saturday, they'd agreed on a price with the old man's heir, and Alaric was the part-owner, in principle at least, of a decrepit vineyard. Emmy put the bulk of the money in, of course, but when the papers arrived from the lawyers two weeks later, his share of the property had grown from ten to fifty percent.

"Wait a second..."

Emmy shoved a pen into his hand. "Just sign it. I don't have all day."

"You can't give me forty percent of a million-dollar property."

She leaned over to whisper in his ear while the lawyer studiously pretended not to listen. "You can pay me back in orgasms. I'll get my money's worth."

So Alaric had signed. But he hadn't kept up his end of the bargain, and he had no idea what had happened to Casa Malizia. Probably he should have enquired, but he hated to think of those days. Of what he'd lost. And besides, he'd never ask Emmy to sell the place. She'd loved it, and he figured he owed the hundred grand he'd put in as compensation for running out on her. For fucking everything up.

"Why haven't you been there for years?" Beth asked.

"I... I bought it with a previous partner."

Alaric decided to leave out the fact that the partner had been Emmy for now. He got the impression Beth wasn't exactly fond of his ex.

"I see. But you're still friends?"

"It's complicated."

"I'm so sorry."

"Nothing for you to be sorry about. The split was entirely my fault, and things were awkward for a long time. Still are awkward, if I'm honest. And so the estate...just sits there."

Beth gave a high-pitched giggle. "Look at us—the king and queen of tricky break-ups. Speaking of which, did you see Andromeda?"

"Couldn't miss her."

"Sometimes, I wonder if I should have stuck with Piers. Made myself more like her and lived with his cheating."

"You wouldn't have been happy."

"Happy, no, but I understood that life. This...this is, well, sort of scary."

"Don't worry," he murmured as he slid one of her shoes back on, and then the other. "I've got you. Ready to face the world again?"

"Not in the slightest."

He lifted her down from the counter anyway, only to freeze when voices drifted through from the kitchen. Piers. Alaric would recognise that whiny Queen's English anywhere.

"I still can't believe Bethie showed her face."

Another voice, deeper, followed by the suck of a refrigerator opening. "It's her family."

"But she's never really fitted in, has she? Even when we were married, she preferred spending time with that nag to socialising."

"So why'd you marry her?"

Ice clinked in a glass. "Her father's connections, obviously. She may not have used them, but I did."

"And the tits and arse were a bonus, right?"

If someone had said that about Alaric's woman, ex or not, he'd have been taking his teeth home in a plastic baggie, but Piers only laughed.

"You'd think, but she was always something of a cold fish in that department."

"What about Andie?"

"She could suck a golf ball through a garden hose."

The voices faded, and Alaric turned to see tears rolling down Beth's face. Ah, fuck. Yes, he'd sworn off murder, but he was fast rethinking that decision.

"I'll speak to him."

"No!" Beth grabbed Alaric's arm and hung on in a death grip. "Just forget it. Please? I'll skip the cake and go home. Look on the bright side—at least Mother hasn't asked me to serve canapés yet."

Alaric fished the handkerchief out of his top pocket and dabbed at Beth's cheeks. *Don't ruin the mascara.* He needed to keep her presentable.

"No, you won't leave. If you run, they win. You're going to go out there and prove everybody wrong. You're strong, you're beautiful, and you're not a cold fish."

Five minutes with her, and he already knew that. If it hadn't been for his twisted past, for the fact that he was her boss and the balance of power lay with him, at least on the surface, he'd have taken her home and put her to bed with him in it. But life was never so straightforward.

"But he's right. I never sucked him like a hose. I mostly gagged." Beth clapped both hands over her mouth. "Dammit, you didn't need to know that."

He tugged her hands clear and wiped away a smear of red lipstick. "Tonight, you don't need to suck. Just drink a glass of wine..." Or three. "And do what I tell you."

"But—"

"Do you trust me?" he asked softly.

Her eyes unfocused for a moment, and her lips

curved into a tiny smile before she nodded.

"I trust you."

Good. Alaric ran a finger down her spine, then caressed her ass, gritting his teeth when she moaned and leaned into him. This was gonna be hard. *He* was gonna be hard.

"See? If you were a cold fish, you'd have slapped me for that and then stormed out." He trailed his tongue along her jawline. Still no slap. "You're more of a dormant volcano. Hot under the surface, biding your time for the right moment."

"You really think that?"

This time when he slid an arm around her waist, he didn't even pretend to go for decorum. His fingers splayed right across one ass cheek.

"I really do. Let's go."

He only hoped that when she did finally erupt, he didn't get burned.

# CHAPTER 29 - ALARIC

"SO YOU WATCH a lot of movies?" Alaric asked as they walked into the living room. Although "living room" didn't quite do it justice. There must've been sixty people in there, and even with a grand piano in one corner and a string quartet in another, there was plenty of space for the waitstaff to dodge past the groups of partygoers with trays held aloft.

"Too many. Guilty pleasure."

He snagged two glasses from a passing waiter—one of champagne, one of orange juice—and handed the bubbly to Beth.

"Thanks." She drained it without coming up for air. "I needed that."

The waiter headed back the other way and did a double take when Alaric swapped the empty glass for another full one. Did everyone in this place judge?

"Who's your favourite actress, Beth?" Alaric took his hand off her rear for a second to move a stray hair out of her face, then returned it to its new favourite spot. Riding that horse sure gave her a peach of an ass.

"I... My favourite actress?"

"Not Andromeda, clearly."

Beth shuddered. "Andromeda isn't even that good. Her biggest claim to fame is playing a nurse on six episodes of *Casualty*. I guess if I had to pick someone...

I'd have to say Violet Miller. I know she's only done a couple of movies, but in real life, she seems human rather than Hollywood plastic. Or maybe Dana Hansen. She's always so graceful."

"Let's stick with Violet Miller. You saw *Hidden Intent*?"

Beth blushed, her cheeks turning an adorable rosy pink because *Hidden Intent* was *that* kind of movie.

"Yes."

"Tonight, you're Veronica." That was Miller's character, a cop-slash-temptress who always got her man in more ways than one. "Confident, dirty, and sexy as hell. Don't let anyone in here tell you otherwise."

"I-I'm not sure I can do that."

"You can."

"And who are you?"

"I'm just a prop. Is that your sister over there?"

"Priscilla? Yes. And her fiancé. He's basically a younger version of Piers, but she's a social climber who loves to shop, so they're perfect for each other. He's cheated on her already. She knows, and she doesn't care."

"Your family makes mine look normal."

"Please, don't remind me." Beth pasted on a fake smile and held out both hands. "Priscilla! How lovely to see you."

They worked their way around the room, making polite conversation with one conceited idiot after another. Alaric didn't meet a single person he'd want to be friends with, and if he had to spend more than an hour with Andromeda, he'd throw her out of a fucking window. Beth started off stiff, but when he whispered "Veronica" into her ear, she made an effort to relax. By the time they made it back to the piano, she'd downed four glasses of wine, dumped the last empty onto a polished wood sideboard despite a glare from her mother, and pressed a hand against his chest. The other was already underneath his tuxedo jacket, wrapped around his waist.

"That wasn't as bad as I thought," she said with the faintest hint of a slur. "But it's so stuffy in here. Can we get some air?"

A pair of French windows were propped open, leading onto the dimly lit terrace, and Alaric steered her outside. How she was still standing in those shoes, he had no idea.

"Feet okay?"

"A little tired."

There was a chill in the air, so when he lifted her onto the stone balustrade that separated the terrace from the lawn, he wrapped his arms around her too. A good thing, because he noticed Piers glance at them from the corner of the room. The ex had abandoned Andromeda in favour of a group of city-boy types, all standing around with glasses of Scotch as they discussed stock prices or call girls or whatever it was douchebags talked about. For good measure, Alaric leaned down to kiss Beth on the forehead, and she snuggled closer, purring like a cat.

"Better?"

"Mmm-hmm."

"Piers is watching us."

"Who cares? I'm Veronica, and I can do whatever the hell I want."

She grabbed his lapels and pulled him closer, then made him choke when she dropped one hand and palmed his half-hard cock. Fuck.

"Perhaps not that, eh?"

"Why not?"

"Because..." When she squeezed, any reason—let alone a good one—escaped him.

"Because what?"

"Because I'm your boss, and this counts as abuse of power."

"No, no, this isn't abuse. This is fun. I deserve some fun after pretending to be nice to all those people, don't I?"

"Yes, but—"

"But what?"

Two toned legs wrapped around his waist, and her hand left his lapel and hooked behind his neck, dragging his lips down to meet hers. Bloody hell, what had he created?

"This is a bad idea."

"No, it's a great idea. And technically, you're not my boss right now because I don't start until Monday."

When she kissed him, he didn't protest. Couldn't protest. The lipstick had long since worn off, left behind on a succession of wine glasses, and her lips were soft and silky as they pressed against his, her tongue sweet yet insistent as it caressed the seam of his mouth. He yielded. Her breath came in uneven little gasps, and she shuffled forward on the balustrade to grind against his thigh. A monster. He'd created a monster.

Piers was struggling with his conversation now, more focused instead on what was happening outside. Cold fish? Yeah, right. Beth was more responsive than any woman Alaric had ever been with, as evidenced by his cock straining at his fly. But he mustn't take advantage of her.

"Beth..."

"Veronica. Tonight, I'm Veronica."

"I don't want you to hate me in the morning."

Now she looked up at him, so sweet, so innocent, those baby blues surprisingly clear.

"I could never hate you, Alaric. Give this to me. Please?"

He was gonna go to hell for this, but he couldn't stop himself. One hand slid up her smooth thigh, under the folds of black silk, all the way to her centre. He stroked the back of one fingernail lightly over thin panties, barely prepared for the jolt she gave.

"Do it, do it, do it," she whispered.

He took stock of the situation. Most of the action was shielded by bushes. Nobody but the small group of men in the corner could see them at all, and only Piers seemed interested in what was going on. Could he see where Alaric's hand was? Not in graphic detail, but he surely knew.

Did Alaric care? No, he fucking didn't. If Piers wanted Beth, he should have taken better care of her when his ring was on her finger.

"I'm gonna make you come so hard you forget your own name."

Alaric nudged the flimsy scrap of satin aside and found her soaked. If they'd been anywhere but a birthday party, his cock would've been inside her like a cruise fucking missile, but they were where they were, so he had to make do with a finger. A finger that circled and pressed and stroked as she squirmed in his arms, making noises he'd replay in his dreams for the rest of his damn life.

"Almost there?" he murmured.

"Yes. So...close."

He slid his middle finger inside, teasing the orgasm out of her, and as she went over the edge, eyes closed and mouth open, he turned her head to face Piers. The prick had given up on any attempt at conversation, and his expression was a mix of shock and anger. Perfect. Alaric muffled Beth's soft scream with a kiss and held her tight as she melted against him.

"You okay?" he asked.

"I... I... It's never been like that before."

"It should be like that every time." Movement inside caught his eye. "I hate to tell you this, but it looks as if they're about to serve the cake."

"Dammit." She got to her feet, swaying on shaky legs. "I'm not certain I can stand on my own."

Gentleman that he pretended to be, Alaric smoothed her skirt down and then offered his arm, even though he wasn't entirely steady himself. "I've got you. Five more minutes, and we can make a run for it."

"In five minutes, I'll still be staggering."

Step by step, they made their way back into the living room. Someone had lit the candles, all sixty of them, and as they crossed the threshold, a chorus of "Happy Birthday" started. Piers hadn't moved. Nor did he make any attempt to stop staring. What was the matter? Had he never seen a woman come before? For once, Alaric didn't have a smart retort, his brain fried, but Beth helped him out as they passed.

"Close your mouth, Piers. You look like you're about to suck a dick."

Yes, an absolute monster.

## CHAPTER 30 - BETHANY

WHAT WAS THAT pounding? For a moment, I thought someone was at the door, then I realised I had a bell, not a knocker, and the pounding was in my head. How much had I drunk last night?

The evening came back in fits and starts. My father's rudeness towards Alaric. Andromeda's awful laugh. Piers's cruel words. An orgasm on the patio.

Wait.

What?

Bloody hell, what had I done?

I closed my eyes and saw him. Felt him. Heard him. Alaric holding me. Alaric kissing me. Alaric whispering sweet filth in my ear. Alaric's finger inside me. Hot damn. I wanted to believe it was all a dream, but when I rolled out of bed to check, the mess in my knickers suggested otherwise.

My groan filled the bedroom. Drunk me, stupid me, had convinced my hot boss to finger me. At my father's freaking birthday party. In front of my ex-husband! If it hadn't been for Chaucer, I'd have climbed into my car and kept driving until I hit water.

What was I supposed to do? This job was meant to be a fresh start, a way for me to get out of my financial quagmire, and instead, I'd taken the opportunity and left it quivering on a stone balustrade at my parents' house. Thirteen years of school, ten GCSEs, five A levels, a first-class honours degree from Oxford, and I'd still turned out dumber than a box of rocks.

Was there any possibility of salvaging this? What if I apologised profusely and offered to sign up for Alcoholics Anonymous? Or volunteered to work from Judd's home like the previous assistants while wearing a chastity belt? Or... Or...

Holy crap, I caught sight of myself in the mirror. If my behaviour hadn't been enough to send Alaric running for the hills, then my appearance would certainly have done the trick. Streaks of mascara tornadoed around my eyes, my hair stuck out in all directions, and it seemed that at some point, I'd tried to refresh my lipstick and missed my mouth entirely. *Demented clown, reporting for duty.* I was still wearing last night's dress, and when I screwed my eyes shut and thought really hard, I vaguely recalled Alaric carrying me up the stairs and depositing me under the duvet.

What did one buy a man as an apology gift? Aftershave? Too personal. Candy? Too thoughtless. A book? I had no idea what he liked to read. A bottle of wine? *Don't you remember what landed us in this mess in the first place, dumbass?* Okay, so definitely not wine.

*Think logically, Beth.*

First, I'd have a shower. Then I'd go to see Chaucer and use the trip to brainstorm the best way to grovel. When I got back, I'd buy an appropriate gift, and then I'd call Alaric. If he felt anything like I did this morning, he'd want a lie-in, and by the afternoon, hopefully he'd be nice and calm. Yes, that would work.

Or at least, it might have done with any other man.

The first phase of operations went well. I swallowed two paracetamol tablets, shaved my legs, and took a shower. Wrapped my hair in a towel turban. Brushed my teeth. Put on moisturiser. Walked back into my bedroom.

Then screamed.

"What the hell are you doing here?"

Alaric was sitting in the armchair by the window, ankles crossed as he sipped something delicious-smelling from a to-go cup.

"I was worried about you. First you didn't answer your phone, and then you didn't answer the door either."

"I was in the freaking shower!"

He looked me up and down, a slow perusal before he caught himself and snapped his soft brown eyes back to my tired ones.

"Yes, I heard the water, but if I'd gone away and come back again, your coffee would've gotten cold."

"Wait, wait..." I gave my head a shake as if that would somehow dislodge a cotton wool ball or two. "You're in my house. You're in my bedroom. How did you get through the door? *Doors*. There are two doors."

"Peggy let me in the outer door."

"Peggy? Who the hell is Peggy?"

"Your neighbour on the second floor. You don't know her?"

"No, this is London. Nobody talks to each other."

"You should. Peggy's a doll. She's gonna bring you a marmalade cake later this week."

"I can't even... It's too early for this, and my head hurts."

"Have you taken painkillers?"

"They're no match for you." I was on the verge of an Alaric-induced migraine. "What about the inner door? It was locked. I'm sure it was locked."

"Your lock's a piece of crap. Yeah, that's got to go. And you need a door chain. I'll send Ravi over."

"No. No, no, no, no, *no*. It's not even nine o'clock. I'm wearing a towel. I can't deal with this right now."

"Want me to pick up breakfast?"

"I feel sick."

"Hangover?"

"No. Yes. Maybe. I don't know. I don't know anything anymore."

Except what an utter fool I'd made out of myself last night. That was pretty clear. And now Alaric was sitting in front of me, calm and unruffled, and how did he look so good anyway? No bloodshot eyes, no dark circles, and he'd even managed to coordinate his navy-blue cashmere V-neck with his loafers.

I sank onto the bed, head in my hands.

"I didn't know whether you took cream or not, so I got your coffee black."

"Coffee? I can't even think about coffee."

"You need to stay hydrated."

"At this precise moment, withering away and dying seems like an attractive option. How can you act so normal? Do you not remember anything about last night?"

"I do." Alaric's tone went from kind to serious. "And I'm sorry. So, so sorry, Beth. I let things go further than they should have, and I took advantage of you, and... All I can do is apologise and promise that it won't happen again."

"What? *You* took advantage of *me*? I was the one who got drunk and...and...you know. In front of my freaking ex. Do you think Piers saw us? Did he realise what we were doing?"

"You were in his line of sight as you came. He saw your face."

"I'm not sure that would've helped—I faked it every single time with him, so he has no clue what a real orgasm looks like." Dammit all to hell, what was I even saying? "Could you just forget you heard that part?"

"Forget? Not exactly, but I can bury it deep." Now it was Alaric's turn to look horrified. "That came out wrong. It wasn't meant to be an innuendo, I swear."

"Listen to us. Just listen to us. This must be the most embarrassing, cringeworthy start to a new job ever. Uh, do I still have a job?"

"I was worried you'd quit before you even started."

"I need the money."

"Right." He got to his feet, five inches taller than me now that my Louboutins were lined up neatly in front of the wardrobe. How had they got to that spot? Had *he* put them there? "I should go. Now that I know you're okay."

And because I was still wearing a flipping towel. I tugged the bottom edge towards my knees and squeezed my thighs together tighter, not that it did much to curb the ache between them.

"So, uh, where should I go tomorrow morning? What time do I start? Is there a dress code?"

"Do you remember where Judd's place is? I pointed it out in passing, but..."

"I remember."

"You'd better meet him. Wear a nun's habit or a

burka."

"And what if I don't own either of those?"

"Jeans. Flat shoes. A sweater that buttons right up to your chin."

"Is Judd really that much of a womaniser?"

"For some unknown reason, they seem to find him irresistible."

Yet it had been Alaric who made me melt yesterday. And not just me. I'd seen the way the other women in the room gazed at him. Andromeda had practically rolled out her tongue like a drool-covered red carpet.

"I'll resist him."

"You haven't met him yet."

"Do you trust me?"

Alaric had asked the same question last night, before he delivered in the most spectacular way possible. And I hadn't lied in my answer. I did trust him. I might have only met him a few days ago, but he... I... I couldn't explain it. Alaric was a rock, an anchor, and he held me steady. And also frustrated the crap out of me.

He nodded. Reached a hand towards me, then realised what he was doing and hastily shoved it into his pocket.

"I trust you."

"Then know that I'm not interested in being Judd's latest plaything. From tomorrow, I'll be the consummate professional."

Alaric gave a faint smile. "I should let you get dressed. Are you still okay to travel this week?"

"I'll start packing today. And I also need to clean the flat and ride Chaucer." And get Alaric's testosterone away from me so I could think straight. "So..."

"In that case, I'll, er, leave you to it."

"Thanks for the coffee."

He turned to look over his shoulder as he exited my bedroom. Did he catch me staring at his backside? I sincerely hoped not.

"Any time, Beth. Any time."

# CHAPTER 31 - ALARIC

"WHERE ARE YOU?" Alaric asked, his phone pressed to his ear. Albany House was such a maze of rooms that it was easier to call Emmy than hunt for her.

"Second floor—well, third if you're being American today—in what was once the DVD library."

Alaric took the stairs two at a time, trying to remember whether he had to turn left or right when he got to the top. He needed a map. After one mistake which landed him in an empty bedroom, he heard voices from the other side of a door.

"You need to relax."

"Then stop using me as a fucking pincushion."

Dare he look? He pushed open the door and found Emmy face down on a massage table with a tiny towel covering her ass and a row of acupuncture needles sticking out of the muscles on either side of her spine. A small Chinese woman glared at him as he approached.

"*Bonjour*," Emmy said, her voice muffled since her face was stuffed into a padded hole.

"*Bonjour. Ça va?*" He asked how she was out of politeness.

"*À quoi ça ressemble?*"

How did it look? Well, he didn't envy her.

"*Plutôt vous que moi. Pourquoi parle-t-on Français?*"

*"Parce que Ling ne parle pas Français."*

Ah, they were speaking French because Ling didn't. Ling, presumably, was the sadist with the needles, and Emmy didn't want her listening in on the conversation. Since Emmy wouldn't allow anyone she'd decided not to trust into her house, that must mean that Ling was new and the jury was still out on her loyalty.

"Bad back?" Alaric asked, sticking with French.

"I tweaked it jumping out of that house the other day. Ling's part of Bradley's 'new and improved' well-being program."

"It can't be both new and improved."

"You know that, I know that..."

"What happened to all the DVDs?"

"Bradley edited the collection, moved half of them to the snug on the next floor, and repurposed the rest as coasters. He took some of those to the office, and there were a few raised eyebrows when Zander flipped one over and found that copy of *Horny Hungarian Hookers* you got me for a Valentine's joke. Anyhow, shall we get down to business?"

With Emmy staring at the floor, Alaric had the opportunity to take a good look at his ex. The Hungarian hookers hadn't been a patch on her. Still weren't. Emmy had been fit before, muscular and athletic, but she'd bulked up just a little more. Every part of her was sculpted, and either she'd been somewhere hotter than England or Bradley's program included spray-tanning. Alaric suspected the latter. Emmy never had time to sunbathe.

Was that scar on her arm new? Yes. She always got the bigger ones smoothed out, so either she considered the mark too small to bother about or she hadn't gotten around to visiting her surgeon yet. Emmy had always cited vanity for the retouches, but Alaric knew that wasn't it. She just didn't like to let on that she might have chinks in her armour.

"Business...yes. Stéphane Hegler. Do you want to go first or shall I?"

"I might as well. Mack's had a dig around, and—"

Emmy didn't get a chance to finish before Ling interrupted.

"You tense." She pointed at a second massage table, the twin of Emmy's. "Lie down."

Alaric held up his hands. "No, I'm fine. Really."

"You hunch shoulders. Shirt off."

Emmy started cackling. "It's pointless arguing. Believe me, I've tried."

"How about I come back later?"

"Don't be a pussy."

"Tell me Black isn't here? Because if he walks in and finds me half-naked..."

"Relax, he's still in Belize. I half expected him to come steaming back, but common sense seems to have prevailed for once."

Before, the man had half-heartedly attempted to keep his jealousy under wraps, but now that he and Emmy were an item, he didn't bother to hide it. Black staked his claim at every possible opportunity, even though there was no need. Now that the pair of them no longer had an open marriage, Alaric wouldn't touch her.

Ling was standing with her arms folded, waiting, and Alaric sighed and peeled off his sweater. Emmy turned her head to look at him, resting it sideways on her folded arms.

"Don't be fooled by Ling's size. She's vicious with those thumbs." *Now* she told him. "She got her hands on Black once, and the next time Bradley scheduled him a session, he suddenly remembered he had to do an Iron Man and flew to Hawaii."

"Why haven't you tied concrete blocks to her feet and dropped her into the Thames?"

"Because she's also good. You'll feel like magic tomorrow. Now, where were we? Hegler. Mack's been digging, and we've got three possibles. Lucky it was an unusual name. One's an art dealer working out of the free port in Geneva. The second is an aide to Senator Carnes. Well, ex-Senator seeing as he resigned two months ago. And the third's a fund manager in New York. I'm thinking the free-port guy's the best possibility. Those places are stuffed full of stolen loot."

Ordinarily, Alaric would've agreed with her. A free port, one of those fortresses that sprang up around seaports and airports to facilitate the sale and storage of goods without hefty tax penalties, would be the perfect place to hide *Red After Dark*. But not this time.

Alaric winced as Ling dug in. "It's Carnes."

"How do you know?"

There was no accusation that he might be wrong, just curiosity.

"Two reasons. First, I have the log showing every private jet that took off from Heathrow last Wednesday."

"Nice. Mack's still trying to get hold of that."

"You can tell her to stop. Naz had a backdoor."

"Noted. So, who was on the list?"

"Doug Jenks. Multimillionaire philanthropist and long-time friend of Carnes."

"That could be a coincidence. Doesn't he have business interests over here?"

"Yes, and if it had been *Emerald* we were hunting, I'd say the same thing. But it's not. It's *Red After Dark*. Remember that anonymous quarter-million-dollar reward a kind-hearted donor offered for the painting's return?"

"Shit. Carnes?"

The Becker Museum had offered fifty thousand bucks per stolen piece, but then Carnes came along and blew their bounty out of the water. Said he'd seen the painting once and it spoke to him.

"Got it in one. And the museum director told me Carnes had asked to buy *Red* on several occasions, but they always turned him down."

"Reckon he was involved in the original theft? That he was just covering his tracks with the reward?"

A good question, but Alaric had spoken to the man right after the heist. His devastation at the loss had certainly seemed genuine. Plus he had his reputation to protect, not to mention a senate seat. And why take all the other paintings? As a smokescreen, surely that was overkill? But thirteen years on... If *Red After Dark* had come up on the black market, could Alaric see Carnes buying it? Possibly.

"No, I don't think he was involved originally. But at least I know where I need to head next. He lives in Kentucky, right?"

"Not so fast. You can't just go steaming in there. We need a plan. Any idea why he quit the senate?"

"The official line is that he resigned to 'spend time with his family.' Usually, that means there was a mistress involved somewhere and the wife got pissed, but I understand his wife passed away several years ago."

"I'll ask James."

By James, Emmy meant President James Harrison, another of her exes, although their fling had ended long before he landed the top job. And they'd been damn careful about their liaison. Outside of Emmy and Black's inner circle, few people knew their dirty little secret.

Emmy and James had stayed friends, at least from her point of view. If you caught Harrison watching her in an unguarded moment and knew what you were looking for, it was clear his feelings still ran deeper than hers. And if anyone was going to know what was going on with Carnes, it was Harrison. It was his job to stay informed. Although Harrison had run as an independent and Carnes was a Republican, they shared the same views in a number of areas, plus Carnes had been chair of the Crime and Terrorism Subcommittee, so he and the president had worked closely on occasion.

Ling did something with her elbows that left Alaric gasping for breath and earned a chuckle from Emmy. Next time, he'd strongly consider the triathlon.

"So I'll tread carefully," he choked out.

"Why now?"

"What do you mean?"

"Why did the painting find its way to Carnes now? It's been thirteen years since the theft. I just don't get it."

"The heat's died down, and Carnes has taken a step back from the public eye," Alaric said. "But how he might have found out it was for sale, I have no idea."

"This whole case gets stranger and stranger every time we dig into it."

"I keep telling you—*Emerald*'s cursed, and it seems it's contagious."

"Have you been spending time with Bradley's spiritual advisor? She told me my Viper was cursed when the engine wouldn't start, but it turned out Nate had just removed the fuse from the fuel pump as a joke."

Nate was one of her business partners, and that sounded like exactly the kind of stunt he'd pull.

"But—"

"*Emerald*'s a painting. It's not fucking cursed. Do you need a ride to the US? We have to take Lenny to rehab this afternoon, but once he's settled, I'll be flying to Virginia with Sky. Probably Tuesday."

"How is Sky?"

"Stubborn. Nosy. Always hungry. Yeah, we're getting on okay. I'm going parkour training with her tomorrow. Apparently, one of her friends thinks I'm a con artist and he's worried about her coming with me, so I figured I'd go and set his mind at rest."

"A ride would be good if there's room for Bethany too. I hired her to replace Barbara."

"Judd...slept with Barbara? I thought she was, like, sixty?"

"He accidentally exposed himself."

"Casanova should come with a warning. I don't know whether to be pleased or insulted that he's always kept his dick in his pants around me."

Emmy had only met Ravi once and never crossed paths with Naz, but she'd experienced Judd's dubious charms before Alaric did. They'd worked together during Judd's days at MI6, and he described her as "not just a ball-breaker; she'll squeeze your nuts in a vice, then run the soggy remains through a mincer." Fairly accurate if she happened to dislike a man.

"You make him nervous."

"Good. And going back to your question, yes, there's space for Bethany on the plane. Are you sure she's up to the task?"

"I hope so, and I felt bad after we essentially got her fired."

He'd given Emmy an update on Friday evening, leaving out the rescue from Chaucer's stable. She didn't need to know that part.

"Same. She seems okay, and it's not her fault Pemberton turned out to be morally corrupt. Speaking of Pemberton, are we going to have a word?"

"Let's follow up on the Carnes angle first. If Pemberton's handling stolen goods on a regular basis as Beth seems to think, I'd rather save him for the authorities. The Metropolitan Police work with the FBI on occasion. Who knows how many leads he'd be able to give them if they applied enough pressure?"

"You'd hand him over to the people who screwed you?"

"The FBI fired me. The jury's out on whether they screwed me. They don't know where the money went either, and I'm still the logical suspect."

Alaric had watched at the office as the team packed the briefcase containing a million bucks in hundred-dollar bills and nine million in diamonds. Each serial number had been recorded, and the rocks came straight from a safe in the evidence room. Everything had been genuine. After Alaric's boss had selected a combination and locked the briefcase, he'd officially transferred it into Alaric's custody with a warning: "Lose this, lose your damn job."

How prescient.

The briefcase had only been out of Alaric's sight four times between the handover at FBI headquarters and the moment it was opened by Dyson. The first time had been in the office. He'd left it next to his desk while he went to the john, and nobody had gone in or out of the room during that time. Not only had the half-dozen colleagues seated at nearby desks attested to that fact, but a security camera had backed them up.

The second time was when he'd stopped for gas en route to the Riverley estate. Rather than draw attention to his cargo by carrying it to the kiosk, he'd left it locked in the trunk. The car had stayed in his sight until a panel truck parked next to it in the middle of the transaction, blocking the view of the security camera as well. A minute or two, that's all it had been, and Alaric had kept the car key in his hand for the duration.

The third time? That had been at Little Riverley, Emmy's home. With the house secured by a system that rivalled Fort Knox, he'd left the case downstairs in the living room when things got heated on the couch and they moved to the bedroom. They'd been the only people in the house that night, and every door and window was alarmed. The logs showed nobody had snuck in, and the system had been armed for his entire stay. Plus, as if that wasn't secure enough, the whole of the Riverley estate was wired with cameras and motion detectors, and as well as having regular guard patrols, two men monitored the place twenty-four seven from the gatehouse. They'd seen no one, and the only nocturnal visitors to trip the sensors that night had been deer and a low-flying owl. The guards themselves had checked in regularly with the control room at Blackwood's headquarters, none of them knew about the briefcase, and Emmy had vouched for her team. And her husband. When Alaric mooted the possibility that Black had been involved, she'd dismissed the idea completely. Apparently, he had an alibi. And no matter how much Alaric would have liked to get the asshole out of the picture, he trusted Emmy's judgement. At that point, she was the *only* person he'd trusted.

Did he ever suspect her? No. While she'd had the opportunity, she didn't have a motive. Alaric didn't know her exact net worth, but he'd estimated it was at least ten times the pay-off amount, so why would she risk everything with petty theft? Hell, afterwards she'd offered to give him the ten million bucks if it would help. But by that point, his reputation was already in the toilet, and besides, it was his mess, not hers.

The last time the briefcase had been out of sight was as he'd climbed onto the scallop boat. Dyson's men had hauled it over the rail on a rope as Alaric climbed the ladder and tried not to puke. Again, the time window had been short, but could they have made the switch? Dyson was one of the few people who knew the contents, because he'd specified it. The sticking point was the briefcase itself. It had disappeared along with Dyson so they couldn't be certain it was the same one, but it had opened with the right combination, and from what Alaric remembered, it had looked identical.

So, where had the pay-off gone? He had no idea, and neither did the FBI after a two-month investigation involving over fifty agents, plus another fifteen from

Blackwood. The FBI had wanted to charge him, but the lack of evidence either way meant they couldn't have made it stick. So they mothballed the case. Let him off with a promise that he'd never work for a US government agency again.

Which was why he was currently getting his back pummelled by a woman with thumbs of steel and seemingly a grudge against all men. If the massage thing didn't work out, she'd excel as a dominatrix.

"You're still the *only* suspect," Emmy pointed out.

"Thanks for reminding me. But in answer to your question, most of the old Art Crime Team members have moved on, and even if one of the remaining few is dirty, they're probably doing sweet fuck all while they count their diamonds and wait for retirement. The new agents will follow a tip, and people deserve to get their paintings back."

"You're not interested in finding them yourself?"

"Not anymore. I enjoyed the work back then, but now? I've moved on with Sirius. I prefer being my own boss, and even though the income's sporadic, I'm making a hell of a lot more than I did at the Bureau."

Emmy grinned. "Finally. Welcome to the private sector."

"But I still want to find that damn painting. *Paintings*. Now I want *Red* back too."

"Then I guess we'll be paying a visit to Mr. Carnes later on this week."

"You'll come?"

"That asshole Dyson shot at me too. Do you need somewhere to stay in the US until you sort out a place? I've got spare bedrooms."

"Black would be just thrilled about that."

"Black needs to learn to get over himself. If you want some distance, the guest house out the back's empty."

"I can't leave Beth on her own. I'm supposed to be training her in the necessities. Usually, Judd does it, but his track record with staff retention needs work."

"There are three bedrooms in the guest house. Bring who you want."

"In that case, thanks."

Emmy's voice softened, as did her expression. "My motives aren't entirely altruistic. I've missed having you around. Just to talk to, you know?"

"Missed you too, Cinders." Alaric reached across and so did Emmy, and he gave her hand a squeeze. Yes, it was good to be at least partially back in the fold, so to speak. "I've been wondering... What happened to Casa Malizia? Did you sell it?"

"Without your agreement? No. We should get the first commercial harvest this year. Wine and olive oil." She paused, biting her lip. "When you got shafted by the FBI and then your parents, I figured you'd need an income, so I had the place replanted. Twenty hectares of grapes and five of olive trees."

Fuck. That was why he'd fallen in love with Emmy. Not because of her looks or her money or even her brain, but for the heart she kept hidden from most of the world.

"You did all that for me?"

"*I* don't abandon the people I care about."

Her words knifed straight through his chest. "I deserved that."

"Yes, you did."

"What about the house?"

"When you didn't come back, I let nature take its course. I hear the place is still standing, more or less."

A bit like their relationship. Rotten, ruined, but not quite crumbled into the ground completely. Emmy had done the hard work so far. Now it was down to Alaric to shore up the foundations. Somehow.

"Cinders, I'm sorry. Sorry I broke, sorry I ran, sorry I wasn't good enough for you."

"I survived. I always will. We were both broken, but I had Black to pick up my pieces. As time went on, I only hoped you had someone to pick up yours."

A vision of Beth popped into Alaric's head, her lips parted as she moaned out her orgasm. Fuck. She wasn't there to pick up his pieces. He was meant to be picking up hers.

"The first couple of years were tough, but founding Sirius helped. Gave me a purpose again. Now we just have to make it a success."

"I'll do everything I can to help, but Alaric?"

"Yes?"

"Don't you fucking dare hurt me like that again."

Yes, he'd forgotten how mercurial Emmy could be. "I won't, Cinders. I promise I won't."

Abruptly, she sat up, her back to Alaric, the towel slipping from her ass, and switched from French back to English.

"Ling, get these bloody needles out of me. I have a meeting."

Ah, the old meeting excuse. Emmy still didn't tolerate emotion well, it seemed.

"Talk to you later, Cinders. I'll show myself out."

# CHAPTER 32 - SKY

TWO DAYS UNTIL my new life began. Inside, I was nervous as hell, but Emmy told me never to show fear. She certainly didn't.

"Are you ready?" she shouted through the bedroom door. "We need to go."

"Just coming."

I'd sat down with Lenny yesterday and explained where he was going—to the Abbey Clinic. At first, I thought he might refuse, might cause a scene in the hospital, but then he'd slumped back onto the pillows and mumbled something about it being "now or never."

I checked my reflection in the mirror. How did I look? Like the sister of someone who could afford the ten-grand-a-month prices? Smart clothes made me uncomfortable, but Emmy was teaching me about the need to fit in. Last night, we'd gone out for dinner at a fancy restaurant and I wore a dress. A freaking dress! But she was right—people looked at me differently. Treated me differently.

And over a meal of twiddly food I couldn't pronounce, Emmy had started my education. First, she'd had me check out the room. *Discreetly*. Where were my exits? Did I have cover if somebody started shooting? What were the walls made from? Would a bullet ricochet? Were there cameras? Smoke detectors?

A sprinkler system? The ceiling...solid or dropped? How many windows? Were they at street level? If there was a sniper, where would he hide? Or she—don't be sexist. Then she started on the people. The staff first. Did any of them look like they didn't belong? Were they smooth or klutzy? Was it the kind of establishment that paid well? People with money were harder to bribe. What about the patrons? Could I see the couple in the corner? That woman was *not* his wife. The two businessmen—what did the one with the blue tie just pass under the table? And so it went on. For a girl used to grabbing a bargain bucket from The Chicken Hut, it sure had been an eye-opener.

Today, I put on a pair of black slacks and cinched the waist in with a belt. Emmy was the same height as me but heavier, although the extra weight was all muscle. I was making do with her clothes until Bradley bought me my own. And the best part? We had the same size feet, and she must've had three thousand pairs of shoes. Her expensive stilettos were far more comfortable than the cheap ones I owned, plus they looked better too. I finished up with a simple grey silk shell and a low ponytail, already a different girl to the person I'd been last week, and opened the door.

"About bloody time," Emmy grumbled.

"I feel a hundred years old."

"Yeah, well, you look appropriate. Apart from the chewing gum—get rid of that before we go."

"Yes, Mum."

"Stop being such a brat."

Down in the parking garage, I gazed wistfully at the Aston Martin, but we couldn't take that because it didn't have enough seats. I was about to climb into the front of the Land Rover that had appeared from somewhere when the roller shutter slowly began to open. Who was coming in from the outside?

Oh. Bethany, on foot. It was kind of nice that Emmy had lent her a parking space after she lost hers. Gave me hope that Emmy wasn't as much of a hard-nosed bitch as she made out.

Bethany stared for a moment as she tried to work out who I was, and I didn't bother to hide my smirk when she finally worked it out. *Yeah, love, the street girl can do posh.*

"Uh, hello." She held out her keys. "I just came to, uh..."

Emmy gave her an encouraging smile. "Have at it. We're on the way out ourselves. How are you settling in with your new job?"

"Well, I haven't actually started yet. Not until tomorrow."

"Have you met everyone?"

"Not Judd or Naz, although I've heard a lot about them. Mostly Judd, actually." She sucked in a breath. "I'm sure I'll learn to cope with him. And I met Ravi yesterday, but not for work. It was Alaric's daughter's birthday, so we went to one of those escape rooms and then had lunch."

Emmy stiffened. Just slightly, but I was sure I hadn't imagined it.

"Alaric's daughter...right. How old is she now? I lose track."

"Fifteen. And so incredibly smart, just like her father."

"Just like her father. Of course. Crazy how fast they grow up, isn't it? One moment, they're not there at all, and suddenly... Poof, they're teenagers."

"I don't have children of my own, but that's the way it was with my cousin's kids. I bought the wrong birthday card once—eleven instead of twelve—and Mother's never let me live it down."

"Funny what's important to some people." Emmy glanced at her watch. "Sorry, but we need to go."

Bethany gave a cutesy little wave. "See you later. And thanks so much for letting me park here."

The whole car rattled as Emmy slammed the door. What was she so pissed about? My lateness? It was only five minutes.

"What did the door ever do to you?"

"Put your seat belt on."

"Yes, M—"

"Don't say it," she growled.

I clicked the buckle into place just in time as she gunned it towards the barely open gates, clearing each side with less than an inch to spare, then screwed my eyes shut as she skidded out onto the street right in front of a truck. Bloody hell. Then and there, I swore I'd never be late again.

Lenny looked thoroughly miserable when we left him on the third floor of the Abbey Clinic, but since he had a private room nicer than any place either of us had ever lived in, Albany House excepted, I didn't feel too sorry for him. That and he was in the best place to help him recover.

"We discourage contact between patients and their families for the first two weeks," the nurse told us. "We find it can have an unsettling effect, and we prefer our guests to focus on their therapy sessions."

"But you'll call if there are any problems?" I asked.

"Most definitely. And you're welcome to speak to a member of staff if you have concerns—any time, day or night."

This was what I'd wanted—a future for Lenny. But as I followed Emmy towards the elevator at the end of the hallway, I couldn't help the nervousness that fluttered in my belly because I'd sold my soul to the she-devil to get him here. Now I had to perform. So far, Emmy hadn't asked much of me, just a gym session yesterday in between her commitments at the office, and I knew it was the calm before the storm. The real test would begin on Wednesday once we touched down in America. Until today, I'd never even had a passport, but one had arrived by courier this morning with my name and photo but a date of birth two months before my real birthday. I was officially an adult now, and even though I'd been fending for myself and Lenny for years, it still felt like a big step to take. Plus I'd been cheated out of a birthday cake.

The sliding doors closed, and Emmy stared straight ahead. I'd learned she didn't much care for elevators. Earlier, she'd wanted to take the stairs, but the orderly wagged a finger and informed us they were for emergency use only. They needed to keep track of the patients, you see.

The elevator stopped on the second floor, and a nurse got in with a blonde wearing a light-blue tracksuit. I didn't pay much attention until the woman leaned forward to peer at Emmy, getting right into her space. Emmy didn't flinch. I wouldn't have expected her to.

"Do I know you?" the blonde asked.

Emmy gave the faintest shake of her head. "No, you don't."

"Are you sure?"

"Positive."

"But you look familiar. Were you a guest here?"

The nurse gave the woman's arm a light tug. "Julie, you mustn't ask questions like that."

"Why? I'm sure I've met her before."

The door opened on the first floor, and the nurse shepherded Julie out. Emmy's face was blank, but the set of her jaw gave away her clenched teeth.

"Bitch," she murmured when the pair were out of earshot, "you don't have the first fucking clue who I am."

The doors closed with a quiet swoosh.

"*Do* you know her?" I asked.

"Not anymore, and every day, I'm grateful for that."

Emmy folded her arms, and I let the subject drop. Whoever Julie was, Emmy clearly didn't like her, and I didn't want to upset my new boss further by pushing the matter. But maybe I'd ask Lenny later on. My curiosity had been piqued, and he might be able to find out more about the one woman I'd seen ruffle Emmy.

## CHAPTER 33 - EMMY

"WHAT DID THAT punching bag ever do to you?" Black asked, his smooth tones dripping from hidden speakers. It was my fault the speakers were there. I'd ignored a phone call from Nate once, so he'd wired the whole damn house for sound.

"Are you spying on me again?"

"You didn't answer your phone."

"I can't hear it over the music."

"Then turn the music down. People need to be able to contact you."

The sound faded and the music video on the flat-screen disappeared, replaced by Black's impassive face. He hadn't shaved since he got back to the US. Didn't seem to have showered either judging by the streaks of dirt.

"You obviously can contact me, so what's the problem?"

"Why don't you tell me?"

"I'm not in the mood to talk."

"Which brings us back to my first question."

"How was Belize?"

I gave the punchbag a solid kick, and another inch of seam split. Sand trickled out onto the gym mats.

"Stop changing the subject. Does your nose still hurt? Is that what you're pissed about?"

"Not really. I hired the girl who broke it, by the way. She's a pain in the ass."

"You what?"

"Her name's Sky. She starts on Wednesday."

"Rewind. Can we go from the top?"

"Sure. You already know the first part. Found painting. Got nose broken. Lost painting. Then Sky turned up with a lead, her brother took an overdose and died, we resuscitated him, and I offered her a job."

"'We' being...?"

"Me and Alaric."

"Where *is* Alaric?"

The way Black asked the question, I knew he'd already overridden the security system and checked all the cameras in the entire house.

"Who the fuck knows? Probably with his daughter. Did you know he had a daughter? Because I sure as hell didn't."

Black raised one eyebrow a millimetre, which was about as expressive as he got.

"He met someone while he was away? He was gone for over seven years, Diamond. It's not beyond the realms of possibility."

"She's fifteen."

"Oh."

"Exactly. Oh. And I only found out because his new PA, who, by the way, he met less than a week ago, let it slip by accident. He told her and not me. I can deal with most things, but when the people close to me lie..."

"Technically, he didn't lie. He just didn't tell you he had a kid."

"A lie by omission is still a fucking lie, Black. And the fact that Alaric was a father the whole time we were dating is a pretty big bloody deal."

"You've made no secret of the fact you don't want to be a mother. Maybe he was worried about your reaction?"

"Why are you defending him? You don't even *like* him."

Black sighed. "I just hate seeing you upset. Do you want me to find out more about this child?"

"No. I want to find this damn painting—paintings, plural, now that we've lost another one—and get closure on the past. I offered the guest house to Alaric before Bethany mentioned his sprog, so that should be fun next week."

"Want me to un-offer it?"

Did I? It was tempting, but there was enough animosity between them as it was.

"No, I'll suck it up."

Black leaned back in his chair. I could see from the edge of the framed etching on the wall—a rather grim Goya he'd picked up in a private sale a decade ago—that he was in our shared study at Riverley Hall.

"So *that's* why you're upset?"

"Partly."

A piece of the tape on my hand started to come unstuck, and I tore at it with my teeth. Yeah, I probably should've worn gloves, but sometimes, I needed pain on the outside to distract from the pain on the inside.

"Partly?"

"As part of the deal with Sky, I said I'd pay for rehab for her brother. Who isn't her real brother, and is an absolute dick. But she cares for him, and I wanted her to take the job, so there we go. Anyhow, Bradley found a place to put him. The best in London, apparently. The Abbey Clinic. Perhaps you've heard of it?"

"Shit." Yup, Black knew exactly who I'd run into there. "What did she say?"

"Not much. She thought she might have seen me someplace before, but she just...couldn't...quite...think where."

And quite frankly, I wasn't sure what was worse— that my own mother hadn't recognised me, or the prospect of her suddenly realising I was the offspring she'd basically forgotten existed twenty years ago and wanting to talk about all the shit she'd put me through. Was it any wonder I didn't want to be a parent with Julie Emerson as my role model? Not really, but I still felt crappy about it because even though Black assured me that he respected my decision, I knew he liked the idea of being a father.

For the best part of two decades, I'd assumed Julie was dead—she'd taken every drug she could get her hands on back in the day—but Black had mentioned a few years ago that she was still breathing. I hadn't wanted to talk to her when I found out. I still didn't. Quite frankly, I'd rather drop-kick her off a skyscraper than rehash the past.

"Diamond, I'm sorry. Sorry she hurt you then and sorry she hurt you now. Do you want me to cut her off? I've considered it before, but...she's your mother."

Honestly? She deserved it, but if I had her tossed out on the street, that would make me as bad as her.

"Leave things as they are. But I don't ever want to set eyes on her again."

"Noted. You mentioned Sky's starting on Wednesday—does that mean you're coming home?"

I nodded, then followed up with, "I miss you." Which only reminded me that I'd said something remarkably similar to Alaric not six hours ago, and now I wished I could take the words back. "This whole week's been a pile of shit. I'm beginning to think Alaric's right and *Emerald is* cursed."

"It's an inanimate object, Diamond. It can't be fucking cursed."

Yes, I'd said that too.

"Whatever. I need gin and chocolate."

"No, you need orange juice and a salad."

I threw my towel over the screen and put my fingers in my ears. "This conversation is over."

## CHAPTER 34 - BETHANY

SEVEN MISSED CALLS. Oops. That'd teach me to turn my phone onto silent. I'd completely forgotten until I got to the yard and couldn't find either Chaucer or Pinkey. After a brief search, I stumbled across Pinkey in the hay barn, and Chaucer was hiding behind a clump of trees in the field, no doubt feeling work-shy.

I scanned down the list—four of the missed calls had been from Alaric, one came from an unknown number, my father had tried to get hold of me, and what did Gemma want? I tried voicemail and found four messages, all from today, starting at seven a.m.

*Beth, it's Alaric. Shit, I'm sorry about last night. Not sorry I went to the party, but things shouldn't have happened the way they did. Can we talk?*

That was followed by another message at nine.

*It's Alaric again. I'm outside your door. Are you okay? Can you call me? Five minutes, and I'm coming up to check you're okay.*

Well, I already knew how that turned out. He'd overstepped boundaries, but it also felt strangely comforting to have somebody looking out for me. He cared. Even though we were colleagues and nothing more, he cared. I forwarded to the next message.

*Good morning, madam. A thousand apologies—good afternoon. My name's Phillip, and I'm calling from Global Wealth Investors with a limited time offer...*

Delete.

*Bethie, I need to speak to you. Call me.*

Short and not so sweet, as always. I hated calling my father. It only meant another lecture or possibly a browbeating. I'd need to psych myself up for that one.

*Bethany? It's Gemma. From the gallery? You always said I could call you if I needed to talk, and...I... It's probably me being silly, but I just feel really uncomfortable, and— Shit, he's coming. I'll call you back.*

All the hairs on the nape of my neck prickled. Not so much from Gemma's words, which were worryingly vague, but from their tone. Gemma had sounded...not scared, exactly, but definitely nervous. When had she called? Two hours ago, according to the log. I tried to ring her, but it went straight to voicemail, her cheerful greeting a sharp contrast to the message she'd left earlier.

"Hey, it's Beth. Sorry I missed your call. I'm about to ride Chaucer, but I'll be around all afternoon if you want to talk. This evening too. Come over for dinner if you like."

Chaucer spooked at a squirrel as we trotted through the woods, but apart from that, he was reasonably well-behaved. As I rode, it struck me that this would be the last time I saw him for a month, possibly two months depending on how long I needed to spend in America. I'd never been away from him for so long, but I had to do this for our future. If I didn't take this job, who knew when another opportunity would come along, let alone one that paid double my previous salary.

"Don't be naughty for Pinkey," I told him. "And she's under strict instructions not to give you too many treats."

He tossed his head in response, which showed what he thought of those ideas.

I'd hoped Gemma might try to phone while I was out, but even after I'd untacked and given Chaucer his tea, my phone remained silent. I dialled again. Still no answer.

Was she okay? Should I call someone? I'd never met any of her family, which meant I'd need to speak to Henrietta or the police. Neither prospect appealed. Was I overreacting? After all, I'd gone radio silent for the entire morning and part of the afternoon today, and there I was, absolutely fine.

To hedge my bets, I tapped out a text message. Maybe she'd notice the screen light up?

*Me: Hi, I'll be home soon if you want to catch up. Let me know either way?*

When Gemma hadn't replied by the time I reached Chiswick, I began to worry more. Perhaps she was busy, out with friends, having a great time and just too busy to check her phone. Or perhaps she...wasn't. I might not have known how to contact her family, but I did have her address. She'd been off sick for a few days soon after I started at the gallery, and I'd got the details from Hugo so I could send a Get Well Soon card from all of us. We'd gone halves—Henrietta said it was a waste of time and refused to chip in, but I liked to think well-wishes cheered people up.

Gemma lived in North Acton. It wasn't the nicest of areas, but if I turned around now and the traffic gods were kind, I could be there in half an hour. Maybe she'd be at home watching Netflix? If she was, I could stop worrying, and I might actually get some sleep tonight.

Sod it. I'd go.

Anslow Place turned out to be a fifties-era concrete box, four storeys of stained grey walls, tiny windows, and terrible curtains without a balcony in sight. I wedged my car in between a skip and a BMW with no wheels on the other side of the street and prayed it would still be there when I got back. And also that I didn't get murdered. Logically, I understood that many, many people survived living in Acton every day, but my parents had spent my entire childhood warning me that anyone who didn't look like us and talk like us was bad news, and although I was trying to re-educate myself, sometimes my baser instincts took over. I hated myself for that.

I'd worried about getting into Gemma's building if she didn't answer the intercom because even if I met a Peggy, what on earth would I say to her? But then a lovely chap with dreadlocks held the outer door open and waved me through.

"The lift's dodgy, love. Best to take the stairs."

"Uh, thank you."

It turned out the place wasn't as unpleasant inside

as I'd imagined, and I hurried up to the second floor, my footsteps echoing in the stairwell as my riding boots clomped on the tile. Now that I was out of my car, which still reeked of Shimmer even though I'd left the windows down overnight in Emmy's garage, I realised I smelled a little too much like Chaucer for comfort. Perhaps I should have taken a shower first? Stinking out Gemma's flat would hardly endear me, would it?

But I needn't have worried, at least about the eau de cheval. Nobody answered my knock, and when I pressed my ear against the door, the flat was silent. Wait, was that a creak? Or—

"Reckon she's out, hun."

Oh, shit. Busted. Could I have looked any more guilty? Probably not, but Gemma's next-door neighbour didn't seem bothered, not while she was trying to fit a twin buggy out of her front door and also avoid the massive bag hung over her shoulder getting stuck on the frame.

"Here, let me help."

I grabbed the bag and nearly tore my biceps off the bone. Wow. She sure didn't need to go to the gym, not if she carried that around all day.

"Ta. It's a nightmare when their dad's out at work."

"I'm not sure the lift's working either." The look of despair on her face made my heart lurch. "Maybe if I took the front of the buggy...?"

"Would ya mind? Bloody stuff's always breaking around here. The management don't do nothing. Gemma lends a hand, but like I said, she's not there. When she's in, she always has the telly on, and I can hear it through the wall."

"When did you last hear her? I work with Gemma—

used to work with her—and she left me a slightly odd voicemail message earlier. I just want to check she's okay."

"She was here this morning. I heard her hoovering right before the kids' cartoons came on."

"What time was that?"

"Just before ten, would've been. But the telly was on for mebbe an hour after that. What'd she say? In her message, I mean?"

"Not an awful lot, to be honest. Just that she was uncomfortable about something. Then she said *he* was coming, and she'd call me back. But she never did."

"He? She probably meant Ryland. He's a right tosser, that one. Or the bellend before him. Even after she dumped that loser, he kept texting."

"Why would you say Ryland was a..." The word stuck in my throat. I cursed, yes, but mostly in my head and never that particular word. "A tosser?"

"He spends, like, an hour every morning on his hair, the vain prick. And when he's not primping, he's lifting weights. Or scoring steroids. No way he got those muscles without them. They met at the gym, did you know that?"

A muscle-bound hulk—that description certainly matched the man I'd seen waiting outside the gallery for Gemma.

"No, I didn't know. And what about the other one? The loser?"

"Kev, Trev, something like that. He just didn't seem to get that she was done with him, so she said. But that was months ago."

"I don't suppose if you hear her come home, you could give me a call? Only Gemma's battery might've run out, or..."

"Sure, hun. Gimme your number."

She entered it into her phone without asking for my name, and I noticed she stored it under "posh bird." Then I nearly put my back out carrying the front end of two fidgety children in a buggy down the stairs. Good thing I'd paid for an annual gym membership up-front last year—it still had a month left to run, and until my world fell apart again last Wednesday, I'd gone religiously three times per week, which had at least prepared me in some small way for today.

Out on the street, I was relieved to see my car, including its wheels, was exactly where I'd left it, and I locked the doors as soon as I climbed in. The chances were, Gemma was just out with her boyfriend, maybe taking a spinning class or jogging, but I still couldn't shake the nagging feeling that something was wrong. The question was, what should I do about it? What *could* I do about it?

# CHAPTER 35 - BETHANY

"WELCOME TO SIRIUS."

Judd set a mug of coffee on the table in front of me, and I surreptitiously moved it from the polished wood to a coaster. It seemed his dining room doubled as a conference room, dominated as it was by a large TV on one wall. Naz grinned at me from the screen, his own drink some kind of purple concoction in a highball glass. He took a sip and grimaced.

"Beetroot smoothie," Judd murmured. "If he ever offers you one, decline."

There was no danger of me accepting a smoothie this morning. No, today I needed caffeine. There was still no word from Gemma or her neighbour, and last night, I'd barely slept from worrying.

"Thanks for the tip."

"Any time." Oh boy, that was one smooth smile. "Day or night."

Naz guffawed from wherever he was. Russia? He sounded Russian. "Ten minutes she's been here, and already you're making the moves. Alaric will kick your *zad*."

"I'd like to see him try."

Ravi walked in, his hair still damp from the shower. "I'd pay money to watch. We could get you both leotards and make an evening of it."

"I don't do Lycra."

"And it wouldn't just be Alaric kicking your ass—it'd be me and Rune too."

"Rune?" Judd clapped both hands against his cheeks. "Oh no."

"Small but mighty, remember?"

"In that case..." He turned to face me. "Ms. Stafford-Lyons, please accept my deepest apologies for my inappropriate comment."

The back-and-forth banter was all in jest, and I realised working for Sirius would be a world away from the quiet grandeur of Pemberton Fine Arts. Yes, Judd's comment had been slightly inappropriate, but I'd been warned what to expect, and his interest was oddly flattering after years of Piers telling me to be grateful I was his wife because no other man would want me. I wouldn't take Judd up on his offer, of course, but it was nice to know there were options. And I couldn't deny he was pleasant to look at. Short dark hair, a day's worth of stubble, hooded brown eyes that practically invited a girl to the bedroom. Dimples that popped out when he smiled. Oh my.

The front door slammed, and Alaric appeared a moment later with a large paper bag in one hand. The first thing he did was scowl at Judd.

"Is he behaving?"

"Mostly."

"Mostly?"

"A wrestling match for my honour was mentioned, but I think we're past that now. Which is a little disappointing—I mean, the two of you are quite evenly matched, and the outfits..." My cheeks heated at the thought, and I gave my head a hurried shake. "So sorry.

Now I'm the one being inappropriate."

Judd's grin grew even wider. "Actually, I think you'll fit in quite well around here."

"Does this mean I don't need to buy popcorn?" Ravi asked. "The CIA versus MI6 would've been worth the effort."

Now I was confused. And also surprised. I suppose I should have guessed that anyone running a private intelligence agency would have a background as some sort of spy, but Judd had been an MI6 agent?

"Who's CIA?" I asked Alaric. "I thought you used to be in the FBI?"

"CIA then FBI. None of this information goes any farther than this room, okay?"

I nodded. I'd had plenty of practice at keeping my mouth shut over the years—not once had I ever blabbed about either of my parents' affairs, even after I accidentally walked in on Father balling Mother's yoga teacher. Thankfully, they'd both been facing away from me. I might have had to wash my eyes out with bleach afterwards, but I'd never breathed a word.

"I understand."

Alaric pointed at Judd. "Ex-MI6, much to his mother's irritation."

"She didn't approve of your career choice?" I asked. "I know that feeling."

Judd snorted.

"No, she didn't want him to quit," Alaric told me. "Naz is former SVR—Sluzhba Vneshney Razvedki Rossiyskoy Federatsii, also known as Russia's foreign intelligence service—but to all intents and purposes, he no longer exists." He waved to his left. "And Ravi came from the circus."

"I'm sorry?"

"You should see him on a trapeze."

At first, I thought Alaric was joking, but he looked dead serious, and then I remembered the way Ravi had jumped and flipped over the laser beams in the escape room. Maybe there was some truth in it? And what about the other revelations? Why didn't Naz exist anymore? And why did Judd's mother hate that he'd quit MI6? Surely she should have been relieved if the James Bond movies were anything to go by?

I pointed at myself. "Former housewife. I might not know much about intelligence services or, uh, trapeze, but I'm organised, and I make an excellent cup of tea."

"Well, I can't make tea for shit apparently, so welcome aboard," Judd said. "I'm afraid I'll have to love you and leave you, though. My train to Brussels leaves in an hour."

"He always puts the milk in first," Naz muttered.

I gasped. "That's sacrilege."

"So I've been told."

Judd walked around the table and leaned down to kiss me on the cheek, then poked Alaric in the forehead. "Stop frowning, old man. There were no tongues."

Weirdly, I thought I might actually grow to like this job.

At least until late morning, when I was so tired that I couldn't stop yawning. Four cups of coffee hadn't made a dent in my exhaustion, but I needed to focus. Alaric had already talked me through the scheduling system twice.

"Could you just go over the colour codes again?"

"Red is me, green's Naz, blue's Judd, and yellow's

Ravi. If it's something all of us are involved with, colour it black, and personal tasks are purple. Are you okay?"

"I'm so sorry—I just didn't get much sleep last night."

His expression morphed from businesslike to concerned. "Because of...? You know, Saturday?"

"No, not that. I'm fine with that. Honestly. All in the past."

"Do you often have trouble sleeping?"

"Only when I'm stressed." I didn't want to bring my personal problems to work, especially on my first day, but I didn't know who else to talk to. "A friend left me a voicemail yesterday morning, and she sounded...uh, just listen to it."

I fumbled my phone out of my handbag and clicked play. Would Alaric think I was overreacting? I'd been flipping and flopping all night about whether to call the police. In the end, I'd decided to give Gemma until this evening to get in contact.

Alaric listened to the message once, then a second time. "You called her back?"

"I didn't pick up the message until yesterday afternoon, and her phone's been off since then. And she hasn't been home. I checked, and her neighbour's keeping an eye out for me."

Despite the circumstances, I was proud I'd spoken to a stranger. Usually, I shied away from anything more than small talk at parties.

"She's not at work?"

"I-I'm not sure. I can hardly call Hugo."

Alaric didn't press me, just pulled out his phone. "Does Gemma have a boyfriend?"

"Yes, Ryland."

Alaric dialled and listened for a second. "All right, mate? It's Ryland. Gemma's boyfriend?" His accent had changed again. This time, he sounded like David Beckham. "Yeah, yeah, I know she's not there. She's ill. That's why I'm calling. She won't be in today." A pause. "Dunno, I'm not a doctor. ... Sure, we'll keep you updated." He hung up. "She's not there."

I got that, but where the heck was she? At least now that Alaric had called in sick for her, she wouldn't get fired.

"Now what?"

"Did you try the cops?"

"Not yet. She hasn't been gone for a full day. Doesn't a person have to be missing for at least twenty-four hours before the police will take a report seriously?"

"Generally, unless there's evidence of foul play. It's a crazy rule. If someone's come to harm, the first twenty-four hours are the most critical. You said you'd been to her apartment?"

"I tried knocking, but nobody answered, and I don't have a key to go inside."

"We'd better get over there. Ravi?" he called. "Are you busy?"

A chill ran up my spine. "You think Gemma might have come to some harm?"

"No friend leaves a message like that if everything's fine, and only the most callous of fools would leave you to fret over it for a day afterwards."

Ravi materialised in the office doorway. "You called?"

"One of Beth's friends is missing. We need to take a look in her apartment."

He didn't even question Alaric. "Two minutes. I'll get my stuff."

On the way to North Acton, I filled Alaric and Ravi in on the conversation I'd had with Gemma's neighbour.

"Two questionable boyfriends?" Ravi mused. "Bad run."

"Has she been herself at work lately?" Alaric asked. "Did she become quieter? Or jittery?"

"She became sort of...scatterbrained. And a little cagey. And I saw a bruise on her once."

Alaric's hands tightened on the wheel. "Don't worry; we'll find her."

Why did his words make me worry more?

When we arrived in North Acton, Alaric parked the SUV in the next street and we headed for Anslow Place. The place looked just as grim as it had yesterday, albeit quieter.

"A man held the door open for me last time. But there aren't many people around today, so maybe—"

I'd been about to suggest that we try the intercom for flat 2e, Gemma's neighbour with the twins, but Ravi stepped ahead, fiddled with the handle for a second, then pulled the door open.

"What do you know? It was unlocked. After you."

Alaric ushered me through with a light touch on the small of my back. "Second floor, right?"

"Uh, yes. I hear the lift isn't very reliable."

"Taking the stairs is a good idea anyway. It gives you more options."

"Options?"

"It's harder to throw somebody down a lift shaft. All those pesky safety features."

I laughed, but nobody else did. Alaric *was* joking, wasn't he? I mean, he had to be.

From the outside, Gemma's flat looked exactly as it had when I left last night. The same tired blue paint on the front door, a scratched white plaque alongside telling me I was at 2d. And it was still silent inside. Perhaps I should have slid a note under the door, just in case?

Alaric knocked, and we waited. Nothing.

"Maybe the management company has a spare key," I said, then glanced towards the window at the end of the hallway. Filthy, and it even had a crack in it. "Not that the management company seems to do much around here."

"Is that a spider?"

Ravi pointed at the ceiling behind me, and I spun around.

"Where? *Where*?" Yes, I understood spiders were a valuable part of our ecosystem, but they still gave me the creeps, okay? I backed away and trod on Alaric's foot by accident. "Sorry! Where's the freaking spider?"

I heard a quiet *click* behind me, and when I turned, Gemma's door was creaking open.

Ravi chuckled. "Guess I must've been mistaken."

"How did you do that? How?"

"Practice. Shall we take a look?"

Ravi was already wearing thin black leather gloves, and Alaric handed me a pair of disposable ones as we stepped over the threshold, the kind you got in hospitals. It felt wrong to be walking into somebody's home uninvited, and somehow, dressing like a burglar made it ten times worse. But if Gemma really was in trouble, she'd want us to investigate, wouldn't she?

"What if a neighbour calls the police?" I whispered.

Another chuckle from Ravi. "In this place? They won't."

There spoke the voice of experience, which should've worried me a bit seeing as I was now working for this man. He clearly had a shady past, and I barely knew him. But honestly, having Ravi and Alaric along made me feel secure. If I'd come alone, I'd still have been standing outside, jumping at my own shadow.

Inside, the flat was, well, not exactly pristine, but there were no signs of a struggle or anything untoward. It appeared for all the world as if Gemma had just gone out to get milk and never returned.

"Can't see a purse anywhere," Alaric said. "Do you know what Gemma's looked like?"

I racked my brain. "Pale pink, medium-sized, not flashy or anything."

Ravi tapped lightly on the counter dividing the living room from the kitchen area. "There's a purse-sized gap here. And mail from Saturday."

"Anything interesting?" Alaric asked.

"Just a loan circular and a discount coupon for a nail salon."

"Search the place?"

"I don't know what other options we have."

They'd clearly done this before. The pair of them checked Gemma's whole flat, combing through everything from her bathroom cupboard to her underwear drawer with a clinical efficiency that left me cold. Alaric made me check in the pockets of every item in her closet while they lifted the mattress, checked beneath cabinets, and even dismantled part of the toilet tank.

"Are you done yet? This is horrible," I whispered.

"Horrible that your friend's missing?" Alaric asked. "Or horrible that we're looking for her?"

When he put it like that... "It's just so invasive."

"The police would do the same thing. Hey, what's this?" He'd been thumbing through a folder full of paperwork, and now he held up an official-looking document. "Hmm. A restraining order, expired last month. Ever heard of a Kevin Waite?"

A chill ran through me. A restraining order? "No, but her neighbour mentioned one of the men she dated was a loser called Kev or maybe Trev who wouldn't leave her alone."

"Sounds like our guy. He got banned from coming within a hundred metres of her." Alaric quickly checked the rest of the papers. "Nothing else of note. I'll take a picture of this."

Despite the thorough search, the flat looked the same when they finished as it had when we'd arrived. Perhaps Gemma herself would notice something out of place, but I couldn't.

"Anything else?" Alaric asked Ravi as he emerged from the bedroom for the final time.

"Just a gym membership card. Beth, didn't you say she met the current boyfriend at the gym? Figure that'd be a good place to start if we need to find him."

"Let's pay Kevin Waite a visit first," Alaric said. "Maybe he just couldn't stay away?"

Couldn't stay away? Well, wasn't that a creepy thought?

# CHAPTER 36 - ALARIC

A MISSING WOMAN was precisely what Alaric didn't need at this moment, but he couldn't just abandon Beth's friend. Instinct told him there was a problem, and experience told him the police wouldn't exactly bust a gut to look into it. It was the same the world over —good cops were overworked and underpaid, bogged down by paperwork plus the crushing weight of public expectations. They'd focus on the big cases—the ones that would garner them favourable headlines—and the easy wins that would improve their statistics. Bad cops? Well, they were a whole other issue. And a disappearance where the only suggestion of foul play was a vague voicemail would be lucky to get an officer assigned.

But the court paperwork gave an address for Waite. In East London, by the looks of it—Emmy's old stomping ground. Alaric had visited with her a time or two. Despite her current lifestyle and the size of her bank account, she still fit right in on the Mile End Road. Jimmy, the ex-boxer who acted as a father figure to her, always said you could take the girl out of East London but you'd never take East London out of the girl. If Alaric and Ravi left now, they could drop Beth off and be in Aldgate in a couple of hours. In terms of distance, Acton and Aldgate weren't far apart, maybe ten miles, but traffic in central London backed up worse than in DC. Could they get there faster on the Tube? Probably, but if you needed to escort a new "friend" to another location, using a vehicle was a damned good idea. Putting a gun to a man's back on a train was something Alaric wanted to avoid. Yes, he'd done it before, but not in London, and the presence of the public brought a whole new level of risk.

"Are we going straight to see Kevin?" Beth asked.

"If when you say 'we' you mean me and Ravi, then we're going right now."

"You think you're leaving me here? Not likely. Gemma's *my* friend."

"Of course we're not leaving you here, my sweet. We'll take you back to Kensington."

Beth folded her arms. Uh-oh. "Okay, you try that. I have an Oyster card."

Normally, loyalty and determination were qualities Alaric admired in a woman, but today, he had to concede that obedience and a propensity to shy away from confrontation were also desirable traits. Now what? Should they take her home anyway? Ravi could pocket the damn Oyster card without her noticing, but she'd be mad, and Alaric really didn't want to lose yet another assistant. Plus he liked Beth. More than he should have—he admitted that—and he hated to see her upset. But nor did he want to see her get hurt physically, and if Waite was involved in Gemma's disappearance, he might not appreciate a visit from a group of concerned strangers.

Ravi put an arm around Beth to steer her past a group of youths, a move that made Alaric bristle on instinct, but...there, he had her wallet. If Alaric hadn't known him so well, hadn't been on the receiving end as Ravi practised the move a hundred times, he'd never have noticed.

"Beth, at the very least, Waite's a stalker who's already been taken to court once. If he *is* wrapped up in this, the chances are he won't go quietly. I'm used to being in these situations, and so is Ravi. You're not."

"I'll be quiet and keep out of the way."

"Yes, in Kensington. I want you to stay safe."

"I will be if I'm with you."

It was nice that she had confidence in him and Ravi, but unfortunately, the world wasn't quite that simple.

"Today, you'd be a distraction. We need to focus one hundred percent of our attention on Waite and what he is and isn't telling us."

"What if I stayed in the car?"

Beth's tone held an edge of desperation, and Alaric understood why—when Gemma had called yesterday, Beth hadn't answered, and now the misplaced guilt was eating away at her. But he still wasn't taking needless risks.

"Actually, that's not a bad idea," Ravi said. "We might need the car moved to the back of the building if...you know."

If they needed to bundle Waite or Gemma into it. Yes, Alaric knew. And sooner or later, Beth would come to understand that not everything he or the other men of Sirius did was strictly law-abiding. Perhaps it was better the revelation happened sooner? Days like this, he regretted breaking up with Emmy. That way, she could've done the dirty work while he played getaway driver, and kidnapping a kidnapper wouldn't even raise one of her perfectly plucked eyebrows.

Beth managed a tight smile. "If I'm in the car, at least you won't come out of the building and find it clamped."

"Okay, fine. You wait in the car, and you keep your phone in your hand. If one of us gives you an instruction, you need to follow it, no questions asked."

Her throat bobbed as she swallowed. "I will, I promise."

If Gemma lived in the armpit of the world, then Kevin was well within sniffing distance. Ravi tried the handle of the building's outer door as Alaric gave one last glance towards Beth, sitting behind the wheel of the SUV in the side street opposite. Her face was in shadow, but he felt her eyes on him.

"Hey, this door really is unlocked. Great security."

"Probably nothing worth stealing."

According to the paperwork, Waite lived in a first-floor apartment—second-floor if you were American—and the stairs stank. Alaric skirted a suspicious-looking puddle gleaming in the light from a single bare bulb and pushed open the door to Waite's floor.

"Nice," Ravi muttered. "Makes the apartment in Thailand look like a palace."

For a moment, Alaric thought back to the hovel they'd shared with Judd and Naz for a few weeks, a cheap two-bedroom place chosen for its location rather than its decor. Yeah, it had been grim, but it had served its purpose, and at least the four of them had known how to use a bathroom. Thanks to Naz and his OCD, the place had reeked of bleach rather than piss with an underlying note of marijuana.

"Where's Naz when you need him?"

"He wouldn't have made it through the front door."

Speaking of front doors, Waite's looked as though it had been kicked in more than once and patched back together again. When Alaric nudged it with a foot, it wobbled.

Should he knock or not? After a moment's hesitation, he rapped on the flimsy wood with his knuckles, then stood to the side as they waited. And waited. And waited. Nobody answered, and he didn't hear any movement inside either.

Ravi reached into his pocket for the set of lock picks Alaric knew he kept in there.

"'Twas the night before Christmas and all through the house, not a creature was stirring, not even a mouse." By the time Ravi finished the second line of the poem, he had the door open. "After you."

"Gee, thanks."

Inside the minuscule apartment, the only light came from unwashed windows, and the place had a feeling of stillness about it. Nobody home. Nobody alive, at any rate. Alaric sniffed the air. Sweat, the musty smell of unwashed bed linen, and a hint of damp. Nothing that indicated decomposition. He took that as a good sign.

But where was Waite?

Ravi opened the fridge. "Two cans of Red Bull, a jar of pickled beets, and an unopened block of cheese. Either Kevin's not much of a cook, or he cleared out for a while."

Alaric eyed up the tiny counter. Knife block,

chopping board, empty fruit bowl. Two recipe books—*100 Meals for Students* and *Family Favourites for Under a Fiver*. The cupboard beside the fridge was stacked full of cans—chickpeas, baked beans, plum tomatoes, sliced carrots...

"It's the latter. But where the hell has he gone?"

A possible answer came when Alaric flattened out a piece of paper from the trash can beside the desk. At some point, the printer had run out of ink, and the list of "*50 free things to do in Marbella*" had cut off halfway down the page. Had Waite gone on vacation?

It didn't take long to search the apartment. The place was basically one room plus a bathroom not much bigger than an old-fashioned phone box. A logoed baseball cap and two polo shirts that smelled of fried chicken hanging in the closet suggested Waite worked at a fast-food joint along the street, and he didn't own much else in the way of clothing. Jeans, tracksuits, half a dozen pairs of branded sneakers. According to the bank statements in the desk drawer, he was overdrawn, and he had indeed purchased airline tickets recently, plus paid three hundred Euros and change to a hotel booking website. His phone bills showed texts and calls to Gemma's number, hundreds a year ago, plus a dozen or so in the last month. Recently, another number had borne the brunt of his obsession, it seemed. Alaric photographed each page for follow-up.

"Anything?" he called out to Ravi.

"Not unless you count the photos in his nightstand —twenty or so of two different brunettes. Cheap paper. Appears he printed them at home."

"Posed?"

"Some of them. But the majority look covert."

"Got pictures?"

"A nice selection."

Then it was time to leave. Waite wasn't there, neither was Gemma, and Alaric was conscious of Beth sitting in the car alone. Despite the fact that Waite was obviously disturbed, Alaric had bumped him down the suspect list.

"Let's go. Waite feels wrong. He's definitely got a problem, but I'm not convinced he's our man."

"Agreed. Pick up lunch on the way back?"

Ravi always thought with his stomach, but it *was* almost dinner time. "Sure. How do you feel about fried chicken?"

By the time they headed back to Judd's place, Waite's colleagues at The Chicken Hut had confirmed he was indeed sunning himself in Marbella for two weeks. Left last Friday, apparently, which put him out of contention for abducting Gemma. Could he have faked a vacation? Possibly, but yesterday, he'd sent one of his buddies a photo of himself burned to the colour of a baked ham, and there was no way he'd turned that colour in England, not in the last couple of days. The heatwave had given way to showers.

"Now what?" Beth asked from the back seat.

She'd wrinkled her nose when Ravi offered her a piece of chicken and muttered something about a salad instead. Alaric offered her a French fry, and she hesitated before reaching out a hand.

"Maybe just the one."

"Take the bag. I got extra."

"I really shouldn't."

"You haven't eaten today."

"Because I'm worried."

"Lesson number one—you have to eat, whatever happens. You need to keep your energy levels up. And in answer to your question, now we move to the second suspect on the list. What do you know about Ryland?"

"Hardly anything. Just that Gemma seemed happy with him at first, but then she gradually got more and more miserable. She mentioned one time that she always attracted the wrong sort of guy."

"You said you saw him once—would you recognise him again?"

"Yes, I think so."

Alaric hated to involve Beth, but he saw little choice at the present time. "Then tomorrow, we join a gym. That was where Gemma met him, right?"

"Both of us? Don't you need to travel to America?"

"If you think I'm leaving you here to hunt for a possible kidnapper by yourself, you've got another think coming. *We'll* find Ryland, and then *we'll* go to the US. I'll call Emmy and tell her we'll fly commercial in a few days."

"Are you sure? The painting..."

"Is less important than a living, breathing woman."

At least, Alaric hoped Gemma was still living and breathing. Otherwise, he might have to brush up on some of his old skills.

Beth reached between the seats to touch him on the shoulder, and he suppressed a shiver at the contact. The effect she had on him...it wasn't healthy.

"Thank you. I...I don't know what else to say."

"Like I said, we look after our own."

"How was the parkour, Cinders?"

Alaric was sitting at Judd's dining table with his phone and a glass of wine, checking Gemma's social media accounts. She didn't post much. There was no mention of Ryland, or Kevin, or any other man either, just the occasional cat meme and a bunch of "Happy Birthday!" messages from friends back in February. Mind you, if Kevin *had* been stalking her, then the lack of content made complete sense.

"Okay."

One word, but Emmy sounded offhand. Distracted.

"Just 'okay'?"

"We got chased out of an abandoned factory, which was kind of ironic since it was Blackwood's people doing the chasing. Those guys need to get in better shape. Probably I should draft a memo. Or get Toby to replace the office biscuits with broccoli again."

Toby was Emmy's nutritionist. She often bitched about his rules, but deep down, she liked to stay healthy. That didn't stop her from hiding candy all over the place though, like the chocolate she habitually left in Alaric's car. Which was okay in Virginia, but not so good when he drove south to Florida and the damn stuff melted.

"Delegation—an exercise in plausible deniability?"

"Something like that. Are you calling about the flight tomorrow? Because it'll have to be later rather than earlier. I need to fit in a couple of meetings before I leave, and the Japanese dude can only do the afternoon. Plus the client booked in for eleven never shows up on time."

"And you put up with that?"

"I bill him top whack for every wasted minute, but since he's a government guy, he doesn't seem to care." Alaric could picture her nonchalant shrug. "I think of it as a deduction on my taxes." A pause. "Anyhow, tomorrow?"

"Thanks for the offer, but we'll have to fly commercial later in the week. Something came up."

"Work? That's good news."

"Not exactly. Remember Gemma from the gallery?"

"Ditzy brunette? Too thin?"

"That's her. She's disappeared, and Beth's worried about her. Frankly, I am too."

"Why?"

Emmy's curiosity: piqued.

"She left a cryptic voicemail saying she was uncomfortable, then mentioned 'he' was coming and said she'd call back."

"And she didn't?"

"No, and now her phone's switched off. Doesn't look as if she's been home either."

"And you want to find her."

A statement, not a question.

"You know me—I've never been able to turn down a damsel in distress."

"I know you?" Emmy gave a hollow laugh. What was all that about? "Right. Look, I'll push the flight forward to Wednesday. If you've finished damsel-saving by then, give me a shout."

"Is everything okay?"

"Fine." Uh-oh. "If you need any input from

Blackwood in your hunt for Gemma, give Sloane a call. She'll sort it out."

Sloane? Now Alaric was being referred to Emmy's assistant? Something was wrong, very wrong. Even when he'd returned from his hiatus, she hadn't pushed him away like this.

"Cinders..."

"I'll speak to you tomorrow."

She hung up. She actually hung up on him. Fuck. Now he wasn't sure which was the bigger problem—Gemma's vanishing act or Emmy's stone-cold attitude. Boy, tomorrow promised to be fun.

# CHAPTER 37 - BETHANY

"REMEMBER, IF YOU see Ryland, don't speak to him."

"I understand."

I'd understood the first five times Alaric briefed me too. If I recognised Gemma's boyfriend, I wasn't to react at all, just carry on with whatever I was doing and tell Alaric at the first opportunity. Honestly, I wasn't convinced we'd even find him. If he *had* been involved in Gemma's disappearance, would he really make it a priority to go to the gym just two days later? And it was morning too. What if he preferred to work out in the afternoon? Or the evening? I clutched the handles of my gym bag tighter, grateful for the energy drink that Alaric had tucked in there before we left Judd's townhouse. I'd need it. If we didn't find Ryland today, I foresaw a lot of exercise in my future.

Alaric held open the door to Workout World, his hand on the small of my back as he ushered me through. He did that often—those fleeting touches—but I'd come to realise it didn't mean much. That was just the way he was. A part of me hated it. The part of me that still wanted more, not all those little teases disguised as chivalry. The other part? Well, I'd take what I could get.

Workout World wasn't like my regular gym—the front desk was manned by a hairy guy in gym shorts rather than an animatronic mannequin in spandex with D-cups she'd earned by sleeping with a cosmetic surgeon. The mannequin's teeth had been perfect as well, veneers I doubted she could afford on her salary. Had *she* screwed Piers too? He'd been a member before our split, and honestly, it wouldn't have surprised me.

I'd need to find a new gym in a month because I wouldn't be renewing my own membership—not only was it too expensive now, but I was also sick of the bitchiness. Could Workout World be a viable alternative? Not the Acton branch—that was too far—but I'd checked the website and there was one in Hammersmith. The hairy guy—Wayne, according to his name badge—greeted us with a pleasant smile.

"Haven't seen you here before. Are you members?"

Alaric took over. "No, but we're hoping to join."

Another plus point—the joining fee would be classed as a legitimate work expense. Wayne slid forms towards both of us, and I noticed Alaric didn't use his real name when he filled his in. *Rick McDonald.* Hmm. If I worked with Sirius for long enough, could I get an alias too? I'd ditched Fortescue-Hamilton before the ink on the divorce papers was dry, but what I really wanted was a surname without a hyphen. Bethany Althea Margaret Constance Stafford-Lyons was such a mouthful, and it didn't fit on the form either. Beth Lyons. There, that would have to do.

"We're short-staffed today," Wayne told us, sending a smile in my direction. "Hold on a sec." He waved at a girl heading for the door. "Hey, Kate! Can you watch the desk?"

"I just finished my shift."

"Five minutes?"

The girl sighed, then nodded. "Five minutes."

"Thanks, babe." Wayne turned back to us. "Okay, I can show you around. You've used a gym before?"

Yup. We both nodded, and I returned Wayne's smile. Why was Alaric's jaw clenched?

"In that case, follow me."

Workout World was easily three times the size of my current gym, over a hundred stations, half of them full even at ten in the morning. No swimming pool, no juice bar, no tanning beds. The only spa facilities were a sauna and steam room, both packed with half-naked men, although that wasn't entirely a negative. The tour took fifteen minutes, and then we were on our own.

"Seen any sign of Ryland?" Alaric asked.

"Not yet." And I'd been looking, believe me, which was slightly awkward because each time I paused my gaze on a man, they either winked, gave me a top-to-toe once-over, or in one particularly unpleasant case, patted me on the shoulder with a giant sweaty paw. If I did venture back into Workout World, I was never making eye contact again. "Now what? Should we hop on a treadmill or something?"

"Yeah, but take it easy. We might be here for a while."

"I need to put my bag in a locker."

"Same. I'll head upstairs to the weights after. You said Ryland was built, right?"

"I think so. He was wearing a jacket when I saw him, but he was definitely bulky around the shoulders."

And so was Alaric when he peeled off his sweater to reveal a tight black vest. Surprisingly so. The outline of his torso in the cashmere sweaters he tended to favour had suggested he was no slouch, but in the flesh, so to speak, he was smooth and sculpted. A work of art. Before I married Piers, I'd always had a weakness for good arms. Hell, I'd even dated a rugby player for a while. But my parents had hated him, or rather, they'd hated his family background, his financial status, and his lack of a "proper job." Back then, I'd been too scared of losing their approval to follow my own path, but the irony was, Johnny had gone on to play for England while Piers was still reliant on his trust fund.

Damn, I missed those arms.

The changing room was basic but functional, the surfaces plastic instead of marble, the lighting harsh rather than tasteful. In short, the place was another reminder of the privileged life I'd led, of the gilded cage I'd now escaped. I picked a locker near the showers and squashed my bag into it, then unzipped my sweater and bundled that in too.

"Hey, I love your top. Where'd you get it?"

Was somebody talking to me? Apparently, yes. I turned to find a pretty Black girl standing there, a year or two younger than me with her hair neatly braided into cornrows.

"Uh, thanks. Yoga Life in Chelsea, I think."

She made a face. "Bit out of my price range. Are you new here?"

"How did you guess?"

"You're using one of the small lockers, and they don't have room for nothin'. Bigger ones are on the other side by the hairdryers. I'm Shereen, by the way."

A nervous giggle bubbled out of me. This was like the first day at a new school, and my only friend was outside lifting weights. "And I'm Beth. Yes, I'm still finding my way around. Wayne gave me a quick tour of the main floor, but he couldn't exactly walk in here."

"Oh, I don't know—he must've seen half the women in this place naked, and most of the rest would invite him in with open arms." Shereen rolled her eyes. "Workout World is hook-up central."

I spotted a ring on her finger. "But not for you?"

"Hell, no. I'm just here for the sauna. I already got a man, and he'd kick Wayne's ass if he looked at me funny."

I put a mental check in the "negatives" column. Perhaps Workout World wasn't the right gym for me after all? I didn't want a hook-up, and I most certainly didn't want a hook-up with Wayne. I liked men who knew how to use a razor.

Shereen must have noticed my grimace. "Taken? Or just not into Wayne?"

"Er..."

My self-appointed buddy grasped my wrist and led me across the room. "Because he's not the only trainer here. Behold..." She waved her arm towards a huge noticeboard. The left half was covered in ads and flyers —dog-walking services, flatmates wanted, stuff for sale —and the right half had neat rows of photos, thirty men at least. "This is the current selection."

"Wow."

It was like browsing through model agency headshots, except each picture was accompanied by notes of the classes the man taught.

*Gavin Hughes, spinning 7-8 a.m. Mon - Fri.*

*Jake Mandell, registered personal trainer, works weekends.*

A banner at the bottom invited us to "Book at Reception!" Did they not have female trainers? Or were their pictures all in the men's changing room?

"What do the numbers underneath mean?" I asked. Most of the men had a line of handwritten red digits under their bios. One or two had a black X, and a couple had sad faces.

"Scores out of ten," Shereen said, and I choked. "What, you think they don't know? They definitely know." She tapped one of the sad faces with a red-painted fingernail. "This means they're gay, and if there's a black cross, it means they're spoken for at the moment. Engaged, married, whatever."

I scanned the photos again. One guy looked kind of plain, but he had tens across the board. My insides clenched just thinking about that achievement, and Shereen gave a throaty chuckle.

"Malcolm has a waiting list, hun. You could try Robbie if you need to loosen up. Nine-point-two average and the stamina to match, by all accounts."

What on earth had I walked into? I tried to focus on my goal, but my vision went fuzzy as I thought of the last man to "loosen me up." I didn't want a quickie with a gym instructor, not in the slightest, but I wouldn't say no to a mysterious American-slash-Brit who went out of his way to save my shoes from certain death.

"You're looking at Ryland?" Shereen asked.

"What? No!" Wait a second... "Ryland?"

"Because I'm, like, ninety percent sure he's got a girlfriend, and he didn't turn up for any of yesterday's classes anyway. I reckon they're gonna fire him."

I stared at the board, willing myself to concentrate on the job at hand rather than Alaric. The picture next to Robbie popped into focus, a vaguely familiar face framed by dark hair, his lips twisted into a slight sneer.

Yes! *That* was the man I'd seen waiting for Gemma outside the gallery. *Ryland Willis, Fat Blaster 11 a.m. and 2 p.m. Sundays, Body Sculpt 8 p.m. weekdays, personal training available.* He'd scored half a dozen sevens and three eights before a black X appeared under his name. For Gemma?

"Saturday?" I tried to keep the excitement out of my voice. "He hasn't been here since Saturday?"

"So I heard. How about Saul? A nine-inch—"

"Actually, I have a boyfriend. He's upstairs waiting for me, but thank you so much for the introduction. At least I know where to find the class details in future."

Shereen seemed vaguely disappointed, as if she enjoyed experiencing vicarious pleasure through other people's one-night stands. Or possibly she was just a gossip-monger, albeit a friendly one.

"You're welcome, hun. And don't use that shower at the end. The thermostat's busted, and it's always freezing."

"I'll be sure to avoid it."

I practically ran out of the changing room. Where were the weights? Upstairs, turn left, *oof*. Alaric caught me as I ploughed into him not six feet from the door.

"What's the hurry?"

I steadied myself on his bare arms and forced my gaze upwards, away from his chest to his face. Men shouldn't be allowed to wear vests in the gym. It was far too distracting.

"Beth? Did you forget to get dressed?"

Huh? I glanced down at myself, relieved to find I was still wearing a sports bra and leggings.

"This is what I always wear to the gym."

Alaric leaned in closer, his lips grazing my ear.

"When you're house-hunting, add a private gym to the list of must-haves."

"Really?"

"We're not coming back to this one. They score the women out of ten on the wall of the men's locker room, and I'm not letting you become a fucking statistic."

He wasn't *letting* me? The ratings thing was horrifying, but shades of Piers triggered me to snap back without thinking.

"What if I *want* to become a fucking statistic?" I clapped a hand over my mouth almost immediately, but the damage was done. "I'm sorry."

Rather than fire me, Alaric just laughed. "I'll give you eleven out of ten. Hell, I'll even make you a certificate."

"But we've never..."

*Shut up, Beth.* This was a conversation I definitely didn't want to be having.

"No, but I've got good instincts." He tugged me closer, and I drew in a sharp breath. "And right now, those instincts are telling me not to set a gazelle loose among the lions. The moment we find Ryland, I'm burning both of our membership cards."

Shereen walked out of the changing room, and I gritted my teeth as I sagged against Alaric. This undercover thing sure was awkward. She gave me a thumbs-up from behind his back, then headed towards the sauna.

"I already found Ryland," I mumbled into Alaric's shoulder.

"Come again?"

*Please, no, it was awkward enough the first time.*

"His picture's on the wall in the ladies' changing

room. Ryland Willis. Average score of seven-point-three, currently unavailable. And he hasn't been to work since Saturday."

I felt Alaric's smile as he kissed my hair, and that made me smile too. I'd actually achieved something in my new job, and it felt better than selling the most expensive painting at the gallery.

"Bethany, I love you, in a purely work-related way, of course." His words were playful, but I still shivered in his arms. The air conditioning was on too high. That was it. "Now that we've got a surname, let's find out where he lives and get the hell away from here."

Find out where Ryland lived? Sure. Piece of cake. No problem.

"How the heck do we do that?"

# CHAPTER 38 - BETHANY

I LIMPED AROUND the corner towards the reception desk, leaning on the wall as I went, hoping to goodness that I looked suitably in pain. Wayne leapt up the instant he saw me.

"Are you okay?"

What do you know? I was a better actress than I thought.

"Fine, fine." I let out what I hoped was a convincing groan. "I just twisted my ankle on the treadmill, that's all."

"Do you need an ambulance?"

"Gosh, no." I tried a smile. "But if you have a bag of ice..."

"Uh, I'm not meant to leave the desk unmanned. Perhaps someone upstairs could give you a hand?"

"I asked a guy upstairs. Gary? But he said he was right in the middle of a training session and that you'd be able to assist."

"The freezer's in the break room, and that's in the basement."

"I'll stay right here. If anyone arrives, I'll tell them you'll be back in two minutes." I put a little weight on my "bad" foot and winced. "I'd be ever so grateful."

"Two minutes..." Wayne weighed up the options—leave a new member in agony or abandon his post for the briefest of periods. In the end, chivalry won out. Shereen's friends had him well trained, it seemed. "Just ask anyone who comes in to wait, okay?"

"Absolutely."

The instant Wayne disappeared down the stairs to the left of the desk, I beckoned Alaric forward from around the corner.

"Did you hear? Two minutes."

"Got it."

He gave a hop-jump like a basketball player leaping for a shot and knocked the overhead security camera out of range before sliding into Wayne's seat behind the desk. The first thing he did was jam a USB drive into a slot on the side of the computer.

"In case we can't get what we need right now," he explained. "The stick contains a program that'll give Naz a backdoor into the system if we need it."

So Naz was the IT guy, and his activities weren't entirely above board. Did that bother me? Apart from the parking tickets Piers used to berate me for and the animal-rights-related indiscretion in my teens, I'd always been a law-abiding citizen, but now I realised the rules weren't entirely black and white. Yes, hacking might be technically illegal, but Naz would only be doing it to find Gemma. And I'd lied my own ass off this morning to help her as well as stealing Ryland's photo from the noticeboard in the changing room.

I positioned myself by the stairs, thankful they were tiled rather than carpeted so I'd hear Wayne when he came back. My whole body tingled with nervous energy. Fear of getting caught versus the excitement of doing something slightly illicit. Was Alaric worried? He looked cool as a cucumber as he tapped away at the keys.

Oh, shit. The front door swung open, and a guy walked in. Early twenties, walked with a bit of a swagger, and he definitely needed to hitch up his tracksuit bottoms because I could see most of his underwear.

"Hey, brother. You new here?"

Alaric glanced up. "Yeah, I'm covering for Wayne."

As usual, his London accent was on point, and how on earth did he stay so composed? I was shaking.

"Look, I know the rules, but I forgot my membership card. Just this once, could you let me in?"

"Aw, man. I'm meant to do things by the book." Alaric glanced both ways. "Go on. Just don't tell anyone, yeah?"

The guy gave him a fist bump on the way past. "My mouth stays shut."

Whew.

Another minute passed, according to the clock on the wall. Every second felt like an hour, and a bead of sweat rolled down my back just as I heard footsteps approaching. Uh-oh.

"He's coming back."

"Almost done."

"Now! He's halfway up the stairs."

*Move, move, move!*

Alaric waited until the last possible moment to leave the desk, utterly unruffled as he strolled in my direction. Me? I was hyperventilating.

Wayne held out a bag of ice. "Are you sure you're okay? You've gone kinda red."

"Yes, really. I just need to go and lie down."

But Alaric helped me over to a chair instead. "Sit

here with the ice for a minute, babe. Don't push things."

Oh, this was excruciating. We were literally hanging out at the scene of the crime, and Alaric was discussing football with Wayne, not a care in the world. Had he got the address? Please say he'd got the address. Was Alaric in the habit of pulling stunts like this often? Because if I did this more than, say, once a year, I'd have a heart attack before I hit forty.

The pair of them must have discussed half the clubs in the Premier League, and my perfectly mobile ankle had frozen solid by the time Alaric helped me to my feet. I gave Wayne a wave, then limped out the door, which was made far easier by the fact that I couldn't feel my left foot anymore.

"Nice," Alaric murmured. "Are you looking for a promotion already, my sweet? Secretary to spy?"

"I think my heart's about to give out. Did you find Ryland's details?"

"According to his membership information, he lives in Hounslow."

Thank goodness. "Can we go straight there?"

"Not without doing some research."

"But what if Gemma's being held against her will?"

"If we go in unprepared, the risk to Gemma's well-being would be greater than the risk of us taking a few hours to plan properly."

"How do you know that?" Alaric hesitated, so I pushed harder. "Please, just tell me what's going on. I can handle it. The not-knowing is a hundred times worse."

He waited until we were back in the car until he answered, and with hindsight, I was grateful to be sitting down.

"Acquaintance kidnappings account for twenty-seven percent of abductions, and of those, seventy-four percent of the victims are killed within the first three hours. That goes up to eighty-nine percent after twenty-four hours, and we're already past that window. Working on the slim possibility that Gemma's still alive, how do you think Ryland will react if we knock on his door? Based on past experience, he's more likely to go on the offensive than invite us inside."

My blood chilled to an icy paste, and I fought for breath as my heart struggled to push the viscous liquid through my veins.

"Oh."

"At Sirius, we work on the basis of the six Ps."

"What are those?"

"Proper Planning Prevents Piss Poor Performance. I want to find Gemma, and we will, but I'm not walking into that building blind. I don't find getting shot at quite as exhilarating as I used to."

The icy paste froze solid. "You think you'll get shot at? But guns are tightly regulated in England."

Although my father and Piers had shotgun licences, and they were both pillocks. The amount of Scotch they drank before shooting meant they rarely hit what they were aiming at, which was both a good thing and a bad thing, depending on how you looked at it.

"There are more guns around than you'd think, and I don't particularly enjoy knife fights either."

"Perhaps we should call the police? If we told them everything we know..."

"It wouldn't be any faster. They've got more red tape, and they rely on warrants rather than breaking and entering." Alaric reached over to squeeze my hand, and the warmth brought a hint of life to my circulation. "This is our priority, and we'll move as fast as possible, I promise. Will you trust me?"

For the third time since we met, I nodded in answer to that question. After the number Piers did on me, I barely trusted anyone, but yes, I trusted Alaric.

"Please could I get three portions of koshary and three falafel sandwiches?"

With Alaric and Ravi busy studying satellite photos and maps of Hounslow, I fell back into the role of errand girl. Everybody needed to eat. The new place around the corner allegedly sold authentic Egyptian street food, but Alaric said it was nothing like the real thing. Cairo was a dusty hubbub of people and cars, apparently, not gentle sounds of sitar music and clinking china. But service was quick, and within ten minutes, I was on my way back to Judd's townhouse with a bag of food.

Or at least, I was until my father rang. The thought of answering made my stomach sink, but I'd already put off calling him for two days, and he didn't take kindly to being ignored. What did he want? Was my presence required at another get-together? Had my sister suffered a wedding-related crisis?

No, it was much, much worse.

"Bethie, why didn't you call me back?"

"Because I was working."

"I thought you got sacked?"

"I got a new job. And I had prep to do for this

week's tasks."

I wasn't about to mention Gemma—rather than concern or sympathy, I'd most likely get a reminder not to associate with somebody who lived in North Acton.

"Not much of a job if you don't get weekends off, is it?"

*Gee, thanks for all the support.* "Did you call for a particular reason, Daddy?"

"As it happens, I did. Piers raised concerns regarding that McLain chap you were with on Saturday." I bet he did. "Concerns I share now that I've done some digging."

"You did *what*?"

"You're my daughter, Bethie. I care about you, and it's not good for you to be associating with that con artist."

Oh, this took the biscuit. Why couldn't my father keep his nose out of my life, just for once?

"Alaric isn't a con artist."

"He's a con artist and a thief. Ambassador McLain tried to get it brushed under the carpet, but his son stole ten million dollars, then did a moonlight flit with the money. Goodness only knows where he's been for the last eight years."

I almost dropped the bag of food, and a blonde woman swore at me as I stopped dead in the middle of the pavement.

"Ten million...*what*?" I was beginning to sound like a stuck record.

"The man walked off with ten million dollars in cash and diamonds, money that was meant to pay a ransom by all accounts. He kept the lot, and rumour says he almost got several of his colleagues killed in the process."

My legs threatened to give way, and I slumped against a wall as if I'd had vodka for breakfast instead of coffee.

"No, you're wrong. Alaric didn't do that."

"I heard it from a friend of the ambassador."

"Then he lied. I mean, if Alaric *had* stolen that money, he'd be in jail, wouldn't he?"

"My source said he's a sneaky son of a bitch. The FBI could never prove he'd done it, but they sure as hell fired him."

Could it be true? Alaric himself had told me that he used to be an FBI agent, but he wasn't anymore. And he hadn't been particularly forthcoming about his past, even when I'd unloaded on him about my troubles with Piers.

I gave my head a quick shake to clear the insanity. What was I thinking? Alaric wouldn't steal a bloody ransom of all things. Look at what he was doing for Gemma—he was in the business of saving people, not putting them in danger. And he didn't exactly live extravagantly. Surely if he had millions in cash lying around, he'd be sunning himself on the beach instead of working? He didn't even own a house, for crying out loud.

My father's words didn't add up.

"Daddy, that's just not true."

"Has he brainwashed you? I thought I taught you to be smarter than that."

Actually, schoolteachers and a succession of nannies had taught me to be smarter than that. My father had had little input into my upbringing. And Alaric hadn't brainwashed me. He'd helped me. Yes, our initial meeting had been a bit fraught, and he'd made me lose my mind somewhat at the party on Saturday evening, and okay, he was a seriously smooth liar, but a thief?

*I* was the one who'd been transporting stolen goods, something else Alaric had been remarkably understanding about.

"There's no way Alaric stole ten million dollars."

"Are you saying I associate with liars?"

"Of course not," I said on instinct, years of placating my father ingrained in my psyche. People in his circle lied all the time, usually about affairs, but what was another fib between friends? "What if perhaps they made a mistake?"

"It's McLain who made the mistake by betraying his employer. Bethie, you need to steer well clear of that man."

"But...but..."

How could I? I worked for Alaric now, and what's more, he was helping me to find Gemma.

"Are you saying you won't do this one little thing for me? Your mother and I have been remarkably patient with all your silliness about getting a job, but this nonsense has gone on for quite long enough. The country club's been holding your seat on the social committee, but they won't do so forever. It's time to come to your senses. Look at Piers—he's moved on already."

My father's words made me see red. Silliness? He thought me wanting to earn my own money and live my own life was *silliness*?

"I'd rather fend for myself than spend every day pretending I care about table decorations. And I happen to like Alaric. He's been kind to me."

"He's been brainwashing you for his next scam, more like. Does he know how much this family is worth?"

"It's not something that's ever come up in conversation."

"I bet he knows. Believe me—he's bad news. And I can't entrust half of our fortune to somebody who exhibits such bad judgement. If you refuse to see what's already obvious to the rest of us, then I'll have no choice but to cut you off. You won't get another penny from me or your mother."

That...that *asshole*!

True, my father hadn't given me any money recently, but the safety net had always been there. A stable for Chaucer and a roof over my head if things got really bad. I'd never been truly alone before. Could I handle it? A tear rolled down my cheek, and another, and another, until I was crying in the middle of bloody Kensington.

"Cheer up, love." A street sweeper paused to fish a packet of tissues out of his pocket and offered it to me. "Might never 'appen."

Do you know? He was right. The worst might not happen, and if I gave up the little bit of freedom I'd found and crawled back to my parents, I'd always wonder "what if?" Better to be poor and happy than forever miserable.

"Thank you," I mouthed at the sweeper and wiped my face as he continued on his way. Then I made myself straighten, even though my father couldn't see me. "Daddy, I don't need your money. Give the whole lot to Priscilla. She can spend it on a third holiday home and a thousand manicures, or better still, you could send Mother on a shopping spree or ten to distract her from the fact that you're fucking yet another mistress. You're such a hypocrite. Your friends are all slugs in fancy clothes, corrupt to the core, and as for Piers... He screwed me over, your *daughter*, and still you take his side. I wish I'd been swapped at birth."

"How dare—"

I hung up before my father could finish the sentence, then stared at the phone in horror. What the hell had I just done? Anger had made my innermost thoughts tumble out, one insult after another, and I couldn't take them back even if I wanted to.

I was on my own now, with just a possible super-thief for company.

Was I scared? Terrified. But also strangely exhilarated.

# CHAPTER 39 - ALARIC

GUN OR NO gun? In the US, that wouldn't even be a question, but in London, where handguns were banned, the risks of being caught carrying could outweigh the benefits. Not that Alaric planned to get caught, of course... In the end, he liberated a Beretta from Judd's collection and secured it behind his back in a covert holster. He always had his sport coats cut to hide a weapon, but he'd have to be careful not to get too close to Beth. Until this afternoon, she seemed to have taken his bending of the law in her stride, but since she got back from lunch, she'd been acting differently. Cooler. More distant. Off in the same way that Emmy had been on the phone yesterday. Unless it was Alaric's imagination? He'd avoided entanglements with women for the past eight years, so maybe his intuition had degraded?

Four p.m., and they were about to head to Ryland's apartment. They'd studied photos and maps of the area, and Naz had come up with a floor plan of Bellsfield House North, showing the layout of apartment 504 on the fifth floor. The seventeen-storey block dated back to the fifties, the northern-most of two identical towers set on a housing estate a ten-minute walk from Hounslow West Tube Station. When the place was first completed, it had been touted as the future for modern families, but in the intervening decades, urban decay had settled in, along with a local gang and a motley crew of drug dealers. The local newspaper mentioned the Bellsfield Estate most weeks, but rarely in a positive light.

Alaric didn't want Beth with them, not remotely, but given that the latest news story had detailed the theft of a catalytic converter, stolen in under ten minutes while the vehicle's owner ran into the local Co-op to buy a sandwich, it seemed a good idea to leave somebody in the SUV if they wanted to drive it away again afterwards.

"Ready to go?" he asked.

Beth and Ravi both nodded from the other side of the table. Ravi was supposed to be on his way to the US to snoop around a media mogul's Hamptons home for one of Judd's projects, but that had been put on hold. They'd all agreed that finding a missing woman took priority.

"How long will you be inside?" Beth asked.

As little time as possible. "If Willis is home, long enough to assess whether he's a likely suspect. If he's not there, we'll take a view on whether to wait, or talk to the neighbours, or leave and regroup."

"And you'll definitely keep me updated?"

She sounded nervous, and Alaric wished Judd was around, or even Naz, and Naz's driving was appalling. Should he call Emmy? Her driving wasn't much better, but nobody would steal the damn wheels off the car if she was sitting in it. He almost reached for his phone, but then he recalled the way Emmy had distanced herself. No, Sirius could handle this.

"All the way, Beth. Just keep your phone ready."

Alaric had been born with not just a silver spoon in his mouth but a whole set of cutlery. At first, it had seemed normal, being driven in a limousine to the international school near whatever embassy his father happened to be posted to at the time, but an insatiable curiosity combined with teenage rebellion had led him to sneak away from the sanctity of wealth with increasing regularity. He'd seen how the other half lived, and when he walked out of his own life with little more than the cash in his wallet and the clothes on his back, he'd experienced it for himself. Six weeks in a Brazilian favela, a trip to Palestine, passage across the South China Sea on a fishing trawler, a month picking grapes in a Spanish vineyard while drinking too much Rioja, the stint as a deckhand in the Similan Islands...

He'd travelled the world, but he'd never seen any place as grim as Bellsfield House North. Kevin's apartment block was luxurious in comparison. Many of the apartments on the Bellsfield Estate were now in private hands, but the outside of the building and the communal areas made North Korea look vibrant. The two towers, no more than six or seven metres apart on their short sides, cast giant shadows over the rest of the estate and plunged gloomy corners into full-on darkness.

"Was that a mouse?" Ravi asked.

"More like a rat."

They'd dressed down for the occasion in jeans, lightweight rubber-soled boots, and plain dark-coloured T-shirts, but Alaric still felt out of place. A hazmat suit would have been more appropriate. The elevator yawned open like the gate to hell, so he opted for the stairs instead, jogging up the ten half-flights of bare concrete steps that led to Ryland's floor. The stairwell was in a permanent state of twilight, most of the lightbulbs blown, the echoing space shaded by the monolithic south tower. Alaric caught a glimpse of a pale silhouette in the window opposite and paused. A teenager in a white hoodie stared back with mild disinterest, almost within touching distance. From his stance, he appeared to be urinating.

Alaric kept climbing.

He had two options if the man answered the door—firstly, he could pretend he was looking for someone else, that he'd made a mistake with the address, and use any resulting conversation to fathom Ryland out. Would he be glib? Shifty? Downright hostile? Or Alaric could push straight away and ask about Gemma. He'd have roughly five seconds to decide which path to take based on first impressions and a lifetime of honed instincts.

The trouble was, both Emmy and Beth had Alaric doubting those instincts today.

On the fifth floor, Ravi paused outside the door, listening while he checked out the lock—a simple mortise by the look of it. "All quiet inside. Wanna knock?"

"Yes, to start with."

In the absence of a doorbell, Alaric rapped lightly on the wood with his knuckles.

Silence. Ravi was right. Either there was nobody home or Ryland was lying low. The question was, which? If they went in uninvited, they had no plausible excuse for being there whatsoever. Logic said to back away, but what if Gemma was incapacitated inside?

Ravi raised an eyebrow. He already had his picks in his hand, so his opinion was clear.

Ah, fuck it.

"Let's go in."

Twenty seconds later, the lock clicked open, and Ravi peered through the crack.

"What the...?" He pushed the door open wider. "Shit."

Shit indeed. The apartment was empty. Devoid of life and furniture. Apart from a trail of rat droppings on the beige carpet, the place was bare. Except...

Ravi made a face. "What the hell is that smell?"

Had a rat died in there? Alaric glanced around the living room, then checked the kitchen, bathroom, and bedroom. No decomposing carcasses, but the odour reminded him of his first solo job as a CIA agent. He'd found the missing informant he'd been sent to locate, but unfortunately, it had taken a DNA test to identify the poor bastard.

"I don't know. I'm not sure I *want* to know." Alaric tapped the floor with a heel. Concrete, not wood. Nothing in the built-in bedroom closet either. "But it's safe to say Ryland isn't here and neither is Gemma."

"Try the neighbours?"

Something buzzed past Alaric's face, and he smacked a fly away.

"Might as well. The worst that can happen is they'll tell us to fuck off, and this apartment gives me the creeps."

At least, Alaric hoped that was the worst that could happen. Almost unconsciously, he checked the gun at his back was still within easy reach. He didn't plan on using it, but...

"Left or right?"

"Left," Alaric said out of habit. Back in the days of Emmy, she'd joked that she was always right so he must be left. It had stuck.

Again, he knocked and waited. And waited. Just as they were about to give up, he heard footsteps, and the door opened an inch, blocked by a chain. The girl could have been anywhere from eighteen to thirty, slight in build, and she barely looked strong enough to hold the baby on her hip.

"Hallo?"

"Good afternoon, Miss. I'm from Hounslow Borough Council, and I'm hoping to speak to your next-door neighbour—Ryland Willis—but he doesn't seem to be in. Could you tell me when you last saw him?"

"The council?" She repeated the words haltingly. "I have papers. I am allowed to be here."

"We're just looking for your neighbour. Next door." Alaric waved his hand to the right for emphasis, and as air wafted past, he sniffed. Smelled like soup. "We had a complaint that he's keeping a cat in there."

More puzzlement. "Next door? There is nobody next door."

"A man? A tall man? Big?"

"Nobody. Empty."

"Empty how long?"

"Since I came here. Three weeks. Nearly four."

So Ryland had left a month ago at least? Dammit. Where the hell had he gone?

"I appreciate your help." They stepped back to leave, but the door opened a fraction wider.

"Speak with Eunice. The other side. Five-zero-five. Eunice, she knows everything."

This time, Alaric's smile was genuine. "Thank you."

Except Eunice wasn't in. He knocked and waited, then knocked again. The tower was far from silent—footsteps echoed in the stairwells, and a couple was arguing on another floor—but nothing stirred in apartment 505. They had no choice but to cast the net wider.

By the time darkness fell, Alaric had been spat at by a kid on a skateboard, shouted at by a group of teenagers, and narrowly avoided a broken nose when the living incarnation of Homer Simpson slammed the door in his face. Ravi materialised at his elbow as he paused in front of yet another apartment. At least Beth was holding herself together. She'd sounded nervous each time Alaric checked in with her, but the car doors were locked, and he heard the engine running in the background so at least she could make a quick getaway if necessary. Still, he didn't want to leave her on her own for much longer.

"Anything?" Ravi asked.

"Either the guy's a ghost or people here just like keeping their mouths shut."

"Or perhaps it's a case of see no evil, hear no evil."

"That too."

Alaric pressed the doorbell, and a scratchy tune rang out, entirely too jolly for the surroundings. *Please, let this one be a woman.* Women had less of a tendency to threaten bodily harm in response to a simple question. Nobody answered, but out of the corner of his eye, he saw a girl barely older than Rune pause at the other end of the hallway, her grip tightening on the hand of the toddler beside her. She wanted to run, but the kid prevented her from doing so.

Alaric tried a smile. "Is this your place?"

"Maybe. Who's askin'? I don't want no trouble."

Her gaze flicked between Alaric and Ravi as she sized them up, and Alaric dropped his hands open at his sides, going for non-threatening.

"There's no trouble, honest. I borrowed a weight belt off a guy in the gym a few weeks ago, and I need to return it, only he hasn't been back for a while."

"What's that got to do with me?"

"He was one of your neighbours, but he seems to have moved out. Ryland Willis? In flat 504?"

"Don't know him."

Alaric held out a copy of the mugshot Beth had taken from the noticeboard at the gym. "Are you sure? He's a big guy, and he was dating a pretty brunette."

The girl glanced at the photo, dismissive at first, then leaned forward an inch to take a second look.

"Oh, yeah, Ry. I do know him. Want my advice? Keep the belt."

"Why do you say that?"

"'Cause he's a creep."

"Really? He always seemed okay to me."

"That's 'cause you're a bloke."

So Ryland was creepy to women? That fit with Gemma's "uncomfortable" description on Beth's voicemail.

"He did something to you?"

"Not to me. My friend. He offered her a lift to Currys to pick up a new TV, then tried to drive her somewhere else."

"But she got away?"

"Jumped out at some traffic lights."

"Your friend—is she around?"

"Nah, she's in prison." The girl tried to skirt past, dragging the toddler along with her. "I shouldn't have said nothin'. People don't like snitches round 'ere."

"As I said, I'm not looking to cause trouble. Do you know where Ry moved to?"

"No, but he ain't gone far. I seen 'im around."

"You think he's still living on the estate?"

"No other reason he'd be here."

"When did you last see him?"

"Yesterday." The girl paused, considering. "No, the day before. Walkin' past the kebab shop."

"The kebab shop on the other side of the south tower?"

She made it to her front door and took three attempts to get the key into the lock. Still nervous?

"Yeah. But like I said, just keep the damn belt."

The door slammed behind her, and Alaric heard voices from inside—not another occupant, but the canned laughter of a TV sitcom. Just another evening in paradise.

"Is there any woman you haven't managed to wrap around your little finger?" Ravi asked as they headed for the stairs.

Only two. And as luck would have it, one called as they hit the ground floor.

"About that flight..." Emmy started.

Shit. He should have updated her. "We can't make it. Not tonight."

"Ditto. The dude I was meant to be meeting got delayed in Tokyo. Now he's not arriving until tomorrow afternoon, and it's easier for me to wait than reschedule again."

"Tell me you're not taking on the Yakuza?"

"No, I want to add a saké line to my portfolio. I'm gonna call it Four Fox. Four Fox Saké—get it? Did you know I bought a distillery a couple of years back? No Fox Given Gin, available from selected retailers and the wet bar at Riverley."

"I didn't know, but it doesn't surprise me in the slightest. I'd better put an order in. We'll all need it before this job's over."

"The missing girl? She didn't show up yet?"

"No, but we've narrowed down our main suspect's address to a few square blocks in Hounslow. I don't suppose you could spare anyone to help tomorrow? Somebody who wouldn't look out of place wandering around the housing estate from hell."

"You can borrow Sky, and I'll see if there's anyone else free. What time are you starting?"

"First thing."

The sooner they started, the more chance they had of finding Gemma alive. The clock was ticking in the background, an unrelenting march towards an outcome Alaric didn't want to contemplate.

"Text me the address, and I'll send her over for eight. Good luck. You'll need it," she added under her breath.

Good luck with Sky or with the search? Either one had the potential to be a nightmare.

# Chapter 40 - Alaric

SKY CERTAINLY CAME dressed for the part. When she fell out of an Uber on Wednesday morning, she looked as though the love child of a hangover and influenza had staggered through a branch of Sports Direct and barely lived to tell the tale.

"What the hell happened to you?" Alaric asked.

She rubbed bloodshot eyes. "I stayed up late helping Emmy to prep for a meeting."

Hmm. Exactly what kind of prep did one need to do to import Japanese rice wine? "You were taste-testing saké?"

"I swear I'm never drinking again."

"You shouldn't have been drinking in the first place. You're only seventeen."

"Not anymore. Emmy got me a new passport."

Of course she did.

"That's not the point."

"You're telling me you never touched alcohol before you were eighteen?"

Ravi laughed, but Beth just looked worried. Alaric hated seeing her like that. She should be safely behind her desk at home, tidying up reports and making sure Judd flew to Paris, France, instead of Paris, Texas, this time. Barbara's predecessor hadn't been hired for her brains.

"Here, have my coffee." Beth held the travel mug towards Sky, who sucked most of it down without pausing for breath, then passed the mug back. "Do you want to sit for a moment?"

"Nah, I'm fine. Just tell me who we're looking for."

Alaric gave her a copy of Ryland's picture, then did the same with two foot soldiers from Blackwood who turned up shortly afterwards. They'd start at the edges of the estate and work inwards while Alaric, Ravi, and Sky focused on the centre.

It was slow going. A handful of people thought they might have seen Ryland around, but most either shook their heads or ignored the questions completely. Every hour, Beth tried calling Gemma just in case she resurfaced, but her phone remained off, its whereabouts unknown. Alaric had taken Ryland's number from his file at the gym too, and that was out of service.

He was losing hope when his mobile rang.

"I just saw him," Sky said, breathless. "A minute ago. I'm sure I did. Massive bloke. That photo doesn't do him justice."

"Where?"

"Walking past the kebab shop. But by the time I got outside, he'd gone."

"Which direction?"

"Towards the skateboard ramp."

"We're on our way."

Dammit, the man was a ghost. Sky was right—he'd vanished. But at least they knew he was still around, and between the stink in his old flat and the "creep" factor, they couldn't afford to let up in the search. Alaric considered calling the police and explaining the situation, but from what he'd heard, the Bellsfield Estate was considered a problem child and they avoided it whenever possible. He tried Emmy instead.

"How's your hangover?"

"I'm rethinking the saké idea. How's your search?"

"Frustrating. Sky spotted our guy, but he disappeared again. I've got a bad feeling about this."

A long pause was followed by a heavy sigh. That was new. Old Emmy had never sounded so weary.

"My meeting's done. I'll come over."

"Is everything okay?"

"Why wouldn't it be?"

"I don't know. It's just..."

"What?"

"Never mind." Now wasn't the time to have that conversation. "I appreciate the help, Cinders."

The breakthrough came later that afternoon. Funny how you could spend hours chasing your own tail only to catch the prize when you least expected it.

It happened when Alaric gave in to his hunger pangs and stopped at the Co-op for a sandwich. Ryland's not-quite neighbour, the girl from 503, was ahead of him in the line with her baby in one arm and a basket of food in the other. Instant noodles, plain yogurt, jars of baby food, a loaf of bread... No luxuries, but when she got to the checkout and saw the total, she stared at it in shock.

"I will put something back."

She pulled out two apples and put them on the counter, then a package of pasta and a box of laundry powder. Fuck. Nobody should have to choose between clean clothes and healthy food. He slid a twenty-pound note across to the cashier.

"Take it out of this."

The cashier did a double take. "What, all of it?"

Alaric nodded. It wouldn't exactly break the bank.

When the girl realised what was happening, she turned to him, eyes glistening.

"You can't..."

"I just did."

She opened her mouth. Closed it again and sniffed before blurting, "Thank you." Then her eyes lit in recognition. "I remember you. Did you find the man?"

"Not yet."

"Eunice didn't know?"

"Eunice hasn't been home."

"Oh. She is probably with her daughter. Over there." The girl pointed out the window, past the towers and the dilapidated playground.

"Here on the estate?"

"Yes."

"Do you have the address?"

She shook her head. "But I can take you there?"

Sandwich and change forgotten, Alaric grabbed the girl's groceries and motioned her out of the store, hoping, *hoping*, that this would be the lead they were looking for. Over three days had passed since anyone heard from Gemma, and statistically... No, he didn't want to think about it. The stench from Ryland's old apartment still lingered in his nostrils.

"Let's go."

"It really is not allowed to keep a cat?" the girl asked.

"Huh?" Sometimes, it was hard to keep all the lies and half-truths straight. Alaric had almost forgotten his initial pretence. "It's a condition of the tenancy. No cats."

"What about a dog?"

"Dogs are fine as long as they're quiet." Probably.

"Then perhaps one day I will get a dog."

A fur-coated burglar alarm. "Good idea."

They wound through the graffiti-covered maze, skirting groups of loitering kids and the occasional vagrant. In Alaric's old life, he'd heard acquaintances from the other side of the tracks ask, *How can people live like this?* But now he knew the answer. They'd been failed. Failed by politicians out for themselves, failed by a society conditioned to accept other people's suffering, failed by a belief that this was their destiny. Too often, people valued material possessions above happiness, and the result was misery that spread like a plague. No one person could fix the problem. It would take an army.

But today, he had to focus on a different issue. Gemma. The girl stopped in front of a dilapidated maisonette and pointed at a set of stairs leading to the second floor.

"Up there."

"Thanks. Do you want to wait for me to walk back with you?"

"No, it is okay. I need to go home."

She vanished without another word, leaving Alaric to speak to Eunice alone.

When the door of the maisonette swung open, Alaric thought he'd taken the red pill and ended up in *The Matrix*. The woman in front of him looked just like

The Oracle, and if the girl from 503 was correct, she might just have the knowledge to match.

"Eunice?"

She folded her arms. "Who are you?"

Alaric tried his spiel again. "Good afternoon, ma'am. I'm from Hounslow Borough Council, and I'm hoping to speak to Ryland Willis. Your neighbour from 503 pointed me over here in case you could help. I believe he used to live next—"

"Bull-sheeet. You ain't from no council. Councilmen don't come around here, not unless it's an election year, and even then them cowards don't make it past the ground floor."

Alaric had to laugh. Eunice *was* a perceptive old battleaxe, and she had the spine to match.

"Okay, you got me. I'm not from the council."

"Ryland owe you money? He owe every other sucker money."

"Yes, exactly that. I wish I could let it go, but..."

"Then everyone would take the piss, I get it. But you're out of luck, toots. Ryland upped and left six weeks ago. Something about a problem with the plumbing. The water wasn't draining properly. He used to call and complain every damn day, eight o'clock, right before I went to work. I heard him yelling through the walls. The poor bastard of a landlord finally gave in and moved him to another place."

"Are your drains okay? I noticed a bad smell in the hallway outside Ryland's flat."

"Had a fall when I was six. *Crack*. Banged my head on the kerb, and now I can't smell a thing. Hevrin said there was a stink the other day, but she don't complain none."

"Hevrin?"

"In 503. She won't rock the boat, that girl. Too scared of gettin' sent back home."

"Where's home?"

"Syria. They killed her whole damn family."

"They? The government?"

"The Turks. She watched her parents die, her brothers, her sister, her husband, and they said she was one of the lucky ones. What kind of world is her daughter gonna grow up in? You got kids?"

What kind of world, indeed? It was a question Alaric had considered many times after he met Rune. Sirius had been born out of the unpalatable answer. When he'd formed the partnership with Judd, Ravi, and Naz, they'd made a vow to each other—any job they took would be for the greater good. Any line they crossed would be for the benefit of humanity. Selling information had proven to be a profitable business, but money couldn't buy the sense of satisfaction that came from empowering people who'd fight for the right causes. Their research had put an ethically challenged logging firm out of business, helped an idealistic pharmaceutical start-up to quash their Goliath of a competitor, and exposed illegal practices in a network of private detention centres, to name but a few projects. Corporate research was their bread and butter, but politics was a profitable sideline. Alaric had lost count of the number of corrupt officials they'd exposed. He didn't much like oligarchs either.

"Yeah, I've got a daughter," Alaric told Eunice. "Doing my best to avoid her following in her old man's footsteps."

Eunice chortled, then went into a coughing fit, and

Alaric caught a whiff of old cigarette smoke over the delightful aroma of fried food drifting from the maisonette.

"Preyin' on the desperate, you mean?"

Alaric shrugged and answered with a chuckle of his own. "Supply and demand."

"I like you. I shouldn't like you, but I do."

"You got any idea where Ryland went?"

"Not far. They put him in the other tower."

"Don't suppose you know what number?"

"Top floor. Not sure which unit. But you didn't get any of this from me, understand? I ain't no narc, but Ryland never had a good word for nobody."

"My lips are sealed. He didn't have many friends?"

"Friends? No. Sometimes women. The man looked after himself, you know? But once they found out what was underneath, none of them stuck around for long."

"There were arguments?"

"Not that I ever heard. They'd be there, and then they wouldn't be, and a new girl would show up." A child's cries came from inside the maisonette, and Eunice backed away. "My granddaughter just woke up."

"Thanks for your help."

She closed the door without another word.

# CHAPTER 41 - ALARIC

THERE WERE EIGHT doors on the top floor of Bellsfield House South. One led to the roof, according to a yellowed sign, and another to a janitorial closet that couldn't have been used for years if the state of the place was any indication. That left six. And they'd tried five.

Two tenants had answered, and neither of them was Ryland Willis. The other three apartments were empty, but Ravi had worked his magic and they'd snooped around inside. Two clearly belonged to families, and the third to a female.

They stacked up outside the door of apartment 1706, Emmy and Sky on one side, Alaric and Ravi on the other. Alaric questioned the wisdom of Sky being there, but Emmy had made the call and he trusted her judgement. The other two men from Blackwood were watching the stairs and the elevator respectively, both to prevent unexpected visitors and to stop Ryland from escaping if he somehow managed to slip past the four of them and make a run for it.

Was he inside? Alaric could hear a TV, so it was a good possibility.

Emmy raised a hand and quirked an eyebrow at him. He nodded. She could do the honours.

She knocked.

No answer. Then silence as the TV shut off. The door stayed closed.

Shit.

They'd had two options—knock and hope Ryland opened the door, or let themselves in. They'd chosen the former because most people tended to answer the door. But it seemed Ryland was antisocial, and now they'd lost the element of surprise.

Emmy tried knocking once more.

Was it Alaric's imagination, or did he hear the quiet shuffle of a footstep on the other side of the door?

"Denise? You in?" Emmy yelled, slurring slightly. "I need a cigarette." She banged on the door again, harder this time. "Denise?"

"Wrong place, lady."

So Ryland *was* home.

"Who are you?"

"Get lost."

What a charmer.

"Fuck you too, asshole."

Emmy clomped along the hallway, then tiptoed back again. Two minutes passed, four, nobody moving a muscle, and then she pointed at the lock picks in Ravi's hand. They were going in. Adrenaline had been simmering through Alaric's veins for a while, but now it surged as his body prepared to fight. He'd seen the size of Ryland's shoulders in that mugshot from the gym's noticeboard. The man wouldn't go down easy.

A quiet *click* was the only giveaway that Ravi had done his job, at least until Emmy slowly pushed open the door, keeping her body to the side. Did she have a gun too? If not, she'd certainly have a knife, and she knew how to use it.

The door inched open to reveal a surprisingly tidy living room. Beige carpet, two low cream leather couches at right angles to each other opposite the mother of all TVs. Matching coffee table and sideboard that looked as if they came from IKEA. Dining table with four chairs and one used plate. Drapes pulled tight across every window. No Ryland.

Alaric's mind fired through the possibilities. Two doors opened from the left side of the room, and another on the right. Bedroom, bathroom, kitchen? Emmy headed left with Sky in tow, leaving Alaric and Ravi to take...yes, the kitchen. The smell of cooked chicken permeated throughout, and a collection of unwashed pans lay jumbled in the sink. No sign of a woman's touch in the room. No magnets on the fridge, no rubber gloves, no moisturiser near the faucet. And unless Ryland had squashed himself into a cupboard, he wasn't there either. Which meant he was in—

*Oh, fuck.*

A crash sounded from the other side of the apartment, followed by the *slap, slap, slap* of feet on tile. Since the living room was carpeted, that could only mean one thing. Ryland had escaped.

Alaric shot out of the front door in time to see Ryland dragging a woman along the hallway in his direction, the door to the janitor's closet swinging open behind him. What the...? Gemma. It was Gemma, and her hands were secured in front of her. A piece of duct tape hung from one side of her face, a gag loosened in the struggle, and her eyes were ringed red from crying. Alaric fumbled for his gun, got it up, but Ryland had already swung around, putting Gemma between himself and a bullet.

"Stop!"

But Ryland didn't stop. He backed away, his arm a steel band around Gemma's chest. She struggled, kicking her feet, then squealed in pain as he squeezed harder. A trickle of blood ran down her neck where Frankenstein's monster pressed the tip of a knife against it.

"Shut up, shut up, shut up!"

Alaric felt rather than saw a presence behind him. Emmy? Ravi? Sky? He didn't take his eyes off Ryland to check. Sky was right—the man was a giant, and right now his gaze roved wildly like a cornered bull's as he shuffled backwards towards a dead end. What would he do when he reached the wall? Gemma was sobbing now, but Alaric couldn't shoot without risking her life.

"Put her down. You've got nowhere to go."

Except that was a lie.

As Ryland passed the door to the roof, he quickly moved sideways, hitting it full-force with one shoulder. The flimsy lock didn't stand a chance. And the man could move. The door bounced off the wall and slammed shut, and by the time Alaric got it open again, Ryland was on top of the damn building.

Gemma's sobs turned to screams as the wind hit them. Seventeen floors up, it was blowing a gale, and Ryland was still backing up, this time towards the north tower. The full moon glinted off the knife as shadows danced like ghouls in the gloom.

"Stand still."

Ryland glanced behind himself, judging the distance. He was ten yards or so from the edge, but unless he planned on jumping, he really was out of options. He was also unhinged—that much was clear.

Alaric lowered his gun and paused in front of the door, hoping that if he stood his ground, Ryland would calm down. It seemed to work to some degree. Ryland stopped moving.

Ravi took up a position beside Alaric, but where were Emmy and Sky? Alaric's heart stuttered. That crash downstairs... He'd just assumed that since Emmy was involved, they were both okay. But what if one of them had been injured? Knocked out, or worse?

*Shit, double shit, triple shit.*

He needed to check on them, but he couldn't, not with a hostage situation on the roof demanding his attention. He hated hostage situations. The last one he'd been involved with had gone on for almost two days and only ended when an FBI sniper had gotten a clear shot. Alaric didn't have a clear shot, and he was unlikely to get one with the wind blowing in unpredictable gusts. And if he tried to shoot and missed, there was a cinderblock plant room Ryland could jump behind.

The other problem was the knife. Alaric was ten yards away, too far to intervene physically if Ryland decided to take his fear and anger out on Gemma. If the worst happened and he cut her, she might bleed out even if they put all their efforts into saving her life and let Ryland get away.

"Now what?" Ravi whispered.

Good question. Alaric would have to take the lead on this. Ravi was smart, but he was a cat burglar, an acrobat, and a thief, not a hostage negotiator. And they were in a stand-off. There was no choice but to talk.

"Well, Ryland, this is an awkward position we find ourselves in..."

It was times like this that Alaric wished he was still bumming around on a beach in Thailand.

# CHAPTER 42 - SKY

"WHERE ARE WE going?"

Some crazy-ass freak was carrying a crying brunette across a roof, Alaric had a fucking gun aimed at said freak, and yet Emmy was dragging me away. What the hell?

"Shh."

Quite frankly, I was still trying to work out what happened. We'd nosed through the bathroom in Ryland's apartment and found it empty apart from a dozen air fresheners, seven bottles of bleach, three of drain cleaner, four spare shower curtains, a lifetime's supply of shower gel, and two toilet brushes—then moved into the bedroom, which was also pretty spartan. A man who liked housework? Well, that was a novelty. The bed was unmade, too low for a man of Ryland's size to hide underneath, and the laundry hamper was on the small side as well. The only place left to check was the double wardrobe. As Emmy approached it, there'd been a sort of...squeak from inside, followed by a crash, and we tried to get the door open but it was jammed shut. By the time we broke it off the hinges and found the hole through to the janitor's-closet-turned-prison-cell on the other side of the wall, Ryland was halfway up the bloody stairs.

And now we were halfway down them.

"Hello? There's a woman being held hostage up there. Shouldn't we be calling the police?"

"Oh, sure, so they can show up in an hour and make a bad situation worse."

"Well, how exactly are *we* helping? You just left Alaric and Ravi up there on their own."

"Alaric's a big boy. He can handle it. Now, this is one of those rare and memorable occasions where we get to use the elevator."

"Everything okay, boss?" one of the Blackwood men asked as Emmy tugged me through the sliding doors. The thing stank. If I lived in this place, I'd take the stairs every day.

"There's a hostage situation on the roof. Once we've hit the ground floor, call the elevator back up and hold it here, okay?"

"Roger that."

Why were we leaving? I thought Emmy was supposed to be a fighter, but this felt more like a disorganised retreat.

"Did you see the knife?" I asked as the lift rumbled into life.

"Yeah, I saw the knife. Did you see the serial killer starter kit in the bathroom?"

Ah, fuck. All that bleach. The extra shower curtains. Now I felt sick. "What if he stabs her while we're...while we're..."

"While we're flanking him. Don't worry—Alaric's got the gift of the gab. He'll keep the lunatic talking for a few minutes. We just have to hurry up."

"Flanking him? What are you talking about?"

As we slowly descended into the bowels of Bellsfield House South, Emmy laid out her plan, and I realised a harsh truth. Ryland Willis wasn't the crazy one. No, my new boss took gold for that. And me? I was in silver medal position, stuck on the second step of the podium since I'd just signed my life over to her for what promised to be six long, long months.

## Chapter 43 - Bethany

WHAT WAS GOING on? Half an hour ago, Alaric had called to say they'd got a lead on Ryland, and everyone except me had headed into Bellsfield House South, but since then, it had been radio silence. Should I try calling? I didn't want to disturb Alaric if he was in the middle of something important, but the waiting was unbearable.

For most of the day, I'd been hiding out in a car park on the far side of the play area, but as darkness fell, a group of youths had appeared, and they kept kicking a football against the side of the vehicle. On purpose, I suspected. So after Alaric's call, I'd moved the SUV, slotting it in between a dumpster and what had once been a sofa before rain, vandals, and mould got to it. The position gave me a good view of the south tower, and for that, I'd put up with the rotten smell.

I was checking the phone—yet again—when movement caught my eye. Two blondes burst out of the door. Was that...was that Emmy? And Sky? They weren't hanging around. The pair of them ran right past the front of the SUV, and before I had time to think what a bad, bad idea it was, I jumped out and sprinted after them. Something was wrong, wasn't it?

"What happened?" I gasped as I burst into the lobby of the north tower behind them.

Emmy cursed under her breath, and I wasn't sure whether her words were aimed at me or the out-of-order lift.

"Go back to the car."

"Where's Alaric?"

"Busy. The car, Bethany."

She headed for the stairs, and I followed. She may have been rich and she may have been powerful, but I'd be damned if she was going to give me the brush-off like that. Not when a man I cared about was involved. Yes, even after my father's warning, I still cared about Alaric. Against my best efforts, my heart had overruled my head and fallen a tiny bit in love with him, and if he was in trouble... I ran after Emmy and Sky.

For seventeen floors. Seventeen *freaking* floors. My heart threatened to give out somewhere around level fifteen, but if there was one thing I was good at, it was stairs. After Piers made a throwaway comment about my butt being saggy, pride had led me to spend hours climbing on the StairMaster, a hundred floors at the start of every gym session. I may have sounded like a dying walrus by the time we reached the top of the north tower, but I wasn't far behind.

"Tell me what happened!" I choked out.

"Shitting hell. Are you incapable of following directions?"

Oh, that made me see red.

"Actually, I'm really, really good at it. I kowtowed to Piers for years which, if you think about it, was how we all ended up here in this delightful place. And do you know what? I'm sick of doing what I'm told."

"Well, while you're getting butt-hurt and wasting my time, your friend's being held hostage, so how about you sit the fuck down, shut the fuck up, and let me get on with my job so she doesn't end up dead instead?"

The anger blew out of me, and I slithered down the wall like a deflated beach ball. Gemma was a hostage?

"I'm sorry," I whispered, but Emmy and Sky were already gone. Farther along the corridor, a door clanged shut, and I was alone again. And scared. Gemma was in danger, I still didn't know where Alaric had gone, and I might have made things worse by interfering. I wasn't cut out for this. I shouldn't be working for a company like Sirius. Hell, I couldn't even sell paintings without screwing up.

What now? More than anything, I wanted to go home, but I couldn't just drive off with Alaric's car, and I didn't fancy walking to the Tube station on my own at night either. No, I needed to wait for Emmy to finish whatever she was doing, then apologise and beg for a ride back to civilisation. And tomorrow, I'd have to call my father, apologise profusely, and offer to rejoin the country club social committee.

If nothing else, at least I'd still have Chaucer, and as I hugged my knees against my chest in the gloom, I prayed that Gemma would be safe too.

## CHAPTER 44 - SKY

"UH, YOU'RE GONNA die."

Emmy had picked the lock on the door to the roof, and we'd crept across the moss-covered asphalt and hidden behind some sort of ventilation unit. From there, we had a prime view of the action, not to mention the large gap between the two towers.

The gap Emmy thought she was going to jump.

See? Crazy.

Ryland had his back to us, his arms wrapped around Gemma, and Alaric was still standing with Ravi by the access door. Not much seemed to have changed during our wild run up the stairs except for the fact that my heart was fast heading for cardiac arrest. Emmy wasn't even out of breath. If we both survived until morning, I definitely planned to spend more time in the gym.

"Aren't you just a fountain of positivity tonight?"

"Just sayin'."

"I'm not going to die."

"The gap's, like, six metres? Seven? And the towers are the same height. It's too far."

"The wind's with me."

And gravity was against her. "It's not enough."

Every so often, a snippet of conversation drifted across, and it seemed to me that Ryland was unravelling by the minute. Gemma had gone quiet, and I wasn't sure whether that was a good sign or a bad sign.

"We all want to walk out of here," Alaric said, his voice calm. "All you have to do is let Gemma go."

"I want a helicopter!"

Yup, looney tunes.

"I can't promise a helicopter, but I have a car downstairs."

"You'll come after me! I'd rather jump than go to jail!"

"Alaric had better have a tracker in his car," Emmy muttered.

That sounded hopeful. "Does this mean you're not jumping?"

"You're right. It *is* too far." I'd never heard Emmy sound so dejected before. "I'd need more height."

"So should we cover the car? Or do you want me to stay here and keep you updated while you go downstairs?"

"Dammit, I don't want Ryland getting off that roof. He's insane. What if he takes another hostage on the way down?"

"Should we clear the way or something? Tell people to stay in their flats?"

"Ravi would need to stay on the roof with Gemma. That only leaves five of us to go after Ryland, and this estate is a maze."

"Six. What about Beth?"

"If we let Beth 'help,' she'll probably get taken hostage herself. She's got no street smarts. Zero. But..." Emmy's gaze settled on something behind me, and a sickening dread poured itself into my stomach. Her smile... It was cunning in a terrifying sort of way. "I have a better idea."

"Does it involve calling a SWAT team and letting them deal with the problem?"

"SWAT? Depending who's on duty, you'll get either 'Sit, Wait, And Talk' or 'Shoot Without Any Thinking.'"

On the other roof, Ryland took a step backwards. How Alaric remained calm, I had no idea. And where was his gun? I couldn't see it in his hand anymore.

"So what's your idea?"

Emmy turned me around and pointed at a wooden board, just visible in the darkness among the piles of junk dotted all over the roof. There were flapping bags of building materials, rusty satellite dishes, concrete blocks, even a manky old mattress.

"Simple. You're gonna give me the extra height I need."

She wanted a fucking ramp? Oh, hell no. "Maybe I could book you an appointment with a psychiatrist instead? I hear the room next to Lenny's is free."

"Sky, Sky... Always so negative." She picked up one end of the board, careful to keep the ventilation unit between herself and Ryland in case he turned around. "Now, what's the best way to hold this?"

I took the weight. The good news was that the board wasn't rotten; the bad news was that it was bloody heavy. If I hooked it over my forearms, I wouldn't be able to hold it with Emmy's weight as well. If I knelt on my hands and knees with it on my back, there wouldn't be enough height. I considered bending forward with my hands on my knees and balancing it on my arse, but that would give us a stability problem. Beside me, Emmy twisted and turned and judging by her sour expression, came to the same conclusion.

"What we need is another volunteer," she said. "Then we could have one person each side, arms bridged."

"How about that dude by the lift? He's big."

"Too far away."

She jerked her head at the tower, and I saw Ryland had taken a few steps closer to the edge. The sound of Gemma's sobs drifted across, and I wanted to take the board and smash it over his deranged head. Shame it wasn't long enough.

We both looked at each other, and I knew Emmy was thinking the same thing. So near, yet so far. We had to do something, but what?

She spoke first. "Beth. She's closer."

"I thought you said she was a liability?"

"Mentally, she's fragile, but she stayed with us all the way up those stairs, and she rides horses. Physically, she's tough. See if she's still there."

Ryland took another step as I crept back to the stairwell. Whatever we did, it had to be fast.

# Chapter 45 - Alaric

RYLAND HAD LOST his damn mind. Alaric saw it in his eyes. He wouldn't listen to reason, and at this stage, the only option left was to walk away, to let him go and try to catch him downstairs. The blood was running freely down Gemma's throat now. One wrong move, and he'd nick an artery.

Alaric hated to lose. It felt like being back on the Seaduction, knowing the job was turning to shit but unable to do anything about it. At least he had Ravi at his back rather than a bloodthirsty agent with an itchy trigger finger—that was some small measure of comfort. But where the hell was Emmy? For five long minutes, he'd been asking himself that question, each time Ryland yelled out a crazy demand or took another step backwards.

Then he found out the answer, and suddenly, he didn't want to know anymore.

What the fuck? Why was she on the other roof? And what was Beth doing there? She was meant to be locked in the car, out of trouble and definitely not carrying... What *was* that? Some sort of plank?

*Don't react, don't react, don't react.*

If he reacted, if Ryland turned to see what he was looking at, then Gemma was dead. Alaric glanced sideways. Next to him, Ravi had his eyes firmly fixed on

Ryland too.

"We can still sort this out. Right now, Gemma isn't hurt." More or less. "You won't go to the police, will you, Gemma?"

"N-n-no."

"We're moving away from the door now. See?"

Alaric went left and motioned Ravi to move to the right. Whatever Emmy was planning, he wanted to cover all bases. Then he realised what she was planning and wanted to cover his eyes instead. Fuck, no. Tell him she wasn't going to... She was. She was going to jump.

He wanted to shout, to tell her to stop, but he knew it was pointless. If Emmy had made up her mind to do something, she'd do it. She'd done exactly the same thing when she leapt the gap between the Seaduction and the scallop boat to rescue Alaric eight years ago. Her single-minded determination was one of the things he both loved and hated about her.

But what about Beth? She appeared to have been roped into this cockamamie plan, and he'd thought she was more sensible than that. What if he yelled at her to put down the plank? Then Emmy couldn't jump. Except... Except now Emmy was on her run-up, and it was too late.

Alaric's heart threatened to quit as she sprinted up the plank and leapt, arms outstretched to keep her body upright. Oh, shit! She wasn't going to make it... At the last second, she flicked her legs to the side, tucked, and rolled like a demented hedgehog. A stone skittered across the roof. Ryland snapped his head around, but Emmy had already vanished behind the plant room, thank fuck. Sky and Beth had disappeared too, melted back into the darkness on the south tower. He'd be having words with Ms. Stafford-Lyons later. Sky's involvement, he could understand, but Beth should have known better.

"You won't let me go," Ryland said, turning his attention back to Alaric. "I know it. You'll call the cops, and—"

He took another step back, and Emmy struck. The knife went flying as she ripped Ryland's hand away from Gemma's neck, Alaric leapt forward to pull Gemma from the psycho's grip, and they rolled out of the way. But it wasn't over. The guy must have been twice Emmy's weight, and he was hopped up on adrenaline and steroids and fuck knew what else. They grappled, getting perilously close to the edge of the roof as Emmy fought for the upper hand. Finally, she wrenched herself free and booted him in the chest. He overbalanced, arms flailing, but Emmy teetered too.

Ryland toppled over the edge.

And with Gemma sprawled on top of him, Alaric could do nothing but watch in horror as Emmy followed.

He closed his eyes. There were a thousand things he wanted to say to her—I'm sorry, I wish things had been different, I love you—but the words stuck in his throat.

Then he heard a whoop, and his eyes popped open in time to see a crouching Ravi swing Emmy up into the air as if the pair of them had rehearsed the act a hundred times. She landed like a cat.

Nine lives. The crazy bitch had nine fucking lives.

Alaric helped Gemma to her feet, and he had to hold her up, she was trembling so much. His knees weren't much steadier. Emmy produced a knife—Alaric had been right about her carrying—and sliced the tape off Gemma's wrists.

"We need to get out of here. Ryland's splattered across the walkway, and I don't fancy spending the night in an interview room."

Vintage Emmy. She'd come close to death, yet she was the calmest of all of them. Ravi looked more shaken up than her. Alaric glanced across to the south tower. Sky and Beth were wrapped up in a hug, whether out of joy or relief he wasn't sure. Emmy caught Sky's eye and motioned her down the stairs.

"W-w-what's happening?" Gemma asked. "Are you the police?"

"Not exactly." Alaric scooped her up and headed for the stairs. Could she feel his heart pounding against his ribcage? It was threatening to crack a bone from the inside out. "We'll talk about that later, okay?"

By the time they got to the lobby, a small crowd had gathered between the two buildings. Most of the onlookers had smartphones out, filming and taking photos, and nobody paid Alaric and company the slightest attention as they regrouped outside.

"Go and get the car, would you?" Emmy said to her Blackwood guys, and they vanished into the night.

"Where's the SUV?" Alaric asked Beth, and she pointed a quaking finger into the darkness. At that moment, Alaric was glad she'd been on the roof with Sky because otherwise, she'd have had a front-row seat for Ryland's swan dive.

"You okay?"

"Not really."

He had to appreciate her honesty.

"Have you got the key?"

She fumbled in her pocket and held it out.

Ravi took it from her. "How about I do the honours?"

That left Alaric with the four women. He set Gemma on her feet again, keeping one arm around her waist because she still didn't look too steady. Hardly surprising after the debacle on the roof, and who knew what hell Ryland had inflicted on her over the past three days.

"Beth?" Gemma rubbed her eyes. "Is that really you?"

"Yes, it's me. Don't worry, we're going to take you away from here."

"Is he dead? Is Ry dead?"

Beth looked to Alaric. She must've known Ryland was spread out across the concrete, but Alaric understood she didn't want to be the one to break the news.

He mustered up a sombre tone as he herded them both towards the SUV. "I'm afraid he is."

"Good. I hope it hurt."

Pain scored through Gemma's words, and Alaric realised that whatever Ryland had done to her, it was both worse than he'd hoped and as bad as he feared. He helped her into the back seat with Beth and then turned to Emmy.

"You okay, Cinders?"

"Fine."

*Fine.* The word was a warning klaxon coming from Emmy. She wasn't fine, not by a long shot. Anyone else might have assumed the near-death experience had unsettled her, but she'd been acting weird before that.

"Liar."

She didn't even bother to deny it. "It's too late to fly

tonight. I'll reschedule for tomorrow. Text me if you and Beth want a ride, okay?"

"You're leaving?"

"No point in hanging around." Ravi got a bigger smile from Emmy than Alaric did. "Thanks for the acrobatics lesson."

Ravi still looked unnerved. "If you wanna try that again, a safety net would be a good idea."

"Don't you get it? In this swamp we swim in, *we* are the safety net." She turned to Alaric. "Do you need anything more from me tonight? Counselling? Medical care? Someone to run interference with the cops?"

"I'll get Gemma back to Judd's place and assess the situation." It was closer than Emmy's mansion and probably less intimidating. "Do you still have a friendly doctor on call? Somebody who can keep their mouth shut?"

"Sure. Just let me know, yeah?"

"I will." Alaric squeezed her hand, holding onto it for a beat longer than he should have. He'd almost forgotten how terrifying Emmy's fearlessness could be. "Thanks for tonight, Cinders. You're crazy, you know that?"

"It's been mentioned a time or two." Her car pulled up, and she followed Sky towards it, pausing to glance over one shoulder. "Laters, Prince Charming."

## CHAPTER 46 - BETHANY

THE SIRENS STILL echoed in my ears as Alaric parked the car in front of the garage at Curzon Place, Judd's home. We'd passed three police cars and an ambulance on the way, all speeding towards the Bellsfield Estate. The ambulance crew might as well have gone home.

So many thoughts tumbled through my aching head. Ryland Willis was dead. Emmy had somehow survived. *Death wish. Miracle. Knife. Gun.* Alaric had a freaking gun! A blur of Ravi. Sky... She'd kept her head while I was losing mine. *How did I get down those stairs?* And Gemma, Gemma was alive. Was she all right? She hadn't said a word since we got in the car, only cried. I hugged her tighter.

"Are you okay?" Ravi asked, opening the back door.

Seriously? "No."

"Sorry. Stupid question."

Gemma gripped my arm. "W-w-where are we?"

"Somewhere safe," I told her. Far away from death, and that was all that mattered. "Can you walk inside? Or... Or..."

Perhaps one of the men could carry her again?

"I can walk."

She gripped my arm as I steadied her up the front steps and into the living room, and when she slumped back onto the sofa, I got my first proper look at her.

This wasn't the Gemma I knew. She'd always been fussy about her appearance, but her hair was lank and greasy, her face pimply and blotchy from crying. Dirt from where she'd fallen on the roof streaked one cheek. Before we left the estate, Alaric had stuck a dressing on her neck to stem the bleeding, and even though she'd kept a hand pressed to it the whole way back, a dark blossom of blood had seeped through to the outer layer. She was thin too. Had Ryland been feeding her? I looked her up and down, then noticed the torn waistband on her jeans. Oh no. *No.* Tell me he hadn't...

"Did he...?"

She followed my gaze and burst into great racking sobs.

It was a good thing Emmy had pushed Ryland off the building, because in that moment, I could have easily killed him myself and taken pleasure in the act.

"It's okay." I sat down and tried to soothe her, then realised I'd said almost the same dumb thing as Ravi had earlier. Of course it wasn't okay. And I was way, way out of my depth here. I looked to Alaric.

"What do we do?" I whispered.

He took a seat on the coffee table and flicked a glance at Ravi. "Tea?"

Ravi nodded and disappeared.

"So..." Alaric started. "We met briefly at the gallery, Gemma, but you probably don't remember me." She stared at him blankly. "I'm a friend of Beth's, and I'm here to help you with whatever you need. Do you feel up to talking?"

A long moment passed before she whispered, "Yes."

"Any time you want to take a break, just say the word. We can go as slow as you like."

"Okay."

"Then let's get the big stuff out of the way to begin with... Firstly, do you need to see a doctor? Can I take a look at your neck?"

Gemma didn't move. Underneath the dirt, she was pale as a ghost, and I feared she'd gone into shock. I reached up to the bandage.

"Can I...?"

She gave the faintest nod.

"Do you know first aid?" I whispered to Alaric as I peeled the edges of the dressing away from clammy skin.

"I've had a reasonable amount of medical training." Gemma shrank away as he leaned closer. "It's not as bad as it could have been."

"Does she need stitches?"

Rather than one big incision, it seemed as if the point of Ryland's knife had jabbed into Gemma's neck over and over, leaving a nick each time. The cuts ranged from pinpricks to a centimetre or so.

"A stitch or two might not be a bad idea."

"Where's the nearest hospital?"

"A mile away. But if we take her there, they'll ask a lot of questions, and not just about the knife wounds."

"What choice do we have?"

"I can get a doctor here, no questions asked."

And we didn't want questions, did we? Emmy might have been the one to throw Ryland off the building, but we'd all had a hand in his death, even me. By rights, I should have been puking my guts up at the memory, but what I actually felt was peace of mind. Yes, a man had died, but justice had been served. And I also didn't want any of us to get arrested for murder. If we went to the hospital, the staff would surely call the police, wouldn't they?

"What about the other stuff?" I hated discussing Gemma as if she wasn't there, but I didn't know how else to ask. "I... I think there's more than the cuts."

"Gemma, did Ryland rape you?" Alaric asked, his tone as kind as it could be under the circumstances. His words hurt, but perhaps it was better than beating around the bush.

Another tiny nod.

"Then we'll need to get you checked out properly."

"Not the hospital."

"But—"

She came to life a little more. "No! My friend Andrea got...she got *attacked*, and she said going to hospital was almost as bad as the...as the..." Gemma couldn't say the word. "They poked at her, and stuck things inside her, and...no."

"What about the police?" Alaric asked. "That's the other big thing—do you want to speak to them?"

"What's the point? Ry's dead, and Andrea said they didn't even believe her."

Oh, thank goodness. Not about Gemma's poor friend, but that Gemma didn't want to involve the authorities. I'd never have pressured her not to report her ordeal if she wanted to, but... Phew.

"Maybe you should call that doctor?" I suggested to Alaric. "And then I could help Gemma to take a shower."

"Has anyone got a cigarette?" she asked. "I haven't smoked for days."

"I don't think so." When I glanced at Alaric, he shook his head. "Sorry."

"I guess I should quit anyway." Another sob burst out of Gemma. "What about food? Do you have any food? I'm so, so hungry. Ry hardly let me eat."

"Anything you want. If there's nothing in the kitchen, I can go to the supermarket or we can get something delivered."

"A pizza? Can we get a pizza? I can pay..." She paled again. "Ry's got my handbag. It's somewhere in his flat."

Oh, crap. The police would be crawling all over the place by now.

Alaric didn't panic. He never did get worked up, I'd noticed. "No, he hasn't. Ravi picked it up before we left. Beth, can you order the pizza? Use my credit card."

I used to hate it when Piers told me what to do, but now with Alaric, I just felt relief. Overwhelming relief that he took charge and kept me sane when the whole world was falling apart around us.

"What toppings?"

"Why don't you order a selection? I'll find some clothes for Gemma to change into." He gave her hand the lightest brush as he got to his feet. "It might not feel like it right now, but you're going to be okay."

And because he'd said it, I knew she would be.

# CHAPTER 47 - EMMY

HOLY FUCK, MY shoulder hurt. The biggest miracle in tonight's adventure was that I hadn't dislocated it. Although losing my arm completely would still have been preferable to falling seventeen storeys and splattering myself across the concrete. I'd seen the aftermath of Ryland's nosedive, and it hadn't been pretty. The crime scene techs better have brought a shovel, or they'd never get him into a body bag.

"You okay?" I asked Sky after we'd dropped the other two guys back at the office.

"Shouldn't that be my line? You were the one who almost died."

"The HR people are pushing well-being at work this month. Figured I'd better ask."

"Yeah, I'm fine. Is your arm sore?"

"Nothing a few sessions of physio won't fix." And possibly a kilo or two of oxycodone. "But you're not fine. When you're upset, you're not so good at bullshitting."

Sky stared straight ahead. Yes, I'd been younger than her when I started in this game, but not only had I come face to face with my first dead body when I was fourteen, I'd also had several months of training under my belt before I watched a man die in front of me. Just this week, Sky had dealt with Lenny's near-death experience, and now Ryland. She was shaken.

"I... I don't think I can do this. The job, I mean. What you did tonight... I'm not sure I could make that jump and then...you know."

"You couldn't, not today. But that's where the training comes in. I've spent over a decade pushing myself to the limits, learning exactly how fast I can run and how far I can jump. With the ramp, I *knew* I could clear that gap. And as for Ryland's tumble off the building... Well, that was just gravity."

"You nearly followed him."

"But I didn't, so what's the point in dwelling on the past?"

Although I did owe Ravi a debt of gratitude. If he hadn't been there, I'd be strawberry jam right now. Who was Ravi, anyway? I'd met him once before when I was briefing Sirius for a job in the US, and Alaric mentioned him from time to time, but he didn't seem like your usual ex-government agent. I'd always trusted Alaric in the past, so I hadn't pried, but now I was curious. About Naz too. Naz was Russian and sketchy as fuck, but beyond that, I had no idea. Judd? Judd I knew. In fact, I'd probably known him for longer than Alaric had. Judd was a lunatic. Ex-MI6 with nerves of steel, skin of Kevlar, and an ego of epic proportions. Which matched his dick, if the rumours were to be believed. I'd only worked with him once or twice, but I dealt with his mother regularly, and the woman was a cold-hearted bitch. Stella Millais-Scott was number two in command at The Circus, as MI6 was nicknamed, just waiting for the current head to retire or die so she could take over the top job. I was half-surprised she hadn't helped him on his way.

The phone rang. Alaric. I put him on speaker.

"Hey."

"Gonna need that doctor."

"She's on standby—I'll send her over. How's Gemma holding up?"

"About as well as can be expected considering what the bastard did to her."

"Rape?"

"If you hadn't killed him, I would have."

"Then I'm glad I saved you the trouble. Alaric, I owe Ravi one. How is he?"

"Physically or mentally?"

"Both."

"He's used to acrobatics, but...he's slightly rattled, although he won't admit it. Ravi's normally in acquisitions, not disposals."

Translation: Ravi was a thief. Well, that explained his mad skills with the lock picks. The acrobatics? Hmm.

"Anything I can do?"

"No, I'll take care of him."

Something about the way he said it... Alaric did *care* about Ravi, and not just as a colleague or even as a friend. They'd been together at one time, hadn't they? Were they still? I didn't think so. If anything, Alaric had been paying a little too much attention to Bethany this evening.

"Well, I'd better call Roxy."

"Roxy?"

"She finished her medical degree recently, and she's more than capable of suturing Gemma's cuts. Or if you want someone with more experience, I can see if Dr. Phil's free?"

"Dr. Phil? Seriously?"

"It's short for Philippa. She's great at stitching people up, but her bedside manner sometimes leaves a bit to be desired. Roxy... Let's just say she'll understand what Gemma's been through."

"I trust your judgement."

I wished I could still say the same, but learning that Alaric had a kid... I couldn't get Bethany's revelation out of my head.

"Talk to you later."

Sky stared at me when I hung up. I was watching the road, but I felt her gaze boring into the side of my head.

"Rape?" she asked.

"I only wish I could've castrated Ryland before he went splat."

"You know what?" Her voice sounded a lot stronger now. "I think I actually *can* do this job."

Thank goodness. "Attagirl. Wanna pick up dinner on the way home? Pizza? Chinese? A curry?"

"Pizza."

"What kind? I'll phone the order through."

"Hawaiian."

What the actual fuck? I stomped on the brakes and skidded into a bus stop, leaving a trail of rubber behind us. Surely I must have misheard?

"What did you just say?"

"Hawaiian. You know, ham and pineapple? Thanks for the whiplash, by the way."

"You put pineapple on pizza? Oh no. No way. We *cannot* be friends."

"What's wrong with pineapple on pizza?"

"It's a fruit. Fruit doesn't belong on pizza."

"Tomatoes are fruit."

"Utter bollocks. To everyone except nerds and gardeners, tomatoes are a vegetable."

Sky folded her arms. "Well, I like pineapple on pizza. I bet you have pepperoni."

"Of course I do."

"Ugh. Pepperoni's too chewy."

"Heathen."

"You barely complained when I smashed your nose, you killed a man without breaking a sweat, and then you almost died, yet this is what you get upset about?"

"It's just wrong."

"Tell you what—you can sit at the other end of the kitchen, and we'll barely even be able to see each other."

Had I totally misjudged Sky? I mean, I didn't mind her breaking the law, but this was a crime against taste, quite literally.

"Well, you'll have to order it. I don't think I can bring myself to utter the words."

"Fine."

I handed over my credit card. "Just don't come running up to me when your taste buds shrivel up and die. And get extra pepperoni on mine. I need something to counteract the horror."

"Do you want anything else? Chilli peppers? Double cheese? Anchovies?"

"Anchovies? Ugh. I suppose you eat those too?"

Sky wrinkled her nose at the prospect, and I breathed a sigh of relief. At least we agreed on something.

# CHAPTER 48 - BETHANY

ROXY WAS A miracle worker. Not only had she stitched Gemma up, but she'd also talked to her about her ordeal in such a kind, understanding manner that Gemma had calmed down enough to fall asleep in the spare bedroom next to Judd's after eating an entire large pizza and a carton of Ben & Jerry's. Apparently, Ryland had been criticising her diet for months—too much fat, too many carbs, not enough protein—as well as telling her that she looked chubby.

He'd started off charming, she said, sweet and attentive, complimenting her at the gym until he finally asked her out. She'd thought he was a real catch, only for his dark side to emerge as things got more serious. He became controlling, abusive, and when she tried to break up with him, he'd snapped. Nobody left him, he told her, at least not alive.

I dreaded to think what that meant.

Apparently, they'd found the little room on the other side of the wardrobe when he moved into his new place. It seemed an enterprising former occupant had been short of space and decided to create a makeshift extension. Gemma had even helped Ryland to carry the old mattress and bedding left behind in there down to the dumpster several weeks previously, as well as scrubbing the whole flat because Ryland didn't like dirt or germs. At least that phobia meant he'd used a condom when he forced Gemma to do the unthinkable.

But it was over. Now we just had the broken pieces to fit back together. I only hoped there weren't too many missing. Ravi had offered to drive Roxy home, which left me alone in the living room with Alaric, a large gin and tonic, and a whole boatload of awkwardness.

"Talk to me, Beth. It's not good to bottle things up."

I'd carefully sat in an armchair to give myself some space, but my plan backfired because he came over to sit on an arm.

"I..." Where did I start? "At first, on the roof, I was barely thinking straight. Emmy told me to hold a wooden board to help save Gemma's life, and I just did it. And even after Ryland fell, I was... I guess I was sort of numb. Is that normal?"

"Perfectly normal."

"Then when I saw those people gathered around his body on the ground, I was horrified. A man *died*. Somebody's son. Perhaps somebody's brother. Except when Gemma told us the details of what Ryland did, all I felt was anger. And then relief. I still feel desperately sorry for his family, but I'm glad he's not here anymore."

There would be no hospital exam, no investigation, and no court case. Gemma had been spared from that ordeal, and she could start to heal rather than prolonging the agony. Death provided closure. She said she wanted to put it behind her, that she refused to let Ryland ruin her life. I think that was Roxy's influence. They'd talked alone for half an hour, and Gemma seemed much better for it. Roxy had promised to come back tomorrow too, just to check how she was getting on.

"And now you feel guilty for that?"

I hadn't got as far as analysing my discomfort, but yes. I nodded. "I can't help it."

"That's good. It shows you've still got your humanity."

"Emmy didn't seem affected."

"Emmy's had a lot of experience at hiding her feelings."

"And you?"

He looked me in the eye. "I'm out of practice, but yes, I have too." He laid a hand on my shoulder, and I jumped out of my skin. "That bothers you."

"You've killed people?"

"I used to have a job I can't talk about."

But I understood from what he didn't tell me that the answer was yes. "How did it make you feel?"

"There's a reason I'm not doing that job anymore."

That was good, right? It showed Alaric cared and had integrity. But holy shit, he'd killed people. I was sitting in the same room as a man who had blood on his hands, but weirdly, I didn't feel scared. Not at all. Not after the way he'd moved heaven and earth to save Gemma.

"Okay," I said.

"Okay?"

"I'm okay with that."

"But you weren't okay earlier."

"Well, it was all so fresh, and I was shaking, and Gemma was crying, and..."

"No, I mean before that. Before we went anywhere near the roof. You've been walking on eggshells around me since yesterday lunchtime. What changed?"

Oh, hell. *My father's phone call.* I'd been trying to block it out, but it had been there the whole time, tugging at the edges of my subconscious, yet another layer of shit making the day stink.

But what was I meant to tell Alaric? And how should I react to my father's accusations?

"It's nothing."

"Beth."

One word, and it cut me to the core. I couldn't lie to Alaric. Since our second meeting, he'd done nothing but help me, and we couldn't move forward with this huge secret between us. The only other option would be for me to quit my job and leave myself and Chaucer destitute.

"It's...honestly, I'm fine with all the Gemma stuff. But...but there's something else."

He brushed the hair away from my face. "I'm listening."

At first, I couldn't speak, but then it all came out in one big vomit of words. "My father called. Yesterday while I was out fetching lunch. And he said he'd spoken to people who knew your father, and in your past...that you'd stolen a ransom, ten million dollars, and I said you wouldn't have done that, no way, but he said you definitely did, and that if I don't keep away from you, he'll cut me off completely. And I said some nasty things and then hung up, and now...now I don't know what to do."

"Fuck."

"It's not true, is it? Is it?"

Alaric moved away, back to the sofa, putting distance between us. I began to get a bad, bad feeling about whatever he had to say. A prickling in my spine, like ice crystallising from the bottom up.

"It's true that I was accused of those things."

"Did you do it?"

"You've got good instincts, Beth."

"So you're saying you didn't?"

"No, I didn't." He shook his head. "I won't lie to you. I promise you that."

"Then what...? Why...?"

"I don't know. Eight years later, I'm still no closer to the truth. The payment was for a painting, not a person, and somebody set me up to take the fall."

The ice in both my spine and my drink melted as Alaric told me the story of *Emerald*, of the heist, the investigation, and the botched exchange. When he got to the part about people shooting at him, I almost threw up.

"You could have been killed."

"And yet here I am. So you see now why I was so interested in *Red After Dark*?"

"You think it can lead you to *Emerald*."

"If I achieve nothing else in life, I want to get that damn painting back. The diamonds were practically untraceable, and the chances of someone spotting a serial number from the cash are slim, but the painting...there's only one *Emerald*. She's unique." He managed a half-smile. "And I hate losing."

When I was a teenager, I'd felt that way too. Every time I rode into a dressage arena, or cantered over the line towards a course of showjumps, or waited in the start box for a cross-country round to begin, I'd wanted to win. Marriage to Piers had almost made me forget what it was like to come out on top.

"Me too. So we're going to keep looking?"

Alaric picked up his wine glass, swirled the now-warm Pinot Grigio, and drained the remainder.

"I'm going to keep looking."

"But what about me? I'm part of this too, and I work for you."

"I can't be responsible for you losing your inheritance. Beth, I'm not worth it." He held up a hand when I opened my mouth to protest. "Right now, you could still resolve things with your family."

"What if I don't want to? What if I want to stay with you?" Shit, wrong word. "I mean, work for you?"

At that moment, I was glad Alaric had put some distance between us; otherwise, I might have been tempted to throw myself into his arms. The thought of never seeing him again wasn't one I wanted to contemplate.

"It's too big a decision to make in a heartbeat. You were under a lot of pressure yesterday. And if you're worried about money, I won't see you stuck. I'll pay you six months' severance and loan you any more you might need."

"But I haven't even done any work yet."

"You helped to save Gemma's life. I'd say that counts." Alaric got up and headed for the door, but before he reached it, he turned and looked right at me, his gaze intense. "Take some time to think about this. I live in the shadows, Beth. I'm no Prince Charming. And I'm not the kind of man you throw away your entire future for. It's only a job."

No, it wasn't only a job.

Alaric had said he wouldn't lie, but he just did. If I was going to give up everything, then he was exactly the kind of man I'd do it for.

## CHAPTER 49 - ALARIC

ALARIC HEADED UPSTAIRS, his heart heavy. One week. One week, and he'd gotten in so deep with Beth that it would hurt like hell to see her go.

He hated that her old man had given her an ultimatum. For one crazy moment, he considered trying to talk to the asshole, but he quickly saw sense. Bertram Stafford-Lyons had the same character as Alaric's own father. There was no reasoning with either of them.

And Alaric knew how difficult it was to walk away from everything. There'd been times in that first year—like the weeks he spent in a Mozambique hospital, shitting his guts out from malaria—that he'd wished he could turn back the clock and go begging to the people he'd left behind. Life alone had been hard. Beth wouldn't be on her own, not completely, but when she lost her inheritance, would she grow to resent him for splitting up her family?

It wasn't a decision she should make lightly.

And then there was his lifestyle. He'd always danced on the edge, and he didn't know how to live any other way. Didn't *want* to live any other way. Tonight, Emmy had diced with death, but next week, it could easily be his turn. Of course, all the risks he took were calculated, but they were still just that: risks. Plus he didn't need any emotional entanglements, not right now, and Beth was the very definition of temptation.

Damn, he wanted her.

That slip of the tongue downstairs, the way she'd looked at him... He'd had to leave because otherwise he'd have dragged her into his arms and made the decision for her. His dick still disagreed with his choice. Sex had always been his favourite way to relieve stress. But sometimes it caused more problems than it solved. Like that last night with Emmy at Riverley, for example. If he hadn't been so busy fucking her, perhaps he'd have done a final check of the pay-off, and then they'd know for certain whether the switch had occurred before he left for the handover. No, he couldn't afford to get distracted by a woman again, not now. Not when the trail to *Red After Dark* was still so fresh.

Beth would have to make her decision, and he'd have to live with it.

Since he'd offered her his bed tonight—without him in it—and Judd was due back in the early hours, that left him two choices: wait until Beth went to sleep and then take the couch, or share with Ravi.

It wasn't hard to make up his mind.

Ravi was sprawled across the bed, face down and buck naked, but when Alaric slipped into the room, he mumbled into the pillow.

"Thought you'd be with Beth."

"We talked. She knows."

"Knows everything?"

"About *Emerald*. And a little of my past."

Ravi rolled onto his side and propped his head up on one hand. "How'd she take it?"

"Better than I thought, but it's complicated. How are you holding up? It's not every day you see a man reduced to his component parts."

"Wired. Fuckin' wired. I drank a couple beers, but I still can't sleep. I might go out for a while. Unless..." His gaze settled on the bulge in Alaric's pants. "Unless you want to take my mind off things?"

Alaric's history with Ravi was complicated. They'd first hooked up in Phuket seven years ago. A double-booking at a hostel led to them sharing a room and later a bed. It was meant to be a fling, nothing more—a week of sex and snorkelling and the kind of companionship Alaric had missed since he left the US. A week turned into a month, then fate intervened. Naz and Judd showed up one evening, and all hell let loose.

Now, Alaric and Ravi were colleagues above all else. They'd never gotten into deep-and-meaningful territory, but occasionally when they needed to blow off steam, their relationship slipped into friends-with-benefits. It looked as if tonight would be one of those nights.

But as Ravi got to his knees and reached for Alaric's belt buckle, it didn't feel the same as it had in the past. No rush of heat, no release of tension. Why? There was nothing between Alaric and Beth. There couldn't be, not with circumstances as they were. Alaric forced himself into the moment. Ravi had done this dozens of times before, and they'd both enjoyed it. Nothing had changed, had it? *Had it?* So this time, why did Alaric feel as if he was cheating?

# Epilogue

THE WOMAN WHO called herself Hevrin Moradi shifted her baby in her arms as she walked across her flat. A fly buzzed past her face, and she waved it away. No matter how many she caught on the sticky spiral of flypaper hanging in the kitchen, there were always more. Probably because there was something dead in Bellsfield House North. Every so often, she caught a whiff of it, and it reminded her of home. Of Rojava.

The smell had grown worse over the last week, and she'd finally plucked up the courage to contact the council and let them know. Probably just a rat, the lady told her. She'd agreed to send out a pest control man, but so far, there'd been no sign of him. Eunice had promised to call if he didn't show up. Last time there was a rat, she said, it had turned into fifty rats, and besides, she had a problem with her plumbing so she had to phone anyway. The water in her bath wasn't draining properly, and this morning, her toilet had nearly overflowed when she flushed it.

The knock at the door came again.

"Who's there?" Hevrin called.

Living on the Bellsfield Estate left her uneasy. Even before Ryland Willis's death, she'd hated the place, but where else could she go? As an asylum seeker, she wasn't allowed to work, and even if she could earn money, childcare cost a fortune. She volunteered at a homeless shelter once a week, serving food with Indy on her back, but back in Syria, she'd had a very different job. War had forced her into the tightest of corners.

She missed the old days at home. She missed sitting in the sun with her grandma, eating dates and listening to music on their tinny stereo. She missed growing her own vegetables. She missed the warmth, not just of the sun but of the people in her neighbourhood. Her old house was gone now, reduced to rubble along with her hopes and dreams for the future.

But now... Now, a neighbour was dead. Everyone felt sorry for the man who'd jumped from the roof. For a tortured soul who'd been in such despair that he saw no other way out. The police only took a day to rule it death by suicide, but Hevrin wasn't so sure it had been an accident. Why? Because first, a man claiming to be from the council had shown up, asking questions. Eunice said he was a debt collector, but Hevrin wasn't so sure about that either. Debt collectors didn't buy people groceries.

And then while everyone else was staring at the body, she'd seen him helping the brown-haired girl into a car. The brown-haired girl with blood running down her neck and bruises covering her face.

*That smell...*

Hevrin didn't need a badge and a uniform to know that Ryland Willis had been bad news.

"It's Mahmoud from UPS."

"What?"

"I've got a delivery for you. A parcel."

"I didn't order anything."

"Hevrin Moradi? 503 Bellsfield House North?"

"That's me, but..." Was this a trick? The door may have had a chain, but the wood itself was flimsy, and there was no peephole. Security wasn't a priority for the landlord, despite the estate having the highest crime rate in the area. "It's not mine. I can't open the door."

"Well, I'm not taking it down all those stairs again, Miss. I'll just leave it here."

Footsteps receded along the hallway. What should she do? A whole five minutes passed, and from habit, Hevrin slipped the knife out of her waistband and opened the blade with a quiet *snick*.

*This was England. It was supposed to be safe.*

Her heart thumped as she opened the door, but the man had gone. Only a box remained, a big box, and when she tried to move it inside, it was too heavy for her to lift. No wonder Mahmoud hadn't wanted to take it away with him. He must have used superpowers to get it there in the first place.

In the end, Hevrin shoved the package through the door, then checked she was safely locked inside before she examined the box more closely. What was it? Her details were typed onto a white label stuck to the top, but there was no return address.

She used the knife to slit the tape, standing back, half expecting a bogeyman to jump out, but there was nothing. Nothing except a bunch of Tesco bags.

Groceries?

Instant noodles, plain yogurt, jars of baby food, a loaf of bread, apples, pasta, laundry powder... And at the bottom of the box, an envelope. She opened it, hoping to solve the mystery, but what fell out was cash. A pile of twenty-pound notes that floated to the floor like giant confetti. Hevrin's jaw dropped. She'd never seen so much money in her life. Five thousand pounds.

And a note.

*Groceries will come each week for six months. I hope the money makes your life a little easier.*

Was this a joke? There was no signature, and no explanation as to why someone should send this package to her of all people. What if they asked for the money back? Or worse, expected something in return? Hevrin didn't want to touch the stuff, but she was hungry. So hungry. By the time she paid the bills, she could barely afford to eat, and breastfeeding Indy left her drained. Maybe if she ate the food and then replaced it...?

It was only as Hevrin stacked the items onto the kitchen counter that she put the pieces together. It was the second time she'd done this recently, tidied away a gift from a stranger, and the items were the same. Different brands, but it was as if somebody had used an old receipt as a shopping list.

She thought back to the handsome man who'd bailed her out in the Co-op. The man who'd been looking for a monster. The man she suspected may have had a hand in Ryland Willis's death.

One day, she'd find him and thank him. For both actions.

# WHAT'S NEXT?

**My next book will be _Red After Dark_, the thirteenth novel in the Blackwood Security series...**

_Red After Dark_

_A missing girl from the past. A monster from the present..._

When Bethany Stafford-Lyons accepted a position as personal assistant at Sirius Consulting, she didn't expect to become embroiled in the murky world of American politics within a week of starting the job, but with money tight, she has little choice but to follow her new boss Alaric McLain overseas.

Together with Emmy Black, Alaric's ex-girlfriend, they find themselves back on the trail of a stolen painting, but that's not the only mystery they have to solve. Fourteen years ago, teenage homecoming queen Piper Simms disappeared, and finding her might be the only way to stop a criminal from stealing a seat in the US senate.

Catching a killer is all in a day's work for Emmy Black, but her world is rocked by a betrayal from somebody very close to her. Can she fight back? Or will a ghost from the past destroy her future?

For more details: www.elise-noble.com/dark

**If you enjoyed *The Girl with the Emerald Ring*, please consider leaving a review.**

For an author, every review is incredibly important. Not only do they make us feel warm and fuzzy inside, readers consider them when making their decision whether or not to buy a book. Even a line saying you enjoyed the book or what your favourite part was helps a lot.

# Want to stalk me?

For updates on my new releases, giveaways, and other random stuff, you can sign up for my newsletter on my website:
www.elise-noble.com

**Facebook:**
www.facebook.com/EliseNobleAuthor

**Twitter:** @EliseANoble

**Instagram:** @elise_noble

If you're on Facebook, you may also like to join Team Blackwood for exclusive giveaways, sneak previews, and book-related chat. Be the first to find out about new stories, and you might even see your name or one of your ideas make it into print!

And if you'd like to read my books for FREE, you can also find details of how to join my advance review team.

Would you like to join Team Blackwood?

www.elise-noble.com/team-blackwood

## END OF BOOK STUFF

Ah, I have to admit, it was lovely to write a Blackwood book set in England again. I'm sure by now, most people have realised I write in British (proper) English, although there are still a few folks out there who think I just can't spell. Those reviews are the absolute best, lol. Having British characters also means I don't need to "translate" so many bits into American at the end, and also Brits have a far superior selection of expletives.

As parts two and three of Alaric's story will also feature a smorgasbord of British characters, I thought it might be useful to include a brief explanation of my second-favourite swear word (I'm sure you can guess what number one is) for my US friends:

*A man's bollocks - His balls*
*The (dog's) bollocks - Fantastic*
*Bollocks - Darn and blast*
*Utter bollocks - Nonsense*
*Bollocking - A telling off*
*Stark bollock naked - Nude*
*Bollocks to it - I shall ignore that*
*Bollock all - Nothing*
*Bollocksed/bolloxed - Messed up, beyond repair*
Related: *Bellend - an idiot*

Oh, and if you're gonna shop someone, you're reporting them to the police, not taking them on a nice trip to Oxford Street.

I hope this helps, and perhaps one day, you guys on the other side of the pond will learn to curse properly ;)

In Emerald, not only did I get to swear in technicolour, but thanks to Beth being a dressage diva, I also got to write another book with horses. Polo was named after my old horse, who I had to sell in my teens after I got ill. I lost track of him after that :( He was a bit of a sod—he sometimes bit people, although mostly people I didn't like so I couldn't get too mad, and he also used to stop at fences and let me go over them first. And he loooooved mud. But he taught me a lot, and I still miss him. Even today, I wonder where he ended up.

Now I have Trev, who'll be with me for life, even thought he's besties with the vet and eats me out of house and home. As I write this, he's in pony prison again because he went on a rampage through some rhododendrons on the way to the field and managed to kick his own leg. Pinkey, the lady who looks after Chaucer for Beth, is named after the lady who cares for Trev when I'm at work. Hi, Pinkey!

Well, I'd better carry on with the next instalment... Alaric, Beth, Sky, and Emmy will be off to the US, but will things go smoothly? Of course they bloody won't. *Red After Dark* was due to be released at the end of October, but since that's right before the US election and everyone'll be busy shouting at each other on the internet, I'm planning to bring it forward by two weeks as long as I can get the dreaded editing finished in time...

Happy reading, and stay safe,
*Elise*

Carbon
Rhodium
Platinum
Lead
Copper
Bronze
Nickel
Hydrogen (TBA)

## The Blackwood UK Series
Joker in the Pack
Cherry on Top (novella)
Roses are Dead
Shallow Graves
Indigo Rain
Pass the Parcel (TBA)

## Blackwood Casefiles
Stolen Hearts

## Blackstone House
Hard Lines (2021)
Hard Tide (TBA)

## The Electi Series
Cursed
Spooked
Possessed
Demented
Judged (2021)

## The Trouble Series
Trouble in Paradise

Nothing but Trouble
24 Hours of Trouble

## Standalone
Life
Coco du Ciel (TBA)
Twisted (short stories)
A Very Happy Christmas (novella)

## Books with clean versions available (no swearing and no on-the-page sex)
Pitch Black
Into the Black
Forever Black
Gold Rush
Gray is my Heart

## Audiobooks
Black is My Heart (Diamond & Snow - prequel)
Pitch Black
Into the Black
Forever Black
Gold Rush

Printed in Great Britain
by Amazon